WERE-

Other Anthologies Edited by
Patricia Bray & Joshua Palmatier

After Hours: Tales from the Ur-Bar
The Modern Fae's Guide to Surviving Humanity
Clockwork Universe: Steampunk vs Aliens
Temporally Out of Order
Alien Artifacts

WERE-

EDITED BY

Patricia Bray
&
Joshua Palmatier

Zombies Need Brains LLC
www.zombiesneedbrains.com

Interior Design (ebook): April Steenburgh
Interior Design (print): C. Lennox
Cover Design by C. Lennox
Cover Art "Were-" by Justin Adams

ZNB Book Collectors #7
All characters and events in this book are fictitious.
All resemblance to persons living or dead is coincidental.

Kickstarter Edition Printing, July 2016
First Printing, August 2016

Print ISBN-10: 1940709105
Print ISBN-13: 978-1940709109

Ebook ISBN-10: 1940709113
Ebook ISBN-13: 978-1940709116

Printed in the U.S.A.

COPYRIGHTS

TABLE OF CONTENTS

Introduction
by Joshua Palmatier   1

"Best In Show"
by Seanan McGuire   2

"We Dig"
by Ashley McConnell   13

"Eyes Like Pearls"
by Susan Jett   27

"Among the Grapevines, Growing"
by Eliora Smith   34

"A Party For Bailey"
by David B. Coe   46

"Cry Murder"
by April Steenburgh   59

"Missy the Were-Pomeranian vs. the Masters of
Mediocre Doom" by Gini Koch   71

"Paper Wasp"
by Mike Barretta   92

"Point Five"
by Elizabeth Kite   107

"The Promise of Death"
by Danielle Ackley-McPhail   111

"The Five Bean Solution"
by Jean Marie Ward   123

"Witness Report"
by Katharine Kerr   145

"Attack of the Were-Zombie Friendship
With Benefits" by Sarah Brand   153

"The Whale"
by Anneliese Belmond   162

"Anzu, Duba, Beast"
by Faith Hunter   179

"Shiftr"
by Patricia Bray   198

"Sniff For Your Life"
by Phyllis Ames   210

About the Authors   223

About the Editors   227

Acknowledgments   228

SIGNATURE PAGE

Patricia Bray, editor:

_____

Joshua Palmatier, editor:

_____

Seanan McGuire:

_____

Ashley McConnell:

_____

Susan Jett:

_____

Eliora Smith:

_____

David B. Coe:

_____

April Steenburgh:

_____

Gini Koch:

_____

Mike Barretta:

_____

Elizabeth Kite:

_____

Danielle Ackley-McPhail:

_____

Jean Marie Ward:

_____

Katharine Kerr:

_____

Sarah Brand:

_____

Anneliese Belmond:

_____

Faith Hunter:

_____

Patricia Bray:

_____

Phyllis Ames:

_____

Justin Adams, artist:

_____

INTRODUCTION

When Patricia and I sit down at the bar, order our drinks, and begin brainstorming anthology ideas, as depicted on the cover—I'm the guinea pig, Patricia is the goat—we often get a ton of ideas, none of them good. However, during one such session, we both agreed it would be cool to have an anthology based around the idea of "shifters," people that could shift into animal forms. But we also agreed that we didn't want an anthology filled with werewolves. They've been done before, have become a standard trope of urban fantasy, and we're always more interested in something different, something unique. But how could we get that across to the reader and the writers with the least amount of fuss?

Thus, WERE- was born. It seemed obvious to me that if there were werewolves, then there were likely werelions, weretigers, and werebears out there as well. (Oh my!) Why weren't we telling their stories? What would those stories be? How would they be different from the standard werewolf story?

As soon as we announced the project, we had authors knocking on our door to participate. The results are the seventeen stories you have here, stories that take a were-something and tell its tale. We hope you enjoy.

In the meantime, Patricia and I have slipped into our alternate forms, slid onto our barstools, and ordered our next round. It's time to start brainstorming again.

BEST IN SHOW
SEANAN MCGUIRE

The office was dark. Michael had found that the sort of clients who went looking for a private investigator in a strip mall rather than hiring one online wanted that classic Phillip Marlowe vibe as part of the service. They wanted to open the door and feel like they were stepping into a noir movie, complete with leggy dames, liquid lunches, and the threat of being gunned down at any moment.

Michael would have preferred bright lights and an ergonomic desk. But that would have been bad for business, and he liked his job. He liked setting his own hours, and he liked the fact that no two days were the same. If he had to live in the city until he'd saved up enough to buy himself a farm, a degree of enforced noir was a small price to pay for doing it the way he wanted.

Except on days like this one. The couple currently sitting across from him looked like they'd stepped out of a movie, and not one where the heroic detective saved the day with quick thinking and legwork. No, they were from the sort of murder mystery where a little old lady with blue-rinsed hair came along after half the cast was dead, declared that the butler had done it, and went home for tea. The man was tall, thin to the point of verging on cadaverous, and wearing a suit that was easily thirty years out of style, but was still impeccably pressed. The woman was slightly softer, with enough meat on her to keep her skin from actually sticking to her bones, and wearing a sensible pantsuit that was probably pale lavender. Under the dim office lights, it was exactly the color of grave dust.

Michael frowned. "I'm sorry, you want me to do what, exactly?"

"We want you to find proof that the Harrisons are cheating," said the woman, as if it were the most reasonable thing in the world.

"At cat shows."

"And dog shows, although that's less important at the moment." The man smiled, the smug, self-satisfied expression of someone who had always been able to get what he wanted out of life, and wasn't intending to change that any time soon. "Westminster is months away. The North American Grand Championship title will be awarded this coming weekend. I'm sure you can see where time is of the essence."

"Of course," said Michael slowly. "But if you're so confident that these people are cheating, why not bring it to the attention of the governing board of your association? I'm sure there are rules."

"We *have* brought it to their attention, and they've informed us that there are no signs of impropriety," snapped the woman. "It simply isn't true. No one has a cat that well-groomed, that well-behaved, and that obedient. Cats aren't like that. Dogs, maybe—"

"Although even the best dog will act up more than Thea Harrison's Great Dane," said the man, cutting her off without a trace of apology. "These people are doing *something*. Witchcraft, robotics, drugs, I don't know, and I don't care. It needs to stop. You're going to find out what it is, and then we're going to put a stop to it."

"I'm afraid this isn't my normal area of expertise," said Michael carefully. He didn't like refusing work, and more, he didn't like refusing work offered by the sort of entitled, arrogant customers who'd think it was completely appropriate to leave him bad reviews on all the website aggregators. Sometimes he thought wistfully about burning Yelp to the ground. Not because the company itself had done anything wrong, but because the mere existence of a public review system had turned the entire world into a baying pack of hostage-takers, willing to dangle a good review or threaten a bad one for the slightest infraction.

"We were told you were the best," said the woman. She sniffed, gaze turning suddenly sharp. "Were we mis-informed?"

"If you could tell me who referred you—"

"Elizabeth Denkinger."

Michael frowned. Elizabeth Denkinger had been an embezzlement case: she was a small business owner whose profits had gone into freefall after her new boyfriend's teenage son had figured out how to access her accounting software. She'd lost the boyfriend but gained a great deal of peace of mind, and a much better safety net, after using Michael's services.

"I'm not sure her case relates to yours," he said.

"Of course it does," said the man. "Those titles are ours. They're being stolen from us. Every time we come in second—or worse, fail to place at all—our business is devalued. It's embezzlement, plain and simple."

"I see." If he thought about it that way, he could almost see where they were coming from. And being able to pay his bills would, as always, be a rare thrill. "My usual rates apply."

"Naturally. We've brought the first payment." The man offered an envelope across the desk.

Michael took it, opened the flap, and looked inside. He managed not to whistle at the figure on the check, instead mustering a professional smile and asking, "Where do you want me to get started?"

* * *

According to his clients—the Sanfords, of the Rhode Island Sanfords, although what East Coast old money was doing in California was anybody's guess—the Harrisons never appeared together when there was a show. One of them always stayed home with the animals, while the other went to smile at the judges, greet the onlookers, and keep the cats or dogs that they had on display from going completely out of their minds. Because this weekend was a cat show, Nathaniel Harrison would be present, along with a selection of the couples' Maine Coon cats...and of course, their three-time International Grand Champion queen, Unto the Maine's Lady of Shallot, more commonly referred to as "Shelly." He'd been showing her for nearly five years, and it seemed like there wasn't a ribbon or award in North America not claimed by that cat.

(That wasn't quite true. There were awards reserved exclusively for kittens, and Shelly had done her first show as a two-year-old adult. The more Michael read about the dizzying web of rules and regulations governing the world of show cats, the more convinced he became that he wanted absolutely nothing to do with it.)

Getting into the show was easy. Michael paid his forty dollars at the door, electing against the upgraded eighty dollar ticket that would have come with a goodie bag and early access to the judging rings, and he was in. The woman in charge of taking his money smiled as she affixed a plastic band to his wrist, dropping her voice to a conspiratorial whisper as she said, "You made the right choice. I'm supposed to upsell you, but we've sold so damn many 'VIP' bands that it won't make any difference at this point. Save your money, get yourself something nice."

"Thank you for the advice," he said, with a polite nod. "Do you think you could point me in the right direction? My sweetie's been asking about getting a Maine Coon, and I thought I'd come and have a look at the local breeders."

"Oh, you'll want aisle six in the main show room." The woman beamed, bright as a fluorescent bulb. "There are some incredible cats there. Wonderful bloodlines on display. I'm sure you'll find what you're looking for."

"I hope so."

That had been a good fifteen minutes ago. When he'd been approaching the cat show, he had expected this to be an easy assignment. Get in, find the Harrisons, take some pictures, maybe ask a few pointed questions about whether anyone other than his clients felt the couple cheated. Instead, he'd found himself wandering through a maze of makeshift rows formed from folding tables, collapsible cat cages, and portable awnings that wouldn't have looked out of place in a flea market or Renaissance Fair. There were vendors selling cat-themed merchandise everywhere he looked, their products ranging from sweaters and embroidered pillows to portraits of your pet painted while you wait.

And of course, there were the cats. Everywhere cats. So many cats. Most of the fancy awnings belonged to the breeders, creating little enclaves of cat-dom where a single expression of a single breed could reign supreme. Fluffy cats, naked cats, big cats, little cats, cats, cats, *cats*. More cats than Michael had ever seen in his life. More types of cat than he had been aware *existed*.

He stopped in front of a sign proclaiming "FairyTail Siamese: We Put the Wow Back in Meow." There was a woman in the booth on the other side of the sign, dangling a feather on a string above a playpen filled with Siamese kittens. They were mostly snowy white at this age, with sooty paws and noses. Michael wasn't sure he'd ever seen anything more adorable, and was equally sure that there would be something twice as cute on the next aisle. Which was why he needed to get out of here. He was going to suffer permanent cuteness overload if he didn't.

"Excuse me, ma'am?" he said.

The woman looked up and smiled, dazzlingly bright. She had the sort of teeth that really qualified more as an investment, white and straight and perfectly aligned. Michael fought the urge to shy back from the glare.

"Yes?"

"Can you tell me how to find the Maine Coons? I thought it was going to be simple, but all of this," he waved his hands vaguely, "is more complex than I'd expected."

The woman's expression softened, the frighteningly white teeth vanishing behind expertly painted lips. "Oh, you poor dear," she said. "First cat show?"

"Yes, ma'am."

"Go to the end of the row. Make a left at the kiosk selling catnip tea, go down two aisles, and turn right. You'll come to the Maine Coons. Although if you're here because you're looking for the perfect cat for your lifestyle, may I suggest the Siamese? You look like an active fellow. Maine Coons need a lot of brushing, on a daily basis, and they won't appreciate it if you need to leave the house for work. A Siamese, on the other hand, will be a devoted companion who understands that sometimes you need your own space. The best of all possible worlds."

"I'll take that under advisement, ma'am," he said. "Thank you for the directions."

"Think nothing of it," she said, and went back to dangling the feather over her bushel of kittens. They jumped and swatted, tempting in every possible way, and Michael found himself thinking about how nice it would be to have a cat at home.

No, he silently scolded. *Bad.* He had a job to do, and besides, white cat hairs on a black duster didn't really go with the "big, bad noir detective" reputation he was trying to cultivate. It might be attractive to a very specific sort of clientele...but working for those people might wind up dumping him in more situations like this one, where he was expected to prove cheating by a cat. Could cats even cheat? Most of the cats he knew spent their time sleeping in the sun and complaining about the state of their food dishes. Not much cheating there.

The woman's directions were good: in no time at all, he found himself walking down an aisle filled with the sort of cats that weren't actually supposed to exist outside of horror movies. The smallest one in sight had to weigh at least fifteen pounds, making it look more like a long-tailed bobcat than anything that belonged in a private home, and according to the tag on its cage, it was competing in the kitten category. The *kitten* category.

"If that's a kitten, I'm the Queen of Denmark," he muttered, staring at the cat. The cat stared back with unnervingly pumpkin-colored eyes and licked its lips, like it was considering what a private investigator casserole would taste like.

"I assure you, that's a kitten, Your Majesty," said a friendly voice.

Michael looked away from the cat to find himself facing a tall, slender man cast in varying shades of brown, from tawny skin to chestnut hair, with eyes that were somewhere in the middle. He swallowed, hoping the action would be enough to keep him from flushing. It wasn't fair how people were allowed to wander around being so damned attractive all the time.

"It's enormous," said Michael.

"Yes, she is," said the man. He cast a fond look at the cage. The kitten, in turn, looked up at him and made an odd chirping noise. "This is Unto the Maine's Sweet Lady May. She's on the track to place this show, which would be lovely for both of us. I assume you're here because you want to see Shelly?"

It took Michael a moment to remember that "Shelly" was the name of the cat he was supposedly here to spy on. He still didn't know how a cat could cheat. He also, upon some minor reflection, didn't know why this man was offering to show her to him.

"How did you know?" he asked.

The man grinned. "Because everyone is here to see Unto the Maine's Lady of Shallot. I could come with just her, and she'd still have admirers dropping by every five minutes to ooh and aah over her. It's giving her a swelled head, if you ask me, but what do I know? I'm just the human who changes her litterbox. I'm Nathaniel Harrison, by the way. I assume you have a name, apart from your royal title?"

Michael blinked at him for a moment before he remembered his comment about being the Queen of Denmark. This time, he couldn't keep his cheeks from turning red. "I mostly try to keep a low profile on the whole 'royalty' thing," he said, as solemnly as he could. "You can call me Michael."

"Well, Michael, what's your interest in the Maine Coon?"

That wasn't a question he'd been anticipating. Michael froze before blurting the first thing that came into his head: "They're *huge*! I didn't know domestic cats could be this big. It's amazing."

"Ah. 'Huge' and 'amazing' are both accurate descriptors for the Maine Coon or, as some more old-school aficionados call it, 'that Yankee cat.' Come with me." Nathaniel stepped back, fading into the stall and leaving Michael with little choice but to follow him.

Unto the Maine had one of the simpler setups in this area: it was just Nathaniel, a single chair behind a low table, and the cats. Three kittens, three adults. The adults were big enough to make the kittens seem like they were actually to scale. The adults...

Michael had been more right than he knew when he'd looked at Sweet Lady May and declared Maine Coons to be huge. The adults were at least four times her size, still proportionate to themselves; they looked more like longhaired bobcats with raccoon tails than domestic cats.

"May I introduce my pride and joy, Unto the Maine's Lady of Shallot." Nathaniel gestured grandly toward the largest cat, a smoky gray tabby with hints of orange. "I'm afraid I can't ask if you'd like to hold her, for health reasons—hers, not yours, although she might scratch you if you're as bad at holding cats as you look—but I can answer any questions you have, and I'm happy to brush her if you want to see whether her color comes off."

Michael blinked. Nathaniel smirked.

"Oh, come now. I appreciate that the Sanfords have at least gone outside the cat show community for their latest spy, but you couldn't be more out of place if you were carrying a large sign that read 'I have been hired to poke my nose into your business, please show me your secrets.' We have nothing to hide. Shelly is exactly as she appears. I can't blame you for taking a job—one assumes you need to make a living like everyone else— and you haven't done anything truly offensive as yet. That doesn't mean you won't."

Michael's cheeks flushed red again, this time with mortification. "I'd try to tell you that they have honest concerns, but really, I can't," he said. "They just sounded like sore losers to me. Sore losers who'd been referred to me by a good client, which means I have to at least pretend to take them seriously. Like you say, I need to make a living like everyone else."

Unto the Maine's Lady of Shallot made a squeaking noise that wasn't quite a meow and wasn't quite a warble. Michael stared at her.

"I think your cat is malfunctioning."

"No, that's what a Maine Coon is meant to sound like," said Nathaniel. "Look. I have to get Sweet Lady May to judging, and Shelly is up this afternoon. I don't mind your spying on us as much as I probably should, but I don't have time for it right now. How do you feel about coming by the house early next week? We can show you around the property, and you can make up your mind for yourself?"

Michael thought about it for less than thirty seconds. "Absolutely," he said. "Just give me the address."

Nathaniel smiled.

* * *

The Harrisons lived almost an hour's drive outside of city limits. Michael drove down a series of increasingly rural roads with the windows of his car rolled all the way down, breathing in the scent of green growing things and unprocessed air. People who'd seen his office tended to assume that he didn't care for sunlight. The reality was that he didn't like *city* sunlight. It was too sterile, too...stale after being filtered through windows and crammed into the spaces between buildings. He'd rather sit in the dark than stand in city sun. But this, this was sun the way it was meant to be, clean and unfettered and falling on the grassy fields to either side without anything to slow it down.

The urge to pull over, climb over a fence, and run was remarkably strong. Michael forced himself to keep on going. Running around in other people's fields was a good way to get arrested, and *not* a good way to do his job.

Maybe later. On the way home.

The Harrisons lived in a converted farmhouse surrounded by a perfectly cliché white picket fence. There was what looked like a barn out back, and several large dogs playing in the field, which had an equally traditional, if less suburban cattle fence around it. Michael parked behind the single car that was in the driveway, wiping his hands nervously against his jeans, and went to ring the doorbell.

The door opened. A woman with ashy blonde hair smiled at him through the screen, saying, "You must be Michael. Nathaniel told me you'd be dropping by today. Please, come in." She opened the screen door. "I hope you don't mind dogs."

"No, ma'am, although sometimes they mind me." Michael stepped into the front room. It was as traditional as the yard: floral couch, bookshelves, television neatly tucked away in an antique wood cabinet. It looked almost fake, like it had been copied out of a magazine. Only the battered cat tree in one corner made it feel like a real place. There was a cat curled there, massive and orange and fluffy.

Ms. Harrison's eyes narrowed. "Dogs don't like you?"

"Some do. I guess I've just been around a lot of, you know." He gestured helplessly with his hands. "Small dogs. They get skittish when there are new people around."

"Oh." She smiled, looking relieved. "Small dogs aren't going to be an issue here. I'm Thea. It's a pleasure to meet you. Why don't you come with?" She turned and walked out of the room, heading down a short hall to the kitchen. Michael followed.

The impression that the front room wasn't real was just reinforced by the kitchen, which was *so* real that it could have made anything seem artificial. There was a large dining table, piled high with paperwork and with cats; Michael could see three of them sleeping among the paperwork, including Sweet Lady May, who was sprawled on her back with her belly exposed to the ceiling. A pair of braided rag rugs blunted the hardwood floor, and the appliances, while all reasonably modern, were clearly well-used.

There was also a dog, a Great Dane the size of a small pony, with dark brown fur, sleeping in the middle of the larger of the two rugs. Fiona stopped, giving it a fondly exasperated look.

"May I introduce Unto the Maine's Sketchy Character—we call him 'Stretch.' I'm assuming that when the Sanfords hired you, they mentioned that we also show dogs?"

Michael nodded.

"I mostly handle preparing and showing the Great Danes. Stretch here has taken three Grand Championships, and he's gearing up for a fourth. Great Danes are relatively mellow dogs, which makes them a good match for Maine Coon cats. They just get on with things. Unlike the Sanfords, who essentially embody the concept of the little yappy dog. They'd bite the ankles of the universe if they thought it would get them something."

"I don't have any trouble picturing that, ma'am," said Michael. He crouched down, looking at the Great Dane. "You don't do anything by halves, do you? Giant cats, giant dogs. It's all big around here."

"We enjoy sturdy things."

Michael looked at the dog for a few more seconds, taking in the shape of its bones, the angles of its long face. Then he whistled softly. The dog opened its eyes.

"Huh," said Michael. He stood, turning back to Fiona. "Where's Mr. Harrison, ma'am?"

"He couldn't be here today."

"So he's out?"

"That's what I said, isn't it?"

"No, ma'am, it isn't, quite. I was just wondering, you see, if he messed up his count when he asked if I wanted to come for a visit. I'm guessing he's a quarter-moon type of guy, since I assume he'd be on two legs right now if he could."

Fiona blinked. There was a low growl from behind him. The dog was up, then. Good: this was always easier if everyone heard it at the same time.

"I wasn't sure," he said apologetically. "I mean, it seemed odd that you would show both cats and dogs, but I don't know much about the show world. It could have been perfectly normal. So I did a little digging. You came out of nowhere, the pair of you, with the best cat and the best dog anyone had seen in years. No kitten or puppy pictures, though. It was like you'd just found them. No one's ever seen a picture of the four of you, or of you with Lady of Shallot, or Nathaniel with Sketchy Character. You don't breed them. You don't appear with them. You missed a cat show last year when it fell on the quarter-moon. Do you not have a backup handler for when Nathaniel isn't available?"

Fiona said nothing. Her eyes blazed hatred. That was answer enough.

There was a bump as Sketchy Character—Nathaniel's—nose hit the back of Michael's knees. Michael smiled a little. "I guess the logical thing here is for one of you to bite me. Can't give you away if I'm one of you. There's just one problem."

"What's that?" asked Fiona, through gritted teeth.

"It won't work."

"I assure you." She smiled. There was nothing pleasant about it. "It will work just fine."

"No, it won't." He held up his hand. How he hated this part. Only going partway was like thinking about masturbating: frustrating and ultimately fruitless. But it was what had to happen next. He concentrated.

The skin of his hand rippled, darkened, and began to spread, first fusing his fingers into a single mass, and then pulling back as his nails became thick and pink, expanding into a hoof. A few wispy strands of fur accompanied the change, but it stopped short of becoming true fur: if he let it go that far, he'd burst his clothes, and pants weren't cheap.

"You can't infect another therianthrope, ma'am," he said, still apologetic.

Fiona stared. "You're a *horse*," she said.

"Yes, ma'am."

"They...those fools hired a werehorse to figure out whether we were cheating. A *werehorse*. What are the odds?"

"I don't know, ma'am." He shrugged. "There are four P.I.s working that beat, so I suppose one in four." His hoof rippled, melting back into a hand. He grimaced. "Wow, that itches."

Fiona's stare softened. "You poor thing," she said. "You live in the city, don't you?"

"Yes, ma'am."

"When's the last time you really got to run?"

Michael blinked at her before slowly, shyly, beginning to smile.

* * *

Some people were surprised when Unto the Maine expanded to begin showing Friesian horses alongside the dogs and cats they already had. Others felt it was a good thing: that sort of overreach would inevitably result in their quality slipping and other people being able to snatch up the prizes that were rightfully theirs. No one was quite sure what the relationship was between the Harrisons and their new live-in trainer, Michael Collins, but the three were thick as thieves. Michael took over the cat shows, while Fiona continued to show the dogs, and Nathaniel showed the horses.

No matter the phase of the moon, they never missed another competition. And if some people swore they'd seen a black Friesian racing around the Harrisons' farm with a blue tabby Maine Coon clinging to its saddle and a brown Great Dane running at its heels, well, fresh country air can be intoxicating to those who aren't accustomed to it.

WE DIG
ASHLEY MCCONNELL

They felt the rumble first, a rise and fall like an ocean wave carrying them up and then down again, as if earth had momentarily become sea. Men's eyes looked up from their breakfast eggs and met their wives', and then went back to their plates. Forks scraped up the last bits just a little more quickly, and the women went out for water without saying anything. It might, after all, have been a planned detonation.

The church bells started tolling as the men were coming out of their homes, carrying their lunch boxes, kissing their wives goodbye. The sound froze them all in their tracks, as one and all they turned to look up at the hills around the town of Silverfield, seeking the column of smoke that had to be there.

The bells did not stop. The men shook themselves, started for the square between the church and the town hall, while their women and children clung to the doorways or windowsills, staring at the smoke, brown and gray against the blue sky.

A horseman came down the hill in a lathered gallop, shoving through the men, and the bells kept on tolling, tolling as they gathered, watching him spin the horse around, stand in his stirrups and wave frantically at the bell tower. It was not until all the men had gathered that the bells stopped.

"Half a dozen, I think," he gasped. "In the Tolliver. We need...diggers."

"What happened?" came a voice from the back of the crowd.

The man shook his head and licked his lips, trying to find enough moisture and air to answer. "Bad blast," was all he said.

A mutter ran through the crowd: "Third time in six months!" Still, several men shouldered their way to the front, yelled for horses. Others did not wait, but started up the road, up the hill, toward the column of black smoke smeared against the blue sky.

By the time they made it to the mine head, at least twenty Flickers had joined the group and gathered in the open space before it. A frame office building stood perpendicular to the abrupt slope of the hill; across from it a sorting warehouse was open to the winds, and in front of it a set of railroad tracks ran into the mine. The entrance to the Tolliver mine shaft itself was a large hole, a black, forbidding square perhaps twice the height of a tall man framed by rough, squared-off timbers. Dust still hung in the air before the opening.

Next to the shaft was a tumble of huge rocks, waste from the excavation. On one of them, five men stood, arguing among themselves. Finally one of the foremen stood forth from the rest, his forehead creased, his face pale. "All right," he said, raising his voice over the general mutters. "What do we have here? Diggers?"

"Macaque!" one man said indignantly.

"Pangolin," Smetse—Smitty to his friends—Katangazu said, raising one hand.

"Moles," chorused half a dozen others, squinting against the light.

"Armadillo," another called from the back of the crowd.

"Fox!" someone yelped.

"Where the *hell* did we find a pangolin?" the foreman muttered to himself. "Never mind. Where's Tom Mitchell?"

"Here." Tom came up from the back of the crowd and elbowed his way through to the front. "What have you got, MacDougal? What happened here?" He was a relatively short man, grizzled hair at his temples, even though he was a young man, not yet twenty-five, with dark hair and dark, dark eyes, wide shoulders, powerful arms. He walked with his chin thrust forward, as if daring anyone to take a swing at him. His clothes were the same as the rest of the diggers': worn jeans and short boots, stained cotton shirt. The crowd of diggers made way for him as if it was his right.

MacDougal tugged on his suspenders—a nervous habit that had long since resulted in suspenders stretched out beyond any use for holding up his trousers, leaving them sagging on one side. "Blest if I know. Far as I can tell, some charges went off when they weren't supposed to, and we had half a shift down there. We got six out, but there are six more, near as we can tell, behind the collapse. We need to dig them out, boys."

Another man, standing behind him, stepped forward. He was tall, red-haired, dressed noticeably better than the men he looked down on, in a clean, if dusty, coat with good trousers, and diamond links for his sleeves.

"We've got to clear that tunnel," he said. "I'm paying you men good money to get in there and get it done."

They stared at him. Gillings was a Still, one of those who didn't change, had no second soul. He made no secret of the fact that he thought that made him superior to those who Flickered between one phase and the other. He was not well liked. He also owned the mine.

"That's suicide," one of the moles said. "You've got a blast, no way to know what supports are still good, no way to know what else is going off? Just like the last time and the time before that?"

"Yeah," Tom said, lowering his head and glaring at the mole under knitted brows. "And if it's you *next* time? I'll do it."

"Damn badgers," someone muttered. "More teeth than brains."

Tom smiled, showing teeth. The crowd jostled back a half step, starting with the moles. "I'm going for it. Who's with me?"

"I'll go," Smitty said.

"And I." "I'm with you." "I'll go."

MacDougal nodded, clear relief washing the worry from his expression for at least a few seconds. "That's good. Good. Look, boys, sign up before you go change, so Mr. Gillings here will have a record—"

"Because he has to have a record of every breath we take, in case we inhale some silver in his mine," someone shouted from the back. Gillings' head jerked up, and he stared at the crowd of diggers, looking for the speaker. The crowd stared back at him, sullen.

"What are the chances there's anybody alive in there, really?" Mitchell asked. He had jumped up on the rock beside MacDougall and Gillings, brushing his hands together as if to get the dust off, and lowered his voice. "Why do you think they're alive?"

"I heard them," said another man at the foot of the rock, craning his neck to look up at them. His face and one leg were soaked in blood. "The roof came down right in front of us, but we could hear screaming. We were down the main shaft, past the store rooms, right where it branches. There's a good vein there."

"So what happened?"

The man shrugged and winced, putting one hand against the platform rock as he staggered. "We were setting charges. Mikey, he said he thought they were greasy, but—"

"It couldn't be," Gillings said. "I knew we were opening up a new shaft. New equipment, new everything. Somebody made a mistake. Somebody lit a short fuse."

MacDougal shook his head. "Look, boys, there are six men still in there. The reason why doesn't matter. Can we go get them? Now?"

Tom Mitchell looked at him consideringly. "It matters if it means there's going to be another explosion that will take the rest of us out, yeah." The Flickers behind him nodded, and a few yells of agreement echoed. "But you're right. If someone's still alive down there, we're going to try to get them out." He jumped down from the rock and started up the slope to the hole in the side of the hill. The other diggers looked at each other, shrugged, and followed. Behind them, MacDougal waved papers. They ignored him.

The first few yards past the timbers were illuminated by the sunlight through the opening, and their shadows stretched before them. When the shadows disappeared, they turned as a group into a small room carved into the guts of the hillside. There was barely light at all, as if light was only a memory from the outside.

They stripped, bundled their clothing in careful piles against the wall, and Flicked. In one instant they were men, scruffy, muscular, poor. In the time it took to look away and back again—in the Flick of an eye—they were not men any more. Not, at least, in shape.

The mine Flickers shook themselves and looked around the darkness, and a chorus of snorts and sniffs filled the space around them as they oriented themselves by smell. Tom Mitchell growled low as someone brushed by him—Smitty, by the feel of the scales that covered his body. The scent only confirmed it.

He could smell the moles, clustered together in a corner as far from him as he could get, and the human still within him grinned without humor. Badgers ate moles. Flickers didn't eat each other—generally speaking— but the animals remembered. Tom wasn't planning on eating anyone today, but the moles' caution still amused him. The same magic that gave him, as a man, the proportionate strength of a badger—as well as the short temper, aggression, and weak eyesight—gave him a man's ability to think, to reason, in his animal form. He was never one or the other, but always both.

Whelford was the macaque. Almost useless, really, in mines, but he did have one gross advantage over the rest of them: he still had hands. He also had a monkey sense of humor, and Tom found himself being used as a springboard as Whelford leaped from the floor, to Tom's back, to a shelf above their heads. For a blind leap, it wasn't that much of a risk; he'd done it before, knew what was stored there, and like the rest of them had been there before with a lamp.

And there *was* a lamp on the shelf. Whelford brought it to the floor, fumbled with a match, and lit it. His job was to carry it down the shaft, hang it on a hook, and then leave. The single flame would provide enough light for the moles, who were nearly blind anyway, and the badgers, and the rest of the diggers to see where they were going, and more importantly, the way back out.

Tom let Whelford scamper well ahead before padding out of the change room, Smitty at his side. He couldn't smell gas, and the flame should be safe enough, but he didn't like fire, and he liked it less in fur form. They passed several more rooms, used to store carts, tools for the Stills—the ones who couldn't change—and crates of explosives. Tom paused to look inside, sniffing deeply of the scent of dirt, explosive, wood, primer cord, the scent of the men who had carried the boxes here.

Smitty snorted and shouldered past, his long tongue touching here and there across the crates. Whelford, insatiably curious, came back to see what they were looking at, but there was nothing, nothing but the skittering of long gray insects across the crates. Smitty caught up a half dozen on a long, flexible tongue. The labels, with their large red warning text, were relatively bright against the wood, even in the impossibly dim light from the lantern. Tom snarled, and Whelford scampered away. Reluctantly, Smitty turned back to go with him down the shaft, wobbling a bit as he went. Pangolins walked on their foreclaws, huge and curved and impossibly sharp. Tom's claws, by comparison, merely scarred the dirt and rock floor, a mixture of earth, rock, and guano under their paws. All the bats had fled when the collapse had started. The path sloped gently, and then not so gently, downward into the earth.

With a happy chirp, Whelford hung the lamp from a hook and took down another waiting in a niche beside it and continued leading them downward into the dark. They followed the railroad tracks laid down for ore carts until they veered away down the tunnel and a new hole appeared. This one was round, rough, without the relatively smooth finished sides of the mine shaft; rock outcrops jutted up from the ground and hung down from the ceiling. The scent trail said that miners had gone this way.

New lamp niches appeared every twenty feet, leaving tiny flames to provide more hope than illumination, marking support beams that grew shorter and shorter as the tunnel narrowed. The Tolliver mine contained mainly silver, with some gold, zinc, lead, and even an occasional turquoise outcrop. The group of Flickers straggled into single file, ducking under outcrops that hung down from the ceiling, scrambling over knots of rock that had been too hard and too unproductive to bother removing from the floor. Three niches down, the macaque stopped and chittered. The shaft before them was completely blocked, with support beams sagging and splintered across boulders bigger than any one of them, and a fan of dirt poured out at their feet. As they surveyed the damage, the pile shuddered.

More rocks fell, and more earth whispered down the sides of the tunnel. Whelford squeaked again, set down his lamp, and scampered back up the tunnel. The opening before the rock fall was too low for a human form to stand comfortably, even one as short as most of them were.

The moles moved up, with nearly supersonic squeaks, and Mitchell snarled. One turned blindly toward him, still squeaking, and he reached out with a casual paw and batted it against the far wall of the tunnel. Every Flicker froze in place.

Mitchell listened.

A badger can hear the sound of an earthworm moving, smell the memory of a prairie dog's passing. A Flicker could do that, and more. He could hear the air moving in and out of the lungs of the Flickers around him, the tiny, uncontrolled moan of the mole whose leg had been broken by his blow, and taste their fear in the air. He could hear the shifting of the earth above him, before him. He could smell, through layers of rock and dirt, blood and death and the stink of explosives. Stretching up on four short legs, he raised his head and focused on the rock fall before him. Next to him, Jerry's long, wide ears swiveled forward to scoop sound out of the air.

When he had heard enough, he Flicked back into human form, coughed once to clear dust from his lungs. "I hear them," he said. "Moles, take your friend back up and have him looked at. Next time," he snarled at the protesting moles, "shut the hell up when you're told to. Now move. Jerry and I will start here. Send us some Stills to move earth."

One of the moles Flicked, hunched over in his human form, and spat on the ground between them. "We can help," he said. "They're our people, too. Even if they are Stills, they're miners."

Mitchell's face twisted, as if to issue a snarl more suited to his other form, and then took a deep breath and let it go instead. "All *right*," he said. "But take care of him first." He looked the injured Flicker in the face. "I'm sorry."

The tiny, blind eyes blinked, as if in surprise. His human-form kin picked him up, carefully, and started back up the tunnel, bent double with the mole tucked against his chest. The rest of the moles gathered, shoulder to shoulder, and settled in, oozing stubbornness.

"I'm going up to the top of the slide," Mitchell said. "I'll let you know if—*when*—I need you." There was general grumbling, but they kept it quiet, and Mitchell Flicked into his badger form. His real form, the form where he could breathe and move and dig.

He sniffed at the pile of dirt and rocks, then swarmed up the slope, ignoring the way the rock fall slid and shifted under his paws. In this form, he weighed only about thirty pounds, and it wasn't enough to move the bigger boulders.

The ground wouldn't stay still, though. He had to scramble to stay in place, get to a rock that would hold long enough for him to sniff deep at the place where the ceiling had given way. The Flickers below and behind him were silent. Silent as the tomb, he thought, and his lip curled, showing fangs. Some jokes weren't so funny. Tombs were only supposed to be six feet deep.

Poised at the top of the collapse, he reached out one paw to test the consistency of the dirt, and snarled to himself. There wasn't room for him to Flick back, not up here, and he'd wind up sliding all the way to the bottom and bringing more of the ceiling with him if he tried. He couldn't talk in this form, and he really wanted Jerry's claws right now to rip into the dirt and rock.

But he'd Flicked, he'd climbed, and now—he stretched out his front paws, armed with five long flat claws each, four of which were two inches long, and he took hold of the earth, and he began to dig.

His front feet scooped out the dirt, while his back feet shoved it clear behind him. In the right dirt, a badger could dig faster than a man with a shovel, and no man with a shovel could get in the places he could go. He could hear the Flickers below him chittering and talking—some of them must have Flicked back—but that didn't matter now. What mattered was the movement, the resistance of the earth, the eagerness with which he sank into it, swimming through it, snarling as he hit rock, shaking dirt from his nose, digging deeper and deeper toward the voices and the howls and cries he could hear on the other side of the earth.

He could feel the earth pressing down against his back as he clawed at it. To either side he could feel the heat of other bodies that had followed him up the slope of the rock fall and were digging as well.

The ground shifted under his paws, and he stopped and growled a warning. Around him, the others stopped too, waiting for Earth to decide whether it would bury them today.

As they waited, Earth shuddered, and they could hear the frightened cries from the other side of the rock fall clearly now. They were close, close enough that the smell of blood and terror of the trapped Stills—all of the living ones Stills, according to his nose—filled his nostrils, and Mitchell reached farther, harder, to pull away the rock and grit separating them from him.

Off to one side a Flicked fox yelped as rock tumbled and slid. Mitchell forced himself to slow down. They didn't have to remove the entire fall, only enough to allow the trapped men to get through. Behind him he could hear voices of Flickers in human form, talking about stretchers. He felt a shiver in the fur of his left foreleg, reached over, and snapped. A spasmodic quiver of life and blood between his teeth told him it was a mouse, and he swallowed without pausing in the steady reach, claw, swing back, shove rhythm of his excavation. His paws were bleeding now. Even badgers rarely tried to tackle rock.

Bugs, he thought, in some distant corner of his mind. He needed to talk to Smitty about the bugs.

His claws reached and pulled, narrowly avoiding the other Flicks around him.

A mole was the first to punch through, announcing its achievement with a startled squeak as it fell into the chamber on the other side. For an instant there was silence, and then they could hear voices, moans, cries from the miners on the other side. A single lamp's-worth of light glowed feebly from the blocked chamber.

There was still no room to change to communicate. Mitchell growled and redoubled his efforts, nearly following the mole into the next room when he emerged at the top of a mass of rock that dropped off abruptly on the other side. Earth rumbled.

The trapped miners screamed as fresh air came in the opening and began clawing frantically toward it, and Mitchell, and the mole. Mitchell moved to one side as one by one they scrambled through.

All but one man, not much older than Mitchell, but with softer hands, and a left leg that clearly could not bear his weight. Mitchell growled down at him as the man tried again and again, with human hands and human feet, to climb up, but his injury was against him.

A rumble shivered through the air, and a fine patter of dirt and rock fell across them.

"Help me!" the Still screamed up at him. "Help me!"

This man didn't belong here, down in the mines; he was too soft, his clothes too good, and Mitchell could smell the incipient panic in him from the closeness and darkness pressing in on them. But here he was. And here Mitchell was. The mole beside him squeaked a shrill warning as the ground shifted again, and fled.

"Hel—"

The man didn't have the chance to finish the plea before Mitchell slid down the pile of rocks and Flicked. "Lie down on the slope, face up, and *shut up*," he said. And then he Flicked again, and badger jaws clamped down on the rough collar of the Still's shirt, and he began backing upward.

A fine patter of dirt rained down from the roof of the chamber. The Flicks at the top of the rock fall screamed, and Mitchell set his jaws hard and yanked, pulling nine times his own weight uphill, backwards, with only the man's good leg pushing to help as he pulled, and now rocks were falling on them both. One chunk of ore, almost as heavy as he was, smashed down next to the man's shoulder, and he arched up in panic, carrying the badger with him. Mitchell snarled again through the mouthful of cloth and slapped the man's arm, and he settled into pushing as Mitchell pulled. They were nearly at the top when the roof caved in.

* * *

A week later, Tom Mitchell was summoned to the offices of the Tolliver Mining Company. MacDougal had sent a runner, a child of seven or eight years, down to Silverfield to find him as he prepared to join his shift for the first time since the rescue.

"What does he want?" Mitchell asked.

The child shrugged. "Don't know. Just says, they want to see you in the big boss's office." He gave the man a sideways glance. "Trouble, maybe?"

Mitchell's lip curled. "Maybe." For whom, though?

Once again he trudged the familiar path up the hill to the square, the warehouse, the mine shaft. This time there were no crowds milling around, just the miners gathering, waiting to be checked into the mine for their shift in the bowels of the earth. He raised a hand to them, but instead of joining them, climbed the wooden steps to the door of the office building.

MacDougal, smiling, met him in the foyer and led him down the hall to the office in the back. "It's a great thing today," he said, "a great thing." Mitchell lifted an eyebrow and did not bother to respond.

Six men were waiting in Gillings' office, including Gillings, four well-dressed strangers he thought were members of the Board of Directors—their portraits lined the hallway—and another, younger man he could not place. By their scents, they were all Stills; they stank of cigars and wool and sweat. They were all seated in comfortable leather chairs, with Gillings behind a broad desk and the rest in a semicircle to the right and left, with a gap in the middle so the visitor would be properly awed. Gillings and the Board members glanced at each other as Mitchell came in and stopped in the middle of the room, hands on his hips, waiting. He was wearing his work clothes and boots, and a rough bandage was still visible under the collar of his flannel shirt. There was not, he noted, an extra chair available for him, or for MacDougal either.

"Mr. Mitchell!" Gillings said, rising from behind his desk and coming around it, a broad smile fixed on his face. "Thank you so much for joining us. This is a very special day. These gentlemen here are from the Board of Directors for Tolliver Mines, and they've all come together today just to meet you."

The younger man cleared his throat. A shadow of annoyance flashed across Gillings' face. "And of course this is Mr. Norris, from the Bureau of Mines."

The last time Tom Mitchell had seen "Mr. Norris" was when he had dragged him by main force through a hole in the ground, just as the roof collapsed in the chamber where the miners had been trapped. Now Norris was cleaned up, smiling, levering himself out of his chair with a crutch, limping forward with hand outstretched. "Mr. Mitchell. I can't tell you how glad I am to see you again."

"We're all very grateful," MacDougal said from behind him. "We're still trying to find out what happened; nobody wants this to happen again. Mr. Norris has been trying to discover what's behind this." He started to say something else, Mitchell thought, but Gillings made a sudden movement and MacDougal fell silent.

"We'd like to make a little presentation," Gillings said, still smiling. "The Board has decided that we should show our appreciation for your courage in recent events."

Mitchell looked around. The Board was nodding and smiling. Norris was still holding out his hand.

Mitchell waited a second before taking it. He could feel some calluses, but they weren't from handling a shovel or pickaxe. Evidently men from the Bureau of Mines did not actually work in mines very often. The grip was not soft, though. It was the grip of a man who was sure of himself, and Mitchell thought he liked Norris, soft or not.

"I wasn't the only one digging," Mitchell said directly to Gillings. "Aren't you going to call the rest of them in?"

Gillings laughed, taken aback. "Well. It was you who led them, Mac tells us. So we're going to make our presentation, our thanks to you, and we'll count on you to convey it to the rest of the...men. And of course you can share this with them, as you see fit." He had turned back to his desk, picked up an envelope, and now offered it to him.

"As I see fit," Mitchell said flatly. The news would be all over Silverfield, of course. "You can't give each of them an award, can you." He had not taken the envelope.

"Well." Gillings laughed again. The Board members looked at each other. Mitchell had the feeling that this was a surprise to them, too. "That would be pretty expensive. And we're really not sure just how many of you there were, of course. We wouldn't want to overlook anyone."

"Of course."

"What we really want," Norris said, "is to find out exactly what happened. That's why I was here. I've been investigating the recent explosions at the Tolliver mines. I'd like to talk to you about that—"

"So you were spying on us?" Mitchell asked, his voice carefully neutral. "What were you looking for?"

"Spying? No, not at all. I was investigating. We've been trying to find out what's behind this series of mine explosions."

"Really." Mitchell smiled suddenly, showing teeth. "That's very interesting, Mr. Norris. I'm glad to see you, too. Very glad. Because I think I've got some answers to your questions."

The Board members stirred and looked at each other. Gillings, still holding on to the envelope, went back around behind his desk and stood, holding the back of the desk chair. His smile was still frozen in place.

"Really, Mr. Norris, it's very unlikely Mr. Mitchell can give you any help on this. He's a brave man, of course, that's why he's here, but he's just a miner. And I've been trying to explain, sometimes accidents happen. It's unfortunate, really terrible, but these things are unpredictable at best. Human—" he paused just an instant too long after the word— "error, gas pockets, any number of things can cause—"

"Or bad dynamite," Mitchell said quietly. "Maybe you should be looking at that, Mr. Norris."

Norris raised an eyebrow. "Really? Tell me more."

"What? What are you talking about?" Gillings snapped. "There's no bad dynamite in my mines!" The smile had finally, finally disappeared.

Tom Mitchell looked around at the group of men, Stills every one of them, staring at him as if he'd Flicked and a badger stood before them, talking.

"We lost three men in this last accident at Tolliver One," he said. "Three of them didn't make it."

"Three Flicks," Gillings interposed. "A tragedy, of course," he hastened to add as one by one the directors looked at him.

"Three men," Mitchell repeated. "I'm a miner, Mr. Norris. I don't know the legal ins and outs. But it seems to me that if somebody tries to hide something, he must have a reason. And our Mr. Gillings here, he's been hiding something.

"He's careful with his coin, is our Mr. Gillings," he went on. "Just you look at the charges in the company store. Or what our families are paying to bury their dead. He'll even save money on the coffins." Or on "rewards" and "recognition", he did not add.

"That's not what you're here for," Gillings said harshly, coming around his desk. "You ungrateful Flick, you show some respect..." His voice trailed off as Norris raised one hand.

"Mr. Gillings, here, found a cache of old dynamite and decided to use that in the mines instead, even after the frost we've been having," Mitchell went on, ignoring the owner. "Instead of blowing it up in place, he slapped new labels on it. Smitty saw the bugs."

"What? What are you talking about?" Gillings yelled. Layers of composure were falling away, like earth sliding from a cave wall. "What kind of nonsense—"

"Now, Gillings, let the man talk," said the oldest of the directors, pointing a half-smoked cigar at the other man. "This is interesting. I want to hear more."

"So do I," Norris said, stepping back to give him room, to let everyone see him. "Old dynamite? Why was the frost important?"

"Dynamite's tricky stuff, Mr. Norris. Especially old dynamite. It goes unstable pretty easy when the temperature changes. Starts sweating nitro. Tastes greasy, that stuff.

"If it wasn't old, it might not have mattered so much. Gillings here, he likes to save every penny. Makes him look good to these gentlemen, I'm sure. He thought he'd save money buying older explosives, and it might have worked for a while. But then the freeze hit."

"That's ridiculous. It's my job to watch costs, keep them under control. That's what they pay me for, to run this place at a profit. You can't prove it was old," Gillings sputtered. He was directing his words as much to the directors as to Norris. "I've been buying all along. It's in my monthly reports. If I got old stuff, I didn't know. It was labelled, dated. You saw the dates on the boxes."

"New labels, pasted over old ones, in case anybody checked," Mitchell riposted. "Look for yourself, if you want to take the risk. We knew the old labels were there. Like I said, Smitty Katangazu saw the bugs. He's a pangolin. He knows bugs."

"What bugs?" Norris was trying to follow, laboring to keep up.

"The little silver ones, the ones that go after the glue on the labels. Those bugs like the old glue, and he tasted them, but the labels were fresh.

If the bugs were there, those fresh labels had to be pasted over old ones, ones that had old glue."

"You can't prove it!" Gillings yelled. "You can't take the word of, of an animal!" His face was almost as red as his hair, Mitchell thought. Mitchell bared his teeth in a badger's grin.

"That's what we thought you'd say," Mitchell replied. "Knowing how you feel about us. So a couple of nights ago, a bunch of us went to the records room. You've got Flicks guarding the warehouse, Mr. Gillings. Did you know that?

"We found the books," he said, his lip curled. "We found your monthly reports, and we matched all those expenses you carefully recorded for the company's Board of Directors." He gave the seated directors a nod. "But we found no entries for dynamite in the books, not for the last six months." He dug into his pocket. "You haven't been buying explosives recently.

"But we did find an order to the printers, and their invoice." He held up a piece of paper. "You made yourself a private deal. You ordered a new set of labels, with new dates, and pasted the new labels on your old boxes. It was all in your records, your papers. You never throw anything away. Too cheap."

"I didn't do it!" Gillings shouted. "It was all—MacDougal handles all that! He did it!"

Behind him, Mitchell could hear MacDougal take an indignant breath. Norris was looking at the invoice, and back at Gillings. One of the directors held out a hand for it.

"Yeah, Mac handles your orders and your invoices. We could tell, you see, because we could smell it. His scent was all over them. But not on this one." The Flick had to swallow back a snarl, and the urge to swipe the look off the other man's face. "He never touched that order. Or this invoice, either. The only scent on it from this end is yours, Gillings. You handled this deal all by yourself. You found a way to save some money, and to hell with the risk to the men. Even after the dynamite started exploding off schedule, causing cave-ins."

"It's a lie," Gillings said. He looked around at the directors. "You can't believe him."

They had passed the invoice around. They looked at him stonily.

"I think I'll pass on *your* reward, Mr. Gillings," Mitchell added. "Maybe the directors can find a better use for it."

"How did you find it all?" Norris asked, as his deputies led Gillings away in handcuffs. "I've been in there. There are thousands of invoices and records in that warehouse. It must have taken you—"

"I'm a badger, Mr. Norris," Tom Mitchell said, showing sharp teeth again. "We follow our noses. And we dig."

EYES LIKE PEARLS
SUSAN JETT

Mara looked around her room at the scatter of pebbles and bits of dried kelp littering the windowsill. She wanted to bring it all home, every broken seashell and grit of sand, because it had been a perfect summer, despite this afternoon's fishing fiasco. Tomorrow morning, just before they left, she'd sweep everything into a suitcase. She didn't want to risk leaving anything behind and her mom could just wash the sand out of everything when they got back home.

Ugh. Home.

Today her dad had laughed when she asked if they could just move here, and she'd smiled obligingly because he'd obviously thought she was kidding. But she hadn't been. They'd spent almost a month in the sandy little beach town where her mom grew up, and Mara had expected to hate it. But then she'd met some of the other summer kids. She'd met Garrett, who lived in town, and decided this spot was the most beautiful place in the world. Her best friend Kyla was going to be so jealous.

Mara glanced over at the clock by her bed. 8:30. She'd already missed moonrise. Garrett would tell her all about it though, if she asked him, and she couldn't leave until after her parents came to check on her. They wouldn't bother her after that. Mara heard her dad limping around the tiny family room, his prosthetic leg thumping loudly. He was probably trying to dance and doing it badly for effect, since her mother was laughing fondly. In her bedroom, Mara rolled her eyes. Her parents were such enormous losers.

Her mom had flat-out refused to go deep-sea fishing this morning, but her dad had bribed Mara with a trip to the mall when they got home. It had been kind of fun sneaking away, like they were getting away with something. But being seasick hadn't been fun, and being attacked by a giant fish hadn't been fun either. The barracuda's blood had been pink and watery where it pooled on the deck, and hers was red and disgustingly viscous where it dripped onto the fish's silvery scales. Stupid fish. Its teeth had grazed her knuckles when her dad dragged it over the side while she was puking. When she'd yelped and lurched away, her father hadn't even asked if she was ok, just started whacking it with his cane until the captain of the little charter boat had intervened, scooping the long body up and dumping it into a freezer on the deck. "Keep on like that, sir, and it aint gonna be good for anything but chum."

The memory made Mara want to vomit again. And seven hours later, Dad was still acting like clubbing a fish to death had been the high point of his summer, maybe his life. He'd even served the dead fish for dinner tonight, like they didn't sell perfectly good fillets at the Piggly Wiggly.

"It doesn't work that way, you know." Mara's mother had bitten off the words between her tiny, perfect teeth as she stared at her daughter's bandaged hand. "It's not like you can scare it out of her."

"It was an accident. You know I didn't mean for her to get hurt."

"I know you were so busy trying to punish me—again—that you didn't much care what happened to anyone else. Even our daughter." Her mother had stared at him, her black eyes unblinking, then she'd pushed away from the table, her dinner untouched. Mara watched her go and then she and her dad traded embarrassed looks. Still hungry—though not really for clubbed-to-death fish—Mara went to her room soon after, annoyed with them both. Everyone thought their parents were the most embarrassing humans alive, but surely hers really were.

The bandage itched and Mara rubbed it irritably. At least Mom had been outraged on her behalf this afternoon. Usually it was Mara who made her angry. They'd been clashing more and more this last year, with her mom demanding to know her whereabouts every minute of the day. At least just now it was Dad being scolded like a kid, even if the only real danger Mara had been in was from puking her guts out. If she hadn't been so sick, she certainly could have gotten out of the fish's way, no matter how toothy it was—and it really had possessed far too many teeth for a normal fish, she thought. Trust dad to find a mutant fish to kill. Not that she'd seen many live fish to compare it to. The mountain town they lived in was about as far away from the ocean as you could get on the East Coast.

Mom was right, though, that Dad hadn't seemed to care when she'd gotten hurt. He'd been too busy pretending to be Ahab. Mara felt a moment of resentment directed at him, too, now. Because no matter how many stupid sharky-looking fish he killed, he was still just a frumpy English teacher who'd lost his leg in a car accident long before Mara was born. She'd seen pictures, and he'd been good-looking once upon a time. But now, between all his scars and his leg, Mara sometimes wondered what her mom saw in him anymore. Mom was drop-dead gorgeous, even now that she was old. Strangers turned to watch when she walked by. And when she could be persuaded to perform, everyone listened as raptly as if they heard angels singing.

Mom knocked at her door now and Dad asked her to play Monopoly with them. Fat chance. Though having them gang up on her was more comfortable than listening to them fight. But this was her last weekend here, and everyone had been collecting driftwood for days. Not only that, but Garrett was going to bring his guitar to the bonfire. Mara had never heard him sing, but he could practically be a rock star with that hair, and the way his voice sounded when it went low—it made her insides flip around like a school of little fish trapped in a net.

Which was actually kind of a disgusting comparison.

But there was no way she was going to miss this. And she could be back again before morning with no one the wiser. Tonight would be hers, and if she was lucky, Garrett would be hers, too. All summer long they'd been circling each other—inching together, then drawing apart. He was older than her, yeah, and maybe back in June he'd thought of her as a little sister, but surely by now he knew better. She'd made him laugh last week, a real out-loud laugh, not a big brother kind of laugh. And while her parents might decide to come back here next summer, they might not. And anything could happen between now and then. Maybe Garrett would find a girlfriend. Maybe he'd move away or something. This might be her last chance, and Mara was willing to risk being grounded for a year in order to make it happen.

She caught one last look at her reflection in the mirror as she threw one leg over the windowsill and grimaced to check for spinach stuck to her teeth. Her eyes gleamed like pearls and her lips looked dark in the moonlight. She looked older. She looked like her mom. Then she giggled and the illusion was shattered and she was just fifteen again.

The noise her rubber-soled sneakers made, gritting on the sandy porch, made her cringe, but it certainly wasn't loud enough to be heard over her dad's ridiculous laugh. Practically skipping down the worn steps, Mara hurried to the beach, wending her way through the tight-packed little cottages as easily as a clownfish navigated a coral reef.

The full moon was already up, barely kissing its twin out on the ocean. Faint music came from over by the big pile of rocks, and she headed that way, following the glow of rising sparks from the fire. She hoped Garrett liked her outfit. She hoped he asked her to go for a walk. She hoped she didn't embarrass herself somehow, and she especially hoped that he wouldn't guess she'd never kissed anyone before.

As she got closer, she heard a boy singing, his voice stretching thin on the high notes. She knew it was him. His guitar playing was more assured than his singing, but she thought he sounded as good as anything she'd ever heard on the radio. Better maybe, because he looked up just as she stepped into the circle of firelight and his whole face lit up when he met her eyes. She felt an answering jolt in her own body, like they were connected by a thin line of electricity. Her hand under the bandage tingled. Maybe it's the full moon, she thought. Or maybe this is what destiny feels like.

Picking her way through the crowd, she murmured greetings and accepted a beer some older girl handed her. She sipped absently before remembering how much she didn't like beer. Garrett smiled again and nodded at the empty spot next to him though he didn't stop playing. He was finger-picking a song she'd heard her dad play in the car. Her dad's taste in music suddenly seemed a lot cooler than it had five minutes ago. "I know that one," she whispered as she sat down and pulled her knees up close.

His smile warmed her more than the fire. "No one else here seems to know anything cool."

She hummed quietly, almost under her breath, but when Garrett smiled, she sang louder, and was rewarded by the look of gratified surprise spreading across his face. One by one, all the whispering kids turned to listen, drifting into silence, their mouths falling open. She'd never felt so powerful, so mature. This must be how her mom felt when she performed. No wonder she loved it. Buoyed by everyone's obvious admiration, Mara made sure everyone could hear her, drawing them to her as surely as if she held ropes tied around their necks. By the end of her song, Garrett was barely playing, just strumming random notes, as entranced as everyone else. There was an instant of astonished silence when the song ended, then they broke into applause.

Mara giggled a little, nervously, and felt her face flaming. She wasn't embarrassed, though. She was triumphant.

Garrett leaned over and whispered, "That was amazing." His breath was as warm as sunlight. "You're like a professional. Why didn't you tell me you could sing like that?"

"It's nothing special," she said modestly, though she was rather astonished herself. Her mother always teased her that she could barely follow a tune, but then, her mom hated listening to other people sing. This felt wrong, somehow, like a dream. Surely Mara would remember if she'd suddenly learned to sing?

Garrett held out his guitar but she shook her head. She could no more play a guitar than she could fly to the moon. And she had no desire to ruin the perfection of this night with stumbling, halting attempts to recapture what she'd just done. No, as it stood right now, this was a perfect night to end her summer on. She didn't want to ruin it.

Sighing happily, she wondered if Mom had built a hotel on Park Place yet and won the game like she always did. She wondered if Dad had eaten the last of the fish steaks, and also wondered why her stomach rumbled so enthusiastically at the thought; he was a terrible cook. Of course, she hadn't eaten much of the bruised steak he'd served her, so maybe that was why she was so hungry now. She wondered if Garrett was going to laugh at her for making these embarrassing noises.

Instead, he said the words she'd been hoping to hear for the last month: "You want to go for a walk?"

She set down her bottle while he tucked his guitar safely into its case. If her hand was empty, maybe he'd offer to hold it. They stepped away from the party, and walked in silence until Garrett took her hand carefully and threw out a teasing question about all the boyfriends she must have back home. She felt herself blushing with the effort of acting oblivious. This was it. She was going to kiss the handsomest guy she'd ever met, and she was going to tell Kyla all about it tomorrow. Or maybe the day after. Unless Ky'd had an amazing summer, this was so going to be the juiciest thing they'd ever had to talk about.

She felt his thumb exploring the bandage on her hand. "What happened?" She told him the story of her great fishing adventure, only leaving out the part where she got sick, and he laughed at all the right parts, though she wished he'd leave her bandage alone. Didn't he know that people bandaged things because they hurt? Still, this was Garrett, and she'd forgive him anything if he'd just look at her with those eyes again...

His hand was slightly clammy, but his body radiated heat. She shivered and enjoyed the sensation of being surrounded by his warmth as he pulled her closer to him. When they were far enough away from the bonfire that the individual voices had blurred together, he bent his head down and kissed her gently, just pressing his lips against hers. The shock of electricity that careened down all her nerves startled her, but she felt more alive than she'd ever been.

All her thoughts were centered on the taste of him in her mouth, salty and sweet as taffy. Warm as sunlight on a hot summer day. As delicious as a promise she meant to keep.

"Ow!" He yelped, pulling back hard and wiping the back of his hand across his mouth. His grin was reassuring, though, as he reached out a hand and ran his fingers from her shoulder down the front of her t-shirt. "You're enthusiastic," he teased. "It's ok. I like a girl who does more than just stand there. I can't believe I thought you were such a goody-goody when I met you."

The sound of the waves was overwhelming. It sounded like the ocean was inside her brain, and she longed to be in the water, to bring him into the water with her. Laughing, she dared him with her eyes to follow, toeing off her sneakers and kicking them aside as she went, teasing him with glimpses of her flesh as she pulled her tee shirt over her head and unhooked her bra. Her long hair tickled her shoulder blades as she ran; letting him pursue her, letting him think he could catch her. Letting him think he wanted to.

She dove headfirst into the surf, and it was like coming home. While the summer night's air had been stiflingly hot, the water was perfect, cool and silver. Garrett splashed in beside her, his big clumsy body as out of place here as a bull's, as a human's. Mara reached for him, clinging as her legs grew weak. She cupped the back of his neck, pulling his face down to her in the shallows. He made a noise of surprise against her mouth, and it was like feeling the deep sounds of whale-song echoing in her bones. She felt her lips stretch wide, as if her mouth was growing to accommodate more nerves, more sensation there, at the tip of her tongue and there, along the line of her lips where the flesh was so sensitive...

Her hands were all over his body now, plucking at his clothing, pinching the fat, hot flesh beneath. He tried to pull away, but she held him there easily, nibbling at him, then taking him in, so salty and rich in her mouth. When his moans turned to whimpers, she sang to him so sweetly that her voice harmonized with his ragged breaths until his life faded into the sounds of the sea.

After that, it was a long night of swimming, of singing, of doing things she'd never even dreamed of in her home on top of a mountain. Then at dawn, she coughed and spluttered. The waves flung her to shore, rejecting her, keeping only the fiercest part of her and leaving her bereft, forlorn, completely alone. Gathering up her clothing, Mara staggered home. She did not look at his guitar, leaning against the driftwood log where he'd left it. She did not pause by the dying embers of the fire. And she certainly did not look back to see if anything might still be drifting like kelp in the surf.

When her mother found her lying naked on her sandy, fouled bed, she just stroked Mara's tangled hair and didn't try to meet her eyes. "We'll be home tomorrow, sweetie. It's easier there, I promise. So far from the sea."

Something about her voice made Mara raise her head to stare at her mother's tongue running along the edge of her front teeth, back and forth. "You knew," she rasped, through her salt-roughened throat. "Why'd you bring me here? Why didn't you tell me?"

The hand stroking her hair faltered, then continued its slow soothing motion: as rhythmic as waves, as inevitable as currents, as slow as a heartbeat pulsing through dying limbs. Mara's mouth tasted of blood, and without warning, she vomited over the side of her bed. Her mother held her hair away from her face and dropped a beach towel on top of the mess, preventing Mara from seeing if that had really been a fingertip. His left hand, she thought muzzily. She'd seen the slightly yellowed callus left by the strings of his guitar.

With a sigh, her mother sat up and looked out the window toward the sea. "You're so much your father's child. I didn't know if you had it from me. I had to be certain."

Mara didn't want to say the words, but she blurted out, "Did you ever do something like this?" Her mother nodded, and Mara forced out the question: "Is he still alive?" She was pretty sure Garrett wasn't. She was pretty sure that was a good thing, given the parts of last night that she remembered.

"My first boyfriend?"

Mara nodded her head and her mother said quietly, "Yes, sweetie. But don't worry. Next time it'll be easier to stop before you get so carried away." There was a long silence, broken only by the eternal sound of the waves on the strand before her mother sighed. Bending low she kissed Mara's gritty forehead, like a benediction or an apology. "Let's go tell your dad we're nearly ready to go. He'll need a few minutes to put his leg back on."

AMONG THE GRAPEVINES, GROWING
ELIORA SMITH

I was gardening when it happened. I called it that, but it was a long way from a garden. That summer, the most I managed to keep alive was the few potted plants I brought with me. Those, and the grapevines, and myself.

But the grapevines didn't need my help.

I used to have a marvelous garden, back when I still lived with my grandmother, full of happy flowers and thriving herbs and more zucchini than I knew what to do with. My grandmother raised me. She was always there for me, even before my mother died, before the depression hit, before any of it. She taught me almost everything I know: how to garden, how to cook, how to look things up, and how to fix just about anything that ever broke.

And she taught me how to be alone, too. How to be alone, and how to know you aren't.

She used to talk to plants. She used to talk to everything—but only the plants talked back, she said.

I told her plants couldn't talk.

"You just have to learn how to listen," she told me.

I didn't believe her.

I kept talking to her plants anyway, after she died. And they grew. Not as well as when she was taking care of them, but enough to share. And that, Grandma always said, was enough.

But it couldn't last. With my grandmother gone and her savings spent on medical bills, I got less than a year in her house. Just enough time to finish off one last crop, and see the next year's perennials begin to bloom.

Leaving was bittersweet. I grew up in that house. I had so many memories there, good and bad. I'd sat shiva there three times, once each for my mother and grandfather, when I was young, and then again for my grandmother. It was too many, and some days, in the quiet of the empty house, it was all I could think about.

And besides, I could always start a new garden.

So when I moved out here, I tried to do that. The place wasn't in great shape—some of the plants in the yard threatened to overrun the house, and the wooden porch was unfinished and half rotten in a few places. But it was cheap, and it had a yard, and I wouldn't need a roommate. Besides, there was something almost charming about it, like a house from a fairytale. Set back in the woods, tangled in roots and vines, like the earth was reclaiming it.

I was determined to make it mine.

I started off by hacking away at the vines—wild grapes, invasive bastards. My grandmother had taught me plenty about invasive plants. I started off hopeful, imagining myself a knight, my clippers a magic sword. I could do this. I could hack my way through the brambles to the castle beyond and rescue whatever poor soul lay trapped inside, sleeping away the centuries. The vines were thick in places, some of them an inch or more, and hard, like wood. I fought with them for hours, my muscles aching and my skin stinging as the sharp, broken pieces scratched at it. I heaved the corpses of branches off the side of my deck. I imagined them smothering the rest of the vines until they all lay, dead and dying, in the dirt. It was a satisfying thought.

I went inside, exhausted but victorious, and past ready for a shower. Before I peeled off my sweat drenched clothes, however, I put some potted plants out on the deck—five of the six I had saved from my grandmother's garden. The sixth pot I left in my kitchen window. I needed a piece of my grandmother there, with me while I ate. Food nourishes your body, but meals nourish your heart, and food can't make a meal unless you share it.

That's what my grandmother told me, anyway.

Inside, I undressed and stepped into the shower. Hot water cascaded over aching muscles and gave cuts a fresh sting. For a few minutes, the world melted away. It was only me and the water. I felt new. Refreshed. Slightly raw—but stronger.

Finally, I forced myself to turn the water off. I stepped out of the shower stall, shivering and over-damp. Not so strong now. Just tired.

Tired, and alone.

Feeling empty, I went to my room. I lay on my bed, not caring that my wet hair was soaking the sheets.

When I woke up, the sun was shining.

Sitting up was hard. I felt anchored, somehow, to the spot. My skin stuck to the sheets in places. A little effort removed it, but what caused it to stick in the first place I had no idea. It was like being bound by pinpricks of hot glue. I rubbed at my arms. Everything felt strange, out of place. As if I was not quite myself.

But then, I supposed, it shouldn't be too surprising. The first few nights in a new house always feel strange.

My stomach rumbled, reminding me that I had skipped dinner the night before. Food, though, seemed unappetizing, the very act of eating unpalatable. Impossible. I downed a bottle of water instead, even though it made my stomach slosh, and went about the rest of my morning routine.

I thought briefly that I should finish unpacking. My stomach sank as I imagined going through the boxes with their cold, practical labels. Everything I owned had been my grandmother's.

No, it was too much. It couldn't be approached all at once—a box at a time, maybe. But not yet. First, I would deal with the house. I had gotten most of the grapevines the day before; perhaps today I could finish. If I worked hard, maybe I could be planting by next week.

When I stepped outside, though, my heart sank. The vines seemed so much worse than when I'd left them. They had once more wound their way up onto the deck. They weren't as thick as I remembered, but they were almost as prominent, twisting around the railings and creeping towards the outer walls of the house.

And at my feet, a broken pot, the plant inside it crushed in the grip of the vine.

I repotted the remains of the plant and moved it and the others inside. After that I went back to hacking at the grapevines, the sun seeping into my skin, giving my arms strength for the fight. The vines seemed to twist around my limbs, trying to stop me in my tracks. I fought with them for the rest of the week, barely eating, barely sleeping either, but drinking several bottles of water a day. Every day the plant seemed to come back angrier and stronger than before—and something strange was happening to my body. My arms ached. My entire *core* ached. I kept the blinds wide open whenever I was inside, soaking up the sunlight as though I was starving for it, but I rarely felt hungry—at least, not for food. My stomach seldom complained, and even when it did, its emptiness seemed far away, as though it was happening to someone else. But there was a hunger deep inside of me, a hunger for something I couldn't understand that ran deep into my core and through my veins, filling every part of me. A loneliness, and a longing, and a weakness for lack of whatever was lacking. And there was—*something*—growing on my arm, tiny sprouts of green that grabbed onto things when I sat or slept.

* * *

One week later, I found myself outside in the almost-light of early morning. I was kneeling, naked, my legs pressing down into the ground. The damp of the dew sat, pleasantly refreshing, in my chest and on my skin, and my hands...my hands were buried in the dirt. The hunger that had been growing inside me for the past 2 weeks—the hunger which sat, not in my stomach, but throughout the whole of me—was beginning to wane.

I sank back against my heels, resting my hands on my thighs. I felt alone again. It was only then that I realized that, for a moment, the loneliness of the empty house had dimmed, replaced by a connection that I couldn't define.

Leaves brushed against my skin. The vine had snaked a tendril out around one of my legs. I could feel it squeezing, firm and gentle at the same time, like the hand of an old friend. I lingered in its touch—then moved to yank my leg away. As I did, I found my legs held fast to the ground. And I could feel why: little tendrils of self had tangled themselves in the dirt, breathing in its nutrients. I pulled hard and the roots, still new and shallow, came out. And roots were what they were. This wasn't a fungus or a skin disease, it wasn't growing on my skin like a parasite. This was mine: my body and myself and my being. For a moment, the roots felt more a part of me then my arms and legs themselves.

I got to my feet, feeling displaced and strange within myself. I rubbed my hands on my legs, streaking the dirt across my tanned skin. Still bare—I had forgotten I was naked. Shame seemed foreign to me, but I glanced around, from habit more than nerve. The morning still held the wet grayness that comes when the colors of dawn have leeched away. Perhaps no one but me was awake yet. Either way, the yard was hidden by trees.

"We're not friends," I said out loud. My voice was out of place among the chirping of the crickets and the birds.

I stayed inside for the rest of the day.

* * *

Despite my attempts to stay away from the vine, my sleepwalking continued. Every morning I woke up with my hands in the earth, trying desperately to take my fill before I, in my waking state, denied myself. Trying desperately to soak up what sun I could before I shut myself inside.

But whatever I was taking in, it wasn't enough. I was weak and exhausted, starving no matter how much I forced myself to eat. A hopeless, gloomy numbness settled over me. I had felt this before, or something like it: The feeling of isolation and grayness that cuts into your stomach until pain turns into apathy. I had felt it for most of my life. And mostly, I had learned to cope.

Perhaps that's why it took so long for it to become unbearable, or perhaps it was just that the apathy of my renewed depression precluded any attempt to find a solution. I had plenty of tricks—self talk and socializing and keeping busy—but none of them worked. Not this time. Not when I couldn't even leave the house. And so I fell back on the one thing that required little effort on my part:

I waited.

I began to isolate myself, to lock myself away from the sunlight and the greenery my body was screaming for. I woke up every morning in the dirt, then let the sickly grayness in my mind push away whatever had brought me there. I started keeping a blanket and a set of clothes out on the porch. Each morning I would numbly dress myself, with dead skin and fumbling hands, and I would go inside.

But my body was changing in ways I couldn't ignore, and the strange new urges were growing stronger. The tiny sprouts on my skin had grown into leaves, and the skin itself was beginning to change color, it's ordinarily olive hue becoming more prominent, brightening toward a deep spring green.

Summer had already begun to turn to fall when I finally gave in. I took my dinner out into the early evening, an hour or two before sunset, and sat amongst the vines as I ate. After a few bites I stopped, removed my shoes and socks, and dug my bare feet into the dirt.

The change was immediate. The loneliness and hunger of the recent weeks began to lessen. I looked at the grape vine, which was already beginning to grow around my ankles.

"We're still not friends," I said. For once, I half expected the plant to reply.

The vine said nothing, of course. But I thought I felt it loosen, just a little. After that, we spent the evening in companionable silence. It was the first genuine meal I'd had in months.

* * *

Time passed strangely, the weeks slipping by in moments and eternities, and soon the leaves began to change. The trees outside were beautiful, flame-tipped branches burning to bare cold bones, standing incongruously against the wet grayness of the sky and the thick, squelching muck of the ground. The grapevines were turning dry and cracking, their leaves dropping off and leaving them bare. The few grapes they had produced ripened, then fell to the ground and were eaten by the birds and other creatures. There was something stubbornly undead about the plant beneath, stripped now of some of its verdant and insistent greenness.

I was exhausted. I had started spending more time outside, but the days were getting shorter now, and the cold pricked at my skin and at my leaves and at my bones. Just as the leaves and the green overtook my skin they began to recede, the leaves dropping off and following me like footprints as I walked.

Sleep came every night like a quilt settling over me, wrapping me in warmth. In the mornings I still found myself outside, hands trying to dig their way into near-freezing earth, but I was weary when I woke, and going inside seemed impossible. Waking seemed to take an eternity. I pictured myself staying out there, lying on the ground until autumn turned and the snow began to fall, until I was blanketed and buried and asleep.

But I knew what to do with those kinds of thoughts, and so I pushed them back and went inside.

* * *

By the time Sukkot came I was too weak to do much. When I was younger, my grandmother and I had a sukkah every year. They were small, but the two of us would put one up, and eat dinner in it, and sleep in it if it wasn't too cold out. The year she died, I was too caught up in bills and grief and paperwork to build one for myself. This year, though, I remembered. With my arms covered in leaves I couldn't exactly go to temple for Rosh Hashanah or Yom Kippur, but Sukkot...Sukkot was different.

Sukkot was the harvest.

A harvest I didn't have, because nothing could grow past the grapevines.

A harvest I couldn't do, because I was too weak for picking anyway.

A harvest that I didn't need, because I was barely eating and had no neighbors that I knew.

But a harvest that I was determined to celebrate.

I picked a few of the grapes that still sat on the vine, and collected some of those that had dropped onto the wooden porch below. They were small and sour and mostly made of seeds, but I ate them.

I couldn't build a sukkah, but I slept outside anyway. I was used to waking up to the sky by then, but for Sukkot I decided I would fall asleep to it.   I dug my naked feet into the ground and sucked on sour grapes. The vines wove a roof over top of me, twining with the leaves which remained on my arm, and through them I watched the stars until sleep claimed me.

When the week was done, I found it difficult to go back. My room seemed empty and isolating compared to the embrace of the vines, somehow both achingly vast and stiflingly small compared to the open air. The dimness of the starlight that filtered through the windows was off-putting. I tossed and turned, unsettled in my bed, unable to lull my brain into sleep. Finally, after an hour or so, I got up. One by one, I moved every potted plant that I had into the bedroom.

Only then, reluctantly, did my mind allow me to rest.

* * *

By this time, I was taking all of my meals outside. I couldn't manage anything heartier than broth, but that didn't matter: the damp ground and the sunlight and the company seemed far more important than the food, and even as I resisted the urge to sleep among the vines, the need for these things was one I couldn't deny. So I sat outside, and ate, and talked sometimes— to myself or to the vine, I didn't know. I had developed a sort of routine.

And then came the frost.

I woke one morning in late October with my body numb from cold. I was outside, and naked, as I had been every morning for months, but there was something different. I was...*less* than before, somehow. Smaller. I rubbed my arms with my hands, trying to warm myself up.

My skin was bare.

The leaves and bursts of green which had sprouted from me were gone—all of them. And the grapevines which ruled my porch, even the green ones, hung limply.

I dressed quickly, the cold biting at my skin. Looking down, I could see what had happened to my leaves. The ground around me was littered with them, an array of colors from burgundy to brown to green, leaves in every stage of their senescence.

I knelt, and picked up the vines. They were cold in my hands. There was no life in them. I squeezed my hands around them, shutting my eyes and centering my mind on the cold stabbing into my skin.

The vines rustled.

I opened my eyes and got to my feet. The wood burned like ice, freezing against my skin—I hadn't bothered to put on shoes. Whatever it was, it was coming from under the porch. I started to clear away the plants. It was slow work—even uprooted, the vines were heavy and tangled. The cold didn't help either, my hands were numb after only a few minutes. And whatever was rustling beneath the vines was still there, pulling. We must have been working against each other at least half the time, but I kept going, my body screaming at the tension. My muscles ached, and my breathing grew labored, the cold morning air making my throat raw. Finally, the vines were clear.

On the ground where they had been, there was a woman.

She looked up at me, shaking, and wrapped her arms around herself. "Well?" Her teeth were chattering. "You gonna stand there staring, or are you gonna get me a blanket?"

* * *

Half an hour later we were sitting at the kitchen table, wrapped in blankets, two now-empty bowls sitting in front of us. For the first time in weeks, I actually wanted food.

"So," I said.

"So," she said. A moment passed in awkward silence. "Sorry," she said. "I've been a plant for the last few months. My conversation skills are...rusty."

I nodded and leaned back, drumming my fingers on the table as I tried to process what was happening. Everything that had happened since I moved into the house was catching up with me. It was like watching something on TV. I didn't totally fit inside myself anymore, nor was I entirely certain that I wanted too. "So," I said again, finally. "Care to explain why I woke up this morning to discover that the grapevine which has been taking over my life had turned into a naked woman?"

"Did you expect me to transform wearing clothes?"

"*You were a grapevine*," I exclaimed, exasperated. "The lack of clothes was not the part of this morning's events that confused me!"

She bit her lip, utterly failing to hide her laughter. "You've done pretty well so far. I'd kind of like to see how far you can get with this."

I glared. "This is not funny. I have not left my house since *August*."

"All right, first of all, that is not true, because you've been coming outside all the time. Second of all, let me state once again that *I have been a plant*, and so I am sorry if my emotional reactions are a little out of whack." She took a deep breath. "Just...give me a minute."

I folded my hands and waited, staring at her through the silence. She closed her eyes and ran a hand over her face, thinking. For a few torturous minutes, she said nothing. It was strange. There hadn't been another human in this house since I'd moved in, and I hadn't been going out. Aside from some music and internet videos, the only voice I'd heard since I got here was my own. And for the most part, I'd been okay with that.

Now, though, the silence between us was oppressive. It took everything I had not to break it. But even though there was plenty for us to talk about, I had no idea what I was supposed to say, let alone how to say it. I was getting that feeling again, like I didn't fit inside my body, like my mouth and my brain weren't actually connected. Like this couldn't possibly be happening, it had to be made up, and everything I said was just lines in a film.

Only nobody had given me the script.

Finally, the woman spoke.

"You know how, in movies and stories and stuff, werewolves change shape every month? The details vary, but basically, when the moon is full, they change. And there's nothing they can do about it. While they're wolves they can't control what they do. It's like this...wildness in them, and it just comes out. Man's inner beast."

I nodded.

"Okay, well...this is kind of like that. Except it's not so much 'every month, with the full moon' as it is 'every summer, from last thaw to first frost, whenever the hell that is,' and it's not so much 'man's inner beast' as it is...grapevines." She gave a weak smile. "I'm like...a werevine? And now you are too, so, you know. Congratulations. Welcome to the club." She stuck out her hand.

I didn't take it.

"You can't be serious," I said.

"No, I definitely can. Look, no offence, I get that you're kind of freaking out right now, but could you maybe...hurry up? "

"Oh, I'm sorry, is there a to-do list I'm keeping you from?"

"Yes, actually. We have to figure out what to do about this place, for one thing."

I sighed. "Okay. I get your point. The house is...an issue." I frowned. "I'm sorry, I don't get it. You seem to know what's going on here. If you knew you'd turn into a plant—and I am trying so hard not to think about that sentence—but if you *knew*, why didn't you tell someone? I mean, not the truth obviously, but it was your sister that dealt with everything after you disappeared, right? That's what she told me. Why didn't you arrange something so that she wouldn't sell your house? Or *think you were dead*? Because I don't know if you've ever *had* a family member die, but it *sucks*. And if I was your sister, and I thought you died, and then I found out six months later that you were still alive? I would kill you."

"Wow, judgmental. I didn't *know*, okay? I'm new to this too. Everything you were going through this summer? A year ago, that was me. I didn't change fully until this past spring—I'm guessing it takes a while for whatever this is to fully take root, so to speak. But once it does...well, things become clearer, I guess, when you're a plant." She leaned back in her chair, and I saw her mask slip, just for a moment. Then it was back, a wry veneer of humor obscuring whatever she was really feeling.

"Besides," she said, "How do you think I feel? My sister didn't exactly wait a long time before selling the house. I mean, I know no one had heard from me for a while, but come on, my hypothetical dead body was barely even *cold*."

I bit my lip. "People cope with grief in different ways, okay? And anyway, what about bills? Someone has to pay the bills, and I'm guessing you weren't pulling in a lot of money under that porch."

She huffed. "Yeah, people tend to prefer landscapers who can actually, you know, leave the house. And hold shears." She took a deep breath, like she was trying to center herself. "Look, I don't want to fight with you." She paused. "Actually, that's not totally true. I don't know if it's me or the grapevines—very aggressive plant— but...I'm kind of enjoying this. A little bit. Sorry. But there are a lot of things we have to talk about, and if we can't have a civil conversation about the living situation, we're kind of screwed. It's not like we can really take this to court. So." She stopped, taking another deep breath.

"You bought this house. I get that. And I guess since I stopped paying the bills, probably I have no legal right to it. But on your own...I mean, I know what it's like trying to figure this out without help, and it's hard. Plus, between the fatigue and the six-month cycle and everything else, I'm guessing you aren't going to have a much easier time than me, money-wise."

She was right. I was burning through what I'd gotten from selling the old house way too quick.

She kept talking. "I don't want to have to leave, and I don't really want to risk this same thing happening next year with someone else. I mean, I lucked out. You could have been a creep. But you're not. You seem like...I don't know. Maybe we could be friends. And maybe, if we work together, we can make enough to keep the house. Find ways to cut costs during the summer. Something."

I stared at her, my mouth hard. "You almost killed my grandmother's geranium."

"You tried to hack me to death. Besides, geraniums are tough little bastards."

I didn't smile.

She sighed, her face softening. "I'm sorry. The vine...it wants to live. It wants to *thrive*. I had a garden, too, you know. But after the change...I'd rooted it out by the time you moved in. I couldn't control it. But I'm sorry, anyway."

I dropped my accusing gaze. I couldn't look at her.

"So, what?" I asked. "We both stay? Try to live together? We know literally nothing about each other."

One corner of her mouth curled up, a little half smile, like her mouth had snagged on a secret. There was a brightness behind her face, a light shining through the cracks in her mask. "I know you talk to plants. You've been doing it since you got here. I know you're strong. Stubborn, too. Didn't matter how many times you woke up outside, you kept going back in. I know you grew up surrounded by people you cared about and people who cared about you and now that's gone, and you have no idea what to do with yourself. I know that you think apples smell better than anything, and I know that sometimes when you talk, if it's safe enough, you start to sound like a fairytale. I know the stuff you went through this summer wasn't that new to you—the plant thing, maybe, but not the rest." She reached out, and trailed her fingers over my arm.

"I know that you have sunshine in your veins and earth in your heart. I know that your heartbeat feels like a rocking chair and that when you breathe at night it's like waves lapping at the shore." She grinned and ran her tongue over her teeth. "And I know that you talk in your sleep. It's kind of hilarious, actually. But also adorable."

I could feel myself blushing. I rolled my eyes and looked away, unable to stop myself from smiling. But I let her keep her fingers on my arm, anyway.

"That's what I know about you," she said. "So what do you know about me?"

I shook my head, just a little. "You never talked back," I said quietly.

"Not even once. But you felt me. I know you did. You might not have changed completely yet, but, honey...I've been there. You start to change, after it happens, and all of a sudden you can feel things. Things that were always there, maybe, but they were too far under the surface for you to touch. Like your blood is always pumping in your veins, but you only feel it when you take your pulse. You *felt me*. So what do you know?"

I shook my head again. "I don't know how to..." I trailed off. Then, tentatively, I reached out the hand she wasn't holding. I hooked my finger around hers, curling around it like a vine. "That's what I know," I said quietly. "And I know you still haven't told me your name."

She smiled. "Laura," she said. She drew her hand from mine, then stuck it out for a handshake.

Her grip was firm, her skin soft and warm. I could feel the sunlight through her fingers.

"Nahal," I said.

A PARTY FOR BAILEY
DAVID B. COE

"I'm going to have a party," Bailey said, pumping her legs as hard as she could, the creaking of the swing echoing the word in a sing-song. *Par-ty, par-ty.*

Lucy waved a fly away from her face. "Again?"

At the same time, Chloe asked, "When?" And then "Can I come?"

"Maybe. It depends."

Lucy hooked her legs through the bars of the climber and let go with her hands so that she hung upside down, her pigtails looking like horns. "My mom says you have too many parties, and that's why you get in trouble so much."

"I don't get in trouble that much."

"Yes, you do. You get in trouble more than any of us. She says it's 'cause your parents let you do whatever you want. They're too..." Lucy scrunched her face. "Lean-ant. I think that's what she said." She nodded, pigtails bouncing. "Yeah, lean-ant."

"Well, they're not. And if you're going to say stuff like that, you don't have to come. Chloe can take your place."

Chloe smiled, patting both hands in the dirt.

Lucy grasped the bar, pulled her legs out, and dangled by her fingers. "I wasn't the one saying it. It was my mom."

"But you think she's right."

"What kind of party will it be?" Chloe asked, blue eyes wide.

"I don't want to talk about it anymore." Bailey scuffed her feet on the ground, slowing the swing until she could hop off. "Let's play bears. I'll be the mother."

"You're always the mother," Lucy said. She dropped to the ground. She was taller than Bailey and the others. That was why she was so bossy.

"Not always. Sometimes Emmy is."

Emmy sat on the other swing, walking her feet in tight circles to twist the chain and then lifting them off the ground to let the swing unwind. She nodded as she spun. "Yeah, sometimes I am."

"Well, it's always one of you. I wanna be the mother this time."

As Emmy's spinning slowed, she and Bailey shared a look and a grin. Emmy was the prettiest girl Bailey knew. Bailey's mom said it was because she was mixed up: her mother was American, but her father was Japanese. She had silky black hair and dimples. Bailey had always wanted dimples.

"Have you ever been a bear?" Emmy asked.

"Yeah," Bailey said, fists on her hips. "Have you ever been?"

Lucy's gaze darted from one of them to the other. "No. But neither have you."

Bailey laughed, and a moment later so did Emmy.

"We've been bears lots of times."

"Have not."

"Have too," Emmy said.

"You're lying."

Bailey shook her head, her brown curls whipping around her face. "No, we're not. Just because you don't see it, doesn't mean it's not true." She bent down, grabbed a handful of dirt, and rubbed some on each cheek. "But this time you can be the mother, Emmy. If you want."

"Okay. Thanks."

Emmy dirtied her face, too.

Lucy watched them, frowning. "My mother doesn't like it when I make my face dirty."

"Then I guess you can't play. Too bad. We were going to let you be the grandma bear this time."

"The grandma?"

Bailey nodded, glancing at Emmy again. "She's kind of like the mother, but she's older."

"What does she get to do?"

"Lots of stuff," Bailey said with a shrug. "She cooks and tells stories and takes care of the baby bear."

"Who's the baby?" Chloe asked.

Bailey tapped her chest. "I am."

"Then what am I?"

"You can be the older sister."

Chloe made a face, but then said, "Okay." She bent and put dirt on her face. Her hair was blond, which was usually too light for bears, but she did look good with the dirt on her cheeks.

That left Lucy as the only one who didn't look like a bear.

Bailey lay on her back and cooed like a baby. Emmy and Chloe got down on their hands and knees and began to crawl around her, growling and snuffling. Lucy's frown deepened. She was wearing a pink dress and shiny black shoes. She'd probably get in as much trouble for mussing those as she would for putting dirt on her face.

Emmy pretended to give Bailey honey, and Chloe did a little dance like a bear in the circus. Bailey thought she might make a decent bear.

They tromped around the playground, pretending to hunt for berries, fish for salmon, and search for more honey, which was Bailey's favorite bear food. When they returned to their bear cave under the slide, Bailey decided that winter had settled in. They lay down to hibernate.

Lucy had watched them the whole time, following through the forest and tundra and streams, and asking what they were doing. Bailey ignored her, but Emmy answered, and Chloe did, too. She understood more than Bailey had expected.

They brushed the dirt off their clothes and walked back to the swings.

"Do you think Jonathan will come?" Emmy asked. "To the party, I mean."

"I guess," Bailey said. "I'll invite him."

Lucy stared across the playground at the school. "He's still with the nurse."

"He'll be all right."

Emmy straightened her skirt. "I hope his mom lets him. It won't be as much fun without him."

"You like him," Chloe said with a teasing smile.

Emmy shrugged, her cheeks reddening. "So?"

Lucy grinned at Chloe. Bailey said nothing. She wouldn't tease her friend, but she knew Chloe was right. That was why she'd decided to invite Jonathan in the first place. For Emmy. That was why he was going to be a bear.

The bell rang inside the school, ending recess.

Emmy glanced at Bailey, a serious look on her oval face.

"It'll be all right," Bailey said. "It has been the other times."

"Not always," Emmy said.

"Mostly, though. This time it will be."

"Okay." Her friend gave a tight smile that Bailey didn't believe.

Miss Glasser, their teacher, waved them toward the playground door. "Come on, children," she called.

Most of them ran. Emmy, Bailey, Chloe, and Lucy walked. But Lucy walked faster than the others, and tried to rush them. She hated to be late. And she liked spelling, which is what they did after recess.

"Bailey," Miss Glasser said as they neared the door. "You'll come with me. Mister Donovan wants to talk to you."

The principal. Again. Several of the students ahead of her looked over their shoulders, their cheeks rosy from recess, their mouths fixed in small "o"s. Most of them tried to stay away from her. They were afraid of what she might do to them. They didn't want to end up like Jonathan. Or like Emmy.

Miss Glasser led the others to their room and left them with Patty, her assistant. Bailey liked Patty. She was young and pretty and she sang well. She thought Miss Glasser was nice, too, but only sometimes. She yelled at the class too much, and Bailey didn't think Miss Glasser liked her very well. She wouldn't have admitted this to anyone—not even Emmy—but Lucy was right: she did get in trouble a lot.

She and her teacher walked through the hallway, passing cubbies and science fair displays, the only sounds the clicking of Miss Glasser's heels and the squeak of Bailey's tennies. She'd been to Mister Donovan's office enough times to know she didn't have to be afraid. He couldn't do anything to her. Not really. He'd tell her he was disappointed in her, and that her mother and father would be, too. And then he'd make her sit by herself in the main office for the rest of the day until her mother arrived.

As they reached the door to the principal's office, Miss Glasser paused and gazed down at her, tilting her head to the side.

"I'm sorry about this, Bailey. I wish you didn't make me bring you here so often. But there are some things you just shouldn't do."

"I know."

The corners of her teacher's mouth turned down, and lines appeared in her forehead. "If you know better, why do you do them?"

Bailey lifted her shoulders and let them drop. "I'm sorry," she said.

Her teacher straightened with a sigh, pushed open the door, and ushered Bailey inside.

The secretary, Missus Crandall, was old and scary. Bailey stayed as far from her desk as she could. But once Miss Glasser left, there was really nothing she could do. Missus Crandall peered at her over her glasses, a sour look on her wrinkled face.

"He'll be with you in a minute," she said, in a voice like dried leaves being crushed. "You just sit there."

Bailey sat and stared at her hands. But she knew every moment exactly where Missus Crandall was, and when the secretary was watching her. Sitting out here with her, waiting for Mister Donovan, was always the worst part.

When at last Mister Donovan came out of his room to fetch her, Bailey practically jumped off her chair. He regarded her, his expression very much like Miss Glasser's, brown eyes magnified by his glasses, his bushy moustache making him look friendlier than he was. Without a word, he turned on his heel and disappeared into his office, knowing Bailey would follow. She climbed up into the chair in front of his desk, and he shut the door.

"Well, Miss Browne, here we are again." He took his seat behind the desk, folded his hands and hunched his shoulders, as if trying to look bigger than he was. "Do you have anything to say for yourself?"

"No."

"Can you tell me why you did it?"

Her gaze roamed the walls, skimming over framed diplomas and posters from old musicals. "No."

"Did Jonathan make you angry? Did he do something to you?"

She shook her head. "No. He's pretty nice. We're friends."

His huff of laughter told her he didn't believe this. "Friends don't hurt each other. You hurt him."

Bailey didn't bother to answer. He wouldn't understand.

"I've called your mother. She'll be here after school. How do you think she'll feel about what you did?"

She didn't respond to that, either.

He blew a breath through his teeth and stared out at the street through his window. "You're a bright girl, Bailey. Your teacher says you do well in math and spelling and reading. You seem to have friends. You seem to be happy. So I can't figure out why you keep getting yourself in trouble like this."

The principal leaned forward, like he was hoping to hear whatever she might say. But Bailey only stared at him. Finally, sensing that he wanted her to say something—anything—she asked, "When did you say my mom's coming?"

He sat back, sighed the way Miss Glasser had. "After school. I'm not going to let you return to your class." He eyed the clock on his wall. "It's an hour until final bell. You'll spend that time here in the main office, and I'd like you to think about how you should be treating your friends."

She nodded, scooted down from the chair, and let him lead her back to the main office and that seat near Missus Crandall's desk.

Once there, Bailey looked around the office, at the walls, the phones, the American flag, the drawings tacked to the bulletin board. One of hers was there, a picture of a mama bear and two cubs that had gotten honorable mention in the first grade art contest. She looked at everything except Missus Crandall. But that didn't keep the woman from talking to her.

"I know why you do the things you do," Missus Crandall said after a few minutes, in that same dry, crumbly voice.

Bailey counted the stripes on the flag.

"You think you're the first girl I've seen in this office who does things like you do? I've been here a long time, missy. I've seen plenty."

Thirteen stripes. She started on the stars, even though she knew there were fifty.

One of the other teachers came in, handed Missus Crandall some papers, and talked to her, his voice low. She nodded and smiled, acting like she was simply a nice old lady. But too soon the teacher left, and it was just the two of them again.

"A girl like you doesn't belong in a school. And you can tell your mother I said so."

Bailey twisted in her chair to check the clock behind her. It had only been ten minutes.

"Church I go to—they know how to deal with your kind. They've been dealing with bears for longer than I've been alive, and they'll deal with you."

Bailey kept her eyes on the flag, but tears blurred her vision and her hands shook. She wished the woman would stop talking and leave her alone.

The principal emerged from his office, a manila folder in one hand, a cup of coffee in the other.

"Mister Donovan, my head hurts. Can I lie down?"

He stepped to her chair, looking both stern and sympathetic. "I can't send you to the nurse, Bailey. Jonathan is still there, and I don't think that would be fair to him."

"I just want to lie down. I don't feel good."

He turned to Missus Crandall, but she pretended to be working and didn't look up.

"All right," he said. "Come with me."

Bailey scrambled off the chair, but then slowed, not wanting to act too healthy. The principal led her to the teacher's lounge, across the hall from the main office. It had a coffee maker and a kettle, a table and chairs, and an old torn, plastic couch that was the ugliest shade of yellow Bailey had ever seen.

"No one will bother you here," Mister Donovan said. "Not this late in the day. You can lie down. I'll come and get you when your mom arrives."

"Okay. Thank you."

His smile seemed a little sad, but he said she was welcome and left her there, closing the door behind him.

She lay down on the couch, but couldn't keep still for long. She hadn't stopped trembling, and she could hear Missus Crandall's voice in her head, powdery like the dirt she and the others had put on their faces.

She prowled the room, running her fingertips over the table and chair backs, her eyes straying again and again to the door. It had a window, but she saw no one outside in the hallway, and there were places in the lounge where even someone staring through the glass wouldn't be able to see her. Not unless they were trying to find her.

Her mother would have told her not to, but Bailey always felt better afterwards. Calmer, more like herself. And her mother said that in emergencies it was okay.

She crossed to the farthest corner from the door and sat criss-cross on the floor, remembering to pull off her tennies and socks.

The first thing was to find the moon. That was what her mother said. The moon was where the magic came from. So with her eyes closed, Bailey sent her thoughts into the sky to search for it. She found it more easily than she had expected. It wasn't full yet, but it was close, almost round, like a playground ball that had lost some air.

She could imagine it in the night sky, white as cold milk, surrounded by pinprick stars, and she wrapped her arms around the vision, holding it to her heart, opening herself to the magic.

The first shift of bone brought a gasp of pain, as always. Bailey doubled over, so that her chest rested on her folded legs, and she stifled a cry. Bones wrenched, grated against one another, popped and snapped and reformed. Beads of sweat broke out on Bailey's face and the back of her neck. A scream rose in her throat, but she clamped her teeth against it, even as she felt her mouth and jaw and nose change, grow, distort. Thick, dark fur sprouted from her hands and arms, her tummy and back, her legs; her skin tingled and stung.

But though it hurt, making it seem that her body was being turned inside out, like some heavy old sweater, Bailey welcomed the change. Becoming bear cub was a little like getting in a bathtub filled with hot water. It hurt for a moment, but soon enough the pain tipped over into warm comfort.

Girl-thoughts fled her mind. Bear-thoughts padded in.

Bailey sat up, braced her paws on the hard, straightened. She sniffed the air, caught a scent she knew: powerful, sweet. Close. Other smells blended with it. Harsh, bitter, but the sweet was strongest. She took a step. Claws clattered. She looked down, tapped the claws on the hard. Another step and she slipped. The hard and the claws weren't right together. But the sweet.

She tottered across the smooth cave place, following the scent. She reached a stump-thing. The smells came from on top of it.

Voices stopped her. She stilled, cocked her head, twitched an ear. Voices. Humans. Footsteps. More humans. None were close.

Bailey reached for the sweet smell, batted aside others—the harsh and the bitter. They fell on the hard; the noise startled her, drew a growl to her lips.

But then she had the sweet. Odd to the touch. Too soft and also too hard. She tried to hold it: one way, another, rolling it between her paws. Teeth crushed it, but still no sweet reached her tongue.

She snuffled, listened. The humans weren't nearby yet.

Using a single claw, she poked a hole in the sweet, and a second. Bailey crushed it with teeth again and sweet flooded her mouth. She chewed and more of the sweet seeped in. Golden, sticky, lovely. Bailey rumbled, happy now.

She let the odd sweet thing drop from her mouth and walked, searching for more. Sweet? Salt?

A box smaller than Bailey hummed nearby and something in her thoughts stirred, woke. She batted the box, pushed it, shook it. Nothing. She slapped her claws on its top; they caught on something and she pulled. The box opened.

The inside was like winter. There were hard things, small things, softer things. All were cold. Most she couldn't chew or open, but some she could. There were sweets that were also sours. She decided she liked them. An apple—she had seen apples before. This one was good.

Not so hungry anymore, she settled down on the hard, licked her sticky paws clean, and lowered her head.

* * *

She woke to a shrill screech and many, many voices.

A girl-thought: *That's the bell.* And another. *Time to change back.*

Bailey liked being bear cub; she didn't want to be girl-Bailey again. Not yet. But mother was coming. That she remembered. She sat up and reached again for the moon's magic.

* * *

The change back to human hurt less than turning into bear. Still, when Bailey was herself again she wiped tears from her cheeks. Then she looked around the teacher's lounge and groaned. Her bear could be such a slob.

The small refrigerator had been pulled out into the middle of the room, so that its plug stretched in a tight black line to the wall outlet. The refrigerator door stood open, and several containers of juice and coffee creamer lay scattered on the floor. But at least they hadn't been opened or crushed. She couldn't say the same for the yogurt containers. They looked like someone had come in and stomped on them. All of them. Yogurt and fruit covered the floor, some of it matted with strands of brown fur.

"Oh, Bear!" Bailey whispered. Nearby, packets of tea, instant coffee, and sugar covered the floor, along with cups, stir sticks, and napkins. A container—one of those plastic squeezy ones shaped like a teddy bear—had been chewed to bits and lay in a sticky puddle of honey.

Bailey wanted to cry.

But she gathered the napkins, wet many of them at the sink, and cleaned up the mess as best she could. She threw away the ruined containers and dirty napkins, pushed the refrigerator back in place, cleaned up the honey, taking a bit on her finger and licking it clean.

Her feet and hands had yogurt on them, as did her dress. After washing her hands she ran her fingers through her hair and found honey and yogurt there, too.

"Bear!"

She took the rest of the napkins and wiped herself and her clothes clean before wetting her fingers so that she could untangle her hair. All the while, she mumbled about bear and all the trouble she had made for them. Tomorrow, the teachers would come to the lounge and find their food gone, their napkins used up, their honey bear missing. And Mister Donovan would blame her, even though it wasn't her fault.

Bailey paused, twisting her mouth to the side. Maybe it was a little bit her fault. She knew better than to shift into her bear in the middle of school. If Missus Crandall hadn't frightened her so...

She shuddered and worked the rest of the honey out of her hair.

When at last she finished, she straightened her dress and pulled on her socks. She was still tying her shoes when the door opened and Mister Donovan stuck his head in.

"Your mother's here."

"Okay."

"How's your headache?"

"It's better. Thank you."

He nodded, held the door open while she finished with her shoelaces, got to her feet, and walked to where he stood.

"Why is your hair wet?"

She blinked. "I was...I thought maybe putting cold water on my head would make me feel better. Sorry."

The corners of his mouth drooped, making him look like a walrus. "It's all right. You'll just...You'll need to explain that to your mother."

"She won't mind."

He didn't comment and they crossed the hall to the office. Missus Crandall still sat at her desk, her attention on the papers strewn there. Bailey's mother sat in the same chair Bailey had been in earlier. She stood as they entered. Bailey ran to her and threw a hug around her waist, breathing in her perfume.

"Mommy."

"Hi, Peanut. Are you okay?"

"I'm better now."

Her mother touched her wet hair. Bailey pulled back a little so that she could look up into her mother's dark eyes. They remained that way for a second or two, and then her mother gave the slightest of nods, chestnut hair bobbing.

"I'm sorry to trouble you, Missus Browne," Mister Donovan said. "But I'm afraid Bailey's gotten herself into a bit of trouble. Again."

"I see. What kind of trouble?"

"Perhaps we should speak about this in my office. Bailey you can wait out here for another few—"

"No!" Bailey said, clutching her mother again. She turned her head toward Missus Crandall, hoping her mother would understand. All the while, the old secretary kept her eyes on her work.

"Bailey and I will talk about this eventually, I'm sure," her mother said. "I don't see any harm in letting her hear what you and I have to say."

Mister Donovan scowled at this, and Bailey thought she heard Missus Crandall make a *tsking* sound. But the principal shrugged and waved them into his office. Bailey grasped her mother's hand.

The principal sat behind his desk. Bailey and her mother took the chairs opposite him.

"Well," he said, exhaling the word, "I'm afraid Bailey has hurt another student."

"How?"

"She bit him, which should come as no surprise. You and I have had this conversation before, Missus Browne. The first week of school, Bailey bit Emily Takada. Her parents, of course, were very upset. I believe they would have liked to see Bailey expelled."

"You believe," her mother repeated. "But they never said as much, did they?"

The principal shifted in his chair, gaze dropping to his desk. "No, they didn't."

"In fact, as I understand it, they told you it had all been a misunderstanding, and they asked you to drop the matter."

"That's true."

"And as you know, Bailey and Emmy are friends now."

"Best friends," Bailey said.

Her mother glanced her way and held a finger to her lips.

"Yes, I've noticed that. They do seem to get along quite well. And as far as I know, the Takadas consider what happened an isolated incident."

"Exactly—"

"But it's not," Mister Donovan said. "Just two weeks later, she bit the Gallagher girl. Her parents were so angry, and so disturbed by the incident, they pulled Sarah out of our school and sent her to Saint Mark's."

Bailey chewed her lip. She liked Sarah. She missed her.

"That was...a regrettable choice on their part."

"But understandable," the principal said. "And today, less than a month later, Bailey has hurt another of her...her friends. This time she bit Jonathan Golding on the arm. Jonathan spent much of the afternoon in the nurse's office, and again, I can tell you that his mother is every bit as angry as the other parents have been."

"I'm very sorry to hear that. Obviously, I hope that Jonathan isn't too badly hurt, and I'd be willing to reach out to his mother and talk to her myself."

"I don't know if that's wise just now, but I do appreciate the offer." Mister Donovan pushed his glasses up on his nose. "The point, though, is that this can't continue. The school is responsible for the safety of all students, and at this point, Bailey has established a pattern of behavior that poses a threat to that safety. By all rights, I ought to expel her today."

Bailey gaped at him, and then at her mother. She didn't want to be expelled. She liked this school. She liked her friends.

"But you're not going to," her mother said.

"I'd rather not. I'm going to insist, though, that you take her for counseling. I can give you a list of therapists in the area who deal with behavioral issues of this sort. And I think it best that Bailey not come to school for a day or two. Maybe not until Monday."

"A suspension."

"Yes." The principal turned to Bailey. "That's a lighter punishment than I could have given you, Bailey, and I won't be so lenient again. This has to be the very last time. Understand me? If you bite anyone else, you can't come back to this school ever again."

Bailey's eyes welled and she didn't trust herself to say anything. She simply nodded. A tear slipped down her cheek.

Mister Donovan and her mother talked for a short while longer, but Bailey didn't listen to much of what they said. She had almost been kicked out of school, and she had to be more careful. That was what mattered.

When she and her mother left the office, Missus Crandall was no longer behind her desk. Bailey was glad. That would be the best thing about not biting more people: she wouldn't have to see the old woman as much, or hear her dried leaf voice.

But as they left the school and walked through the parking lot to the car, Bailey spotted Missus Crandall crawling out of a small, green station wagon.

"Mommy?" she whispered, hiding behind her mother.

"It's all right," her mother said, taking her hand and walking on, her back straight. "She can't do anything to us."

"I know what you are!" Missus Crandall said, pointing a bony finger at Bailey's mother. "I know what all of you are."

"And I know you, Helen Crandall," her mother said, allowing a growl to creep into her voice. She opened her mouth just enough to let her bear teeth show. "Your hunters and my kind reached an understanding long ago. Your church is nothing but a remnant of something long dead."

"We don't need hunters. Faith is weapon enough." The words were brave, but Bailey heard a tremor in her voice.

"I think we both know better. Your faith won't protect you if you ever trouble my daughter again." She growled a second time and the woman shrank back against the station wagon.

"Come on, Bailey."

They climbed into the car, Bailey in her booster, her mother behind the wheel.

Her mother steered out into the street and adjusted her mirror so she could look at Bailey. "So who is Jonathan?"

"A boy Emmy likes," Bailey said. "He's nice. He'll make a good bear. As good as Emmy."

"All right. But no more, Peanut. You heard Mister Donovan."

"I know. But I want someone else. Just one other bear. For my party."

"Another party?"

Bailey nodded, smiled. "Before winter. With s'mores. Bears like s'mores."

"Cubs do. That's for certain. Well, you can't make any more bears at school."

"Then can we invite her over?"

Her mother turned a corner, checked her side mirror. "I suppose," she said. "What's this one's name?"

"Chloe," Bailey said. "She has blond hair, but I still think she'll make a very good bear."

CRY MURDER
APRIL STEENBURGH

It starts as an itch over every inch of the scalp—that prickly sensation that comes with the need for a shower and that no amount of scratching will alleviate. It moves down the neck, bringing a shiver and gooseflesh in its wake. It's not long after that joints will start to ache, throat goes dry, and it becomes impossible to hold still.

It usually starts just around dinner time, when the day is settling into evening, a familiar warning that tonight will be just a bit awkward. It was an awkward I was familiar with, at least. And that my family was used to. It was not so hard for a young woman to explain away being just a bit off as being "that time of the month." Honestly I had never found a phrase that killed each and every line of inquiry as quickly or completely.

It *was* my time of the month, just not the one I was alluding to.

It was expected that I would rush and jitter my way through dinner, hardly eating anything. It was understood that I would go to my room early, begging biological indiscretions as to why I was unable to settle in for living room lounging with my parents and younger sibling. My family respected that, bore my idiosyncrasies with indulgent smiles and well wishes. They would most likely be a bit put off by the way I hauled open my bedroom window, slipping the screen free with skill borne of repetition, the way I hung my head out into the autumn night panting like a canine.

The brisk air soothed the itching for a moment, pulled the frantic fog from my brain. It brushed across the cold sweat that covered my body until I started to shiver. The shivering was nothing more than a prequel to the shakes and then bone-shifting and crunching convulsions that rippled and ripped through me. It hurt like a bitch every time. But there is nothing a good preening session cannot solve, and preening was always almost frantically in my mind as I settled out of my human shape and into corvid.

It is wonderfully satisfying and soothing, rearranging each and every feather, making sure everything is in place and well oiled. One good shake and a hop to the windowsill later and I was ready to enjoy the evening.

Crows don't usually fly at night. Nor do they generally appear as the result of a monthly inconvenience. I was a bit atypical—enjoying feathers and flight once a month, dealing with community college the rest of the time. Well, the community college thing was only for another year—I could expect a monthly experience as a crow for the rest of my life. After a quick stretch I took to flight.

I was not pecked in the eye by a crow, or scratched by irritable corvid claws or anything like that. I am pretty sure I put the wrong feather in my mouth as a child and that was all the juju it took to get me feathered monthly. Turns out shape shifting is a communicable disease.

A communicable disease that came with social obligations. I flew over to the town Department of Transportation building and settled onto a fence post, taking a second to assess who was here already. Eric was poking around in the leaf mulch pile, probably looking for something to eat. That guy could, and would, eat anything that moved. I was a crow of distinction—I liked my snacks dead and cooked, preferably cooked on a grill, but a bit of asphalt on a hot summer day would do. The sisters, Ashley and Kim, were chattering up a storm next to what looked like a pile of food waste that had missed the dumpster. Probably trying to pretend they weren't considering a snack themselves. Jack, an older crow who was constantly missing at least one wing feather, was perched on the fence a few feet away from where I had settled. He was the head of our strange little family, and was usually accompanied by Melody, his somewhat grumpy partner and matriarch of the murder. She drifted in with a croaking rattle, our cue to join her where she settled by Jack on the fence.

The evening had officially begun. And by the look on Melody's face, it was a good thing I had gotten my Psych homework done early.

Everyone settled onto sections of fence with a bit of chatter and grumbling, and as we turned our collective attention towards Jack, I noticed little Anthony was absent. Enthusiastic, excitable Anthony. Melody gave a full-body rustle and shake, croaked out her displeasure before calling the evening to order. I fluffed once with a bit of reflexive anxiety, then flapped my way to her bit of fence.

We were bigger than common American Crows, and it showed the most when we perched, when our claws were visible, when we were suddenly put to scale with mundane things like the planks of wood that made up fence posts, light posts, trees. Melody was larger than most of us, and prone to wicked jabs of the beak if the mood struck her, so I did my best to perch far enough away to be out of reach, but not far enough to be considered rude. She eyed me, head turned to the side, for a long moment, then clacked her beak and proceeded to let us know our evening was booked.

We had to go find out why Anthony had missed our family "dinner."

We were usually a tight group, my murder of were-crows. Everyone, no matter how new to the feathers you were, knew it was important not to miss the monthly family meeting. Natural crows were social creatures and were-crows were no different. We usually caught up on what was going on with each of us in our mammalian skins during our full moon soirées, touched base, let everyone know everyone else was doing well. If someone wasn't doing well, we did what we could to alleviate the situation. Anthony was newer, smaller, and never missed our gatherings.

We were a Halloween fanatic's dream as we took to the sky with a rustle of feathers and rattle of beaks at Jack's command, dark wings cutting across the moon-bright sky. We were silent as we flew, apart from the occasional "no luck" or "all clear here." We cut through the territories of sleepy local crow families who called out at our passing, wishing us well, wishing us luck, offering no answers. Until we caught the sound of alarm cries coming from a few blocks away.

Jack and Melody must have seen him first, as they shouted and turned sharply downwards, toward a small thing sprawled beneath a pine. They shed feathers as they landed, slipping out of their crow skin. Jack was a formidable man, large frame, heavily muscled, face lined and hardened by sun and wind. He gathered up the stiff, battered crow that was Anthony, cradling him close. Melody should have looked old and frail, her thin frame nothing but sinew and bone. But her eyes were something ancient and dark and right now very, very angry. We settled on the ground at their feet, quiet.

"Erin."

Melody's voice shivered through the air, hung like a threat. Even though I knew her anger was not directed towards me, I roused once before stepping forward and wriggling my way out of my feathers. Jack and Melody made it look easy—they were old crows and the moon was their friend. I had to really work at it, fighting my body's desire to stay ensconced in the shape of a crow. Gooseflesh peppered my skin as I stood, shivers that had nothing to do with being naked in the fall air and everything to do with the quiet magic of a full moon and the look in Melody's ancient eyes.

"Yes, Melody?"

I would give anything to be able to half-shift like Melody did, pulling feathers to cover socially less acceptable parts of her anatomy. Were's have little body modesty—sort of impossible when you belonged to a social circle that was constantly slipping from one set of skin to another, a process that clothing did not participate in. But there was a certain sort of vulnerability associated with being bare-skinned that was hard to shake, especially when standing in front of a dead friend. But I was the oldest-in-feathers of the others, and as a result, a sort of second in command whenever Jack and Melody required it.

Melody gestured with fingers crooked and boney enough to resemble claws, ordering me closer. Unconsciously walking on the balls of my feet with nerves, I took a few steps forward, stopping suddenly as my brain finally got around to processing what I was seeing. There were few things that truly scared me. A dead friend was terrible, but not terrifying in itself. The sight of the feather, large and barred elegantly in browns, tucked under Anthony's wing, kicked in a panic that was very difficult to deny.

There was an owl in our territory. "Owl. How did an owl find us?"

Eric shuddered and almost slipped his feathers, body rippling as the moon pulled him back. Ashley and Kim huddled close to him, too new to try to ride the adrenaline of pure terror back into human skin. There were few things that frightened my feather family—but the silent death that came with a were-owl definitely topped the short list. It was easy to forget, as we enjoyed the comfort of our suburbs, in our ability to move from one skin to the other, that there were other things out there that preyed on us. The human part of our brain was eternally convinced it was comfortable at the top of the predator chain. It was easy to forget that we straddled two skins, and had to account for them both.

"We will find it." Melody's voice was hard. "We will not let it hunt in our territory, will not let it hunt us."

"They are killers of opportunity. So, we flush it out before it takes another of our family." Jack, voice quiet as ever, shifted Anthony's body in his arms. "Cry murder so that all can hear, rouse the natural crows. Come dawn we start the hunt."

"Now, we hold close and alert." Melody brushed a hand across Jack's neck before taking a step away. "We will roost here until dawn. Jack will take Anthony. Everyone will clear their day. And then we begin."

* * *

Dawn after a full moon night was a strange shivery feeling, like coming out of warm water into chilled air. It always left me a bit short of breath and wondering why I couldn't just curl up inside a crow's body forever. But like all leftover bits of dragging dream, the allure of being a crow full-time dispersed after that first cup of coffee. Granted, this morning it was Dunkin Donuts coffee while sending a very apologetic email to my instructors via cellphone explaining the family trouble that had come up and my resulting absence from class today. I had grabbed my phone and extra clothes from home after I had snuck back in through my window and shed my feathers. I should have dared breakfast, too, as my stomach was busy shouting its displeasure as acidic coffee mixed with the bile that nerves were producing like a champ.

I ignored the news playing on the screen in the corner of the Dunkin Donuts—it was a quiet reminder that in a few days we would start hearing stories about a missing person, about our Anthony. But they would be looking for a young man, not the battered crow skin he had been wearing when he died. They would never find him. His family would never know what happened. It infuriated me. My phone buzzed, letting me know I had a message.

Family meeting. Usual spot.

Eric had apparently been assigned the task of gathering the troops. I shifted my backpack—a smaller sporty thing meant for short hikes—downed the last bit of my coffee, and started out.

The usual spot, in this case, meant Jack's place. It was where the murder gathered when we were inclined towards lounging on the sofa instead of perching. Jack's place was at the edge of town, where suburbia bordered on rural, but you could still get cable internet and public utilities. I settled my bike onto the front of the bus and climbed aboard for the rambling ride towards Jack's. I had this commute down to an art form.

We had an owl. It had only been a matter of time. The last owl had been years ago, when I was a scrawny adolescent just sorting out that flying was not an innate ability—that it had to be learned. The murder had been larger then. Predation had a way of thinning the ranks. Jenny had been a good friend, all shit-eating grins and wild gesticulations. I am pretty sure we more or less were the textbook case of troublesome corvids. I had been so new to the feathers that Jenny had seemed like an ancient sage. I still have no idea how old she had been—you learned not to ask members of the were-community how old they were as you would sometimes get an honest answer. Jenny had been one of the first kills, the first hint something was wrong. I had found her in human form, eyes open and face startled. Jack told me she had been caught just as she slipped from feathers to skin, when even the oldest were- was just that much more vulnerable. Anthony was a clean kill in comparison—wounds harder to make out through dark feathers. Jenny...I still had nightmares about Jenny.

Jenny had at least been able to have a funeral of sorts, though she had no human family to claim her. It had been a parcel of crows dressed in their funeral finery attending her burial. Anthony would be buried at Jack's place, under the old pines in the back yard.

I got off the bus with an absent wave at the driver, unhitched my bike and started on the handful of miles down quiet roads that would take me to Jack and the rest of the murder. I could have pulled on my feathers and flown to Jack's place, but the commute was therapeutic, it let me get my thoughts and my emotions together. It let me tumble through old, bad memories in my own time, in my own space, before I had to support the rest of the family, had to soothe and support crows who were too young to have experienced the hunt. The morning light was   comforting—we had time now to look for the owl. The day was ours and we would use it to our advantage. I had no desire to spend weeks holed up, terrified and hoping the danger would pass. Not again.

I ditched my bike at the end of Jack's long, gravel driveway and started the mostly up-hill walk to the front door. Eric's shiny new sedan was parked in the grass at the top of the driveway, next to the mechanical Frankenstein's Monster that was Jack's truck. Someone must have picked up Ashley and Kim as I could hear their voices from inside, but their well-used, well-loved car was missing and they were new enough to their feathers that they would not have started the day slipping skins, not after a full moon night.

I let myself in the front door, grabbed a soda as I passed through the kitchen, and joined my family in the living room, saluting them with my drink in greeting. "Morning."

"Good morning, Erin." Melody smoothed her skirts before gesturing for me to join her on the couch. I did my best to ignore the way my hair tried to stand on end as I settled beside her. It's not that I disliked Melody, it's just my subconscious gets a bit overwhelmed by the uncanny feel of her—age and something that is far less human than it looks. Old Crows are strange magic. That is the best way I can put it to words. Something to look forward to as I get older, I guess.

The rest of the murder unconsciously moved closer to where Melody and I sat. Were we in feathers there would likely be some reassuring preening going on. We collectively ignored the dirt on Jack's shoes as he came in through the backdoor and took his usual place in the rocker beside the couch. The family meeting was about to officially start.

"It has been some time since we have had a predator in our midst." Melody introduced the business at hand with a deceptively casual air. "Our family is smaller than it was, and we have new members who have yet to join us on the hunt."

"The trick is there are more of us than there are of them. And we use that to our advantage." I leaned forward, hands on thighs. "We hunt together. We bring in the natural crows. The days are ours and we use them to our advantage." And we stay the hell inside at night.

"Erin is right." Jack's chair creaked as he rocked slowly. "We are a good family. Strong. With the assistance of our cousins we will find the owl and drive it from our territory."

Or kill it. I was fond of the killing it option. I did not trust a predator to stay gone. Owls and crows did not get along on a good day. Add in the supernatural nonsense that came with being a were-, all the size and strength and cunning thrown in to keep things interesting, and I don't think scaring the owl off was an option. But then again, I was a bit blood thirsty when it came to owls. We all have our faults. I will give Jack credit—his gentle reassurance settled the family, so I set my bloodlust to simmer quietly in the background. "To drive it out we need to start moving now." I settled back a bit, tried to force my posture to relax.

"Skin or feather, you will know an Owl as you pass it by." Melody's voice was quiet, causing us all to lean in a bit. "You can always feel another were-. Magic calls to magic, and Owls feel like the quietest part of the night, when you want to keep looking over your shoulder, just in case."

"In human skin, it gets the hair on your neck to raise, gets you all goosebumpy. Feathered, you want to hide and attack all at once." And shout, scream, let everyone know there is something dangerous and wrong nearby. There were memories I liked to keep swept under the rug. Staring at an owl, old and half-feathered, as it roused once and then stepped almost daintily off of Jenny's torn body, feeling anger and terror to such an extreme that I was unable to move...that I would be dead if Jack had not arrived then, a monstrous amalgamation of corvid and man...that was one memory I tried to keep buried as deep as possible. "You can't miss it, you will never mistake it for anything else. Trust me."

"So we should be hitting the streets now." Eric managed to sound confident, even as his body language suggested he was more than a little unsure, unbalanced. "Get it before it gets another of ours."

"Eric, Ashley, and Kim—you will start hunting on foot. Stay together. Pay attention to our cousins in the trees. Melody started the alert call as the sun rose—they know to keep an eye out and to let us know what they see."

Jack stood and we all followed, even Melody. The time for talking was over. "Erin, Melody, and I will be flying. Do not try to take on the Owl alone. I buried one family member today. I do not want to bury another."

We reassured ourselves as humans do, touching skin to skin and speaking affection and confidence. I followed the twins and Eric out to Jack's front yard and then reached for my feathers. Slipping from one skin to the other was different when not being coaxed by the siren call of the full moon. It was less of an obligation—instead it was an action of pure joy. Nerves tickled with anticipation as I pulled my magic around me like a blanket, gave a quick shiver and stretch, and unfurled my wings. It still hurt—there was no way to get around the sensation of a body reforming bone and tendon—and I still needed to make sure every feather was where it should be as soon as the shifting settled.

I cut my preening short this time around. As soon as my stomach settled from the mix of nausea and butterflies slipping skins always produced, I took to flight with a croak of parting for my human-shaped family members. Jack and Melody joined me in flight, and we started off, our wings taking us back to where we had found Anthony.

* * *

The tall pines were filled with crows, cousins paying their respects to our Anthony, as well as passing on information, letting each crow that passed through know we had a predator in our midst. That the Crows were going to take care of it, and that we needed to know if anyone had heard anything, seen anything. The cacophony that was a large gathering of crows quieted as we approached, diminishing into occasional rattles and the hiss of feather on feather as they shifted about where they perched. Jack and Melody made a point of seeking out members of individual families, to calm as well as interrogate. Questioning was not one of my more developed skills. I was content to let them sort out who knew what while I took myself higher, giving myself a good view and space to think.

Under all of the local crow conversation, I heard the nasal call of a fish crow, a call that was short and sharp with distress. Leaving Jack and Melody behind, I called out reassurance as I flew towards the pond near the middle of the nearby community park. There, near a patch of scraggly willows, the fish crow stood, feathers raised in distress as she stood near the body of her companion. I circled, assessing the situation. They were young, still waiting to grow into their full adult glossy black. The male was limp and bloody, feathers and flesh having been rearranged by sharp talons. The female croaked and puffed, terrified and furious all at once, and unable to decide what to do about it. Calling for help. Calling for my family.

She had been there, when the Owl had killed. I could see it in her eyes. I knew that immobilizing terror. I knew that self-loathing that crept in after being unable to act. I drifted down, settled next to her, bent to preen, to calm...

She wanted none of it. With a shout she hopped back, rousing and puffing. She did not want comfort. She wanted blood.

And I could not blame her. We were the same, she and I. I had not wanted the comfort of my family, had not wanted to be preened calm. I had wanted blood as soon as the terror had left. I had wanted to see Owl feathers torn free and broken. I had wanted to be the one doing the breaking. She met my eyes, the young fish crow, held me there with her terrified anger until I roused and jumped into flight with a rattle.

It had stepped over a line, the Owl. It was one thing to hunt Anthony, a were-, to work within the somewhat bloody lines established by old conflict. It was another to terrorize my natural cousins. Anthony. The young fish crow. It was too much death, too suddenly. It dug at too many memories. And there would be more death, if we did not find the Owl, and quickly.

I did not want to think about cold, dark eyes or the crunching crush of powerful talons. I flapped higher, as if trying to flee the memory of soft, soft feathers as the Owl brushed a talon-tipped finger across my cheek, drawing blood. Instinct must have turned my flight in the right direction, something just at the edge of conscious perception. In the middle of deciding to turn back and join Melody and Jack, I felt it.

It was unmistakable—the sensation of being watched, a shiver of vulnerability and the feel of the deep woods at night. I did the thing we had spent the morning reminding each other we should not: catching a taste of the Owl, I took off in its direction, calling out to Jack, Melody, and all my natural cousins as I flew, letting them know that it was here, that I had found the predator in our midst.

A Crow will always know an Owl as we pass it by. I could taste it on the air, musty feathers and old blood. I could see it where it sat, bold as could be, on a bench in the quiet corner of the community park, away from the noise of children playing and dogs barking. Nestled in the comforting dark of the tall pines it rested in its human form, tricking anyone who glanced its way into thinking nothing more than an old man rested there.

Magic calls to magic and it noticed me, opening eyes that were too yellow to pass close inspection, lifting eyebrows that were more fine bits of feather than hair. So old it could just barely pull itself down into a human shape. It stood and slipped back into the trees. I shouted as I dove down through the pine branches after it.

This old Owl had nothing to fear, not from a single Crow, but I dove at it, claws extended, screaming and shouting to wake the entire city. It slipped out of its human skin, pulling out talons and feathers, mouth gaping in the bastard cousin of a proper smile. Anticipation gleamed in bright yellow eyes as I struck at its head, as it brushed me away with one arm. A couple beats of my wings brought me back around to strike again. It was slow, not built to be active in the day, and that likely saved me as I dove at it again and again.

This was what had killed little Anthony—so new to his feathers, an eager and excited member of my family. This was what had killed Jenny—mentor and partner in crime. This was what meant to kill me. It might be older than I, larger and more powerful, but I was a Crow.

And Crows did not hunt alone.

Melody dove with a scream that would haunt the dreams of all that heard her. Jack followed, touching ground to slip into the same sort of hybrid form the Owl was holding, providing ground support. I dove again, close behind Melody, who hit home, the scent of fresh blood trailing her as she turned up and around to strike again. I struck the back of its head with a triumphant shout, hitting and cutting before twisting into a turn of my own.

The natural crows gathered, filling the sky with black wings and shouting. They added to our mob, pressing the Owl, giving it no time to counter or plan. Stuck on the defensive, bleeding and sun-slow, the Owl started to gather itself. Jack lunged forward, swiping with one clawed hand, but the Owl was moving away, muscles rippling and arms slipping to wings.

It was going to fly and flee.

I let the rein I had on my fury slip free and came in again, shouting and screaming. The impotent rage of the fledgling I had been sitting on for years bubbled to the surface, mixing with the outrage of an adult who saw their sense of security and safety slipping away. I came down with my hands around the Owl's neck, claw-tipped fingers digging deep into flesh as I strove to strangle it. Surprise filled wide yellow eyes, just before I felt a bone snap beneath my fingers.

I smelled blood as I pulled away, startled, as I blinked at hands that were unfamiliar- black and clawed. Adrenaline left a sense of exhaustion in its wake and I stumbled, catching my balance as the world stopped spinning. Everything was too sharp, all my senses seemed stuck on a high setting. It was disorienting. My throat offered a crow's rattle as I decided, perhaps, it was time to sit and collapsed backwards, my descent eased by Jack's strong arms as he came to settle beside me.

The sky was filled with crows. They would mob for a few minutes longer, making sure the threat was well and truly handled, before heading back to their own territories. The old Owl lay in front of me, seeming smaller now that it was still and unbreathing. I could still feel its neck in my hands. I could still feel its talon on my cheek. A corner of my brain was horrified at what had happened, at what I had done. Another part was content, pleased and preening, knowing my family was safe. Humanity arguing with Crow sensibilities—nothing new. I sensed I would grow out of the sense of conflict the longer I lived feathered, the less human I became.

I exhaled, forcing my way out of feathers, coaxing my magic to relax enough to give me proper hands—and who knew what else—but I was not taking the time to examine just how I had managed that half shift. Jack was kneeling in front of me, eyeing me with a mix of concern and pride. All bare skin and worry.

And here I was, sitting naked in some pine needles, a bit of blood under my nails, wondering how many days I could take off from school before someone got concerned or decided to fail me. It could go either way. "Umph." Not my most elegant statement, but it reassured Jack enough so that he stood and offered me a hand up.

"Not the result I had anticipated, but it will do." Jack patted me on the shoulder after making sure I was steady on my feet. Steady enough, at least. My brain kept wanting wings to fan out and balance with. I had not been this addled since the first time I writhed my way into feathers.

Melody landed beside us, feathers fanning out as she slipped back into her skin. She took my head in her hands and kissed my forehead. "My little fledgling has grown up." Her magic danced down my spine, this time far more familiar than old and strange. I would digest that later—preferably with a side of adult beverage and Netflix. I was not ready to join the ancient and mysterious club.

While Melody was favoring me with some Crow bonding, Jack was dragging the Owl into a decorative cluster of barberry bushes, caching it there to return for later. The crows above us were dispersing, and I could hear the usual sounds of the morning—cars and kids and dogs—now that the cacophony had diminished. I wanted to get back to my pants, and cell phone. Someone needed to call Eric and the twins, let them know they did not have to jump at shadows any more, that things had been handled. That the family was safe.

Safe. I rolled the word around for a moment, letting it settle down deep where terror had been holed up for years. Since Jenny. Letting it take the painful edge away from losing Anthony. We would mourn our losses and rebuild. Perhaps pick up a handful more fledglings along the way so Jack's house would not feel too quiet, family meetings would have more excitement. Melody and Jack, and more than likely myself now, would find the young ones as they fumbled through their first full moon, and bring them home.

I pulled my feathers around me and flapped to a low branch, waiting for the family heads to join me. Jack was missing a tail feather. Melody was, as always, impeccable in appearance. We preened a bit, there in the tree, recovering and reassuring ourselves. When Melody took to the air, Jack and I followed. I was ready for a nap, and Jack's rocking chair sounded pretty damn perfect.

MISSY THE WERE-POMERANIAN VS. THE MASTERS OF MEDIOCRE DOOM

GINI KOCH

Beth loved her Pomeranian, Missy, with all her heart. Missy was pretty and smart and Beth's best friend in all possible ways. Of course, Missy was far more than just a Pomeranian. But then, Beth was far more than just a girl, too. So it all worked out.

Beth lived in the Big City, where crime had been wiped out by the Super Team. Of course, half of the Big City had also been wiped out by the Super Team destroying all the Crime Lords and Mega-Villains of Villainy and all the other Teams of Evil that the Big City seemed to generate on a regular basis. But, as Beth's grandfather liked to say, those were the risks you took in order to live in the best darned city in the world.

And everyone living—well, still living—in the Big City was used to that, too. Sadly, her father's parents had been wiped out when Lord Megaboss had done his run through the Big City when Beth was only seven, which was when her parents had said, "The hell with this," and moved their family in with her mother's parents.

This meant that when danger appeared, which it regularly did, they all trotted down to the basement and moved the family and whoever might be visiting at the time into an impregnable underground bunker her maternal grandparents had built when the first Minions of Evil team had come to town, threatening nuclear annihilation.

The Bunk, as her family called it, was a spacious four-story affair and quite well-equipped. It also had Impregnable Tunnels connecting to the many other bunkers in and around the Big City—what those who lived there called the Underground. So, whenever the Super Team and their latest group of adversaries were having it out, everyone who had enough sense went, as her grandfather called it, Downstairs. Her grandparents lived in the Bunk 24/7, because they'd decided long before Beth had been born that living Upstairs was for thrill seekers and lunatics.

It was difficult to have pets in the Underground, and most had cats, who seemed reasonably content to stay down and inside and just hunt whatever burrowing creatures tried to get into the Impregnable Tunnels. The count was Burrowing Creatures 13,457, Cats 13,450, and Impregnable Tunnels 0, though those who built the tunnels insisted that the tunnels were keeping far more than thirteen-thousand things out.

Beth, on the other hand, wanted a dog, in part to be different. And in other part because one of the Super Team had a Super Dog and Beth had Aspirations.

Her parents had given her Missy on her twelfth birthday. At first Beth had been disappointed—the Super Dog was a Great Dane, after all—but Missy had been so fluffy and adorable that Beth had fallen in love with her within two minutes.

For the first year or so of her life, Missy just seemed like a normal dog, albeit a really smart one. She learned every command right off the bat, and even used a litter box, just like the family cats did.

But when Beth turned fourteen, everything changed. Well, Missy changed. But that also changed everything.

Beth was sitting in the living room with her parents Upstairs, because the television reception was better Upstairs. The family cats stayed Underground, but Missy went wherever Beth went, and she was asleep on a cushion at Beth's feet. It wasn't too late in the evening, but it was the weekend so Beth was allowed to stay up past midnight as long as she wasn't, as her mother put it, "Sullen and unpleasant the next day." So far, Beth had a pretty good record on at least faking pleasantness when she hadn't gotten a full night's sleep.

They were watching the latest exploits of the Super Team's sister team across the country and the fight looked like it was going to go on for quite a while, meaning Beth was glad the fight was taking place on Saturday instead of Sunday. It was always fun to see the Amazeballs in action and, despite their name, the League of Losers were doing pretty well against them, so it was a really good match. Well, as long as you didn't live in Sunshine City. It was harder to go underground there.

While they watched, Beth was also filling in her parents about what her friends were doing, why boys were kind of stupid, and complaining that her teachers never reacted fast enough when the Super Team announced a meet and greet, but acted too fast when the Super Team had to Take the Fight to the Streets.

"It's as if teachers don't want us to even get a chance to *see* the Super Team, let alone meet them," Beth complained.

Her father opened his mouth, but instead of words, a really weird growl came out. He slammed his mouth shut and looked at Beth's feet. She and her mother looked down, too, in time to see Missy jerking around and hear Missy make another wailing growl as she woke up.

Beth dropped down next to Missy. "Are you okay, girl?"

"She looks like she's having a fit," Beth's father said. He wasn't wrong—Missy was jerking all over the place, whining, and growling and acting like she was in pain or sick.

"She looks a little...bigger, too," Beth's mother said. "And she's kind of frothing. Ah, Beth, sweetie, get away from the dog."

"No, Mom! Missy would never hurt me."

"If she's gone rabid she'd hurt you without meaning to." Beth's father stood up and came over to them. He reached for Missy, but she growled at him. Missy had never growled at anyone in the family before.

Beth's mother grabbed the phone and started dialing, but Missy made a new sound. "Nooorw."

"Mom, she's calling for help!"

"Nooorw! Rime frine!"

At this everyone froze. "I could be crazy," Beth's father said, "but that sounded like Missy was talking. In a way, at least."

The Super Dog was said to be able to communicate with the rest of the Super Team, so Beth knew this was possible. "Missy, are you okay?"

"Rort rof."

"Ah, is she saying 'sort of?'" Beth's mother asked.

Missy nodded her head. She stopped shaking and the frothing seemed under control, too. Beth picked her up to cuddle her but Missy wrenched out of her arms. "Nooorw." Missy backed away from all of them.

Missy's mother still had her phone. "Dad, could you come up here? Yes, up. Yes, I know you don't like to take the risk. But we need you." She hung up. "Your grandfather's coming."

"How could Grandpa help?" Beth tried not to cry. Missy didn't look like her normal self. She was still fluffy, but her fur looked thicker somehow. Also, Beth's mother was right—Missy was a little larger than she'd been before. Her lower jaw was protruding now, the fangs sort of jutting out in front of her nose. Her claws looked longer and sharper as well. Her eyes looked a little bigger and a lot more predatory.

Beth's grandfather arrived and took a look. "Oh, fabulous."

"What is it, Dad?" Missy's mother asked.

"I knew we shouldn't have bought a dog from a friend of a friend of those Conasons." He sounded disgusted, but Beth wasn't sure why. The Conasons lived two doors down both Upstairs and Underground. James was Beth's age and they went to school together, and the families were friends.

"What's wrong with them?" Beth asked.

"They know some shifty people," he said with a dramatic sigh. "And one of those shifty types clearly has Evildoer Leanings."

"What makes you say so?" Beth's father asked.

Her grandfather shook his head. "Because apparently what we got Beth wasn't a Pomeranian. Well, not a full Pomeranian." They looked at him expectantly. He sighed dramatically again. "Missy's a Werewolf."

They all looked at her. "I'm not seeing 'wolf,'" Beth's father pointed out. Beth and her mother nodded their agreement.

"Were-dog then," her grandfather said. "Were-something. It's the first night of the full moon, and, from what we learned when the Super Team took care of the Doom Squad a couple of years back, they were doing experiments to create a stronger army. Experiments with animals and, I heard, lycanthropy. Clearly those experiments worked. After a fashion."

"We've had her for two years," Beth's father pointed out.

He shrugged. "Lycanthropy isn't an exact science, my boy. Besides, maybe the Were-something has to mature, and two years is about what it takes for most dogs to mature."

"Does that mean that anyone Missy bites will become a Were-something?" Beth asked. She wasn't opposed to Were-ness, but if Missy was any example, you didn't look better as a Were-whatever. But maybe the Super Team would find it useful enough to add on a new Were-something member.

"Maybe," her grandfather said. "But I don't recommend it. Becoming a Were-Pomeranian doesn't sound like an immediate path to fame, fortune, or the Super Team."

"We don't want Missy biting anyone," her mother said sternly, "least of all Beth."

"Wron't rite," Missy said.

Her grandfather perked up. "So, you can talk a little when you're in Were-something form?"

"Wress."

"And you understand us?"

"Wress. Retter ris ray."

"Excellent. That could be useful. She's still pretty cute, overwhelming underbite or not."

"Grandpa, that's not nice. Missy can hear you." Beth put her hand out. "C'mere, girl. I'm still your person, and you're still my dog." Missy whined, but she came to Beth hesitantly. Beth could tell her parents were ready to leap, but Missy didn't do anything aggressive. Just climbed into Beth's arms and whimpered. Beth hugged her. "See?" She petted Missy's head. "It's okay."

"Rot rearry."

"Oh," Beth's grandfather said heartily, "not to worry. The full moon cycle only lasts for three nights. Missy, you can do some vermin hunting in the Impregnable Tunnels, but don't bite or eat one of the other Underground pets—or the people, obviously—and it'll be fine."

"Rot rit."

"You really think she'll turn back in three nights, Dad?" Beth's mother asked.

"I do. She'll be herself in the daytime, too. Figure she'll want more meat than normal until then. Now, I'm going back to the Bunk where it's safe, and I suggest the four of you do so, too."

Beth and her parents looked at each other. A Were-Pomeranian was definitely an exciting development, and a little more exciting than watching the Amazeballs fight, since that seemed to have moved out over the ocean, which was cool and all, but lacked the building collapses that made superhero team fights so interesting.

"I guess we'd better go Underground," her father said. "Missy seems under control but we don't want her getting out accidentally."

"We don't need a Were outbreak," her mother agreed.

They shut up the house and headed downstairs. "Ungrrry," Missy said, sounding rather urgent. She was drooling a lot and Missy didn't drool normally. Her mother pulled out a whole raw chicken that was supposed to be Sunday's dinner. Missy scarfed it down, bones and all.

"I've never seen her eat so much at one time," Beth said.

Her grandfather snorted. "Weres are big eaters from the little I know about it. But only during 'the change' time."

Chicken rapidly gone, Beth headed to her room, Missy trotting along behind her just like normal. The family cats weren't happy as they passed, though, and a lot of hissing ensued. Missy growled at them and the cats shut up. They headed for higher ground and settled onto the top levels of their cat trees.

Beth put Missy onto her bed, then started a search on Werewolves. TV reception wasn't as good Underground, but the World Wide Web was plenty strong.

Beth found a lot of information about Werewolves, but it wasn't all that helpful. Almost all the texts indicated that a Were was a human who changed into a wolf or other animal, or vice versa. An animal turning into a Were version of itself wasn't mentioned.

"You're extra-special," Beth told Missy.

"Groody." Missy didn't sound thrilled.

"Oh, don't be like that. It says that some Weres can change any time they want, with or without the full moon. So maybe you can, too. We can experiment tomorrow." Beth yawned. So did Missy.

Beth got ready for bed and, despite her mother's worries, snuggled right next to Missy, who heaved a sad little doggy sigh. Beth hugged her. "Don't feel bad. I have a Were-Pomeranian guarding me. Not even the Super Team can say that."

"Rue."

The next morning Beth woke up to see Missy looking normal. Tests proved that Missy couldn't talk in regular dog form, which Beth found disappointing. However, Missy seemed to be thrilled to not have an ugly underbite anymore and she ate normally, though, at her grandfather's insistence, Beth's father went to the store and stocked up on a lot of raw chickens.

As evening came around, the whole family watched Missy and, sure enough, she went through the change again. This time, Beth left her alone until it was over and her mother gave Missy a raw chicken right away.

"Rank roo," Missy said, once she was done eating.

"She is sooo cute," Beth's grandmother cooed. "Isn't she cute? You're so fierce! Fierce, scary doggie!"

Missy heaved a sigh. "Rye ress."

The family all agreed that Missy was still really cute, underbite and drool or no. "What's the point of it, though?" Beth's Aunt Cil asked. "I mean, yes, Were-thing, I get it. But why make a Were-Pomeranian? What can Missy possibly do other than bite ankles?"

"Ro rirea."

"Yeah, we have no idea, either," Beth's grandfather said. "But you can't necessarily understand the Crazed Evil Genius Mind."

The adults concluded that it was probably a useless trait but one they'd deal with because Missy was Beth's dog. Beth felt that a Were-Pomeranian was still cooler than just a regular Pomeranian, but she kept those thoughts to herself.

Monday came and with it school. Beth hugged Missy tightly. "Don't worry. We'll figure it out."

She headed Upstairs and over to the Conasons to pick up James, who was waiting for her. "Did you see the Amazeballs fight?" he asked as they headed for school, keeping a wary eye out for Enemy Attacks. "They really destroyed the League of Losers. Of course, they're not a really good evil group. Not like the ones we have here."

Beth looked at him out of the corner of her eyes and considered how to answer this. Her grandfather was dead set on blaming James' family for Missy being a Were-Dog, but that didn't mean James had anything to do with it. Could she trust him? Maybe. Besides, he was probably her best friend, even though he was a boy.

"Part of it, but then something really exciting happened. Missy turned into a Were-Pomeranian."

James stared at her. "What? Missy, your little girly dog Missy?"

"Yes."

"She turned into a Werewolf?"

"No. She turned into a Were-Pomeranian." Beth waited. Maybe James knew about how this had happened.

"She turned into a Werewolf version of what she already is?"

"Um, yes. She did."

James shook his head. "Girls are weird. My mom warned me that this would happen. She said you'll get through it, though, in a few years, and I should be nice and understanding when you act crazy because you can't help it."

Beth sniffed. "My whole family saw it happen."

"Well, your family is kind of weird, so..."

"Yeah? Well your family knows shifty people."

They glared at each other and walked the rest of the way to school in silence. The rest of the day Beth barely paid attention to what her teachers were saying. She was too upset with James and worried about Missy to pay attention to math or social studies, though she did pay attention in science class because they were talking about genetics. She wanted to ask her science teacher what he thought about lycanthropy but, after James' reaction, she decided to wait a bit.

She debated waiting for James to walk home. Their parents didn't like them walking alone because an Evil Team could attack at any time and they felt there was safety in numbers. However, she was still mad at James. But, the Super Team didn't Shirk Their Duties and Beth figured she shouldn't, either.

She went to where they normally met up to see James with a bunch of other boys and a man she didn't know. The man wasn't a teacher at the school, and he looked vaguely familiar, like she'd seen him maybe once before.

As she neared the group, the man gave her a calculating look. "So, this is Beth?" he asked James.

"Yes," James said, sounding a little uncertain.

"My name is Laurence. I'm James' cousin's girlfriend's brother," the man said. "I hear you're liking your dog."

"Are you who sold us Missy?" Beth asked.

"I am!" Laurence beamed. "James seems to think there's some trouble with her?"

Beth hadn't watched the Super Team all her life not to know when to lie. "Oh, no. I was playing around and James took it seriously. Missy's the best."

"Ah." Laurence looked just a little disappointed and a whole lot suspicious. "Well, that's good then."

"We need to get home," Beth said to James. "You know our parents will worry."

"Ah, I'm going out with Laurence this afternoon," James said, a little nervously. "I forgot to tell you this morning."

"Uh huh. Okay then, I'll see you later." Beth turned to go.

"Oh, why don't you come with us?" Laurence asked. "I'm sure you'll enjoy what we're going to do as much as the boys will."

Beth turned but took a step back, so that she was out of reach of any of them. Ms. Super was quite clear on how a young woman should be prepared for an attack at any time, and Beth didn't trust Laurence at all. "No thanks," she said nicely. "My parents don't like it when I change plans on them. Maybe next time." She nodded to James and the others, then turned again and walked quickly away.

They didn't follow, for which Beth was quite relieved. She got across the street and then looked back at them. They were all watching her. She gave them a little wave, but kept walking quickly, just in case.

Beth got home without incident. Her parents and Aunt Cil were at work, but her grandparents were home and she told them about what had happened.

"Laurence is definitely the man who sold us Missy," her grandfather said, eyes narrowed. "Glad you had the sense to come home."

"I'm glad they didn't try to grab Beth and force her away," her grandmother said worriedly. "You need to be careful."

"I was and I will be. I just wonder what that Laurence is up to."

"No good," her grandfather said firmly.

Beth sent James a text, asking him what he was doing with Laurence. *Nothing*, was the reply. "That's totally suspicious," she said to Missy, who was cuddled next to her. "I don't think that Laurence is a good person."

Missy gave a quiet bark Beth assumed meant agreement.

Beth considered options. Based on what her grandfather had said, tonight was the last night for a month that Missy would be a Were. And James was her friend, and the other boys with him weren't bad kids. But they would be if Laurence got his hands on them.

Beth sent another text to James. *Got permission to hang out. Where are you?*

The reply was slow to come back. *You're sure?*

Yeah.

The next reply was even slower, but an address was provided. *And don't bring your stupid dog.*

Beth stared at that. "Missy, if someone you suspect is being influenced by a bad guy tells you not to do something, should you do it or not?" Missy looked at her questioningly, and Beth shared the conversation and her thoughts. "I think we need to intervene before James Turns To Evil. Laurence is clearly already there."

Missy growled and nudged Beth's watch. "Yeah, I know you won't change for a while. But I just know in my gut that James and the other boys are in danger of going to the Side of Evil. And we can't allow that."

Missy barked what sounded like agreement.

Beth gathered what she thought she might need in a Fight Against Nascent Evil. The Super Team had superpowers, of course, but still they went equipped with the means of communication with the police force and some conventional weapons, too. Beth's family wasn't loaded with weapons, but the neighbor between them and the Conasons was totally prepped for an invasion.

"Going to visit Missus Marconi," Beth said to her grandparents.

They both looked at her suspiciously. "Not going to see James?" her grandmother asked.

"He's not home. I checked. I want to see if Missus Marconi has noticed that Laurence hanging around."

"If she can see anything aside from all those cats," her grandfather said. Mrs. Marconi proudly proclaimed herself to be a Crazy Cat Lady and nothing about her or her home could make anyone offer an argument against this.

"Remember that cats aren't the only way she's crazy," her grandmother added.

Her grandparents couldn't find a strong reason to object to the visit, however, since they were friendly with Mrs. Marconi, cats in double digits and potentially crazy or not, so Beth put Missy's leash on, made sure her phone and Swiss Army knife were securely in her jacket pocket, and headed out of the Bunk.

Mrs. Marconi was older than Aunt Cil and Beth's parents but not as old as her grandparents. She was, as Beth's father put it, still in fighting shape. And she was prepped to fight a lot of things.

Mrs. Marconi was home and happy to see Beth, who told her the whole story while petting cats and having cookies and milk. Unlike James, Mrs. Marconi didn't argue about Missy being a Were-Pomeranian.

"He's at it again," she muttered as she examined Missy carefully. "You're planning to try to stop whatever Laurence is up to?"

"I am, but I know I need help. Weapons at the least."

"As if you know how to use them? Stay here." Mrs. Marconi shook her head and trotted off and Beth wondered if she was going to tell her grandparents what was going on. But that wasn't the case. She came back wearing a full bodysuit. It wasn't leather, but looked a little like it. She handed Beth a suit that looked similar. "Go put this on. It's a protection suit. Put your clothes back on over it."

Beth took the suit and went to the bathroom to change. Missy went with her. "No one just has suits like these lying around," she whispered to Missy. "I wonder if Missus Marconi isn't really Missus Marconi, but a retired superhero!"

Missy barked softly and nudged around the hamper. Beth looked at it. It looked like a hamper. She dressed as Mrs. Marconi had told her to—the bodysuit wasn't very thick and her clothes went on over it easily. She left the bathroom to find that Mrs. Marconi had also put her regular clothes back on. She'd also laid out an assortment of weapons, not just guns, but whips, knives, a crossbow, and things Beth wasn't familiar with.

"Have you ever handled a weapon of any kind?" Mrs. Marconi asked. "Don't lie. I'll know."

Beth resisted the urge to say she had. "I've handled knives. In the kitchen," she added for honesty's sake.

Mrs. Marconi sighed. "Well, we make do with what we have." She handed Beth a couple of knives in sheaths. "Secure those about your person and let's hope they don't get used against you."

"Who were you?" Beth asked as she stashed knives in her jacket and back pocket of her jeans.

"Someone who wants to remain anonymous."

"But I'm working with you now."

Mrs. Marconi grunted. "True enough. I'm someone who has to right a wrong at this precise time. We'll leave it at that for now."

Beth's mind raced. "You know Laurence, don't you? I mean, beyond what I've told you."

"I do. And I know that if he's blatantly recruiting at your school then he's ready to roll whatever nefarious plan he's been prepping." With that, she loaded up on weapons herself, including a whip, a couple of pistols, what looked like a laser gun, and the crossbow. Then she jerked her head and headed off. Beth followed.

They went to the same bathroom Beth had changed in and Mrs. Marconi opened the hamper lid, then moved the hamper ninety degrees. The wall behind the hamper slid open.

"A secret door! That's so cool!" Beth was impressed with the setup and also with Missy, who'd clearly spotted this door earlier.

"Follow me and stay quiet. These tunnels can echo."

While following Mrs. Marconi through a very different set of tunnels than the ones she was used to, Beth ran through all the older super teams she could think of. Mrs. Marconi had been living next to her grandparents longer than Beth could remember, which meant that she was probably from one of the teams from the Golden Age of about twenty years ago.

There had always been plenty of female superheroes, so without anything to go on, Beth came up blank—too many options. She focused instead on Laurence. He didn't look familiar, and he wasn't old enough to have been part of the Golden Age unless he'd been a child.

Of course, there were usually kids helping out the various Teams of Super Goodness, just like Beth was helping Mrs. Marconi. So she focused on trying to remember all of them. Due to her Aspirations, Beth has memorized every Sidekick on both the Side of Goodness and the Side of Evil. She had most of their trading cards, too. She decided to go through them alphabetically so as to be more accurate.

She was up to Noxious Boy when they reached the exit from the tunnels into the Subway. "Don't need to pay the fare," Mrs. Marconi chuckled under her breath. "We'll always get you there."

Beth didn't complain—she hadn't brought any money, so them not having to pay was a relief. Mrs. Marconi verified the address they were heading for and they got on the train that would get them there fastest.

Missy sat in Beth's lap for the ride. She seemed extra alert and Beth was pleased. Missy was clearly a Mini Super Dog and Mrs. Marconi was obviously a Retired Superhero Returning To Duty and that made Beth an Official Sidekick. She contemplated what name to choose, but decided that it would be something that should be collaborative with Mrs. Marconi.

Beth put the rhyme that Mrs. Marconi had said into her phone's search engine, but they reached their stop before the search was done.

They were in a very disreputable part of town, not that this came as a surprise. "Should you go in with me?" Beth asked as they neared their destination, a rickety looking two-story warehouse.

"I've been debating that. They're expecting only you, not me or Missy." Mrs. Marconi pulled them into an alleyway near the warehouse, presumably so they wouldn't be spotted. Beth felt that she should've been taking notes, but that could slow things down, so she'd just have to remember as much as possible.

"I thought you said they'd expect me to bring Missy."

"Exactly, but you're going to play dumb and obedient and not bring her in with you, I think. Missy and I will be the sneak attack."

Being the Bait was standard Sidekick Duty, so Beth had no objections. "How long before I can graduate to full Superhero status?"

Mrs. Marconi snorted. "Let's get through this before you make a decision on having to live a double life forever."

They discussed their Plan of Attack until Beth was clear on her duties. Get inside, engage the enemy, then stall as much as possible. Seemed simple enough. Of course, Beth was also aware that many times Plans Went Awry, but that just meant that she and Mrs. Marconi would have to think on their feet, while Missy thought on her paws.

Beth hugged Missy. "Be good and stay safe. Oh, and find me at the right time." It never hurt to give exact instructions to a Super Dog.

With that, Beth headed out of the alley while Mrs. Marconi and Missy went out the other side so as to slip into the warehouse from the back. Beth went to the front door and made a show of looking around and verifying the address just in case someone was watching.

The door wasn't locked so Beth went in. "Hello?" she called out, just as if she didn't expect a trap. "James?"

The warehouse wasn't well lit, which wasn't a surprise. But while it had looked like two stories from the street, there was only one floor with a really high ceiling. There were a lot of tall stacks of metal sheets and pipes and such that blocked most of the building from view. There weren't any catwalks, which Beth thought was odd, considering the height of the building. This could mean that Laurence could fly, though, so she checked up as much as down and around.

She didn't spot any traps, so she walked in carefully. She didn't call out anymore—either they could hear her and were lying in wait, or they couldn't hear her, so she might as well go the rest of the way in Stealth Mode.

Beth crept around through the maze of metal. It sort of looked like this place was a foundry, only it wasn't all that warm and there were no noises that one would associate with someplace working with metals. It was, in fact, almost eerily quiet.

It looked creepy, too, presumably on purpose. There was lighting, but it was really high up. Whoever had to change the bulbs would need a fireman's ladder or flight ability for sure.

Beth missed Missy a lot right now. Having her dog with her to hold and at least seem like protection would have been nice. But one didn't join a Superhero team by being a scaredy-cat and Beth knew this was her Big Chance. So she forged on, making a note that this was a pun she might want to toss out if, in fact, this place had a forge in it. Sidekicks had pun and riddle requirements, after all.

She finally got into the middle and the stacks of various kinds of metal gave way to an area without a lot of stuff in it. There were still stacks of metal of all kinds ahead of her and to the side, but this area had nothing in it but a dirty concrete floor. Beth figured that the Secret Lair was going to be underground somewhere, though hopefully not connected to Underground. Though if it was, she and Mrs. Marconi could get there easily next time without taking the Subway.

She checked her phone. The rhyme search was a dead end—it had come up with too many options and Beth currently didn't have time to sort through them. "Maybe later," she said to herself, mostly to hear some sound. There was still no one around and, since she was exposed here anyway, Beth figured faking it again was the way to go. "Hello? James? Where are you guys?"

She was rewarded with James finally coming to get her. He didn't come up from beneath, but from the stack of metal to her right. "Hey, Beth." He sounded underwhelmed that she was here.

"Hey." She went towards him, but not too fast, just in case. "What's with all the weirdness?"

"You didn't bring your dog?" He sounded relieved and disappointed.

"You told me not to."

"And you listened to me?" Now he sounded shocked.

Beth sniffed at him. "Sometimes. So, what's going on? Why are you guys at this creepy warehouse?"

"It's where Laurence lives, uh, works."

Clearly James was not as good at the Sidekick Business as Beth was. Sadly, though, he appeared to be Sidekicking for the Side of Evil. There was nothing for it—Beth was going to have to Save Him From Himself. And that meant she had to lull James into a False Sense Of Security and Put Him At His Ease.

"Oh. Okay. Why are you guys here? He's not some weird creeper, is he?"

James laughed weakly. "Not like that, no. Um, you know, you don't have to come in." He sounded a little desperate. "You should probably go home. The guys will understand."

"Understand what?"

"That you're scared here. I mean, you're a girl, it's a creepy building, I'm sure you're not feeling comfortable."

Beth resisted saying all the things she wanted to, starting with the fact that she was less scared of a lot more things than James was and ending with the fact that no one on the Side of Right was supposed to feel comfortable in an Evil Lair. Instead, she gave him what she figured was the answer he expected. "Oh, but you're here to protect me, right?" She managed not to throw up a little in her mouth when she said this, and really hoped Mrs. Marconi had both caught this and was clear that Beth was Faking Out The Evil Sidekick.

"Oh, yeah," James said weakly. "That's right. Totally what I'm here for." With that he jerked his head towards the metal stacks that were opposite from the ones he'd come out of. "Everyone's over there."

"They're awfully quiet," Beth remarked as they walked across the empty space.

"Yeah, well, Laurence doesn't like a lot of noise."

"Huh. And yet he breeds dogs."

"No, he doesn't."

Beth didn't argue. Just because Laurence had been the one who'd sold Missy to them, that didn't mean he was a breeder. Beth really hoped Missy and Mrs. Marconi were nearby, because she wasn't counting on James to back her at all.

They reached the other stacks without the floor falling out from under them and also without a cage dropping on them. Beth was relieved and a little disappointed. Laurence wasn't really impressing in the Evil Lair department.

But then they rounded one of the stacks of sheet metal to find a huge pipe, easily six feet in diameter. James walked into it. Beth followed. They reached the end of the pipe to find the stairs Beth knew had to be here. This was more like it. Time to head into the Secret Lair and see what was what.

"This is weird," she said, in case James was thinking that she seemed too calm.

"Yeah, it's kind of cool, though."

"Oh yeah. Totally." Beth hoped she didn't sound disparaging. It wouldn't do to let on that she was aware that things weren't what they seemed to James. At least, not yet.

Down a long flight of stairs and out into a room that was far more like what she'd been expecting. Lots of laboratory equipment, vats of clear blue liquid in which various things floated, stuff that looked like it was out of a Frankenstein movie, what might have been a small reactor, and other, less easily identified items filled most of this big underground room.

Laurence was in a white lab coat and the other boys from school were near him. They all looked kind of slack-jawed. "What's with them?" she asked James quietly.

"Um, they're listening to Laurence."

"He's not talking."

"Not right now, no. But they're waiting for him to play again."

Beth looked more closely at Laurence. Sure enough, he had what looked like a flute in his hands. She ran through her various Sidekick Cards in her head. There had been one, sure enough, during the Golden Age, who'd played a flute. He'd been called the Petit Pied Piper, Triple P for short. But he'd been a good guy.

She examined Laurence's face as they got closer. He could indeed have been Triple P grown up, he looked old enough without being too old. So, did that mean he was on the Side of Right? Beth's gut said there was no way. The Super Team's headquarters was at the top of a giant skyscraper because Heroes Didn't Hide. So, Laurence was definitely a bad guy.

The other boys seemed more alert. Laurence notice this, too, and played a fast little tune on his flute. Beth wasn't impressed, but the boys all looked kind of glazed again. James didn't, though.

Laurence's eyes narrowed as they reached him. "Where's the dog?"

"James told me not to bring her."

"And you listened to him?" It was official—they'd bet on Beth doing exactly the opposite of what James had said.

"Sometimes."

"It's the last night of the full moon," Laurence said. "If we're to cure your dog of her lycanthropic tendencies, I need her here."

For a moment Beth wondered if Laurence was actually a good guy. But if he was, why would James have told her to leave Missy at home, and as nastily as he had? No, Beth knew that a good Superhero or Sidekick Trusted Their Gut, and her gut said that Laurence wanted Missy for Nefarious Purposes.

"I told you I was joking about that." Now it was time to stall. Beth sincerely hoped that Mrs. Marconi had a plan, because while the rest of the guys looked kind of like zombies, there were a lot more of them than there were of her.

"But I know you were lying about joking about it," Laurence said smoothly. "So, what did she turn into? An alligator? A wolf? A lion?"

"Um, no."

Laurence stepped closer to her. "Understand, young lady. If you don't want to follow in your dog's footsteps and become a lycan yourself, you'll tell me what your dog changed into."

Beth considered lying, but decided there were other ways to stall. "She turned into a Were-Pomeranian."

Laurence made a sound of disgust and put his flute to his lips. He played another tune. Beth winced. "Did you take lessons?" she asked politely.

Laurence stopped mid-tune. "Yes." He sounded shocked. "Why do you ask?"

"You're kind of flat. Or sharp. I'm not sure which, but since I don't think a flute can be tuned, it's got to be you."

"They can, too." He stared at her. "You weren't, ah, affected by the music?"

"Only in that it was painful." Beth looked him right in the eyes. "I know who you are."

Laurence managed a smirk. "And who is that?"

"You're the Petit Pied Piper. Though you've lost the petit part. You're a lot taller than I'd have expected."

"I lost it through my experiments," he said rather grandly. "Experiments you'll be a part of." He grabbed Beth's arm.

She didn't look to James for help. Aunt Cil was big on self-defense and she'd spent a lot of time drilling Beth into how to protect herself. Beth slammed her knee into Laurence's groin, then kicked at his knee while she wrenched herself away from him.

He staggered and Beth backed up. Into James, who grabbed and held her upper arms more tightly than Laurence had. "You have to stay now," he said quietly. "It'll be safer and I don't want you to get hurt. Besides, every team needs a girl in it."

"Why is that?" Beth asked.

"To make the food and bring the snacks and answer the phone. And, um, you know, maybe...you could be my girlfriend."

He'd never been stupid like this before. Beth presumed this was Laurence's influence. "The heck with that." Beth stomped on his foot and slammed her head back into his face while slamming her elbows back at the same time. James let go, howling. Beth leaped away from him, but Laurence was playing his flute and the other boys had surrounded them. They looked more like zombies than they had before.

"You broke my nose!" James was holding his face and there was definitely blood.

"You're supposed to be my friend, not someone trying to force me to do things against my will!"

"But it's going to be so cool," James said, as he used a handkerchief to sop up the blood. "We're going to be the New Masters of Doom, taking up the mantle after the demise of the Doom Squad who took over from the original Masters of Doom. We'll take on the Super Team, and the Amazeballs, maybe both at once. Don't you want in on that? Don't you want to be my girlfriend?"

"No, I don't want to be your girlfriend just so I can get your snacks and act like you're impressive even when you're not. Good boyfriends don't try to make their girlfriends Turn To Evil or force them to do anything they don't want to. And, to make it even worse, the Doom Squad was even lamer than the Masters of Doom. The Masters of Doom were enemies of your team, too," she said to Laurence. She pulled out one of the knives Mrs. Marconi had given her.

Laurence shrugged and stopped playing. The boys looked a little less like zombies again. "Alliances shift. Doctor Megadoom had many interesting...ideas." He went to a metal cylinder that was sort of hanging from the ceiling and flipped one of its many toggles. The knife flew out of Beth's hand and slammed into the metal cylinder. The other knives she had on her did the same thing, even her Swiss Army knife. Laurence smirked. "Now, for the last time, where's your dog?"

"Mrime herrrre!" Missy came bounding in from a different direction than from where Beth had entered the Secret Lair.

"Stop her!" Laurence shouted. He played another painful few notes and the boys lurched into action.

Missy was in full Were-Pomeranian form and she dodged the admittedly slow boys and leapt in front of Beth. Missy's collar wasn't on, so presumably Mrs. Marconi had noted the giant magnet and had Adapted the

Plan accordingly.

Laurence stared at Missy. "You were serious? That's her entire transformation? Into a slightly larger and less cute Pomeranian? How is that even possible? How could the serum fail so miserably?"

"Rooo ruck," Missy said. Accurately, as far as Beth could tell.

Still, Missy was her dog. "I think she's awesome as her regular self and as a Were-Pomeranian. Just because she's not what *you* wanted doesn't make her anything less than Super."

"Still playing with toys that aren't yours, Laurence?" Mrs. Marconi came from the same direction Missy had. Only she wasn't dressed like Mrs. Marconi anymore. She was dressed in her former uniform. She didn't have any weapons Beth could see other than the whip, which made sense, since all the other weapons they'd brought had metal in them. But then, her whip was all she'd need.

"It's Wonder Gal," James said, sounding shocked, as the other boys once again seemed to be coming out of their Zombie-Like Trance. "I thought she disappeared after the Last Battle with Doctor Megadoom."

Beth was thrilled. Wonder Gal was one of the Originals, one of the members of the very first heroes' alliance, the Wonder Team. And Beth was her new Sidekick! "This day could be the best ever."

"Mother, what are you doing here?" Laurence asked. Whined, really.

"Stopping your madness. Again."

Laurence put his flute to his lips. "Attack!" Then he started playing. The sound was still painful, off-key, unappealing, and still totally non-hypnotic for Beth. But the boys all lumbered towards Wonder Gal. James, however, didn't.

"So, his awful playing doesn't work on you?" Beth asked.

James shrugged. "I'm immune, I guess. Like you are." He looked down. "Your Were-dog isn't, though."

Missy was indeed running away from Beth, but not towards Wonder Gal. No, Missy was headed right for Laurence. She grabbed his ankle in her jaws and bit down. And then she flipped him.

One moment Laurence was standing up, the next Missy had him on his side. She shook her head the way dogs do, from side-to-side rapidly, and he went from side-to-side rapidly, too, slamming onto the floor each time. He stopped playing and the boys stopped trying to attack Wonder Gal. She rounded them up with her Whip of Holding and though they struggled, they couldn't get free.

Beth and James stared at Missy flipping Laurence around from side to side. "She always that strong?" he asked finally.

"I don't think so. But, you know, she's a Super Dog, so maybe."

The flute finally flew out of Laurence's hands. James and Beth both jumped for it, but he was a little taller than she was and had a slightly better vertical leap. James came down with the flute in his hand.

"Give it to me," Wonder Gal said. "Let's get this over with."

James looked at Beth but he didn't make a move towards Wonder Gal. "James, give the flute to Wonder Gal. Then we can take Laurence to the police and go home."

"But we're the New Masters of Doom."

"Hardly," Wonder Gal said.

"Yeah, I have to agree. You guys are mediocre at best. I mean, unless you have hidden troops here or something."

"I'm not mediocre," James said angrily.

"Not you," Beth said. Sure, he'd tried to force her to do things she didn't want to, but they'd been friends forever, so he deserved the benefit of the doubt. Not a lot of benefit, but some. "But this team is. Who wants to be in the Masters of Mediocre Doom? You could have a Change of Heart and join with me and Wonder Gal."

He put the flute to his lips and blew into it. Music came out. Far better than the music that Laurence had played. It still wasn't compelling to Beth, but Wonder Gal gasped. "He's got the Ability. Dash it all, we thought it had been bred out!"

The boys started to fight against their bonds in earnest, and even though the Whip of Holding was impressive, there were a lot of them and they got free. Then they dogpiled onto Wonder Gal. She fought bravely, tossing boy after boy off and away from her but, again, there were a lot of them, they were kids, and Beth knew she didn't want to hurt them. Ultimately they got her down.

Meanwhile, Beth was trying to get the flute away from James, but he was running around the room playing, while she ran after him.

She finally got him cornered between a couple of vats of the clear blue liquid. Beth kicked at James, but he dodged it, shoved her into a vat and, as she bounced against the glass, took off.

Beth scrambled to her feet and this time she didn't try to get fancy—she tackled James from behind. They went down, but he kept a hold of the flute. He was a little bigger than her, though, and also a little stronger, and he managed to kick away from her, and get to his feet. To his credit, James didn't try to kick her in the head, he just ran away, once more playing the flute.

"To me, my minions!" James shouted, as he reached the hidden door

Beth realized Missy and Wonder Gal had come through. "We'll show these girls who's the boss!"

The boys ran away from Wonder Gal, and they seemed less like zombies and more like they were really into the whole Masters of Doom thing. At the same time, Missy dropped Laurence, who was unconscious by now anyway, and lunged at James. As a Were-Pomeranian she had a lot more spring. She wasn't quite able to reach the flute, but she got his arm and held on.

James spun, flinging his arm around. Because Missy wasn't on the ground she couldn't bring him down, and he finally managed to shake her off and sent her flying.

Beth didn't hesitate. Super dog or Were-dog or not, Missy could get hurt. She ran even faster than she had after James. She had to jump to make it, but she caught Missy, pulled her in, and did a tuck and cover. They landed against the vat of clear blue liquid Beth had already slammed into and this time it broke. The water splashed all over them.

"You haven't heard the last of the Masters of *Mediocre* Doom, Beth," James shouted. "You'll see! I'll impress you and you'll stop calling us mediocre and you'll join our team because I'm the best and you'll want to be with the best!" With that, he and the boys ran out, carrying Laurence's unconscious body with them.

Wonder Gal ran over to Beth and Missy. "Anything broken? Any cuts?"

"I don't think so," Beth said, as she stood up.

"Rime rokay."

Wonder Gal looked worried. "I have no idea what was in that and with Laurence and the boys gone, we're not going to know for a while. It could affect one or both of you. The protection suit is good, but it's not the best against that much liquid."

Beth shrugged. "I'm prepared for whatever might happen. Those are the Risks when you're part of a Super Squad."

"And the risks when you get bitten by a lycan. We have no idea if Missy's bite will alter Laurence or James, but I think we need to be prepared for it."

"I'm ever ready," Beth said. Missy barked her readiness as well.

Wonder Gal smiled. "I knew you were special, Beth. I'm proud of how you handled things today."

Beth beamed and hugged Missy. "I couldn't have done it without you, Wonder Gal, or our Wonder Dog, Missy the Were-Pomeranian! Missy did the hardest stuff, after all."

Missy licked her face. "Ryyy rerson."

"Yes, I'm your person and you're my dog." Beth cuddled Missy a bit more. "So what's my Sidekick name?"

Wonder Gal snorted softly. "You weren't a sidekick today, Beth. You were definitely a superhero. So, I'm thinking that, based on age alone, Wonder Girl might be a good starting name. After all, I won't live forever and someone should always be ready to take up the whip and become Wonder Gal."

"Really?" Beth could not believe her luck. "I'm really a full superhero now?"

"You are," Wonder Gal said solemnly. "You even have a Nemesis. Who you're going to have to be prepared for. James isn't going to come back and say he's sorry. He's going to try to outdo himself to impress you."

"Rike fowr roo."

Wonder Gal nodded. "Yes, Missy, just like for me. Mister Marconi wasn't on the Wonder Team. He was a mild mannered college professor by day and at night he was...Doctor Megadoom. And Laurence's father."

Beth gasped. "You married your Nemesis?" Wonder Gal nodded. "But why?"

Wonder Gal got a funny little smile on her face. "Oh, you know. Chicks dig the bad boys."

"I don't."

Wonder Gal sighed. "Well, we'll see what happens when the time comes. For now, we have to change into our regular clothes and get back home to our Secret Identities. And I'm going to catch hell from your Aunt Cil, too."

"Really? Why?"

Wonder Gal grinned and put her arm around Beth's shoulders. "I'll tell you all about what your family does on the side on the way home, Wonder Girl."

Beth sighed happily. "I was right. This has definitely been the best day ever. Oh, can we stop on the way and get Missy a chicken?"

Wonder Gal laughed. "Yes, we can. Whatever Missy our Wonder Were-Pomeranian wants, she gets."

"Rye wrant a steak!"

"A steak it is then," Beth said as she patted Missy's head.

"Wronder-roo! Missy's ron the case!"

PAPER WASP
MIKE BARRETTA

Vespa Magillacuddy listened to the party in the next cabin over. Music and laughter drifted through the pines and loneliness pressed on her like a weight. The children were gone, visiting a sister camp on the other side of the lake for the weekend. The supervising adults were in hiding, so the teenage camp counselors were running the show for the weekend. Though kind and patient enough to deal with the kids, she'd never learned how to ingratiate herself to the camp supervisors. Consequently, she was not a counselor and not invited to the party. Working in the kitchen wasn't bad. It certainly wasn't what she wanted, but she made the best of it.

She examined herself in the mirror, trying to find out why no one liked her. The dull and lusterless chunk of glass did not reflect her brighter self, so it was no surprise that no one else could see the real her. Still, she wanted desperately to be loved...or at the very least...liked. Each year, she held out hope and this year, while searching for the tiniest sign of acceptance, she'd found Jack. He said "please" and "thank you" and "excuse me," though she had never really had a conversation with him. He didn't shun her or say cruel things. It could be automatic, unthinking courtesy, but she hoped that perhaps, with him, things would be different this year.

She grabbed her hair and moved it from one side to the other of her pudgy face, seeking a better side to present to the world. Her plastic framed glasses slipped to the bottom of her nose and she pushed them up where they did good service hiding her unremarkable, dirt-brown eyes. She sucked in her tummy and then released. Endless laps around the lake in her glued-up PF Flyers did little to shed the stubborn pounds of baby fat that clung to her body.

She turned away from her sad reflection and stepped out onto the front porch of her cabin to hear the party better. Drowsy paper wasps clung to their fragile gray nest next to a dim 40 watt bulb over the door. Maintenance hadn't taken it down despite her repeated requests. The partiers laughed and yelled at each other, playing spin-the-bottle or Truth or Dare. She fantasizing that someone would come over and invite her to the party and then she imagined leaning against a boy so casually that it wasn't a big deal at all. The next morning, they could walk around the camp with hands tucked into each other's back pockets.

The fantasy faded out, the effort to sustain it too tiring. Back inside, she flopped down on the hollowed out mattress to read.

* * *

"If you like her so much, go over and do her, why don't you?" said Amanda.

"I don't like her," said Jack. "I think, maybe, we should just include her."

"Eww, what for? She's a freakin' toad or something. What are you, some sort of caped crusader?" said Lisa. "I know you're the new guy, but, come on, have some sense."

"Yea, Jack, righting wrongs wherever they may be found," added Eric.

"Shut up, idiot. I'm just saying we should be nicer to her." Eric handed him the bottle of Boone's Farm and he took a long drink of the fine wine.

"She's fat. It's the last group we can discriminate against," said Amanda. "Perfectly legal. They do it to themselves."

"She's not that fat," said Jack.

"Rotund!"

"Bovine!"

"Corpulent!"

"Corpulent? Big words from a little mind."

"She's got some big boobs for a moped," said Eric.

"Moped?" asked Jack.

"Yea, lots of fun to ride, but you don't want anyone to catch ya doin' it."

The group dissolved into vicious laughter.

"Yea, she's a moped," said Jack. He wanted to defend Vespa, but it had risks. He enjoyed the acceptance of the others and did not want to be cast out. "Any more wine? This bottle is empty."

"So spin it," said Eric.

He spun the bottle and it pointed at Amanda.

"Well?" he said to Amanda.

"Well what?"

"You gotta kiss me," said Jack.

"You wish," said Amanda. "I'm not playing this game."

"What do you want to play?"

"Truth or Dare, and I get to ask first," said Amanda.

"Why is that?" asked Jack.

"The bottle picked me. Are you in Jack? Truth or Dare?" asked Amanda.

"Dare," he said. The girl, dull and vain, had no imagination. What could she think of? Jumping in the lake naked?

"I dare you to go next door and ride the moped."

"I'm not doing that," said Jack.

"Pussy," said Eric.

"I wouldn't take that dare. What kind of name is that? Vespa Magillacuddy. It's like hillbilly white trash and wannabe Italian supermodel all rolled into one," said LeeAnne.

"Yea, only without the supermodel part. So are you gonna take the dare, or you gonna be a virgin for the whole summer?" asked Eric.

Jack stood up, wobbled a bit. He'd had more wine than he thought. "One, I am not a virgin. Two." He pointed to Amanda. "When I come back I'm doin' you."

"Oooooh," chorused the group.

"If you think you can handle all this," said Amanda.

"Oh, I can handle it." He plucked two wine coolers from the Coleman cooler and staggered to the door, letting it slam shut. "I'll be back."

"Yea, that's my man, thanks for bangin' the skanks," said Eric.

* * *

Vespa turned the page, realized she hadn't even read it, and turned it back.

Today at lunch, she'd sat down at the table for the counselors and Jack had walked by her and put his hand on her shoulder as he passed, then sat down right next to her, rather than keeping one seat between them. He didn't speak to her, but it had felt like acceptance.

"Hey," said Jack through the screen door.

She sat up in bed, surprised. "Hey."

"We weren't keeping you up, were we?

"No. I was just reading." Vespa held up her book. Her heart pounded. No one had ever visited before.

"Can I come in?"

"Yea, sure."

The screen door creaked when opened and slammed shut on its springs.

"Sorry."

The wasps buzzed, flying short, agitated arcs, bouncing off the screen a few times, before settling back down on the paper nest.

"I didn't know what you liked, so I picked two. Pina Colada or Berry?"

"I don't know."

He sat on the bed next to her, twisted the cap off of the Pina Colada, and handed her the bottle. "Try this."

She took a sip. "It's good."

"Yea."

"Why are you here?"

"Because I think you're nice, not like those phonies."

He put his arm around her, his face inches from her own, just as she'd imagined it would be. She felt awkward and self-conscious. Though in unfamiliar territory, she didn't want it to stop. If she did something wrong or said something stupid, the moment would pop like a soap bubble and disappear. She took another sip of the wine cooler.

He leaned over and kissed her the moment she brought the bottle down. His soft lips pressed against hers. He pulled back, but was still so close she could feel his breath on her skin. "You taste like Pina Colada."

She didn't say anything. The perfect and fragile moment crystallized around her. His left hand rested on her leg.

"Are you alright?" he asked.

"Yes."

"You can kiss me back, you know? If you want."

She did.

She'd kissed family, but never on the lips. Family smelled of old lady perfume, liquor, and cigarettes. Jack smelled like a boy and his kiss felt as wonderful and different from those kisses as anything could be. He tasted sweet and she wanted more. Electricity and warmth coursed through her veins. He leaned into her and pushed her back onto the bed and she let him. He touched her, and she thought that she should tell him to stop or slow down, but then he might go away and that would break her. The impulse towards caution, honed by years of disappointment, abandoned her. It had to happen sometime, didn't it? Someone would come along to love her and make her feel special. Good things could happen to her.

He slipped his hand under her shirt and she gasped.

She was just as good as the other girls that got all the attention and all the kissing and touching and hand holding. Wasn't she? She deserved to have the same sweet summer like the kind in the movies, even if it meant nothing in the long run.

He kissed her again and she felt his tongue in her mouth. His other hand unzipped her pants and pushed them down around her hips.

She didn't feel like herself. She felt wonderful. He reached and turned off the light.

When he entered her, she gasped at the delicious pain. He moved rhythmically and she wasn't a slut like her father called her, because she loved Jack for the tiny kindnesses, like talking to her and sitting next to her.

He shuddered and she felt warmth between her legs. No fireworks or magic. She just felt a bit of pain and a pleasant buzzing in her groin that was growing to something altogether different until he stopped.

She held his face and pulled it down, taking the initiative, so she could kiss him. "I love you."

He jerked back.

"What are you saying?"

He rolled off, got out of the bed, and gathered his clothes.

She lay still. Time buzzed in her ears. "I thought that..."

"Thought what?"

The buzz turned to a terrible blood-roar. Her heart raced out of control. Suddenly aware of her nakedness, she pulled up the sheets to cover herself. They made a thin defense against what was coming. The world lurched sidewise and forgot to take her with it. Despair bubbled to the surface with a strange chemical vengeance. Blind, stupid panic froze her limbs and narrowed her vision to a small gray cone. She needed a lifeline to pull her back from the deep water.

"I thought that..."

"God, you are dense, just like they said. It was just a thing." He put on his pants, pulled his shirt over his head. "A dare. You know?"

"Get out! Get out! Get out!"

He picked up his shoes and left her alone.

Rage and humiliation flooded her body. She dressed with extreme deliberation. If just one more thing happened, she would fracture into a thousand pieces. How did she get to this instant? An abyss yawned in the pit of her stomach, an empty hollow feeling of betrayal and loss. She needed to run, flee into the night and leave the moment behind. Her cheap running shoes squeezed her feet tight. The screen door spring groaned as she pushed it open.

They were waiting for her outside, prepared to pile on the pain and humiliation. They hoisted their beer bottles and wine coolers in celebration and cheered.

"Oh sweetie, did you get your cherry popped?" purred Amanda.

"More like her watermelon," said LeeAnne.

Tears blurred her tormentors into melted monsters. The camp lights starred and smeared her vision. The screen door slipped from her fingers and slammed shut, launching the paper wasps from their nest in search of the source of their disturbance.

She searched for Jack in the crowd, but he blended into them, just another blurry monster.

A wasp landed at the cusp of her neck and right shoulder and stung her. She slapped it away and the angry wasp lapped her head, the buzz of its membranous wings thick in her ears. It flew out of the light and into the enveloping darkness.

"Two pricks in one night, huh, Vespa?" said Amanda.

The pain in her heart and her shoulder flared. She leapt off the porch and ran, splitting the group right between Madison and Ashley, knocking them aside, following the wasp into darkness.

"Watch it, whore," said Madison.

"Piggie," said Ashley.

"Wee, wee, wee, all the way home," said Amanda.

* * *

Vespa ran. Humiliation and anger drove her over every rock and root hazarding the moonlit lake trail. Six miles of trail fell behind her slapping feet. The length of the lake lay between her and the camp and she was still too close. Their laughter and cruelty followed. She slowed, looking over her shoulder, but no one followed. Her breath hitched and her heart pounded loudly in her ears. The wasp stung flesh on her right shoulder felt soft and hot, like a liquid boil ready to burst.

She tried to reconstruct what had happened in her head, but it made no sense. He came over, and took her in his arms, and made love to her, just the way she imagined it would be.

She didn't say no. She didn't say stop.

Did she have to?

Did it matter?

Each year she held out hope that the camp would be a different, better place, but people carried their shittiness everywhere they went. Up until now, she'd taken every bit they dished out. What choice did she have?

At the uninhabited end of the lake, at a sandy beach too small and remote for anyone to visit—especially in the depths of night—she stripped off her clothes, walked into the water, and scrubbed herself between her legs. Later, chilled to the bone, she came out of the water, collapsed on the sandy shore, and sobbed. Wasp venom burned her shoulder and crept through her veins.

* * *

Gray light washed the camp. Lake fog cast a hush over the pines. Vespa walked to the main building that housed the kitchen, each step a bit closer to the dirty looks, knowing whispers, and mocking laughter. The adults moved about sluggishly, recovering from their own partying in town and getting ready for the returning campers. She entered the back kitchen door and put on her apron. It felt too short and too loose, but her name was written on the pocket, so it had to be hers. She wrapped the strings around and cinched them tight.

"Buenos dias," said Louis the cook. "You must have got some good beauty sleep. Lookin' good girl."

Louis, a forty-four year old Costa Rican grandfather, worked the kitchen preparing breakfast, lunch, and dinner with two of his cousins. The other two did not speak English and went about their jobs with silent efficiency. Louis sent most of his money home, keeping enough for cigarettes and the occasional beer. She liked him.

"Morning, Lou," said Vespa. With Jack's true nature revealed, Louis felt like the only real person in the camp. "Stop making fun, I feel like hell and I got stung by a wasp." There was no way she was going to tell him about what happened in her cabin.

"Bad news, bad news," said Louis. "In Costa Rica wasps grow a foot long."

She mustered a weak smile. Her shoulder hurt and her heart pounded in a dreary broken manner. After her return from her midnight run, she'd tossed and turned all night. She'd awoken feverish, tangled in sweat-soaked sheets with aching bones and half-remembered dreams. She'd kicked off her sheets and lay curled and shivering on a bare mattress. The ceiling fan had wobbled and squeaked, pushing cool night air around the cabin.

With the slightest movement, pain flared in her shoulder. The sting had hardened to an itchy knot, but she had work to do so she ignored it. Louis and his cousins spat rapid fire Spanish at each other as they cooked. She set out the hash browns, scrambled eggs, and bacon in the water tray warmers, arranged baskets of silverware, plastic trays, and fruit yogurt and little boxes of cereal. Louis's cousins helped her fill the big coolers with milk, orange juice, and ice water. For the moment, the cafeteria and its cooking smells felt safe and comfortable. She tried to eat a light breakfast of fruit and yogurt, but her stomach rebelled on her.

She unlocked the front doors. The counselors, her tormentors, had gathered in front of the building so they could enter at the same time in a show of force.

She walked back behind the serving counter to take her station and waited for it to begin. Most mornings, they just ignored her, but today she was sure it would be different and the thought of the inevitable taunting and humiliation made her angry.

"I tell you," said Louis. He leaned in and whispered into her ear. "You should poke that little puta, Amanda. You do it, and I see nothing."

The girls came in first, laughing and speaking behind cupped hands. They lined up in reverse rank order, with Amanda at the end.

"Hey, Vespa, did you have a good time?" asked Nicole.

LeeAnne leaned in close, "Vespa, you little slut. What did you get up to last night?"

She slopped food on their trays and stayed quiet, dampening their enthusiasm for insult. Amanda drew closer, like a matador prepared to deliver the killing strike after the less adept at cruelty prepped the bull for slaughter.

"Two sausages," said Amanda.

Vespa speared two sausages with the tines of the fork and scraped them off on Amanda's plate.

"And some bacon. I love to have some meat, don't you?" Amanda picked up a sausage with two fingers and nibbled on it with her perfect white teeth. "Oooh, so good. Remind you of anything?"

Vespa tightened her grip on the twin pronged fork and before she could think, she stabbed Amanda in the webbing of her hand between her thumb and finger. Blood welled from the punctures in bright red bubbles. Amanda dropped the tray to clatter on the floor. The cafeteria silenced. "You bitch. You slutty, little bitch," said Amanda.

Vespa came around the counter with a towel, seized Amanda's bleeding hand, and wrapped it up. She squeezed hard, feeling the bones of Amanda's hand grinding together. "We have to keep pressure on it."

"Let go of me. I said, let go! You're hurting me."

"You should be more careful."

"Careful? You stabbed me, you idiot. My hand. Let go."

"I did, didn't I? What I meant to say is that you should be more careful around me."

"Are you threatening me?"

Vespa pulled Amanda close and whispered, "Yes, I am. I am threatening you. I'll stab you over and over. We should keep this between us. Don't you think?" She let go.

Amanda stepped away, her eyes wide with unaccustomed fear. She spun about and stormed out the door, in the direction of the dispensary. The boys, just entering, caught the tail end of the drama.

"I'm sorry, Amanda. I didn't mean to," called Vespa.

The boys queued up to the counter.

"Hey, I'll have a sausage," said Jared. "Or is that what you want?"

"That is definitely what I want, but you don't have enough for me," said Vespa

She picked up a sausage, bit it in half, and tossed it onto his tray.

"Oh, oh, man, burn," said Bobby.

"Serve yourself boys. I got a whole tray of little dicks for little dicks." She took off her apron, dropped it to the floor, and strode to the back door of the kitchen.

"You feeling okay?" asked Louis.

"Bueno, Louis. Muy bueno."

* * *

She walked across the grass-bare ground to her cabin. She felt strong and purposeful and weird, as if the events of the night had no meaning. Pounds of doubt and anxiety sloughed off her. Jealousy and anger evaporated in the slanting sun. She kicked off her cheap sneakers and left them behind. The ground felt cool and sensual and she wanted to strip off her other clothes and feel the air on her skin. At her cabin, the wasp nest hung empty, save for the capped over cells that harbored the next generation. The adults foraged for prey.

She would not have to work half as hard. The cabin was surrounded by prey. Inside her cabin, the morning light, warm and gold, pushed back the dreariness that typically infested the small room the rest of the day. The heaviness of the room disgusted her. Her cloths itched terribly so she stripped them off and dropped them to the floor. In the shower, she turned the water to hot until the small bathroom billowed with moist steam. Under the scalding water, layers of her old self washed away, gurgling down the drain. When she was all gone, she turned the water off and waited in front of the fogged over mirror. Rivulets of condensation flowed down the mirror, clearing it away so that it reflected her brighter self, just like she wanted it to.

* * *

Someone knocked on the door and she wrapped a towel around herself and exited the bathroom.

"Vespa, it's Mr. Barnes."

"Come in."

Mr. Barnes, the camp administrator, stepped in without looking up. He ruled the camp with malign indifference, only caring when he had to write a report about someone's little darling getting hurt. She imagined stabbing Amanda in the hand qualified. His mouth formed a little "O" of surprise when he saw her.

"Oh, I'm sorry. I can come back."

"It's okay Mr. Barnes. I don't mind."

She walked closer to him, driven by instinct and desire.

"Vespa, did you stab Amanda on purpose? She came to me and I...I know you...you and the other girls don't get along. She needed stitches."

"No, Mr. Barnes I would never do that. Stitches? That's terrible. She held her tray out and then...I just don't know..."

The slick lie, crocodile tears, and the trembling lip convinced him.

"Well, I didn't think...you...Uh...did it on purpose."

She put her hand on his chest, slipping a finger beneath his button-down shirt to touch bare skin and feel the race of blood and the burn of neurons. She could taste him with her fingertips.

Her towel slipped away.

"Mr. Barnes, you're my friend, aren't you?"

She stood on her tiptoes to kiss him.

* * *

Mr. Barnes would have screamed if he could have, but he didn't. When she was done with him, he wasn't even Mr. Barnes any more, but something else, something obedient: a drone. After he left, Vespa fidgeted, collapsed into her chair, confused as to what she'd done and how she even knew how to do it. Old patterns were comforting, so she picked up her book. The worm-like words squirmed across the page, blurry and pointless. She ripped a page free and crammed the tasteless paper into her mouth. More pages followed, until the book was gone. She reached for the next, chewing and swallowing, until gray masticated pulp dribbled down her chin. The eaten books sat in her gut like a stone.

She seized the Bible, the last book—all the cabins had one—and tore the gilt-edged, onion-skinned Word. Slowly at first, and then with greater urgency, she ate the Bible, making it part of herself.

Her stomach rumbled and she pressed her hand against the hard bulge of her belly. She left her cabin, entering into the chaos of yellow school busses disgorging returning campers. The children dispersed to their bunkhouses to meet with their counselors and begin the day's activities. They hollered and screamed and the pointless noise and disordered conduct annoyed her. She escaped behind the kitchen building into relative quiet. Louis was nowhere in sight and she was grateful. When he wasn't working, he napped and smoked in a hammock strung up in the woods. She pulled up the building's wooden storm cellar door and stepped down into the spider-infested gloom. The lower door had a rusted padlock that she twisted off with her bare hand. In the far corner, behind boxes of unknown items, she dropped to her knees and vomited up the chewed up books into a pulpy steaming mass. Her hands reached into the warm pile, feeling the heat and moist slickness. She padded and stretched and carved the digested pulp into graceful hexagonal cells just large enough to fit a child or small person. When finished, she had an array of sixteen cells of translucent, thin paper as strong as sheet aluminum. She stood back, satisfied with her initial effort, and then shimmied off her jeans to lay her eggs.

Jack and Mr. Barnes were worth something after all.

* * *

The next day, she found Louis behind the kitchen smoking and, because she liked him, she gave him fair warning. He looked into her eyes, crossed himself, and left, looking over his shoulder once. He called in Spanish and his two relatives joined him. As he drove off, she forgot he ever existed. The other adults came to her privately and when they left, they all saw her point of view. Each encounter drained her, but it drained them more. Unquestioned, unthinking devotion was all she asked, and they were happy to give it.

The adults did not notice her new self because she told them not to notice. They went about the mundane business of running the camp, but the counselors did notice, especially the boys. They fought to please her and be next to her. At first their attention was flattering, but later, it grew tiresome and tedious. She had a project to attend to, and they were just boys and entirely predictable.

She ate sparingly. The food tasted bland and unsatisfying. After-hours, she hunted in the walk-in refrigerator and pantry. Nothing in the pantry suited her, but in the refrigerator, she found a bowl of hamburger. She sat on the floor, curling her long legs beneath her, and scooped a mouthful of the chilled raw meat into her mouth. Delicious proteins and amino acids electrified her senses. She ate faster, with both hands alternating. Cold juices sluiced down her throat. Better if warm, she thought, but it was all so new to her. She licked her hands clean of the greasy fat and blood with manic insect fastidiousness and then put her lips to the bowl, tipped it back, and drank.

Better, if warm, she thought. Better if living.

More or less satiated, she returned to her nest and regurgitated a small amount to feed her pupae.

When they got bigger they would need more.

* * *

"How do I look?"

"You look fantastic," said Mr. Barnes.

"I do, don't I?" She twisted her body in the mirror. Her lingerie clung to her wasp-waist and flowed down her long legs in a shimmering silken fall. Once, another lifetime ago, she had saved her money and bought a bra from Victoria's Secret. Apparently, underwear came with a lifetime subscription to the catalog. The few times she received the catalog—before her mother threw it away as trashy, or her father took it to who-knows-where—she would pour through the pages, fantasizing about the glamour and eroticism. Now, compared to her, the catalog women—haute and remote and criminally aloof to the world—would be sluggish and dull.

Mr. Barnes took a cautious, hopeful step closer.

"Ah, ah, ah. You can go. Please stop at Nick's cabin and tell him to come over."

She could smell the disappointment and impotent violence buried deep in his body, but he left obediently. He had no choice in the matter.

A moment later, Nick knocked on her door.

Nick should have run, but instead, he entered, eyes wide, mouth agape, like a fish out of water, gasping its life away.

"Nick, you should close the door."

He did.

* * *

"We need to see what she does down there," said Amanda.

"I'm not going," said Jack. "Shit is getting creepy around here. Everyone is acting like drones or something. You go and I'll wait."

He didn't like the idea of being close to Vespa. Her terrifying attractiveness felt evil, and the fact that no one noticed, or cared, about her stunning and sudden metamorphosis freaked him out. One day there was a Magillicuddy in the kitchen, and the next, a Vespa running the camp. One-by-one, everyone had moved onto Team Vespa. The children, unreasonably polite and cooperative, were the creepiest. Homesickness, pointless crying jags, and hurt feelings were banished to wherever they came from. Everyone knew their role and did it without any extraneous emotion or calculation.

"Stop being a coward," said Amanda.

She grabbed him by his hand and dragged him towards the cellar door. He pulled it open and they stepped down, closing the door after them, casting themselves into dark, stygian gloom.

"Let's go back and get a flashlight," said Jack.

"We can see well enough. Let's find out what is so interesting down here."

They walked between boxes, sporting equipment, and discarded hand tools.

"What is that?" asked Amanda. Greasy light from small cellar windows illuminated a pale geometric assembly.

"I don't know."

They walked closer.

Gray, hexagonal tubes stacked horizontally, one onto the other, emerged. A sticky wet mess, black in the dim light, matted the dirt floor in front of the tubes. The tubes were all empty except for one. Jack took out his cellphone; still no bars. He turned on the flashlight app and shined it on the capped cell.

Something inside crawled toward the light. It squirmed and humped down the tube, a rapid, fluttering motion, eager to get out of the paper nest.

"Turn it off, turn it off!" said Amanda.

Jack discerned the outline of a pale triangular head and bulging eyes. Scissored jaws snapped.

A mindless atavistic fear gripped him. White hot adrenaline flushed his blood. He turned off the flashlight app.

Amanda gripped his arm painfully. "Oh, Jesus, oh Jesus, oh Jesus. We need to get out, now. We need to get out."

The basement door opened and he took Amanda's hand and led her away from the thing in the tube into the dark. He pulled her into a far corner and wrapped his arms around her. Amanda shook violently. A scream built in her throat and he covered her mouth.

"Please," he pleaded. "She'll hear us."

* * *

"This way, honey," said Vespa.

She guided Lacy, the last child, to the nest. The child, chemically drained of volition and will, walked without complaint. Vespa knelt down behind the child and lay her down. She reached over the prone child and shredded the cell's paper cap, pulling it away and setting the pieces of paper aside. She reached into the cell and stroked the pupae. The creature cocked its head, leaning into her touch.

"Oh, beautiful. How sweet. See Lacy, see how beautiful?"

The pupae's head extruded from the cell. Its jaws stretched sideways and clacked shut, the serrated edges mated together. The ghastly white pupae—soft, devoid of detail, except for the razor jaws and slicked-back antennae—let out a happy squeal.

Lacy stared, uncomprehending and without fear. She did not make a sound as Vespa fed her to the pupae. The pupae's jaws worked like a bladed machine, slicing and rending. When the last bit of Lacy vanished through the pupae's mouth, Vespa stepped back and waited.

The pupae retreated into its cell and shuddered as violent chemical processes took over. An oozing split ruptured down the center of the pupae's face. Milky fluid and undigested blood ran out the cell, adding to the waste on the dirt floor. The split widened and something inside the pupae protruded from the ruptured wasp head. Vespa reached into the pupae shell and pulled out a child, a pale, wrinkled version of Lacy.

"That's it," she said. "You're a new creature now, born again. All the old things have passed away and become new." She cradled the child, wiped the remains of birthing fluid from her body, and set her down on her feet. New Lacy wobbled for a moment, then took a firm confident stance. Her body plumped smooth and her eyes brightened with purpose. The child leaned forward and butted foreheads with her mother, her queen.

"That's my sweet. You're perfect. Perfect and uncorrupted. You'll go home soon and no one will laugh at you or tease you or call you bad names. Are you still hungry, dear?"

New Lacy nodded

She was hungry herself.

"Jack," said Vespa. "Amanda. I can smell your piss."

* * *

Mercedes, BMWs, and Lexus's filled the dirt parking lot. Parents, dragged about by inordinately well-behaved children, cooed over the lake, the cabins, and various projects. All the fathers wanted to talk to Vespa, but she stood aloof, swarmed and protected by her own kind.

Later, they would find out about her through their children.

At the end of the day, the adult supervisors and the counselors lined up and waved goodbye. Tomorrow, a new bus would bring more campers and replacement counselors for Jack and Amanda, the two that had allegedly run off.

They had a day between sessions to prepare. No worry. They all knew their jobs. Vespa reached over and took a male by the hand. It did not matter which one. The other males seethed with a jealousy they could not express or understand. The females, sterile, had no thoughts on the matter whatsoever. They had work to do.

She led him to the cellar to tidy up and conceive the next perfect generation.

POINT FIVE
ELIZABETH KITE

From: Nia Gonzales (nia@shantyshack.com)
To: Estrella Mendez (estrella@shantyshack.com)
Subject: Padlock on freezer (read me first)
Sent: 0636 Thurs 24 March 2016

Dear Auntie Estrella,

By now, you've probably noticed the padlock on the restaurant's walk-in freezer. Please stay out of there for now. If you absolutely need more salmon fillets defrosted, the key is in the same spot my dad used for storing his collection of "Jerry Garcia" seashells. You shouldn't need more fillets; Neil and I moved enough to the prep fridge before we left.

On that note, Neil and I will miss lunch. I've called Navarro and he super-promised to wait tables through the rush. If he asks you for cash, I've put $40 in his apron pocket. I also paid his phone bill this month. If you need another hand, call Natalie. She didn't respond to my texts.

If you keep the freezer door closed, I promise I'll explain everything when I get back.

If you open the freezer, please don't call the cops. I'm going to send you a longer email while we're on the road. Call Natalie first, then read the other email.

Nia Gonzales
Sous Chef
Shanty Shack
20476 Breeze Blvd.
Seaside, CA 93955

* * *

From: Nia Gonzales (nia@shantyshack.com)
To: Estrella Mendez (estrella@shantyshack.com)
Subject: Padlock on freezer (read me if freezer is opened) (please don't open freezer)
Sent: 0945 Thurs 24 March 2016

If you're reading this, you've opened the freezer and have a few questions.

Please know that I've always considered you my favorite aunt and am immensely grateful to you for paying for culinary school and letting me cook in Dad's old kitchen. I don't know what I'd ever do without you.

That said, I've not been entirely honest. I am only human for 29.5 days out of every 30. During that measly, occasionally important .5, when the moon is full, I turn into a starfish.

Yes, it's Mom's fault. Dad didn't know she was selkie-esque (sealionkie?) when they got married. I don't know how he could have missed the clues. I've seen her clapping for food in the old home videos and she wears her coat everywhere, but you knew Dad. He was oblivious to everything except the fish on the grill.

I'm also not the only one who changes. Natalie turns into a sea lion, same as Mom. Neil becomes a shark. (He's driving right now. Says hi.) And Navarro's a bottom-feeding stingray. I just happened to get the short shrift on the sea creature selection chart before birth.

There is some benefit. I can taste food with my fingers. That is how I can tell if a shipment's too old when I touch it. So, in an odd way, Mom *has* saved the restaurant money.

Well, last night was the family's .5. Usually I spend that time in my own saltwater bathtub with an assortment of mussels stuck to the bottom, but Natalie wasn't having it. She kept barking on about how I "never visit anyone" and I "don't take care of myself" and I "need to spend time in the ocean so I know what it means to be a real were-starfish." Arguing with a sea lion is as pointless as you can imagine. I met Neil at his house and he drove us to the old harbor.

It doesn't hurt to change, Auntie. I know you'd think so if you watched us, but it doesn't. There is a point where my brain slides into my stomach and my sex drive possesses my arms and legs, but if school has taught us anything, it's that humans also get used to their bodies over time. And, when I'm a starfish, clams taste amazing.

I found a tide pool with a great selection of my favorite invertebrates. For the first few hours, I thought everything would be fine. How silly of me to forget that Spring Break is a 'thing' when culinary school doesn't have one.

Something you should know, Auntie: starfish need salt water for circulation. It is their blood. It is their life. If there was a biology major among the crowd of drunken jobless imbeciles, then he failed basic echinoderms. Thanks to both the primitive eye I have at the end of each arm and a game of Ultimate Starfish Frisbee, I can now sympathize with hula hoops.

By the time I unwillingly boarded some frat boy's speed boat, I was half-dead and dizzy enough to vomit. I used my tube feet to grab on to whoever was holding me at the time and expelled my stomach onto their hand. My carrier, also not a biology major, freaked out and tossed me off the back of the boat.

You know the surge you get when you slice your hand, Auntie? That feeling right before the blood escapes? That's what the propeller did to me. After that, I lost all sensation and plummeted.

The tide must have carried me to shore. I woke up human and crawled out of the water. It was still dark out, but late enough that the college students had collapsed into drunken nap huddles in the sand. At the time, I figured some homeless drifter had stolen my clothes and my phone from the locker, so I covered myself in kelp and walked to the nearest landline. Of course, no one in this family answers collect calls. I walked barefoot for two hours before reaching the restaurant.

Oh, the window. I'm sorry. I'll fix that too.

I finally got Neil to pick up his phone. He told me to stay right where I was. I threw out my kelp bikini and put on my chef's jacket. Since I needed to channel the frustration somewhere, I chopped vegetables until the back door slammed open. Neil stomped in and stared at me the same way he stares at horror movies on Wednesday night. I didn't understand his face until my copy walked in behind him.

Another thing you should know, Auntie: starfish can regrow missing body parts after colliding with propellers. All they need is a leg and part of their core.

Now that I've had time to think, I should have put down the knife. My copy must have thought she was me, what with having my clothes and my phone and my brand new Happy-Birthday-Nia Coach bag hanging from her elbow. I'd probably think I was me too. Her eyes darted to my knife. She picked up the frying pan. One of us screamed. I swear she swung first. I nicked a vein in her arm while blocking the pan.

It was all over the moment Neil smelled blood. The moon hadn't set. If you go back to the freezer, you'll see the bite marks under the saran wrap. Don't worry, blood only freaks Neil out during that special .5 time of the month, and he's usually swimming during that time anyway.

Neil says I have to wrap this up. We just parked. I guess all I have left to say is: I love you, Auntie. Please don't let my dead copy freak you out. I'm shaken enough as is. The possibility of three other copies wandering naked through a beach full of drunk college students doesn't help. Neil and I are going to search for them. I have extra outfits with me, just in case. I left the knife in the sink.

If a copy does come in and starts my shift, tell her the veggies are prepped and waiting in the fridge.

Nia Gonzales
Sous Chef
Shanty Shack
20476 Breeze Blvd.
Seaside, CA 93955

THE PROMISE OF DEATH
DANIELLE ACKLEY-MCPHAIL

"It is only the promise of death that makes life worth living." – Robert E. Howard

An Rógaire resisted the urge to rub where a crescent-shaped ivory sliver yet marked his forehead, hidden by a dark shock of once-silken hair now gone rough. Just enough horn remained to serve as a stark reminder of all he had lost. Magic...kin...his true form...even his name. Everything but his life—which felt all but worthless without the rest—and his new-found purpose. A muscle in his cheek twitched as he raised his head and flared his nostrils to sample the air.

He caught a whiff, a mere memory of his quarry's scent, faint and growing fainter.

Tension radiated up his jaw as his teeth clenched. With each passing day the threat grew that Den Jeger—brother to the man who had died severing An's horn—would figure out how to use it. Not an alicorn alive would be safe as long as Jeger held his trophy. Much like a dousing rod, the spire would lead the hunter to anyone nearby with even a trace of magic, alicorn or otherwise.

An would not let that happen. Just the thought drove him closer to the edge of madness as rage flared through him. He was more than a touch mad anyway, as most alicorns robbed of their horns—and thus their magic—tended to be, but for the most part he was able to stay on the reasonable side of sane. In part because of the sliver of horn left to him, in part because he must. Forcing back the pain at the center of his forehead, An turned his focus outward and hunted the hunter, not for vengeance, but to neutralize the threat.

Jeger had to be stopped.

* * *

The energy of Dublin grated on An like a constant jolt applied directly to his nerve endings. He liked the city and had visited often over the years, but this constant exposure wore on him. What he wouldn't give to leave the perpetual barrage of traffic sounds, human voices, and electronic noise for the gentle music of the wild, to run on four legs and not two. Just for half an hour. Instead, Jeger lead him a merry chase through the city. Over the last week they'd stalked one another back and forth across every neighborhood in Dublin.

For now, An had lost track of the hunter. Snarling, he cut down an old, cobblestoned alley heading toward Trinity College, trying with the meager magic still at his call to locate Jeger's trail...or the spire's to be more precise.

An had been both blessed and cursed when he'd been cleaved. Once most rogues transformed to their human form for the final time—the only defense a hornless alicorn had in humanity's world—their ability for magic was spent. Not so for An Rógaire. The sliver he had left allowed him enough ability to glamour his features and cast other minor workings—such as sensing the inherent magic in others...and his horn, which Jeger had taken as a trophy. All An wanted was to retrieve the blasted thing and have done with this half-existence. No...that wasn't precisely true. What An truly wanted was to pound Jeger beneath his hooves until his fetlocks were crimson with the man's blood, to hear the man's screams fade away into the squelch of pulping flesh...

An's footsteps became more forceful in response to the violent thought and his lips twisted in a cruel smile, until those walking toward him began to swing wide to go around.

As he realized it, he abruptly stopped, trembling as a cold, clammy sweat coated him. This was not him. This was not the behavior of an alicorn, whose nature was to heal, not harm. With each day that passed—and with him hardly realizing it—the madness took more control.

He needed to end this before it was too late. Before these impulses extended not just to Jeger, but to all mankind. Once the threat was gone, An could let go and find...release...from this shadow existence.

For that he had to find Jeger.

Recklessly, he overreached himself, grasping for magic beyond his current capability. His stomach churned with the effort and a piercing pain lanced through his head. Slumping against a worn brick wall, he heaved a sharp sigh and pressed the heel of his hand against his forehead where the scar throbbed.

"Soundin' mighty vexed there, sunshine."

An jerked upright, his hand tightening into a raised fist. Aggression briefly surged through him, until he forced it back. As he regained control he recognized Charlie's voice and felt a phantom sensation down his back reminiscent of the tingling brush of another's magic. A sensation An had not felt since his cleaving. As his nerves settled he nearly snorted as the misnomer registered. But then, his friend here tended toward snark. "Nearly missed you today, Charlie," An said in his gentlest tone as he forced his hand to relax. "Not finding trouble out there, are you?" As he spoke, he reached into the messenger bag slung across his shoulder and drew out what would have been his lunch. He managed an impression of a smile as he leaned out and handed it to the waif.

With a sullen look, Charlie jerked a hard head shake as she all but grabbed the sandwich. "Got more sense than that, An Rógaire."

He flinched. Though that alias predated his losing his spire, it was the only name he had claimed since. Being addressed by it left him feeling raw, as if he lost a little more of himself each time it was used.

Charlie didn't even notice, all her attention focused on the food. Deft hands extracted half the sandwich from the wrapper and squirreled the rest away, somehow managing to do so in a way that made it seem nothing was there at all. If not for her age and obvious state of existence, An would have suspected Charlie of being one of his kind, but no foal could have mastered the human transformation this young, and even if one had, they would have been sheltered and nurtured, not cast alone into the world to subsist among humankind at such a tender age.

Still...perhaps somewhere back in her human lineage she had alicorn kin. Despite living on the rough there was a sense of purity there, and signs of mage potential that might develop as she grew older. It was enough to make him wonder.

Of course, Charlie's entire nature was a puzzle to him. A long tenure on the streets had made her age and sex nearly indeterminate. Any tell-tale features were as hidden as the sandwich he'd given her. Most people assumed she was a young boy. An figured somewhere in her early teens and female, but that was just instinct. Her scent was muddied, not clearly one gender or the other. He'd known her for years through a mutual connection to the local Romani clan, but even he couldn't be completely certain, though he was better equipped than most at sensing biological cues.

Without intending to, he leaned a little closer and let his nostrils flare, still trying to make sense of Charlie's scent. She tensed and her jaw stilled. Though they'd known each other a while and counted each other friend,

Charlie never lost the sense of self-preservation that kept her alive on the streets. She looked ready to drop the food in her hand and bolt.

An caught himself before she took off. He stepped back out of reach to lean against the opposite wall of the alleyway, sliding his hands into his pockets and crossing his ankles. It almost wasn't enough, but after a long, taut pause, Charlie lifted the sandwich and made half of it disappear in one bite, never once taking her eyes from him.

"What's the word?" he asked, knowing street kids—especially this one—were better informed than practically anyone else, just as a matter of survival.

That got him an eye-roll and half-shrug as Charlie carefully chewed, then swallowed before answering, showing she had more sense than most of those he sacrificed his meals to. An reached into his bag again and drew out a bottle of water, which Charlie was quick to take, but not snatch. She sipped enough to clear her throat before answering, then squirreled away the rest.

"The yobs are causin' trouble down by the docks, an' a new crop of Paki dossers are settin' shop 'round the market. I tell ya, they could teach them cinema actors a thing or two, they're that good at fakin'. Oh, an' someone's snatchin' school girls, but it's real strange. Always good girls...lily white, if ya get me. They turn up somewhere a few days later loopy on somethin' but otherwise just fine. Three's gone missin', an' two come back so far."

An bobbed his head and let her ramble between bites until her sandwich was gone. Normally this was the point where they'd part ways. An hesitated. What she said about the school girls concerned him, but that didn't sound like Jeger's thing. Yet anxiety twitched down An's back in an instinctive warning he couldn't shake.

It wasn't like anyone would confuse Charlie with a school girl. Hell, as far as he knew no one except him pegged her as female at all. If this was a random snatcher, An was pretty sure she was safe.

But what if this wasn't some random perv? What if gender wasn't the only common identifier between the victims? Jeger was out there somewhere roaming those streets Charlie called home. That made An nervous. He still couldn't say if his young friend had anything to worry about. Might be there was nothing more than the usual; unless his suspicions were correct and she was an aliman, a melding of their kind with threads of magic woven through her humanity. That could definitely put her more at risk from the hunter. The horn fragment Jeger possessed could lead him right to her thinking she was alicorn...and worse yet, if she had any developing mage sense, she might not realize a stranger drew near if she felt An's essence through the horn.

Again violent urges surged through him. He closed his eyes as he felt them begin to roll and clenched his jaw as he swallowed down a bugling scream. Breathing slow and deep, he got himself under control before he spoke.

"There's a man out there you need to stay clear of..."

Charlie scoffed. "Just one, An?"

"I mean it, Charlie," he said, leaning forward to catch her gaze. "This guy's a hunter and might be you have enough in you of what he's hunting for." An quickly described Jeger, from his brush-cut blond hair to his flat brown gaze. He detailed the scar across the hunter's right wrist—for which An was unintentionally responsible—and even the horn shard—though An didn't call it that—which never left its custom-made sheath at Jeger's side. The way the man moved and how he operated. The words came out in a rush because An didn't know how long she'd let him talk before taking off. He could feel himself losing his calm with each word. Already her eyes were wary. "If you hear anything about him...or worse, cross paths with him, stay clear and get word to me through the Clan."

"Don't know what you're going on about." She started to back away and he knew she'd dash once she was clear of the alley.

"I just want you to be careful, Charlie. He's after me, but that doesn't mean you're safe if he notices you...If he notices what I have."

An spoke that last to the empty air.

* * *

Tension rippled through every muscle and drew his brow into a vicious scowl. An felt something looming on the air. As if there were somewhere he should be. Driven, he made his way across the Temple Bar. His hands fisted and his shoulders bunched as his gaze tracked all around him. Where was the bastard? It wasn't like Jeger to drop off the grid. To taunt and tease and try and lead An somewhere society wouldn't interfere, that was the hunter's usual course. But Jeger was nowhere to be found.

Jeger's absence left An agitated. But that wasn't all.

Over the past weeks three more girls had been reported missing. They had all turned back up, in the same condition. Innocent girls, unharmed and intact, but with no memory of what had gone before. He had a bad feeling Jeger, misguided by legends of unicorns and virgins, was responsible for the abductions after all.

That wasn't why An was worked up, though. What had him worried was that there were only six girls reported missing. And seven had been found.

The seventh was a street kid no one knew or cared had gone missing.

An couldn't help but think of Charlie, whom he feared was number eight. The otherness about her reminded him of his own kind. The only other instance a human came close to such a resemblance—without possessing magic—was those who were pure.

Like all the other girls gone missing.

Alicorn had no care for human abstinence; what they sought was their own kind. Unfortunately, one form of purity often mimicked the other, giving rise to the legends.

The thought that the hunter might have targeted his friend kindled rage in An's belly. He felt the urge to roll his eyes and toss his head, rearing up in a display of equine fury, though his body could no longer manage the posture and his rough, shoulder-length locks hardly constituted a lashing mane. He fought the impulse down, but it kicked his ass. Even in the thick of Temple Bar foot traffic, the space surrounding An cleared. His nostrils flared with every heated breath and his lips kept twitching, baring clenched teeth. For a moment he caught his reflection and nearly screamed in challenge.

That snapped him out of it. He was no use to Charlie like this.

He wrestled the madness down and strove to ignore the depression that flowed into its place. He moved more methodically through the city with an eye out for the hunter, but hoping to find his friend. He believed he caught fleeting glimpses of Jeger, occasionally sensing what might have been the trail of his horn, but An could not be certain. The presence of magic in the city and the crowds muddled his senses. There was enough whiff of Jeger's trail to lead An southward, but not give him a clear sense of direction.

Giving up on the hunter for now, An turned his focus back toward finding Charlie.

Gritting his teeth, he crossed the street toward St. Stephen's Green thinking to search the shadows beneath the trees, where the street kids like to hang after dark. Before he could dodge them, a cluster of women intersected his path. He grunted as he collided with a mass of soft curves and flowing skirts. Bell-like laughter rose in the night as two delicate hands gripped his arms to the musical clatter of a multitude of bangles. More laughter, just as loud and melodious rose around him until An cursed at the attention the bevy surrounding him drew.

"Ah, La-La! What a catch! Toss that one here if you even think of lobbin' him back."

"Now, now, La-La! Don't listen to her...family before all others, yeah, *cousin?*"

The catcalls and ribald comments continued as An sought to extract himself, but he stilled as soon as he recognized the Romani lilt to their voices and took heed of the name they called to.

"La-La?" he asked on a bare breath. He peered into the woman's face, finding familiar dark eyes asparkle among a riot of long, thick curls he knew would be a warm honey brown in the daylight. His hands came up to rest on her shoulders and hope seized his breath, scarcely believing to encounter this one here. She was not alicorn, or even aliman, but she knew him and his kind. Her Clan...the Kalderăs Clan, had oft sheltered members of his herd.

Perhaps...but no, he could not sense any kin among those with her. Still, the Clan might be able to help. They held a magic of their own...for tracking, for Seeing. And they knew Charlie. Cared for her. If anyone could help him find the girl, it was the Rom.

The woman stilled, a frown on her face as she peered closer. He watched her gaze lose focus as her Sight kicked in and she saw beyond his glamour. Her eyes crinkled and her smile grew warmer.

"Lor...!" She started to squeal the name she knew him by, only An darted his hand out and pressed it over her lips, giving a sharp shake of his head. Jeger knew that name, but not the face An wore now to hide his own.

The sparkle in her gaze dimmed as she noticed the changes in him, along with his behavior. She scanned around them for trouble. Her forehead creased as none was evident, but any good Rom knew when best to be silent, and to fade from notice. She gestured to the women she was with. With a nod, they swarmed past the two of them, and moved off, their voices rising higher and more exuberant than before as they danced and laughed and drew everyone's eye off of the two they left behind.

An let La-La claim the hand he'd raised and draw him into the shelter of the boughs overhanging the wrought-iron fence surrounding the park. Together they turned and headed off in the opposite direction, both remaining silent and moving swiftly, once the attention of the masses was firmly anchored on the Romani women now playing "gypsy" to the hilt.

"Talk to me, my friend," La-La said once the crowds had been left behind, gently slipping her hand into the crook of his arm and reining him back to a more leisurely pace as they moved off down a quiet cobbled street. Her calm demeanor conflicted with the worry woven through her scent.

An stopped abruptly. He could not help it.

La-La turned back toward him. The worry blossomed in her gaze as she noted his faint trembling. He flinched when she peered closer at him, her brow furrowed. The muscles of An's face twitched as he tried to answer her, but he could not say the words. Could not tell her of his cleaving. She must have read something in his expression, though, because her hand rose slowly, as if not to startle, and gently brushed beneath the locks hanging heavy across his forehead.

He clenched his eyes shut at the sight of her silent tears as she mourned his loss.

"There is a hunter in the city...Den Jeger," An told her, his voice low and controlled, his tone flat. "He has gone to ground. I am afraid he has taken a friend of mine with him to force my hand."

As he filled the Rom in, fury kindled in her gaze. She reached out and took his hand, striding off with a determined gate.

"Where are we going?"

"Phoenix Park," she murmured. "The others need to know. An' perhaps we can help find...your friend."

* * *

As they made their way across the city the crowds lessened as the spaces grew more open. An turned his focus inward toward his meager trickle of magic and allowed La-La to guide him. Centering, he charged his senses and extended them outward, seeking Jeger's trail through the essence of the spire. His spirit surged. As they followed the Liffey toward Phoenix Park the trail strengthened.

La-La tried to draw him toward the Clan's camp, but An tugged his arm out of her grip. His nostrils flared as he caught the faintest trace of Charlie's scent wafting on the breeze. She was here, somewhere. Beyond Phoenix Park. Behind him he heard the electronic tones of a cell phone dialing but ignored it, his stride lengthening as he left La-La behind.

An tracked Jeger to an abandoned warehouse in the Ballymount Industrial Estate, south of the city, past the park. A fire had left the building a burned-out husk not quite a year ago. The walls were solid, but the roof was gone in patches and the windows altogether. The gaps in the walls had been boarded over, but one had been pried away, left prominently propped against the smoke-scarred wall.

Through with games, An Rógaire stalked up the path between the buildings and straight to the way left open for him. He went alone, unwilling to risk the Rom in this private battle. Though he envied them the promise of death they and all mortals held, he would not be the cause of them embracing that state before they must. They'd trailed him anyway, he could tell by their scent on the air, but for now they hid themselves among the surrounding buildings. It galled him that he could not stop them, but he found it a comfort as well.

As he walked past a bunch of brambles closest to his target, La-La's voice whispered from the brush, "No fear, Lorcan. No matter what happens, the bastard won't walk away from this with your spire." Her vow touched him, as did her insistence on acknowledging his former self, but he could not let that distract him from his purpose.

"Go conquer your demon and when you're done you will return to the Clan so we may heal your hurts. You and your friend." He shook off her words and kept walking, but nonetheless they warmed his heart. The Kalderăs Clan might not be his own, but their solidarity lent him strength...and hope, misplaced as it was. An Rógaire wasn't really concerned about walking away tonight, as long as Jeger didn't either, but to know Charlie had a place to be safe. He nearly reeled with the relief he felt at that.

La-La must have Sensed his thoughts. She called after him in a low whisper, only loud enough to reach his sensitive ears. "I mean it, Lorcan. There is one who has joined the Clan who might heal even the most grievous of your wounds. You might recognize her name. She is called Anu..."

Anu? Surely he had not heard La-La correctly. A healer who bore the name of the Mother Goddess...? Powerful enough to restore him? His chest tightened as he longed to believe.

Forgetting the wisdom of silence, he pivoted to meet La-La's gaze. "What?!"

She nodded, but said nothing, as she drew back into her sheltering spot. He read the belief in her bright eyes before she fluttered her hands at him, shooing him toward the building. He continued forward, burying the seed of hope La-La had planted before it could distract him further.

As he drew closer to the warehouse the stench of old ash and moldering concrete assaulted his senses, overlaid by a heavy odor of industrial chemicals he could not identify either by origin or source. He marveled at the strength of it after all this time.

Huffing out his breath in an effort to clear the scents from his head, An climbed through the gap in the wall only to be assaulted by the odors tenfold. How could they still be so strong? As he struggled against the overload, he was unsurprised to discover Den Jeger waiting for him. He locked gazes with the hunter and saw a mad glint in the man's eyes.

Concerned, An resisted the urge to glance toward Charlie, slumped and bound to a chair in the middle of the vacant warehouse.

"Took you long enough to show up," Jeger said with a sneer. "I thought I'd have to try sheep next if neither girls *nor* boys served to lure you."

For a moment An was puzzled until he realized Jeger thought *Charlie* a boy. Puzzled enough that he almost missed the insult. An curled his lip in response, but he did not otherwise acknowledge Jeger's barb.

"You have something that is mine," An said, his voice freely channeling his wrath for the first time since the cleaving.

Jeger's hand moved over the ivory spire sheathed at his hip, as if that was all that could possibly matter here. "Come closer, hellspawn. I'd be glad to give it back to you."

An could imagine all too well Jeger's meaning, envisioning his severed horn resheathed in his own chest, as it had once nestled among the ribs of this man's brother. That image haunted An. Alicorn were meant to heal, not harm, yet in his fear and his thrashing An had impaled the mortal intent on harvesting the very horn that ended him. And yet, Jeger's brother had not failed. Already partially hewn away, An's spire had snapped beneath the corpse's weight to become Jeger's trophy.

It would crush Jeger to know the death he dreamt of dealing this day was doomed to fail if the only weapon he'd armed himself with was the spire. The thought almost amused An, until the hunter interrupted.

"Time to pay for my brother's death, beast."

"There is no payment due, the thief owns the risk when he steals what is not his."

Jeger answered him with a rage-filled scream as he drew the spire and lunged forward. An nearly answered him, but Charlie's safety was dependent on An keeping his head. He flowed away from the path of attack with an echo of the grace he'd once had, barely resisting the instinctual urge to reach out and steady the man attacking him. How ironic, were Den Jeger to impale himself. But no, the hunter pivoted and lashed out again, grazing An's arm. In an instant the wound healed, leaving a rent in An's sleeve, and nothing more, not even a crimson stain. The sensation of magic's caress nearly sent An to his knees as the blow itself had not.

"For you?!" Jeger spat, nearly foaming in his rage. "It still works for you?"

It was true. Once one, always one. Severed or not, the one person the spire would always heal was the one it had been cleaved from, of anything short of restoring the cleaved horn itself. Still, An was not about to try and explain the principle of sympathetic magic to his attacker. They were both haunted by the memory of that same horn jutting from the half-healed wound in the chest of Jeger's brother. The moment it broke free from An, it had lost its ability to heal as far as others were concerned.

He shrugged now, knowing it would infuriate the hunter, make him sloppy. "Maybe it was for old time's sake." In a calculated move, An held out his hand, palm up. "Come on, it is useless to you..."

"But not to *you*, which means I am all the more inclined to keep it." Hatred burned in Den Jeger's gaze. "Of course, there is one condition under which I would gladly return it to you." The hunter lunged and thrust once again. Even knowing it would fail to slay him, for an instant An felt the urge to fling his arms wide and bare his chest to Jeger's thrust. Shoving down *that* madness—more his personal demon than Jeger could ever be—An backed away, slowly circling. He focused every effort on drawing the hunter away from Charlie, who had come to and was working free of her bonds. As he carefully made his way through the wreckage left by the fire, fresh bursts of the earlier stench assaulted him. He glanced down and nearly stumbled as his gaze took in darkened concrete and glistening wood. Glancing back up, he saw two things that chilled him: Den Jeger, lost to madness, clutching a newly struck match; and Charlie, creeping up behind the hunter, hand reached out to snatch An's spire.

In that moment, with La-La's words echoing in his memory, An Rógaire...no...*Lorcan* understood he had no more desire for death.

His or anyone else's...not even Den Jeger.

Leaping forward he grabbed for the match.

Startled, Jeger jerked back, his chemical-spattered clothes going up like a torch.

"No..." Lorcan barely murmured, anguish thickening his cry. "Charlie! RUN!"

She didn't hesitate. Even as Jeger shrieked in agony, with the kind of speed only a kid living on the streets possessed, Charlie snatched the spire from the hunter's grasp and shoved off in the other direction. But even she was not fast enough. An heard her hiss as she stopped short.

Already the fire had spread to every puddle and soaked surface until it crackled and snapped and roared at them from all sides. Charlie turned to An, eyes at once both panicked and trusting. He spied a patch of red, angry skin on her cheek where a bit of flame had licked too close. Crouching, coughing, he dove through the flames to reach her. Tucking her beneath the scant protection of his body, Lor searched for some way out.

He searched in vain.

And then he felt it. On his arm, where the spire Charlie still clutched brushed his skin, magic cascaded across his burns, healing them even as falling embers created more.

Once one, always one.

Dare he hope? Dare he not?

Unable to talk for the coughing, he reached out and took the spire from her hand and found the raw edge by touch. With a prayer to the Mother Goddess, he lifted the horn to his head, nestled it perfectly in place. Everywhere it touched, it tingled like crazy, but he knew it would not stay, and if it would not stay, this would not work. He could not take his true form and still hold the spire in place, assuming this was even possible at all.

Lorcan gathered his courage and vowed to live.

"Charlie...listen..." he lost his words in another coughing fit as the smoke grew thicker and the heat seized his throat. He shielded his face and tried once more. "Up on my back. Hold this in place and no matter what don't let go." He helped her clamber up as he choked out his commands, trusting she would either listen, or they would die.

She clung to him, trembling and crying silent tears, but with her hand steadfast as she held the spire to its base.

Lor closed his eyes against the sting of chemical-laden smoke and prayed again with every bit of faith he could muster.

The tingle became a burn of a different sort as magic flooded through him and Lorcan instantly transformed, tail flagged and mane thrashing, muzzle long and teeth bared as he challenged death with a defiant scream. Bunching his muscular hindquarters, he charged the flaming beast, his hooves ringing like steel on the concrete as they carried them through the open gap where he'd entered out into the cool night air to land among the Rom, who had swarmed the building and looked ready to charge the blaze.

For a brief instant Lorcan was whole again.

And then he was not, as Charlie slid half-conscious from his singed back. Lorcan collapsed beside her, coughing great hacking coughs as he took on his human seeming once more. But, as he reached out a hand to cradle his dropped spire, Lor did not despair.

Because they were alive, and there was hope.

THE FIVE BEAN SOLUTION
JEAN MARIE WARD

Jack Tibbert opened the door to his dorm room and found an opossum wearing his roommate's polo shirt. Since a full October moon rode high in the sky, and blood-streaked ichor reeking of fear sweat and opossum funk oozed from the sleeves of the shirt and the bottoms of the pressed and belted jeans splayed across the bed, there could be only one explanation. Eugene Peterson Braen, the most tight-assed, twenty-something, college freshman ever, was a were-opossum.

This didn't bother Jack as much as it might some people. As a half-breed, biracial cat shifter who'd been adopted by a family of overachieving, shapeshifting foxes, he was used to weird. But why did his roommate have to get were-ed the night before an exam? How was Jack supposed to study, much less sleep, with that thing in the room?

Squealing like a rusty hinge, 'Possum Gene thrashed inside the thick fabric, trying to claw his way out, but his shoulders were stuck in the collar. As usual, Gene had buttoned his shirt all the way to the top. *His polo shirt!*

Jack shut the door and dumped his backpack on his bed. "It's your own fault. Didn't you ever see *The Wolfman*? There's an order to these things. Get naked, *then* shift. Pillage, *then* burn. But *nooo*, you're too much of a *brain* to watch horror movies. You're lucky I'm a nice guy."

Up close, the stench was eye-watering. Gritting his teeth, Jack yanked the shirt off the bed. Gene tumbled out the bottom, onto the sodden bedcovers, and kept rolling. He landed with a *splat* on the carpet next to a page of laser-printed photos, righted himself and waddled toward the door.

A flash of silver in one of the pictures caught Jack's eye. The object curved like the top of a strapless party dress. He snatched the paper off the floor.

Jack had a picture of his adoptive sister Rika Nakamura wearing a silver dress like that. She looked like a star, and she was smiling at him. No, better than smiling—her face glowed like she'd won the lottery and he was the prize. He kept the photo on his phone. How did Gene get it?

He hadn't. The gray thing wasn't a dress. It wasn't even a person. It was a weird silver beehive in a flash-strobed glass case. Jack's secret crush was safe.

He checked the other photos. The biggest one showed the Basilica of the National Shrine of the Immaculate Conception, the super-sized church overlooking the Catholic University of America. The remaining pictures featured a black metal rose on a wood plaque, and a silver sculpture of a veiled woman's head.

"What the hell?" he muttered.

Gene growled in response. Jack whirled. The opossum's head butted the door. His paws tore into the carpet like he planned to dig through the floor.

"Stop it!" Jack lunged across the room and grabbed the opossum by the scruff.

Gene hissed and snapped. Were-spit flew from the corners of his mouth. Jack jerked his hand away. Gene bounced against the door and slid bonelessly to the floor.

"Sorry, man. But were-spit's contagious." To humans. Jack wasn't sure about half-breeds like himself, but he wasn't taking any chances.

Gene didn't respond. He lay on the carpet like a giant hairball. He didn't appear injured, but his jaw hung slack, and his ribs weren't moving. Green fluid bubbled from under his tail. The fetid odor of overflowing restaurant dumpsters filled the room.

"No!" Jack dropped to his knees. "Don't be dead. Don't be dead!"

He prodded Gene's chest. The Nakamuras insisted all their kits, including Jack, learn first aid. But none of his ABC moves worked, and he wasn't putting his face anywhere near a were's teeth—even if they did belong to his roommate. *His roommate who wasn't breathing.*

He grabbed his phone. There was only one person who could help. Rika was training to become an exo-med—a doctor to the fae and other sapients not covered in the standard medical texts. In addition to studying Pre-Med across town at Georgetown University, she was enrolled in a number of specialized courses not recognized by the American Medical Association. If she couldn't save Gene...

He couldn't think about that.

She picked up on the first ring. Her light, musical voice caroled: "This better be good, Cat Boy. I've got lab and lecture midterms in Biology tomorrow, and less than ninety minutes of me time before my roommate gets back."

"Rika, I think I killed my roommate!"

"Oh, Jack," she gasped. "Are you all right? What happened?"

"It's not my fault! It was an accident! I picked him up. He spit at me, and I dropped him. Now he's not moving. He smells dead!"

"Jesus, Jack, I knew you didn't like him, but murder..." She stopped. "Wait, you picked him up? Gene's six-two and ripped. You're barely five-eight on a tall day. That doesn't compute."

"Short jokes, now? Really? He's a were-opossum. Of course I picked him up. He was wrecking the carpet"

"A were-what?"

"Opossum—you know, pointy face, beady eyes, gray fur, naked tail, looks like Jurassic rat. *And not breathing.* What do I do?"

"Um, wait for him to wake up."

Jack opened his mouth. Nothing came out.

"Look, you said he's a were-opossum. He shifted at moonrise, right?"

"I guess. He was human this afternoon."

"What does he look like now?" Rika asked patiently.

"Like a dead opossum."

"Uh huh. Say it with me. What do weres do when they die? They..."

"Change back to human. Oh." And he'd watched all *The Wolfman* movies a dozen times.

"It's called playing opossum," Rika continued.

This was why he kept his crush secret.

"Geez, Jack, you lived in Holcomb Park for months. You never saw an opossum faint?"

"Not close up. Have you seen the teeth on those things?"

"Well, he's not using them now. Dump him in the shower and close the door. I'll see what I can find for the smell." The patter of rapid keystrokes echoed in his ear. "Nothing for opossum, but for skunk you mix a quart of peroxide, a quarter cup of baking soda and a teaspoon of liquid soap. It's worth a shot."

This was why he couldn't let it go. Where would he find a woman who understood how much a part-time cat hated bad smells and immediately help? But before he had a chance to thank her, the opossum's ribs heaved. He sneezed, blinked, rolled over and resumed digging.

"Gene!"

"He's up?" Rika yelped. "Already? Then again, he's a were-opossum. He could be super hungry from the change. Try distracting him with food. Opossums'll eat anything."

Not this opossum. Jack tried Gene's protein bars and his veggies. He tried potato chips. He even tried the slice of pizza he'd been saving for breakfast. Nothing worked.

"Maybe he wants to go somewhere!" She made it sound better than chocolate.

"Ya think," Jack snarled.

The ghost of his cat tail twitched irritably at the base of his spine. Tonight was everything he hated about college—test stress on top of dick roommate stress compounded by the prospect of extra work and more stress. It wouldn't be so bad if he could figure out Gene's problem and save at least part of their security deposit. Then it hit him.

"Crap. The stench is rotting my brain. The Shrine! There was a paper with photos of the Shrine and a bunch of other stuff on the floor by the bed."

"What kind of photos? Were there any notes? Never mind. I'll see for myself. See you and Gene at Visitors Parking in thirty. Bring the papers. It's a *clue*," she warbled. "This is going to be fun!"

Fun? Fun! Phantom cat ears pricked. *Fun with him?!* Jack's inner tomcat roused and stretched. Suddenly the evening glittered with possibilities. The Shrine and the lecture halls facing it were closed for the night. Between exams and the raw evening breeze, the university mall would be deserted. But he and Rika wouldn't feel the cold. They'd be snug inside in her clean, warm car—her clean, warm car with the backseat that folded down—all alone.

Grunting in marsupial frustration, Gene tore through another chunk of carpet. *Yeah, all alone with a crazy were-opossum.* Hell no.

"I'll lock Gene in the bathroom and meet you there."

"No, I need to examine him. Weres aren't supposed to act like this. We have to figure out why the Shrine's important and how he kept his focus through the change. It could rewrite everything we know about were behavior. That's what makes this so exciting."

That's what made their meet-up so exciting—not him? Jack glared at the phone.

"Sorry, Rika," he lied, "the exam'll have to wait. Gene's too big for my book bag, and I'm not carrying him. He bites. Maybe next month we can borrow a pet carrier."

"Who said anything about carrying him? Use the leash in your sock drawer. The halter's adjustable."

He started to deny it, then stopped. This was Rika. She wasn't just a foxy chick with a four-point-oh in everything, including the courses that didn't officially exist. She was a full-blooded shape-shifting fox, what the

Japanese called a *kitsune*, with a black belt in a form of mixed martial arts supposedly developed for ninjas. She once took out a crazed cat sidhe with nothing but a metal tray. Compared to that, what was a little b-and-e in a boys-only dorm at a college she didn't attend?

A neatly coiled red leash and halter set lay on the bottom of the drawer underneath a package of new dress socks. The socks shouldn't have been there, either.

"Damn it, Rika, you're worse than the NSA! A man's got a right to privacy, especially in his sock drawer. That's sacred space! How'd you like it if I went groping in your..."

Drawers. Do not go there. By some miracle, his mouth stopped in time. By an even bigger one, Rika didn't notice the slip.

"I don't see why you're getting so upset," she shot back. "I did you a favor. You should be grateful. Shift happens, Jack, and you need to be prepared. Now are the two of you meeting me at the Shrine, or do I have to come to your room?"

* * *

The Shrine basilica soared above the black asphalt moat of Visitor's Parking like a mountain fortress, complete with massive, pale stone walls, narrow windows and grim doors straight out of the Evil Overlord handbook. But something had happened when the builders got to the roof. Instead of gun turrets or arrow slits, they capped their stronghold with an enormous blue, red, and yellow beanie in desperate need of a propeller. Jack was half convinced it was an epic university prank nobody knew how to fix.

The newly upscale neighborhood shared the basilica's goofy vibe. It wasn't dangerous by Washington, DC, standards. Still, something in Jack's chest relaxed when he saw Rika's old Honda parked under the streetlamp directly across from the Shrine's monumental east portico.

And clenched all over again when she stepped out of the car. She was dressed in black from the crown of her hoodie to the tips of her leather-gloved fingers and the soles of her black-laced dance shoes.

Part of it was jealousy. If brown-skinned Jack stepped out in a hoodie like that he'd be arrested for breathing. The only reason a cop would stop a cute Asian chick with killer legs (not that anybody could see them under those loose knit pants, dammit) would be to ask for her phone number. The larger part, however, was a sinking sense of dread at the thousand different bad reasons Rika might have for dressing like a ninja—a lead weight in his gut that only got heavier when she hauled a backpack (also black) out of the backseat.

Jack spooled Gene's leash around his elbow to keep "Uber Rat" from taking another kamikaze leap off the curb in the direction of the Shrine. He glowered sternly at Rika to forestall the *kitsune* equivalent. "What's in the bag?"

Rika flashed him a smile that made his breath hitch, his heart stutter, and all his tomcat parts sit up and take notice. She hoisted the bag onto the hood of the car, and his brain short-circuited entirely. Her breasts *bounced* under her hoodie. The woman had killer everything.

She produced a penlight from the backpack. "Study tools. We're looking at original research here. I could get a grant. Now try to keep Wonder Opossum still. I need to do a visual exam."

Wonder Opossum. He should've known she wasn't glowing at him. He scowled at the crown of her head as she trained her light on Gene.

The ever-present swish of traffic along Michigan Avenue exploded in a blare of horns. Gene hissed like a leaky balloon and collapsed on the sidewalk. Green opossum poo oozed from his butt.

The timing was perfect. Rika jumped from her crouch and stumbled against the car.

"That's not dead," she gurgled. "That's *decayed*."

"You should smell the room."

"The curse of the five bean brain," she said, fanning her hand in front of her face.

Jack's eyes narrowed. "Five bean what?"

"Five bean brain," she repeated. "An opossum's brainpan only holds five beans. Pound for pound it has the tiniest brain of any mammal anywhere."

"So? Cat brains are pretty small, but I don't crap over everything when I shift."

"Because you *shift*. Born shifters like us go from one form to another without losing consciousness. No matter what we look like, we're still us inside. Weres *change*. They become their animal, with all its strengths and limitations. That's why Gene's fixation with the Shrine is so amazing. His opossum shouldn't remember the Shrine exists, much less seek it out— assuming he did. He did, didn't he? You didn't drag him here."

"Trust me," Jack said drily, "I wouldn't."

"So the big question is: Why the Shrine? Well, the first big question. We can't ask how until Gene remembers how to talk." She slid the penlight into her hoodie pocket and held out her hand. "Show me the pictures."

When she put it that way, he was curious, too. Still annoyed—part of him couldn't shake the feeling were-Gene had simply found a new and improved way of being a jerk—but curious.

"These things are from the Shrine," she said. "I saw them the other week when I..." *When you snuck into my room?* Her cheeks darkened as if she heard his thoughts. She hiked her chin and continued defiantly, "...when I took a tour. The Shrine's a giant art museum. The Madonna is a silver cast of Michelangelo's Pieta. The flower is Pope Benedict's Golden Rose, and the crown is the papal tiara of Pope Paul the Sixth. Is Gene religious? Could he have printed these for his devotions?"

"Not a chance. Lack of religion is the only thing we have in common. If the Shrine's like a museum, does that mean this stuff is valuable?"

She nodded enthusiastically, obviously relieved he wasn't pressing her about her "tour." (*Yet*, he promised himself.) "Oh yeah. We're talking twenty-four karat treasure—gold, sterling silver and jewels by the pound."

"That's bad," Jack said. "Gene was an Army MP—military police. He enrolled at Catholic because the FBI hires a lot of CUA graduates. If you put that together with the pictures and the way he's acting, it sounds like he heard somebody was planning to rob the Shrine but couldn't get a fix on the target."

The color drained from Rika's cheeks. "A robbery?" she whispered.

A sneeze from the direction of the pavement sounded like the opossum version of agreement. Gene lurched to his feet, oriented himself toward the Shrine and resumed plodding, seemingly unaware of the fact he wasn't actually getting anywhere.

Rika didn't smile at his antics. If anything, she grew more alarmed. The musky tang of *kitsune* fear overlay the sewer smell of Gene's faint.

"He's still trying to get to the Shrine. Whatever's happening, it's happening tonight. That's the only way his actions make sense. We've got to call the police."

"Gene would've done that first thing. FBI-wannabe, remember."

"Then where are they?" She swept her arm in an arc that encompassed the parking lot and the five late-model cars huddled near the softly lit apse. A gust of wind ripped the paper from her hand and sent it cartwheeling in toward the Shrine. "Why aren't they here?"

"Probably because he didn't have any proof."

She pulled out her phone anyway.

"Rika, it won't do any good. If the cops didn't believe an ex-MP, they won't believe us."

"We have to do something! Those Shrine treasures aren't just valuable, they're sacred. They've been the object of belief, reverence and concentrated spiritual energy for years. They could've turned into true talismans. That's the magical equivalent of a nuclear reactor. We can't let that on the street. There are evil sorcerers out there who would use a true talisman to open the portal to a hell dimension just for bragging rights."

"Don't worry, we won't," he assured her. "But there's no point calling the cops. They won't listen to you. They'll assume they're being punked. But there are people in this town they *have* to listen to—and a lot of them know your parents. You need to call *them*, get one of their political friends on it. Your parents will believe you, and the cops will believe them."

Hope flared in her eyes, and fizzled an instant later. "Can't. They're in Paris with Uncle Five-Tails. They won't be up for hours. Then it'll be too late."

"Then call your brother and have him hack into their address book. You can fake your mom's voice—though I suggest doing it in the car. It's getting cold, and if we're inside, you won't have to worry about the wind screwing up your illusion."

Jack held his breath. If she went for it, he might save the evening yet. He'd even figured out how to tether Gene's leash to the outside of the door.

She shook her head. "There's no time. But you're right. The cops need something solid. Well, I'll give them solid." She unzipped another pocket of backpack, extracted a blue and gray Hoyas baseball cap and tossed it at him. "You're going to need this."

"Why?" he asked suspiciously as she wriggled into the bag's shoulder straps.

"CCTVs. I'm breaking into the Shrine." She darted across the lot, pulling up her hood as she ran.

"What? No!" he yelled.

But Rika wasn't listening. She had the do-gooder bit between her teeth, damn the torpedoes and any look-outs the bad guys might have posted—and nobody to save her except him. Jack yanked the cap over his hair and gave the opossum its head. Gene chittered and wheezed, pushing his stumpy legs faster than they were meant to go. It wasn't nearly fast enough. By himself, Jack would've overtaken her before she reached the first of the two flights of stairs leading to the east portico. With Gene in tow, he was still halfway down the first flight when she veered right across the intervening terrace.

Gritting his teeth and hoping he didn't get bit, Jack grabbed the opossum by the halter and took the rest of the stairs two at a time. The trees bordering the terrace were shadows on black. A dozen people could be hiding there. All they had to do was stand still. He'd never hear them.

A brass lantern illuminated a descending stairwell tucked against the side of the portico's upper staircase. At the bottom, directly under the lantern, stood two wooden doors. Rika hunched over their handles, a pair of lock picks glinting in the gloved darkness of her hands. Jack jumped the last four steps into the stairwell. He released Gene's halter and captured her wrists.

"Stop it," he whispered hoarsely, praying the shadow of his cap was enough to hide his face from any security cameras. "Wearing black does not make you a ninja."

She flicked her hands from his grasp. "Being a ninja makes you a ninja. It's a Zen thing. Back up. You're in my light. We need to get the doors open.

"No, we don't."

"It's the only solution. The door alarm will buzz security, and they'll call the cops. All we'll have to do is run away." Her arm torqued. "Ah."

The doors were heavy and far too loud. Rika retrieved her penlight and brandished it at the darkness. He glimpsed a corridor and a matching set of doors before the beam settled on a tiny box mounted on the doorjamb.

"Uh oh," Rika said.

Despite the comparative warmth of the stairwell, despite his sweatshirt and the long-sleeved tee he wore underneath, he went ice bucket cold. "What?"

"The sensor's off." She waved her hand in front of the box.

Gene tried to break for the interior. Jack hauled him back.

"So it's a silent alarm. Let's get out of here."

Rika shook her head. He started to protest. She incinerated him with a glare. "I'm a fox. I can hear the heartbeat of a field mouse sleeping in its burrow under a foot of snow. If the sensor was working I'd hear current humming in the wire. I don't. The alarm is dead."

"We're going. Now." He grabbed her arm.

A whiff of stale cigarettes tweaked his nose. Before Jack could parse what it meant, a large body landed in the stairwell. An instant later, something cold and hard jabbed the back of his skull. It felt like a gun.

Rika's horrified gaze angled upward to a point past the top of his head. Gene growled and snapped.

"Control your rat, or he eats the second bullet," a mechanically distorted voice thrummed behind him.

Oh crap. It *was* a gun, a gun behind his left ear. Jack couldn't think past the reality of the gun pressed against his head. Sweat flushed his armpits, worsening his chill. Carefully, oh so carefully, he wound Gene's leash around his hand until the opossum was forced to heel.

"Keep your hands where I can see them," the voice continued.

Rika nodded. She slowly spread her arms to the side. *Please*, Jack thought as hard as he could, *don't try anything. He can't miss.*

The voice said, "We're going to the Crypt. Move slowly, or the boy dies."

Crypt? Jack's mind yelped. Rika gulped and nodded again.

Cigarette Crook directed Rika to open a pair of doors in the middle of the corridor. "No tricks."

No kidding. Dim light radiated from the basement of the church, illuminating a short staircase and a passage beyond.

Gene flopped against Jack's foot. The stink hit a second later. Cigarette Crook didn't flinch. He must be wearing a mask. None of them had seen his face. They might yet survive. They just had to be smart.

The passage ended in a second, wider flight of stairs, which fed into a stone hall bigger than Jack's entire dorm. The overhead lights were off, but hard white light blazed from an elevated stone bridge to his left. As he turned for a better look, two sharp barbs dug into his shoulder. His muscles convulsed. Pain exploded inside him—bone-breaking, muscle-shearing, lung-burning, heart-bursting agony. His vision flashed white and black. The world winked out to the sound of Rika's scream.

* * *

Heaven smelled like incense, beeswax, and polished stone. Jack's cheek pressed against a slick, cold surface. His mouth tasted like dirt, only drier. *Okay, not heaven.* He forced his aching eyelids apart. Soft light dappled a glossy stone floor. There were people on the floor—strangers with zip-tied feet and hands bound behind their backs.

Rika!

He struggled to sit up and crashed to the floor, landing on his bruised shoulder. The pain made him want to throw up, but it cleared his head. He was bound like the others. He strained against the zip ties, but the plastic wouldn't give, and he couldn't wrestle his arms over his hips. Praying his human clothes wouldn't dislocate his cat shoulders, he forced himself to shift.

The change left him sore, panting and nearly smothered by his shirts. When he wriggled free, he found himself in a lamp-lit underground church with pews, stands of votive candles and a low vaulted ceiling. He stood in a rectangular space between the back pews and the triple-arched entrance to a darkened side room. The other captives—a chubby, middle-aged man in

a black suit and clerical collar, and three guys in the gray trousers, blue
jackets and yellow hazard vests worn by Shrine   security—lay on the floor
between Jack and the votive stands to his right. To his left, past the last
opening in the archway, a narrow, gold-tiled alcove framed the mosaic
portrait of a black-haired Madonna. One of her cat-like eyes appeared to be
winking at an unmoving huddle of black dumped at the entrance to the
alcove.

Jack tore across the cold floor. His pulse thundered in his ears. It wasn't
until he crouched next to Rika's face that her slow, steady heartbeat and the
soft sounds of her respiration penetrated the din of his fear. Her scent was a
little crisped around the edges, but okay. She was going to be okay. Cat
knees buckled in relief.

She opened her eyes. Her lips crooked in a small, lopsided smile. His
heart pounded against his ribs as if they really were a cage.

"Pocket," she gasped. "Nail clipper."

He nodded and scampered back to his clothes before shifting to human.
As he skinned into his pants, he glanced at the back of the church and froze.
Three sets of tall glass doors overlooked the hall where he'd been tased. *If
the bad guys had seen...*His heart stuttered. But the hall was empty, and
strain as he might, he couldn't hear anyone shouting or running toward the
doors. The only witnesses to his stupidity appeared to be the Madonna and
'Possum Gene, who was too busy pawing the center doors to notice. Jack
ducked behind the pews and scuttled to Rika's side.

"Left pocket." Her voice sounded stronger.

He reached into her pants pocket, trying not to think of where he was
putting his fingers. A different set of muscles tensed when he saw her hands.
The zip tie dug into her gloves. He couldn't work the clipper under the
plastic without cutting something else. He didn't want it to be her skin.

"Can you shift?"

"Can't. Tried."

*But her abilities were stronger than his. She could even stop shifting
partway.*

She must have seen the horror on his face. She moistened her lips. "Need
more time. Smaller than you."

A fierce protectiveness swelled inside him, filling his chest so fast he
couldn't breathe. Rika was slight, small-boned and five inches shorter than
him. She was also smarter, her animal was stronger, she had martial arts
training, but none of it mattered, because when it came to doing what she
believed the right thing, she had no sense of self-preservation. None. And
with the terrible clarity achieved in crisis, he knew if he couldn't keep her

safe he would die.

A small part of his mind whimpered he was too young to get serious. Yeah, that didn't matter either. It was too late. He was doomed the moment she'd rammed a stainless steel tray into the head of a murderous cat sidhe. To protect him. Foxes were supposed to hate cats. Rika had taken him home with her.

He was so screwed.

Thanks to the gloves, her wrists weren't as bad as he thought. But when she sat up and he saw the bruise on her forehead and the cut on her chin, he wanted to smash something, specifically the thug who hurt her. Jack wasn't a violent person, but right now he was furious. *They'd hurt her.*

He fought to say something that wasn't an angry scream. Eventually he managed: "Anything I can do?"

Rika looked up from massaging her ankles. "I'm okay. Do you see my backpack—it's got my tablet and all my notes for tomorrow." Her mouth quirked in a not-quite smile. "You remember: midterms."

His heart flip-flopped in his chest. *Doomed.*

He found her backpack in the small storage area behind the votive stands. Someone had popped the plastic catches on the straps, but bag didn't appear damaged.

Meanwhile, Rika had recovered enough to assume Medical Mode. She crouched on all fours next to the unconscious priest, sniffing his face. He didn't look too good. Neither did the security guards. Their breathing had a wheezy quality, and their faces were gray, irrespective of skin tone.

"Shocked *and* drugged," she whispered. "Ketamine, I think. Our perps weren't taking any chances. Also, the masked guy who stunned us? Dressed like them."

He motioned her behind the arches and handed her the bag. "Now we call the cops."

Rika nodded absently, frowning at her bag like there was more wrong than disconnected straps. She hefted it twice, then dropped it and slapped her phone pocket. She didn't hit plastic.

"Do you still have a phone?" she asked.

No, he didn't. He had his ID and wallet, but no cash and no phone. The bastards had stolen it. Of course they had. They were bastards.

Rika wasn't having any better luck. Pouch by pouch, she removed the contents of her bag to the floor and checked everything twice. She spat, "Those bastards stole my tablet *and* my phone."

Jack smothered a reflexive spurt of panic. "It's okay," he said, trying to convince himself. "We'll find a phone when we get out. It's a public building. There has to be a way out."

"Ja-a-ack?"

He turned in the direction of her gaze. Light flashed outside the sanctuary's far door. His heart dropped below his knees. He looked at Rika. She nodded. They grabbed their belongings and retreated deeper in to the gloom.

The flashlight flicked left, right, up, and down—the search pattern of someone who wasn't looking for anything in particular and didn't expect to find it. The heavy glass doors splintered the beacon's glow into the blue white corona of a dwarf star. The person behind it was nothing more than another shadow in the hall. He moved like one, too. Jack couldn't hear him, or anything else beyond the sanctuary doors.

Luckily the soundproofing worked both ways. The opossum was going nuts, growling and clawing the glass. The patrol didn't appear to notice. Flashlight and shadow ambled past the doors without breaking stride.

Jack tensed. Was the guy really gone, or was it a fake-out? If he was gone, they needed to find an exit. If he wasn't, should they try to take him down? If Jack had been on his own, he'd simply flee. But Rika would insist on saving Gene, which wasn't going to happen unless the damned opossum calmed his damned self down.

"*Srrkrreeaachk!*" The screech bounced off tile and stone, reverberating into infinity.

Jack grabbed Rika and dropped in a roll, shielding her with his body from the floor and the godawful noise. Through the echoes, he thought he heard a galloping rush of paws, then a thud, followed by the soft snap of a plastic clasp.

He motioned Rika to stay put. Hugging the walls, he scrambled past the cat-eyed Madonna to where the back pews almost met the wall. He peeked around the corner. Caught between the central pair of doors was a familiar leash. Jack craned his neck. The edges of Gene's broken harness were visible just beyond the door.

Shit.

The rough fabric of Rika's hoodie brushed his goosebumps. He dragged her back to the alcove. Her dark eyes seemed enormous against the shocked pallor of her face. "How did he do that?"

"I don't care. As soon as they see him, the bad guys will come running. I'll distract them. You take my stuff and find a way out. I'll meet you at the Student Center."

"I'm not leaving you."

He grabbed her shoulders. They felt so fragile beneath his fingers. How could he make her understand? This wasn't judo or aikido or ninja pretend. These were real bad guys, people who electrocuted and drugged their victims, people who would hurt her. One good blow delivered with intent, and her bones would snap. The thought made him ill.

"You have to. You can't shift. I can."

Her eyes narrowed. "I can take care of myself."

"Then prove it. Go."

She tried to outstare him, but nobody can outstare a cat. Finally she looked away. "I'll get the door."

* * *

The glass panel eased shut behind Jack's feline form with no more sound than a puff of air—air he wished he didn't have to breathe through a cat's nose. From the smell and the relative quiet, Gene had fainted again. If Jack could've trusted his roommate to play dead like a normal opossum, he would've shifted back to human, snatched him and run. Gene's spells never lasted that long, but every minute he was out was another minute for recon.

Camouflaged by his cat's brown and white Snowshoe coloring, Jack darted across the shadowed hall and clambered up the second of the three marble statues facing the glass doors of the sanctuary. He peered around the statue's head. A low-walled wheelchair ramp separated his perch from the elevated bridge. Massive piers framed his view of the center section, where a bevy of high-intensity pole lamps sizzled around a large, peaked display case mounted on a pink, stone-veneered plinth. The glare of their hot, white light made it hard to see inside, but based on the cut-out in the foam-lined equipment chest stationed to the left of the case, Jack guessed it contained the pope's tiara.

A stocky guy in a priest suit knelt in front of a drawer protruding from the right side of the plinth. The drawer must have held the guts of the case's security system. Wires streamed from the drawer to a cluttered media cart next to the last right-hand light. An ersatz security guard sporting a latex Richard Nixon mask and blue surgical gloves monitored a laptop on the cart's highest shelf.

The "priest" lifted his head. He was wearing Kennedy.

"Now?" the ersatz priest asked in a mechanically altered voice.

Nixon responded with a similarly distorted string of letters and numbers. His voice sounded lower than "Father Kennedy's," but that could've been a function of their voice changers. Neither of them sounded like the guy with the gun—or moved like the guy with the flashlight.

How big was this operation? A chill raced under Jack's fur as he realized he didn't know how many people were in the church or their location. The lights on the bridge appeared to be the only ones working outside the sanctuary, but he couldn't be sure. The basilica was too big. The only thing he knew for certain was he couldn't let any of them find Rika, not in her present state. She'd tried to hide how weak she was, but he'd seen her arms tremble when she pushed the sanctuary door open.

For her sake he stifled his cat's primal urge to flee and launched himself at the wall of the ramp. He landed noiselessly, leapt across the incline, wriggled under a spindly guard rail and slunk around the chrome-legged bench set between the center piers.

The uptick in acoustics almost made up for the smell of the dead presidents' socks. Beyond the thieves' cryptic exchanges and the hum of their equipment, Jack sensed a faint, regular concussion—the tread of a single pair of soft-soled shoes approaching from the dark beyond the bridge. One pair. *Could be worse.* Jack flattened himself into the bench's shadow.

A thin, bluish glow swept the eastern end of the bridge an instant before a guy in a Reagan mask appeared. He was taller and skinner than Nixon or Kennedy. *Cigarette Crook?* Jack wondered. Reagan didn't click off his flashlight until he stepped past a dark line of cables that snaked between the two statues framing the end of the bridge. He jiggled the cylinder against his thigh. *No, too nervous for Cigarette Crook. He probably startles easily. Good to know.*

"You said you were almost done." Reagan's altered drone sounded distinctly accusatory.

"I am," Kennedy snapped. "Almost, as in not finished. In. Com. Plete."

"But it's almost two," Reagan said.

"You got a date?" Kennedy sneered.

Nixon relaxed against the media cart. The pose wasn't as casual as it appeared. His eyes tracked Reagan's every twitch. *So Nixon was Kennedy's man.* If the situation weren't so dire it'd be funny.

"No, but I worked security," Reagan said. "Anytime now, they're gonna see their camera feed is crap. We won't even hear them coming."

"That's why we have look-outs and Bluetooth. Now shut up and let me do my job. This is an Eighties-vintage standalone system with custom upgrades. In short, it's a bitch, and the more you distract me, the longer it'll take to hack," Kennedy said.

"Sir, yes, sir," Reagan replied sullenly. He crossed his arms and stared at the west end of the bridge. He didn't tap his foot, but Jack had an excellent view of the toes flicking against the vamp of his shoe.

Kennedy waited a beat before telling Nixon, "Scope."

Nixon handed him something that looked like a single-sided stethoscope. He plugged the earpiece into his mask and eased the disk into the drawer. If Jack had been all cat the rat's nest of wires would've been irresistible. It was pretty fascinating from a sapient standpoint. How much force would it take to pull a plug or dislodge a probe? If he jerked some wires free, would it be enough to trigger an alarm?

If he succeeded, would Shrine security believe the alarm or the monitors showing crap? Mental fingers crossed that Rika had listened to him for once, Jack waited for his chance to act.

A single, melodious chime rang from the plinth. Kennedy struggled to his feet, his breath rasping through his distorter. Slowly the case rose from its plinth, supported on metal struts which creaked beneath the weight of the glass.

Jack expected to see silver, but the first flash was gold: the fringed ends of a gold net scarf embroidered with scintillant hammered gold. He squinted against its fierce brightness. It was a relief when the case finally cleared the stand supporting Pope Paul's tiara.

A spiky gold crown studded with diamonds as big as shirt buttons surrounded the base of a spun silver dome almost twelve inches tall—too tall and too heavy for a human head to bear. In person it looked less like a beehive and more like a giant artillery shell—an image the three jeweled wires circling the dome and the small gold cross at its tip did nothing to dispel. *The world's biggest silver bullet*, Jack thought giddily. *No wonder Gene went nuts.*

But big and unquestionably valuable as the tiara was, the finish was dingy, as if the silver had been mixed with lead and the gold dimmed to match. Jack's gaze drifted to the scarf that hurt his eyes. It was vivid, vibrant, *alive*. For all its jewels, the tiara was a husk in comparison.

Superstitious fear ruffled the fur along his back. Half-human Jack didn't sense magic well, but an ordinary net, even gold net, wouldn't have snared his attention so completely. He didn't know where the scarf's power came from or what it could do. He only knew Rika was right. It couldn't be allowed to fall into the hands of an evil sorcerer—or any kind of magician. *And the scarf wasn't even on Gene's radar.* He hoped it wasn't on the crooks'.

Kennedy grunted as he hefted the tiara from its stand. He lowered it into the padded case, carefully arranging the pearl-edged ribbons dangling from the back so they wouldn't get scratched. Then he returned to the case and reached for the laces tying the gold scarf to the stand.

Shit. Jack couldn't see any way to stop him. But if he could trip an alarm, Rika would be safe. Sure, they'd go after him, but there was nothing to connect a stray cat with the captives in the church. He wished Kennedy and Nixon weren't standing so close to the drawer. If he was going to risk his hide, he wanted it to count.

At first he thought the ragged rhythm in his ears was the result of nerves. Then he heard the distinctive thump of naked opossum feet charging up the wheelchair ramp. 'Possum Gene crested the ramp on the west side of the bridge, shrieking the war cry of his people, ridiculous and magnificent at once.

While everyone else stared, stupefied, Nixon drew a shock baton from under his jacket and strode toward the tiny threat. Gene surged toward his calf, teeth bared and drooling were-spit. With a terrible grace, Nixon evaded the charge. He whipped the baton into the opossum's flank. Gene screamed and collapsed, convulsing. But Nixon didn't let go. He kept the stick pressed against Gene's side until the opossum went limp. The awful smell of charred hair mingled with the stench of voided bowels and worse.

Bile spurted up Jack's throat. Heart hammering in panic, he struggled to choke it down. He had to keep it in. He couldn't let them know he was there. If they fried something as stupid and harmless as a 'possum, what would they do to a cat?

Nixon booted the opossum away from the media cart. Gene's inert form skidded down the aisle, smearing the floor with his waste.

"Where'd the 'possum come from?" Nixon's altered voice sounded bored, callous, utterly indifferent to the pain he'd inflicted on a helpless animal, much less the human within.

All the rage building inside Jack since he'd seen Rika's bruised face, all the fear and the shame of his helplessness crashed together and exploded. Blood roared in his ears—blood demanding blood. His ears flattened and his fur rose. A strange, unnatural howl spewed from his throat.

He shot off the floor. He scaled "Father Kennedy" in two bounds. He grabbed the back of Kennedy's mask in his teeth and wrenched it to the side. Before Kennedy or Nixon could react, he leapt into the open drawer and scrambled out the back, tearing wires as he went.

He dashed around the back of the plinth and charged Reagan. Reagan tried to belt him with his flashlight. The blow went wide as Jack dove between his legs. He wheeled and clawed his way up Reagan's trousers and back. The man yelled in counterpoint to an insistent crystalline pinging Jack barely noticed through his wrath.

His claws raked the back of Reagan's neck. He bit deep into rubber and flesh.

"Get him off! Get him off!" Reagan screamed.

Jack raced around Reagan's shoulders and over his head while the man flailed helplessly. As they reeled, Jack glimpsed Kennedy and Nixon shoving plastic slabs under the glass case, which sank much faster than it rose.

Reagan tripped over the cables leading off the east side of the bridge. An ululating klaxon joined the tinny hammering of the display case alarm. He stumbled against the nun statue at the southeast corner of the bridge. The impact knocked the air out of Jack's lungs. Caught between Reagan and the statue, he fought for breath. Suddenly Nixon stood in front of them. His shock baton shot toward Jack's head.

"No!" Reagan yelled. He pushed away from the statue, but his balance was off. Instead of dodging, he fell straight at the baton.

Jack twisted as he dropped, slamming shoulder and hip against marble limbs. He was so wired, he felt no pain. He raced up the nun's marble robes to the top of her habit, and swerved, back arched, teeth bared to confront his foe.

Reagan's unconscious body slid to the floor. Nixon shoved the baton's handle into his mask's mouth, mashing the rubber features into something monstrous. He grabbed the base of the statue and started to climb.

"Stop!" The shout pealed from the hall in front of the sanctuary.

Jack swayed on his perch. Nixon dropped to the floor, angling his body so he could keep both Jack and the new threat in view. Even Kennedy stopped struggling with the laces and turned toward the church.

A black-cowled figure stood in front of the glass doors. The wavering light of a single votive candle kissed the figure's smooth cheeks, but left the rest of the face in shadow. *Damn it, Rika, you're going to get yourself killed.*

"Throw down your weapons," she ordered.

Two masked thugs burst into the hall from opposite directions. Jack tensed, mapping the quickest route to Rika. But everything happened too fast. The thug who ran in from the east side of the basilica—the same route taken earlier by Jack, Rika, and Gene—slipped and landed on his ass. Rika hurled the still burning votive candle at his mask. He threw himself to the side.

She turned on the attacker bearing down from the west. She hit him with a high kick to the side of his jaw, then spun around behind him and slammed into his back, knocking him to the floor. Rika landed on top of him and dug her thumbs into the sides of his neck. He folded. She yanked the shock baton from under his jacket and jabbed it into his shoulder for good measure.

By now the other thug had staggered to his feet. He eyed her warily from behind a line of burning wax. She lifted the baton and stepped forward. He looked at the bridge, looked back at her, then ran away.

Nixon pulled the shock baton from his mouth. He twisted the base of the stick. Lightning bright sparks crackled between the electrodes. He loped toward the hall.

Jack jumped, shifting in midair. He crashed into his quarry at full human weight. Nixon dropped the baton. It skittered across the floor. Jack got in a couple of punches, but Nixon recovered fast. He bucked, using his greater size and mass to lever them both off the ground. Jack locked his legs around the larger man's waist and his arm around his throat. Nixon went for his eyes. Jack ducked.

Rika ran onto the bridge and swung her baton at Nixon's head. But the crook managed to turn at the last minute. She clipped Jack's arm instead, breaking his hold on Nixon's neck. He jabbed an elbow at Jack's knees. Jack shifted and jumped clear.

Nixon reclaimed his baton. Rika danced away.

"I got this," she yelled. "Stop the priest."

Jack wanted to argue, but she was wearing a crazy, black-lipped grin filled with sharp canine teeth. Her powers were back. Warmth flooded his chest. *Nixon deserved this.*

Kennedy cowered against the display case. He'd pushed the damaged mask past his forehead, revealing a pasty, middle-aged baby face drenched in sweat. His lips moved rapidly, but the alarms drowned out the words. His left hand clutched the winking golden scarf to his shoulder. His right hand quivered on the handle of the tiara case as he stared at the brown and white cat stalking, lion-like, toward him.

Jack swaggered just enough.

Kennedy bolted. He was too tall to notice the 'possum slop or the small body in his path. His left shoe skidded on the muck. The toe of his right hooked under the opossum. He fell across the aisle. His head cracked against a stone pedestal at the far right corner of the bridge.

Jack glanced at Rika. Her chest heaved, but her perspiring face glittered like the golden scarf. She hefted two shock batons. Nixon lay face-down on the walkway.

Jack hurried down the aisle and bent over Gene. The opossum's condition appeared no better or worse than before.

Kennedy was still breathing. There was a goose egg growing on his forehead but not a lot of blood. Jack double-checked the pedestal to make sure he wasn't missing anything important, like more blood. The doll-sized bronze statue of a bearded guy seated atop the pedestal peered back at him. The statue winked.

Jack shifted reflexively. It was a mistake. All his bruises, sprains and the adrenalin crash of too much shifting caught up with him at once. He braced his arms to either side of a brass plaque identifying the statue as Saint Peter, the first pope, and eyeballed the saint's shiny nose.

Despite the ear-numbing yammering of the alarms, he sensed her approach, knew the instant she stood behind him. He shook his head at his own foolishness.

He said, "This church is winking at me."

"You're delusional. It's part of your charm."

"Only part?" he asked the statue.

"Yeah."

He glanced over his shoulder. She was staring at him, her gaze traveling the length of his body, so intent it could have been a caress. Part of him was grateful all she could see was his back. An increasingly insistent part of him damned annoyed. Her lips curved in a mischievous smile. Light flared in her eyes.

It flared in the south end of the basilica, blazed over the bridge, and poured over the hall in front of the underground sanctuary as well. Jack blinked, dazzled.

"Oh no," Rika moaned, "the cavalry."

"Isn't that a good thing?"

"Not when you're naked." She shoved her backpack into his arms. "I'll stall them as long as I can."

He tore into the bag. She'd folded everything. This was why he should never get involved with an over-achiever. Why couldn't she just stuff everything on top like a normal college student? Then he wouldn't have to dig to China to find his jeans. He yanked them over his hips.

He heard her shouting in the distance, her voice pitched so he could hear what he needed. "They tried to steal the tiara!"

She'd balled his socks! *At least they weren't rammed in his shoes.* He shoved his feet into his sneakers.

"They tied us up!"

He'd tie them later.

"I had a nail clipper!"

Crap. He forgot his shorts. Forget it. Where the hell were his shirts? Wait—that flash of cardinal red. He wrestled his sweatshirt from the pouch. His t-shirt sailed across the aisle.

"Then the alarm went off and they started fighting."

He jerked his sweatshirt over his head. Pulled it over his jeans.

"I don't know why. We were in the Crypt Church. We couldn't hear anything. We didn't come out 'til we saw the lights."

He hadn't noticed before, but the alarms had faded to blips. He heard the opossum gasp. He bundled his were-roommate in his t-shirt and held him protectively.

Two Metropolitan Police officers in riot vests mounted the stairs at the east end of the bridge, guns drawn. Jack braced himself, praying his blue eyes would count for more than his brown skin and kinky hair.

The lead cop halted a foot shy of Gene's muck. She was tall, gray-haired and built like a Valkyrie. Her right hand lowered the gun. Her left arm swept to the side, wordlessly commanding her colleagues, Rika, and the Shrine guards bringing up the rear to stay back.

Hoping it was true people responded better if called by name, he glanced at her nametag. It read "Pinckey". He gaped. Pinckey? *Pinckey and "the Braen"? Really? What next? Would they try and take over the world?*

'Possum Gene Braen sneezed, spraying the officer's boots. The good news was if he was sneezing he was probably going to be okay. The bad news was she was a cop, a cop who now had were-snot on her boots.

Her face puckered. "Jesus, kid, what are you doing with that rat?"

* * *

Jack was still pondering her question an hour after dawn when Officer Pinckey booted him, Rika, and Gene out an inconspicuous door on the west side of the Shrine with the warning: "Stay away from the east parking lot. Every kid and their cell phone is there."

He'd worry about his answer later. Right now, easing the sleepy, t-shirt-draped opossum onto the lawn without dropping him was almost more than Jack could manage.

Rika dragged her backpack to the low wall overlooking the west terrace of the basilica. She sat on the wall and stared numbly at the trees across Harewood Avenue.

Chilled and aching, he slumped beside her. "I can't believe I have a math test in three hours," he groaned. "Why the hell did the cops have to ask everything six times? Six fucking times! You don't think they believed Kennedy about me turning into a cat?"

Rika started to shake. He had a sudden, horrific flashback to the moment in the church when he realized she couldn't shift.

Teary-eyed, she grabbed his hand. Her features twisted in misery. "You could've been killed, and it's all my fault." Her voice wobbled into a sob. "I just wanted to see you. I thought we could have fun. Fun!"

She wanted to see him? She wanted *to see* him. Him!

He folded her into his arms. Somewhere in the sobbing and the patting, the small fists clinging to his shirt and the small perfect body wriggling against his chest, she raised her damp face to his, and he kissed her. The knell of doom pealed inside his head, ringing through every warning, caveat, and dire prophecy in the young single man's lexicon. His lower brain didn't care. She kissed back like the world would end if they stopped. *This was why he was screwed.*

Their lungs demanded air, but their bodies refused to part. Foreheads touching, they shared each other's breath.

Something rustled in the grass behind the wall. An opossum's scream deepened into a man's heartfelt groan. Gene sat up. His stricken gaze bounced from the grass to the church to Jack and Rika sitting together on the wall, and finally to his lap. He emitted a tiny, high-pitched shriek. He snatched Jack's t-shirt off the grass. T-shirt pressed to his junk, he stumbled to his feet and raced north toward their dorm.

Rika's gaze never strayed from Jack's face.

This was why he didn't care. She was the star around which his world revolved. He threaded his fingers through her silky hair and kissed her again.

WITNESS REPORT
KATHARINE KERR

Yes, I will tell you how it was then. The worst of it was the way the Nazis deprived me of sleep. Before they threw me in the cell, they stripped me naked. Just beyond the steel bars of the door, the guards walked by during the day, peered in, and made coarse comments about me, a young woman, shivering and naked, just beyond their reach. Who could sleep then?

At night they threw me a blanket, but they shone strong lights into my tiny cell. At intervals, they marched up and down the corridor outside and beat on a drum or sang. I had no bed. I would lie curled up on my one stinking blanket in a corner of the cell and try to sleep while their cracked ugly voices rang out with the *Horst Wessel Song* or some other Nazi abomination. If I did manage to snatch a few hours sleep, guards would fling open the door, and an interrogator would march in. He was a jolly-looking little man with a round face and thick glasses that made it hard to read his eyes.

The questions were always the same and my answers as well.

"You are a werewolf, yes?"

"No." I was telling the truth, of course. "I am not a werewolf."

"You're lying. Tell us the truth. We wish to know how you change."

Silence.

"Tell us." A slap on the face.

Silence.

A raised hand – but no slap.

"Why will you not tell us? Tell us, and you go free."

Silence.

A shrug, a sneer, and he would leave again.

They dared not torture me, you see. They knew enough to know that if they damaged my body, I would never be able to demonstrate the change.

Some prisoners might have taken comfort in this. I was hoping they would kill me. Although I knew that the war had started to go badly for my once-loved Germany, maybe the Nazis would manage to fight back and drive the Allies away. Escape? With all those men going back and forth just outside? Even in the dead of night I heard them. For all I knew, I would be a prisoner in that cell for years.

And never have a decent sleep again. When you are not allowed to sleep, your mind begins to splinter. You go beyond the state we call "being exhausted"—far far beyond. If an insect flew into my cell, I felt rage and slapped it dead. There were always plenty of flies. The smell of my own excrement—my only toilet was a bucket in the corner—made me weep. I longed to pick up the bucket and hurl its contents at the guards, but I couldn't bear to touch the filthy thing. I swore and raged and felt only more tired than before. I wanted to pace back and forth, but my quivering legs refused to let me.

I could no longer remember how long they had kept me in the cell. I could barely remember my arrest. Fragments of memory would rise up, images of our village, of the grain fields all around where we worked, the women and children, prisoners of the Army's need for food to fight a war that had taken all our men. I could see Frau Schnabel's terrified face, half-toothless, her chin dotted with white hairs, as she wept at my arrest. She was the informer, she was the one who'd lied, who had sacrificed me to save her own grandchildren.

Could I have told the truth? Tell the soldiers: no, not me, then point to them, the nine year old daughter, the even younger boy—I could not bear to hand them over to the human fiends who raided our village. In the cell, my hatred of the SS lent me life. So many reasons! They shot our village priest for hiding two Jewish babies, then clubbed the infants to death rather than "waste bullets on them". Oh, that memory kept my hatred burning hot enough! Every time the interrogator marched in, every time I saw the little silver death's heads on his thread-bare black uniform, I remembered what he wanted and how I would rather die than give it to him. Would our village children have been able to lie, treated as I was?

At times, when I chewed my daily lump of black bread or drank the bowl of boiled meat and water they gave me now and then, I would remember eating before the war, the roast pork my mother made with the warm potato salad, the fat chickens, and noodles in gravy. At moments I would weep, remembering, but when I did, the guards would laugh and jeer. I soon learned to smother the grief. At times a rat would scuttle across the floor. I longed to change and leap upon it, rend its hide and feast upon its flesh. Instead I screamed in pretend fear. Let the guards laugh! Better that than they see what they wanted to see.

Why? I asked that question of myself many times a day. Why did they want to know? Why not just root us all out, burn us, kill us with silver weapons as so many others had done down the long centuries? The day came when I found out.

The first hint came from the guards, as they stood gossiping in the corridor. All of these men could no longer fight. Anyone strong enough had long since been sent to the front. Still, they talked about the war. They knew little, only that it went badly. But one warm day, when the spring sun cast stripes of light through my little barred window, they began to talk about despair and revenge.

"Revenge!" the sergeant would say. He would wave the stump where his left hand used to be. "Useless, when you're dead."

"Who's to say we'll be dead?" the boy—barely fourteen he was—would remark. "We could slip away into the forest."

"How can you believe in those stupid superstitions?" The sergeant rolled his eyes.

"But Goebbels said on the radio—"

"As if that makes it true! Do you have shit for brains?"

The other two would shrug and fall silent.

Not long after, the sergeant mentioned that an important man was on his way, an officer of high rank, a personal friend of Goebbels himself—or so some said. The old man insisted that this mysterious officer only knew Obergruppenführer Prützmann—whoever he was. I knew nothing about high ranking officers, but I could guess that this one had something to do with my imprisonment.

Sure enough, after a blurred space of days and nights—maybe three days, maybe four, I could not   tell—two men strode down the corridor and stood in front of the door to my cell. One I recognized as the officer who had arrested me, a middle-aged, swag-bellied gray thing with a moustache stained with food. The other stood tall in his black uniform, youngish, good-looking in a blond, bland way. He set his hands on hips and looked me over, turned his head, looked over the cell, the walls, turned and looked up and down the corridor, and then swung around to face the gray, fat man.

"This will not do!" His voice was low, tight, a snarl. "Do you want to kill the prisoner? How can she teach us what we need to know if she's sick and miserable?"

The gray man stammered a few words. The officer turned to the guards and began to bark orders. They scurried before him like the cell rats. Soon I had   clothing—coarse brown stuff, yes, but warm skirts, shirts, shoes. After I dressed, he opened the door and gestured for me to come out. I took three steps and nearly fell. He swore and picked me up. By then I was so thin that he could carry me down the corridor to another cell, this one with a bunk, a proper toilet, a sink. He set me down on the bunk, then turned and ordered the guards to bring me food.

"Not too much! She's been starved." He looked my way. "Small meals, but a lot of them." He smiled. "Once you're stronger, we'll talk."

His smile had all the warmth of a melting icicle. I nearly laughed. Muddled and sick and splintered as I was, I could see through his ruse, the false concern, the smile. I was supposed to like him, I realized, supposed to see him as my savior, if only I would give him the information he wanted. He wanted me to trust him, to cling to his promises, and then he would throw me aside once he had the truth.

"My name is Wülf," he said and showed strong white teeth with his smile. "Think of it as an omen."

I stared at him and let my mouth sag open.

"Just rest," he said. "I can see you're too exhausted to talk."

He left the cell, but lingered outside for a moment. "By the way," he said, "the man who's been questioning you? He's going to be shot. For mistreatment of Aryan prisoners."

That did please me, but I hid my pleasure from him.

For the next few days I slept and ate. How I slept! Long blissful hours of it, both during the day and all night, wrapped in warm, clean blankets. They brought me decent food, small amounts, but many times during the day. I was surprised they could find so much good food after the long winter of near-starvation we'd all suffered, those of us who farmed and sweated and went hungry so the armies could eat. When I was awake, I planned how I would act, just what I might do in response to the opening gambits that Wülf might make.

Because of course, the day came when he opened the door of my cell and walked in. I was sitting at one end of my bunk. He sat at the other and smiled his icicle smile.

"You know what we need to know," he said.

"Oh yes."

"What I'm wondering is why you won't tell us."

"Would you have told that man anything?"

"Of course not. Very well. What about telling me?"

"What I'm wondering," I copied his words deliberately, "is why you want to know."

Wülf mugged comic surprise. "Didn't he tell you?"

"No, he didn't." As you know damn well, I thought to myself.

"I see." Wülf nodded and arranged a look of sympathy on his face. "Let me be honest. We're losing the war. The Russians are nearly to Berlin. The Führer has shut himself up somewhere." His expression turned to honest grief. "There's no hope. We're going to be defeated." He paused to swallow heavily, to take a few deep breaths and choke back tears. "All we have left is revenge."

That word again, revenge. I began to suspect an ugly truth.

"We'll fight to the end, kill as many of them as we can," Wülf continued. "But they'll take the Homeland. Some of us want to plant bombs, traps, anything we can to make them pay high for it."

"And how many of our people will stumble onto those traps by mistake?"

He winced in another honest gesture. "That's very true. And the rest of us see that. Some of us have to survive to lead the resistance. Otherwise, as you say, who knows who'll take the damage?"

Us? I thought. Who is this "us?" SS officers, I supposed, but of course I could not know until he told me.

"Goebbels himself came up with a better plan. When the Homeland falls, the enemy is going to hunt the SS down and kill us all." He shrugged as if it didn't matter. "Unless we can hide like wolves, in the darkness of the night. Why not be wolves, then? Safe in the forests, the hills, during the day, but at night, we kill. We take our revenge. They will pay in blood for their victory."

He sat smiling at me, a bland-looking youngish man in uniform, calm, relaxed, even, but utterly mad, crazed by defeat. I shivered—oh, I went cold, colder than the snow of the horrible winter past. At that moment I saw my plan. A madman can be led by his madness.

"Do you understand now?" He leaned a little closer to me. "Do you?"

"Oh yes. Of course. But who's going to take the wolf form? Not everyone can."

"That's true. I'm hoping I can, but who knows? We've been reading, searching the old books. Young people are the best. We've recruited some of the boys from Hitler Youth, the true ones, the young men who have the true German spirit. They're eager to learn. Most are twelve and thirteen, still young enough to learn."

To myself I thought: Your god will punish you for that, if Russians don't get you first. Aloud, I said, "I must have time to think. You're asking me to betray a sacred trust."

"Very well. I'll come back tomorrow." He got up and went to the door, only to pause and look back. "But remember, the Fatherland is a sacred trust, too."

I smiled and nodded. He saluted me and left.

In the morning Wülf returned soon after I'd eaten. We talked a little, meaningless greetings, just as if courtesy could still matter after the horrors of the last seven years. Finally I stood up with a carefully arranged toss of my head and a defiant tilt of my chin.

"I've decided," I said, "for the sake of the Fatherland, I'll show you. But we must have the proper place. Moonlight. And outside somewhere."

"Outside?" He frowned, a little suspicious.

"You think I'm going to run away. All right, is there a building here with a flat roof? Too high for a wolf to jump from?"

"Yes, there is, the old stables. Very well."

My turn for the suspicious smile. "I must be naked to effect the change. Can you keep the guards from—"

He patted the revolver at his hip. I smiled.

"Excellent!" I said. "Now, the old books say that the moon has to be full, but that's not true. Well, it's not true if you do the proper meditations beforehand."

"Meditations. Huh, I knew we needed more information."

"Much more, apparently." Which was certainly true. "Let me show you the change first. Then the instructions will make more sense. Tonight will do. I could see the moon last night through the cell window. It's just a quarter moon, but it's enough for you to see by." I paused to think. "Or maybe not quite enough, especially if you want to take notes. You'd better have a lantern there, too. A good bright one."

"I'll do that." Wülf got up and made me an odd little bow. "I'll come here an hour after sunset to fetch you. I'd let you out of this wretched cell now, but it would make the others suspicious if I did."

"I understand. I'll need to rest beforehand, anyway. This will do."

"Heil Hitler!" Wülf saluted as he spoke.

"Heil Hitler!" I said the hated name for the last time. "For the glory of the Fatherland."

And then, thank my own gods, he left.

That afternoon, I slept and dreamt of the mountains. When I woke, I ate the decent meal the guards brought me. I took the blanket from the bunk and folded it neatly into a bundle. I'd need something to lie upon while I changed. Wülf arrived a little while after I finished, and together we walked out of the prison house into the clean sunset air. The quarter moon already hung pale in the sky above the wooded foothills to the west. In the darkening east, the Evening Star glimmered.

Two guards fell in behind us as we walked across the cobbled yard toward a flat-roofed building by a broken stone wall. I had arrived in this place blind-folded. Now I could look around and see that it was a small schloss, an old stone manor house, a single squat tower. Wülf noticed my curiosity.

"My family owned this," he said. "I'm the last of them. Who knows who'll have it now? Probably some stinking Russian."

"Spoils of war, eh? Perhaps you can make them pay for it with blood."

"That's my fondest hope."

A sturdy ladder was leaning against the stable wall, which rose about twenty feet above the cobbles. One of the guards clambered up first. The other ducked into the stable and came out with a lantern. I climbed up to the roof, Wülf followed, and finally the last guard. While the guard lit the kerosene lantern, I spread my blanket out on a reasonable clean spot near, but not suspiciously near, the edge of the roof. I could see that if an animal larger than a rat jumped down onto the stones, it would at the very least break a couple of legs.

"Very good," I said. "Now. Notice that I am positioning myself to look at the moon. You know the face there belongs to one of the old Germanic gods, right?"

"Right," Wülf said.

"So as you lie down, invoke him." I was inventing lore as fast as I could. "His name is Máni. Next, I need to disrobe. The guards—"

Wülf told them to turn their backs. He knelt by the blanket. I took off my clothes safely in front of him, who lusted for lore, not a woman. As I lay down on my back, I spoke the names of three runes. I don't remember which ones. They had nothing to do with the change, but Wülf in his ignorance wrote them down in a small notebook.

By then the night had grown dark. The lantern light cast a dazzling pool around us, bright enough, or so I hoped, to make him night-blind. I stretched my arms out to each side and began to chant some meaningless babble. I repeated it several times to allow Wülf to write it all down. While I chanted, I prepared the hawk image in my mind.

Now the crux—I would have to change faster than ever I had before. I forced the image from my mind until I saw it hovering above me. One deep breath—a shriek—the hawk came to me. Every muscle in my arms and back burned with the shock as I merged myself with the image. I leapt into the air, wings beating, but I had forgotten how weak I was from my long confinement.

A woman's legs hung from the hawk's body, meaty, thick, heavy. I swooped over the roof and beat my painful wings. Hampered by the weight, I plunged down toward the cobbles below, but at the last moment my legs transformed, thin now, and light. I flew. I gained the sky at last. I heard them shouting below, heard shots, too, as they fired at me. I spiraled and swooped in as twisted a course as I could fly. The shots missed.

As I soared into the night, the last thing I heard was Wülf's voice, crying "Come back! Come back! The Fatherland..."

I flew higher and left the voice behind.

* * *

You know how I survived in the hills, until not the Russians but Americans came. Now you know everything. Put it in our village archive so we may always remember to live in fear.

ATTACK OF THE WERE-ZOMBIE FRIENDSHIP WITH BENEFITS
SARAH BRAND

What most people don't understand about the Infected is that they're usually not dangerous unless they want to be. As long as they don't bite you, you won't turn into a vampire or a werewolf, and good luck convincing someone with the fae virus to put her teeth anywhere near you. But zombies are definitely unsafe, and you shouldn't get too close. A friend of mine was only mostly a zombie, and whether we were close is up for debate. Still, it didn't end well.

Adam has this band called Flux Mortician that plays every now and then at the Black Cat, one of my favorite DC bars. The second time I met him, he mentioned how much he was enjoying *Atlas Shrugged*. I paused to check for irony, found none, and agreed that really long books were great. For instance, the seventh Harry Potter book was also long. Which House did he think he was in? To Adam's credit, he went with it.

I don't date libertarians, so romance was never in the cards. But I kept hanging out with certain mutual friends of ours, which meant spending time with Adam, and he grew on me. He loved Flux Mortician with a seriousness I reserve for virology, but whenever one of his bandmates wanted to do something risky—a crazy drum solo, a cover of "Chandelier," whatever— he went with it. I never once heard him ask if they thought they could pull something off.

Also, he checked some important boxes: tall, dark eyes, and a tenor voice that could narrate my physical chemistry textbook and still sound like punk rock. I thought he might be secretly fae. Yes, I'm shallow. Sue me.

Then some dude with feminist views and progressive politics dumped me next to the biography shelf at Politics and Prose—during a werewolf attack, if you can believe it—and I was done. If I was destined to fall for emotionally unavailable losers who just saw me as a distraction, I wouldn't fall for anyone. I'd protect myself by sleeping with someone with whom I could never, ever possibly fall in love.

I got to the Black Cat early that Friday night. Adam was always the first one there, and I found him at his usual spot at the bar. Two chairs over, a fae boy and a pretty werewolf were holding hands, talking to each other in low voices. I let my gaze linger on the couple for just a moment, then pushed my envy aside. I wasn't going to get hurt again, which meant a boyfriend was the absolute last thing I needed.

Adam nodded at me. "Lexie said you broke up with that guy," he said. "You doing okay?"

"Yeah." I kept my voice light. "But my life is pretty tragically devoid of kisses right now. I'll have to do something about that."

He snorted. "I bet Marcus would help you out."

My face scrunched up before I could stop it. Flux Mortician's drummer had a thing for me...and every other woman in our group. "Is he actually a vampire?"

Adam raised his hands. "Don't ask, don't tell."

"Well, I have pretty specific requirements for friends with benefits," I said. "First, it has to be someone I'm attracted to. Second, it can't be someone I secretly want to date. Third, I have to trust him not to be an asshole." I had never actually had a friend with benefits, but those rules seemed sufficient.

"Makes sense," he said, draining the last of his beer.

I hesitated, but backing down has never been my style. "So, uh, how about it?"

He narrowly saved us both from a spit-take. When he recovered, he just looked at me for a moment, eyebrows raised. "Is that an actual offer?"

I could feel my face heating up, but I nodded.

"Our friends come first," he said. "I don't want things to get weird. We'd act normal around everyone, I assume?"

I hadn't even considered letting our friends know what was going on. "Yes, please," I said.

He was dangerously charming when he smiled. As our friends straggled into the bar—much too close to sunset, curfews to protect us from the Infected be damned—I pushed that thought to the back of my head. This was going to work.

* * *

After the bartenders kicked all the known Infected out, Flux Mortician's show lasted for two hours, and the party afterward went until morning. It was too dangerous to roam the streets after dark, the logic went, so we might as well be in an amazing bar, with wonderful people, having a fabulous time. And drinking, which can help everything seem more amazing, wonderful, and fabulous.

By sunrise, I was mostly sober. I bought one last bottle of water from the bartender, made sure I had my things, and waited awkwardly on the corner of 14th and U until Adam shuffled up to stand beside me. "Still want to do this?" he said.

Even bleary-eyed and unshaven, he was beautiful. "I do."

As soon as I said it, I flinched—did that sound too much like a wedding thing?—but Adam didn't seem to notice. "You're closer, right?"

We rode the metro in silence, which might have been companionable if I hadn't been wondering the whole time whether it was awkward. When we were back out on the street, about a half-mile from my apartment, Adam glanced over at me and burst out laughing. "What?" I demanded.

"Well, you have to admit this is pretty surreal, right?"

"More surreal than the Infection bringing on the Twilight universe?" There were probably better literary comparisons, but I've never been a fan of urban fantasy, especially not once it turned into urban fact. "Vampires, werewolves, zombies—"

Which, of course, was exactly when a zombie crashed out of the bushes and lurched toward us. It was fast, just like the government had warned us about, and it smelled like my brother's refrigerator. Adam stepped in front of me, and the zombie halted. It sniffed the air, an uncannily human look of confusion on its rotting face. Then it turned and loped away.

Adam kept walking, like nothing had happened. "I knew it!" I said. "You're a fae, aren't you?"

He laughed even harder at that. "Nope, just me."

One street over from my apartment building, there's a brick wall next to the sidewalk that comes up to my shoulder, which is to say it isn't very tall. As we walked past, without warning, Adam picked me up and swung me onto the ledge. Then he reached up just a bit to kiss me, his lips warm and soft against mine. I bent my head and kissed him back.

"Sorry," he said. "I saw the height differential and I had to take it."

"No need to apologize at all." Clearly this had been the best idea ever.

We reached my apartment building, and I led him inside.

* * *

We didn't sleep together, mostly because after the night at the Black Cat, we both really needed some actual sleep. "See you tomorrow afternoon?" Adam said.

Some friend of Adam's had an alt-rock band, which was playing over on H Street. "I'll be there." And I would. But first things first: I had science to do.

I had originally partnered with the NIH to do my dissertation research on flu vaccines, but then my lab had been drafted into looking for ways to prevent   Infection—especially with the zombie virus, given that zombies had almost no self-control when it came to biting people. They left other zombies alone, but that was about it. So, we were developing a disease model that would let us simulate potential vaccines.

Even setting ethics aside, getting blood samples from zombies was tricky, but the principal investigators thought we could develop a vaccine with the data we already had. After months of fighting with our aging CAD software, I wasn't so sure, but I was willing to keep trying. Scientists all over the country were working on the problem, so even when I was the only one on duty at my lab, I never felt lonely for long.

Maybe I could just marry molecular biology. Our children would be beautiful when viewed through a microscope.

I spent the entire night at the lab, drinking far too much coffee and analyzing the latest promising virtual molecules until mid-morning. A few hours before Adam's friend's show was supposed to start, I went home and changed into my cutest dress, the skirt of which is probably a tad too short, but I'll only be in my mid-twenties once. I put on eyeliner, which I never do, and carefully packed my purse with everything I could possibly need if I wound up at Adam's place after the show.

There's no good way to get to H Street, but even running late, I made it just before the friend's band went onstage. Adam was already there, along with our friend Lexie and a couple of others, not to mention the dozens of strangers that were crammed into the tiny bar. *Act natural*, I told myself, even though I'm a terrible actress. Fortunately, once the band started playing, no one was paying any attention to me.

Unfortunately, Adam wasn't paying attention to me, either. He had one drink, then another, and he barely said anything at all. That was my first clue that something was wrong. Normally, when we're out with our friends, he never shuts up. As the music pounded in my ears, he leaned against the nearest wall, then slowly slid to the floor.

By the end of the concert, he had recovered enough to stand upright. "I'm heading home," he told me. "Go with Lexie. We can hang out later."

I couldn't argue without breaking the "act normal" rule, or worse, being a pushy jerk. I swallowed my disappointment and nodded.

It was about five o'clock, with the sun on its way down but not quite there yet. As Lexie and I walked into a nicer, less crowded bar, my phone buzzed. It was a text from Adam, and autocorrect had not been kind to it. *Whey ate you guys?*

Like an idiot, hoping that somehow this day would still turn out the way I wanted, I told him. About ten minutes later, Adam staggered in, made straight for the bar, and then came over to our table with two shots in one hand and a beer in the other. He did the shots in rapid succession, then cracked open the beer. "I thought you went home," I said. He wobbled when he shrugged.

Lexie stepped forward and pried the beer out of his hand. "Adam, you are *drunk*. Go home."

He stared at her for a moment, and then without a word to me or anyone, walked out the door. Something about his gait was familiar, but I couldn't place it.

When the sun really was about to set, we settled our tab and stepped out onto the sidewalk. Ahead of me, I saw Adam, who apparently hadn't made it home after all. But why were people running from him and screaming?

Then he turned around and I screamed, too.

He was a zombie. The flesh on his face was rotting away, and when he moved, he lurched. He took a step toward us, and I froze, some moronic part of me not wanting to leave him like this.

He turned and ran, and Lexie pulled me into the nearest cab. She was crying, and it occurred to me that she had known Adam for much longer than I had. As I awkwardly patted her shoulder, my biologist brain went into overdrive. The zombie virus had a forty-eight hour incubation period. Even if Adam had been bitten immediately after he left the bar, he shouldn't have started decaying that quickly. And I had seen him with his shirt off less than forty-eight hours ago. Besides, while Adam had flaws, somehow I didn't think coming to a concert after a zombie bite was one of them.

What was going on?

After the cab dropped me off, my phone started buzzing with texts from Adam, nonsense that I couldn't decode no matter how hard I tried. Every time my phone went off, I wanted to throw up. His phone was just going haywire. That had to be it. I turned my phone off, and somehow, I went to sleep.

* * *

When I woke up, one more text from Adam was waiting for me. *I need to talk to you.*

My hands were shaking so badly that I could barely type out my reply. *I thought you were Infected.*

It took a few minutes for him to answer. *I am in a relationship with Infection and it's complicated.*

Let's meet at Starbucks, I said. *But it has to be soon. Lab duty this afternoon.* I was freaked out, but I was curious, too.

I arrived before he did, bought a cup of tea, and snagged the one empty table. Between the music and the conversation around us, whatever he had to tell me, we probably wouldn't be overheard.

And then Adam was sitting across from me, a venti coffee in one hand, looking profoundly hungover but otherwise normal. "About last night," he began.

I raised an eyebrow. I wasn't going to help him out.

"Last year, I was bitten by a werewolf," Adam said. "But she had the zombie virus, too. So instead of turning into a wolf at the full moon, when I lose control, I turn into...that thing you saw last night."

I had to take a minute to process this. "You're a were-zombie. I've never even heard of that."

"For all I know, I'm the only one," he said, talking at a point just over my shoulder. "I haven't asked around. I'd end up locked in a lab somewhere." Finally, he met my gaze, and I could tell he was wondering if he would be locked away after all.

I wasn't sure yet whether I could reassure him on that point.

"It's interesting, though," I finally said. "If your flesh can regenerate itself, then the effects of the zombie virus might be reversible." He tilted his head warily, and I took pity on him. "At least give me a sample of your blood."

"Won't your coworkers wonder where it came from?" he said.

"Let them wonder," I said quietly. It was stupid, and I knew it. For everyone's safety, Adam would be better off in quarantine. And if I took his blood secretly, on my own, without so much as making him sign a consent form, I would be breaking about a million rules. But were-zombie or not, he was my friend, and I wasn't going to force him into becoming a lab specimen.

Adam stared at me, then shook his head, as though to clear it. "That's not why I came," he said. "The thing we talked about before...it would be complicated. Probably not a good idea."

I shouldn't have been disappointed. "Okay."

If I had anything approximating good judgment or common sense, the story would have ended there. But it didn't.

* * *

That week, I couldn't stop thinking about Adam. Partly it was because I was spending every spare moment staring at his blood under a microscope, and partly, I felt terrible for him. But some of it—too much of it—was the way I had felt when I was kissing him, perched on top of that brick wall.

My brilliant plan was failing in every way possible. The one saving grace was that I still didn't want to date him.

I didn't talk to Adam, even when I saw him online. But when Friday came around, as I was getting ready to go to the Black Cat, I shaved my legs, even though I was planning to wear jeans. That was my first mistake.

My second mistake was thinking that our other friends would be there. Flux Mortician wasn't playing, and I guess the rest of our group had other things to do. Adam and I stood around awkwardly until I hit upon the idea of going to buy a drink. But then he came to the bar with me. "Don't worry," he said when I stared at him. "I know my limits now."

The problem with making yourself feel more comfortable with the power of drink specials is that eventually, you get too comfortable to remember that you need to stop drinking. I tried to be responsible. I really did. I closed out my tab when I felt the alcohol kicking in. Then Adam offered me one more.

"I can't," I said. For someone who occasionally died, he was far too pretty. "If I have another drink, I'm going to hit on you."

"If you have another drink," he said, "I will let you."

The next morning, I would know that he shouldn't have said that, and I shouldn't have agreed. I would know that I had just been staving off the inevitable feeling that I had no one and would probably die alone. But right then, my princess was at the top of the castle, and I just had to climb the ladder of one more drink. I didn't see the barrel coming to hit me in the face.

"Good," I said. "I've been thinking about you all week, you know."

His eyes widened, but he bought me the drink anyway.

I remember asking him if we could leave. I remember waiting for him near the front entrance, clutching my purse in my arms. I remember Lexie bringing me a bottle of water, and I remember being too far gone to wonder when she had shown up. She helped me toward the bathroom and told Adam to get lost. And just after the bathroom door closed behind us, I bent over the sink and retched up that last rum and Coke.

The worst part was that without Adam, I couldn't go home until sunrise. And the last thing I wanted was to go back into the bar. But Lexie didn't make me leave the bathroom. She just sat with me, one arm around my shoulders, while I cried my eyes out. And slowly, as my vision cleared, I began to think that maybe I wasn't so alone after all.

* * *

By sunrise, I also felt really fucking embarrassed.

I had tried to go home with a part-time zombie. I had made questionable relationship decisions before, but even for me, that was a new low. I had been more intoxicated than at any previous point in my life, and I had no idea how many people had seen me. I had even less idea how many people had seen me with Adam. If Lexie had figured out what was about to happen, other people might have, too.

Also: "I've been thinking about you all week"? Really? Did I have to say that?

Adam had apparently also done some reflecting. After I got home, he texted me to say, again, that he didn't want a casual thing with me. *Okay*, I replied. *I should have taken no for an answer the first time around.*

I left his blood sample outside a principal investigator's office with an anonymous note. Maybe someone could help Adam with his occasional rotting and lurching problem, but that someone wasn't me.

The principal investigator discovered that she could use the data from Adam's blood to synthesize an experimental antiviral drug that could cure him, and maybe others. She also found out that I had brought the sample in. Her gratitude wasn't enough to save me from getting kicked out of my program. Since I had violated most of the protocols for collecting human blood, I knew better than to try to fight it.

Three weeks later, on my last night at the Black Cat, I told my friends I had quit from burnout. I was leaving DC—trying to live on a tiny stipend had been bad enough, so there was no way I could afford the rent now— and I had to tell them something. "Why didn't you say something sooner?" Lexie said.

Adam was standing a short distance away, close enough to hear but far enough away that no one watching would think he was part of the group.

He had told everyone he was cured now, but our friends were still pissed, and I couldn't blame them. "It's complicated," I said. "There's been a lot going on."

I went up to the bar, like I was about to order a drink, and if that put me right next to Adam, I wasn't complaining. He glanced over at me, not quite making eye contact. "You didn't burn out."

I shook my head.

"Thank you," he said, a little clipped, still not looking at me.

"Of course," I said. "We're friends, okay? Some things are more important than a job."

Finally, he smiled. "Friends. Yeah."

For just a moment, I wondered if maybe I had wanted to date Adam all along. But even cured, he wasn't right for me, and wanting something doesn't make it a good idea. And I was leaving town anyway.

Still. "We've got a few hours before sunrise," I said. "Want to dance?"

THE WHALE
ANNELIESE BELMOND

Mara could still hear the elephant's screams as she stared at his human body. The weight of eyes hung on her, perhaps comparing her negative weight to his positive. Both extremes. Wondering if she would break too, if the weight would be too much. They didn't need to worry about her changing; she would be too small for harm, and lightweights had more control than heavyweights. Than the big heavyweights, at least.

Mara knelt and smoothed Caleb's hair. He looked peaceful in death. Light. She swallowed the lump in her throat and apologized for not being enough.

* * *

"How much weight do you carry?" Mara asked. The customary introduction felt heavy in her mouth. The purpose was transparency, but she dreaded the exchange.

"Twenty," Overseer Gemma said. "And you?"

"Negative one-hundred."

Mara hated the widening of the woman's eyes, like she was staring at a bomb. At positive twenty, the Weight Agency Overseer's burden must be a minor blip in her day. Mara focused on the tight pull of her bound hair, and found her voice remained steady. "What's this about, ma'am?"

"One of our own has gone missing off the coast of California. A child. She and her family were sailing when they were overtaken by another boat. The parents sustained minor injuries and their daughter was taken. The FBI is investigating but we need to send one of our own in. We can't risk the possibility that she was taken by politicals."

Mara nodded and glanced toward the rest of the police station, where the humans worked at desks behind the windows of her captain's office. She caught a few eyes before they were directed away. Having no idea about the existence of the Weight community and Mara's other work, they probably thought she was being reprimanded by their captain and deputy chief. She wished it didn't bother her. There was only one other Weight in the department, other than Captain Rye. "I'll contact Hardy about joining—"

"No," Gemma said. Her mouth pulled down, adding lines to her face and betraying her age. "It's dangerous enough sending one person. The town is crawling with suits, we can't risk drawing attention. You won't be able to get anywhere near the parents, or their lawyer."

Mara glanced at her captain, but if he had concerns, he was keeping them to himself. "I appreciate your confidence in me, but I'm not sure there's much I can do on my own."

"There's one of ours in the town. He's met the girl. He'll assist you." There was something off about the way Gemma said "assist."

"A civilian?"

"A fisherman," Captain Rye added. He smiled at what wasn't being said, amused where Gemma was stiff.

There could be only one reason for that. "How much weight does he carry?" Mara asked. It came out like a demand.

Gemma swallowed. "100 tons."

"What?"

"He's a Whale," Rye said. "He's *the* Whale."

"No way," Mara said, a grin inadvertently appearing. "What breed?"

"Blue."

"That's impossible," she said, voice flat. "He would be catatonic."

"He's quite functional," Gemma said. "And safe. He's the only one ever to make it to adulthood. He'd be in the Guinness World Records, if we were out. He prefers anonymity among our own kind and very few know he exists. He'll help you with anything you need."

Mara stared at her, trying to imagine what carrying that much weight would be like. "Yes, ma'am," she said. "I'll leave today."

* * *

From the backseat of a taxi, Mara read over Herman Henley's file. He'd been in and out of psychiatric and rehabilitation facilities for most of his life. His medication history was long and ever-changing, with his last prescription being filled over two years ago. Surprisingly, he had a steady income and didn't need the support that the Weight government gave to those carrying a truly terrible weight. He sounded more stable than many lighter people Mara had met.

More stable than her.

Mara deleted the file from her laptop and looked away, her exhale restrained. The cab had been an opportunity to read and thus avoid looking at the coastline. She had delayed the anxiety for as long as possible.

The town could have been pleasant, even sweet, were it not for recent events. Seagulls called from the docks at the end of town, and while the ocean was silent, the winds carried its scent. Salty and fresh. It made Mara breathe deep even as the familiar longing built pressure in her chest.

She left her bags in the room of a quiet inn before having the cabbie take her to the cliffs. The road became steep and troublesome enough for the man to grumble under his breath. Mara was busy fighting the perverse urge to watch the water get farther and farther away. Heights. Not watching was almost as bad.

The road leveled out and Mara directed the cabbie onto a driveway, more a path than a road. It led to a little house that sat nestled between two hills of green, unseen from the main road. They gave the place a secluded look, and there was a simple beauty to the grass around it.

"You sure?" the cabbie said when Mara passed him his pay. His eyes were on the house and, while maintained, it did have a "cabin in the woods" feel.

"Yeah," Mara said. "Quite sure."

She changed her mind as she approached the door and the cab's engine faded. She felt like she was walking into silence. There was the breeze on the grass and the distant crash of the ocean, but for a moment she was utterly alone. The only one on earth. It wasn't until she reached the house that she realized how close it sat to the cliff. There were maybe fifty feet from the door to the drop off. She forced her legs to keep moving, even though they felt like they were walking on thin ice.

The door opened as she climbed the porch steps. She paused on the last one, knowing better than to get too close without permission.

Herman Henley smiled at her, a thin-lipped expression that only lifted one side of his mouth. A natural tan covered his pale skin, proving he wasn't a recluse. He was tall, but despite his youth, his back had already started to curve forward, making him look perpetually hunched. If it weren't for the tremble in his hands and the twitch in his left eye, Mara would have thought this was the wrong man. Most people carrying more weight than their human form tried to wear some of it as fat, but this man had the body of a cocaine addict. Thin and wiry. When he leaned into the door frame and extended his hand to her, there was strength in his shoulders, but the door supported too much weight for the movement to be anything but necessary.

"Mr. Henley," Mara said, taking the last step so she could reach his hand. "I'm Detective Mara Kendell."

His grip was firm despite the perpetual tremble. To Mara's relief, the frantic patter of her heart ceased under the man's calm.

"Herman, please," he said. "The irony's good for me." His smile widened, and his left eye fluttered shut and then open again. "How much weight do you carry?"

It was harder than usual to say. "Negative one-hundred."

"I hear that can be hard," he said. Mara couldn't tell if that was sarcasm or not. She kept her head high. Her human weight was perfectly average, heavier than many whose animal side was small. Not an easy feat.

"I'm here about the kidnapping of Katherine Young. I was told you'd be willing to assist."

"Any way I can." He straightened and went into the house, motioning for Mara to follow. "What do you need?"

"How well did you know her?"

Herman waved a hand to the living room and headed toward the small kitchen to the right. Mara settled on the edge of the closest chair and shook her head when Herman held up a glass of water.

"We met a few times," he said as he took the chair across from her. "They've been vacationing here for two years now. Her parents are carriers of the gene only. She'd wanted to meet another of her kind so the agency put us in touch. She would have had more in common with another lightweight, but..." He took a sip of water to hide the emotion that had made him stop, and placed the glass on the table between them before his shakes could make it spill. "Does the agency think she was targeted by politicals?"

"That's what I'm here to determine. The agency doesn't want to risk drawing attention until we know for certain."

"Not many people knew about her," he said. "Her parents made sure she didn't tell anyone, and she knew better than to show herself to an outsider. She's a smart girl. And this town is ignorant, as far as I know."

"If she was targeted, it could have been someone who followed them here."

"They would have needed to know how to make a boat disappear."

"So it wasn't spur of the moment." Mara caught herself staring at him and forced the frown off her face. What a sharp mind for someone so heavy.

His mouth quirked. "Say it," he said. "You've held out longer than most, but I'm tired of that look."

"I'm not here to bug you."

He just stared at her, and Mara gave in.

"You don't look like a whale," she said.

"I think whales are sexy, so fuck you, too." Genuine amusement made his grin wide enough to show imperfect teeth.

"How do you do it? I knew an elephant once. He made it to fourteen." She didn't need to say the rest. Understanding made Herman's next blink slow, denting his humor but not removing it.

"Yoga," he said. At Mara's look, he amended, "Work helps. Exercise. People." He paused but Mara couldn't determine what in his eyes had made him stop. "Surprisingly," he said, "drugs are counterproductive. I gave them up two years ago. Alcohol is still a problem. How do you cope?"

He'd been so frank, the least Mara could do was be honest. "Rehab. All through high school." She forced her fingers to stop fiddling with the hem of her shirt. "It took a while to accept the fact that no matter how much weight I lost, I would never be small enough to equalize my weights and make my other form easy." Or take away the anxiety that her human form left her with.

"I tried to gain for a while," Herman said. "But it actually added to my depression. And it's hard to keep weight on when your only interest is milk and powder." His smile was lazy, amused rather than bitter. "I have a boat," he said abruptly, "but the docks are closed. The FBI is checking the islands, but that could take forever."

"Could the kidnappers' boat be sitting out there?"

Herman nodded. "That's what I would do. Wait."

"They would need supplies," Mara mused. "It's a long shot but if the boat originated here, they could have stocked up in town. I need to know where the boat came from."

"I have a friend who can help," Herman said. "And these people love gossip. It shouldn't be too hard to find out if they bought their supplies here."

* * *

The walk down was mildly less terrifying than the drive up. The ocean was still too close, but the fresh air brought calm to Mara's heart. Herman didn't talk much and Mara encouraged the silence, though she spent much of her time focused on him. His legs seemed in a constant state of nearly giving out, and she had to watch her step to make sure it didn't surpass his slow trek. Despite his unnatural movements, he kept his head up.

He'd been quiet so long, Mara nearly jumped when he did speak.

"We're bound to get some stares in town. My pasty white ass next to your chocolate brown, they'll wonder why you're bothering with me. What's your cover?"

Mara rolled her eyes, fighting a smile. "Private investigator. Being the friendly guy you are, you're showing me around."

"Well, that's boring."

Eyes found them as soon as they entered town, but most rolled off Mara to settle on Herman. Her back ached with suddenly tense muscles, anticipating the judgment Herman would feel. Her instinct was to meet the stares with a glare, but it proved unnecessary. Smiles followed the eyes and often a greeting.

Herman stopped outside a rustic little convenience store and pointed to the sign over the door. "'We Got It,'" he said cheerfully.

"This town loves you," Mara said abruptly. It didn't sound like a compliment, though it actually was. Human connection didn't often agree with the side-effects of weight.

"Yeah," Herman agreed. He entered the shop and Mara caught the door behind him.

"Herman!" the woman behind the register raised her hand high in greeting. She leaned against the counter and smiled at Mara. "Who's your friend?"

"Detective Kendell, Shelly."

Mara shook her hand and the woman let the touch linger.

"You investigating that missing girl?" Shelly asked.

"Yes," Mara said. "I'm not with the FBI."

Shelly nodded wisely. "Private investigation. Gotcha."

Herman said, "We were wondering if your cousin had heard anything." To Mara, he added, "Dock security."

"Yeah!" Shelly straightened with excitement before leaning down again, close and conspiratorial. "He said the suits were really interested in a boat that arrived a couple weeks ago and left two days before that girl was taken. It was a white fishing boat named *Surprise*. Ironic, huh?"

Herman grinned his appreciation and Mara said, "I don't suppose your cousin knows who it belongs to?"

Shelly shook her head. "I don't think so. Things are really shut down now."

"We're also looking for anyone who might have bought a lot of merchandise recently," Mara said. "Have you heard anything odd?"

Shelly shook her head. "Tackle, energy bars, the usual."

"Thank you," Mara said. She gave her a smile to counteract the dark thoughts that were probably showing on her face. This was definitely premeditated. But there was no proof it had anything to do with Katherine's identity.

"So," Shelly said to Herman, "you mentioned yesterday you had a number for me?"

Herman pulled a slip of paper from his pocket. "You know," he said, "I think you might have a shot with this one. Lawyer, out of town. Barely looked at me."

Shelly rolled her eyes. "You can't determine if a woman is gay based on whether she finds *you* attractive."

"I have some lawyer jokes lined up," Herman told Shelly as he followed Mara from the shop, "just in case." When the bells over the door chimed its closing, Herman jerked his thumb toward the shop. "The Youngs' lawyer is pretty cute. For a lawyer."

Mara hardly heard him. Her thoughts were with the missing girl.

"Did Katherine tell you what she was?" Mara asked.

"A bird." Herman's face fell and for the first time Mara thought she saw the weight. "She didn't specify."

Mara took a deep breath as an ache settled in her chest. Birds tended to have the greatest difference between animal and human weight. Katherine had a hard future ahead of her. "It's a long shot, but if she was taken for what she is, maybe that's all the kidnappers knew too. They could be keeping her in that form. I need the numbers of anyone here who might sell bird food."

* * *

From a small restaurant overlooking the sea, Mara used Herman's phone to call the few relevant shops in town. They were all in his contacts, grouped helpfully together. He also seemed to have the number of every local and many tourists. Their home state was in parentheses next to their names.

"Yes, hello. My kid brought an injured bird home, and I was wondering if you had any bird food?" Mara narrowed her eyes at Herman's grin. "No? Okay, thank you. I'll tell him. Yeah. Bye." The call ended. "What?" she demanded.

"You do this often?" he asked.

"No." Mara ran her hand over her hair, still snug, and went to the next number. She didn't do this often. She shouldn't have been chosen for this. The tremors in her stomach had made her food go cold long ago. The phone trilled and, out of the corner of her eye, her plate shifted closer to her. Herman had the decency to be looking away.

"Hello? I'm looking for bird food. I'm not sure, my kid brought it home. That many?" Mara stabbed a piece of fish with her fork. She faked a laugh. "Wow, I wouldn't think you'd sell much of that here. Really? My grandma has one of those. Uh-huh." Mara smiled as her shoulders relaxed. "Thank you." She hung up and took the bite of fish.

"Good news?" Herman asked.

"That was the owner of Pets N' Cats. Last week two men bought a bag of every brand she had."

* * *

As they left the pet store, Herman said, "This is bad, isn't it?"

"It implies they knew what she was," Mara said. "Which is not good. We're stretched thin, but the agency will try to get more people involved now." Despite what it meant, Mara felt lighter. At least they had a definite answer now.

"You haven't asked me the obvious."

Mara raised her eyebrows at him.

"If I could change and find her." He stared at her and the serious set to his eyes revealed the darkness humor had covered up.

"I wouldn't do that," Mara said. "If you haven't done it already, you must have a reason."

He didn't answer.

Mara ventured, "I do wonder why you choose to live this way. Most heavyweights try to stay away from their human forms."

"When I change, the weight is gone. But it's worse." He swallowed and Mara's gaze was drawn to his hand. The shake had increased. "I am alone. The other whales won't have anything to do with me. At least here, there are people. Even some who care. It's easier if I pick a shape and stay in it."

The memory of Caleb returned to Mara. He couldn't go more than an hour without changing, his other shape tearing through him without warning, but he never stayed long as an elephant. He'd said it was lonely, an unbearable loneliness that no one could fix, not even Mara. He avoided going out, avoided people, but accidents happened. He killed himself a week after two people died. Mara swallowed the old pain and tried not to think about how much damage a whale could do.

Herman entered the inn with Mara but stayed by the front desk, his voice following her as he exclaimed over some change the owner had made.

Mara settled herself on her bed and called her captain. When she'd finished giving her report, he heaved a sigh that made Mara lean away from the phone. Some enthusiasm entered his voice as he asked, "How's the Whale?"

Mara hesitated, at a loss for words that could explain Herman. "Stable," she said simply. "Helpful."

"Impressive," he mused. He said something else but Mara moved the phone from her ear. The murmur of voices outside her room had changed.

"Excuse me," she said, and hung up.

Mara straightened her back as she walked down the hall and allowed herself two deep breaths to bury the jitters in her gut. The voices were too calm. Training kept them that way, and something else. A measured threat.

Two men stood in the entrance with Herman and the owner of the inn. Their posture made Mara want to bite her tongue.

"Herman would never do anything to hurt a child!" the woman objected.

"Ma'am, this doesn't concern you," one agent said while the other asked Herman, "Why did the Youngs meet with you?"

"The girl was interested in learning how to sail. They got my number from someone in town." Something was wrong with Herman's voice.

The suit who had addressed the innkeeper caught sight of Mara. "Nothing to see here, ma'am."

Mara held her badge up. "Really?"

"This is a federal investigation. What is LAPD doing here?"

"Vacation," Mara said.

"Really," the man drawled. "That's quite the coincidence, don't you think? A girl goes missing and you decide this is the spot to relax?"

"Funny world," Mara said. She stopped at Herman's side, and only then realized how uncomfortably close the suit had been. She kept the awkward distance and smiled up at him. He stepped back.

"Where were you Wednesday night?" the other man asked Herman.

"AA," Herman said, and snorted a laugh that was anything but stable. "It's not exactly anonymous here. You shouldn't have too hard a time finding someone who will admit to being there." He hugged his arms to his sides and didn't meet the man's eyes. Not good. He was considerably taller than the agent but his posture determined who controlled the situation. The tremors owning his body had changed to something Mara recognized. The elephant's screams echoed in her ears.

"Unless you're charging him," Mara said, "this man is showing me the town."

"You keep strange company, Detective."

"So that's a no? Nice to meet you." Mara grabbed Herman's elbow and led him from the inn. The Whale leaned into her as they walked. "It's okay," she said. "Hang in there."

"Get me to the water," he said between his teeth.

"The harbor's closed."

"Why do you think I live on a cliff?"

"I'll get a cab," Mara said, knowing it was hopeless the moment she said it. The town was too small.

Herman laughed, a high, broken sound. "You don't want me in a box."

"What was the trigger?" Anger gave the words an accusatory edge, but the hatred was directed at the men who had started this.

"Confrontation," he said. He was panting now. "You can imagine how fun family reunions were."

Mara nearly laughed from the stress of it all. But she felt eyes on her back. A few people approached them, worry written all over their faces, but when Herman cringed into Mara, she rebuffed them with an excuse about bad shrimp.

The walk to his house was the longest of her life. When he had to stop to curl in on himself, he tried to get her to leave. She refused, even as her heart threatened to run from her chest.

When they arrived, Herman went to the edge of the cliff and stood there. Mara stayed by the porch steps, close enough, with her arms crossed. She was trying very hard not to think about how much weight it would take to send the cliff into the ocean, and the house with it.

After a few minutes of tense silence, Herman called, "How the heck did they know I'd met with Katherine?"

"I've been trying to figure that out. Who knew about the meetings?"

"Her parents. If they were involved in this—" Herman bit off the end and ran his hand through his hair. "Shit."

"I'm sorry," Mara said. "You shouldn't have had to go through that."

"No," Herman agreed. He didn't look at her. "I've seen how you watch the water. Heavyweights fear themselves, and lightweights fear everything else. If you had to change, would you?"

"I don't know."

"It's not your fault the feds showed up."

Mara shook her head and stifled a sigh. She shouldn't be here. "I'll go," she said. "I need to think. Try and figure out who set the feds on you."

"I still want to help." He looked back at her this time. "If you need me, don't hesitate."

Mara nodded a lie and left.

She'd reached the town, covered in that strange pastel light of dusk, when her phone rang with her station's number. She bit back a curse and pressed answer. "Yes, sir?"

"What the hell, Kendell?" Overseer Gemma's voice, level, but harsh enough that it was only a matter of time before the volume rose. "Get back home. Immediately."

"Excuse me?"

"When I gave you the Whale's contact information it was not so you could introduce him to the FBI!" Definitely a yell now. "Half the town saw him as a wreck. He was on the verge of changing. That entire town could have died. He could have died. You almost lost us the only Blue Whale in existence!"

The grief of what that loss would mean made Mara swallow, but she bristled at the accusation. "There is someone in this town who knows about the abduction. And they set the feds on Herman because they knew we were asking questions. This was a premeditated kidnapping, and they knew what she was. I can't leave now."

"That's exactly what you'll do. We'll take it from here, Detective." She spoke the title with belittlement. It was clear she believed Mara didn't deserve the rank, and that it had been a mistake to send her here.

"Who told you?" Mara demanded.

"What?"

"Who told you what happened? How did you know about the feds?"

"The Youngs' lawyer. She heard you'd been openly questioning the town with Herman and then the FBI happened. She was concerned about your treatment of this case and how it might affect our people. She rightly assumed Herman was one of ours."

Mara stilled, her stomach turning. "And you confirmed it?"

"What does that matter? You nearly outed—"

Mara hung up and ran back the way she had come. She pulled her gun from her lower back and took the safety off without pausing. The lack of light made her squint and her breath came too loud in her ears, making the bushes on either side of the road hold countless dangers that she couldn't hear.

By the time Mara reached Herman's driveway, a layer of sweat separated her skin from her gun. She calmed her breathing and listened.

Steps in the grass. Hushed voices. She crept up the hill, keeping close to the ground. At the top she peeked out from behind a bush, hardly caring when it poked her cheek.

Two men stalked into Herman's yard. The Whale stood by his door, hands up and chin high. They were too far away for an accurate shot. So was Mara. But if they got any closer to Herman, she wouldn't be able to risk it.

She fired three shots. They hit by the men's feet, causing them to dance backward. One nearly lost his gun. Not professionals. Mara started over the top of the hill and prayed she wouldn't trip.

She shot again before they could compose themselves, a warning only. They threw themselves to the ground, but bullets broke the air, flying by Mara's cheek.

"Run!" she yelled to Herman at the same time wood exploded across his front door. Something brushed her shoulder, like a wet hand. Probably a graze. The pain would come later. She kept running, toward Herman. If she could get between the shooter and him—

Herman's gait was wrong, stilted, and when he jumped, still twenty feet from the cliff edge, for one horrified moment Mara thought he'd been shot.

The Whale tore through his body with a ripping sound like the heavens splitting. His enormous belly brushed the grass but didn't settle. His tail flew over Mara's head and she threw herself to the ground as it met his house with a shattering crash. Mara covered her head, curling herself into the grass, an animal's certainty of death owning her heart. She forced herself up on shaky legs, turning a scramble into a run.

The Whale vanished as abruptly as he had appeared and Herman rolled on the ground. "Mara!" he shouted. It was command and plea. To follow. Without elegance, he threw himself toward the cliff and the Whale appeared again, arching over the ridge but tail smashing into the earth and severely shortening the distance between the house and the sea. Between Mara and the sea.

The ground sagged under her feet, slipping away, and Herman's tail disappeared from sight. She followed it, not only letting herself fall, but jumping into it.

She screamed and the rush of air carried it away. Below her, the Whale hit the water with a splash that touched her as she fell. Her two fears warred with each other, a battle of wills, and the deeper one, the one she'd feared longer, came out on top of death.

Her inner self ripped through her human form, a searing pain that was both freeing and terrifying. Her sight blurred, her hearing turned muddy, but when she hit the water, clarity struck her. The water held peace.

She wiggled out of her over-sized shirt and tasted her own blood in the water. It was barely a scratch.

Herman was a massive shape beside her, a danger only in size. His breath rippled the water around her and her instincts told her to back off. But she swam closer to the eye watching her.

The Whale shrank, as if a vacuum had been placed over his center, sucking him inward. Mara was pulled toward him as the water rushed to fill the empty space. When Herman's pink form swam to the surface, Mara followed at a safe distance and changed.

"A shark?" Herman exclaimed once her head broke the surface. He was treading water with too much effort. He laughed and slipped under before fighting his way back up. "A little shark!" he crowed.

"I'm a shark that's bad at being a shark," Mara said. The words came fast, grateful to be freed. "My human weight transfers to fear in the water. I'm defenseless. My own prey isn't scared of me."

"Curse of being a lightweight." Herman's teeth flashed in the dim light. "If it helps, I'll be scared of you."

"We have to find that girl."

Herman struggled in the water, watching her. He finally said, "Come with me."

Fear weighed Mara down and she spat out the water that slipped into her mouth. "I suppose no one's going to attack me if I'm with a whale."

"No one will approach us." The words were meant to comfort her, but the pain in his voice ruined it. The ocean was a lonely place for a whale that wasn't quite right.

"I'm not very fast," Mara warned as she started placing some distance between herself and the Whale.

"I'll go slow."

* * *

Herman coasted in the water, sometimes pausing for Mara to catch up. Eventually they worked out a speed that didn't leave her behind. After the first mile, Mara realized she'd stopped looking for danger. She listened with ears that hadn't heard in years and reveled in the water going to her lungs. If she were human, she would have laughed.

Beside her, Herman's eye tracked her and his long mouth twitched in a whale's smile. His breathing shook the water and eventually became a calming presence. He would sway away from her, at first a terrifyingly far distance, to breach the surface. Miles passed before he stopped jumping. He drew close to Mara, who was panting as only a shark could pant, and kept quiet. She thought they must be nearing the boat.

He stilled and the Whale was sucked inside again. Mara fought the current and swam to the surface. She floated on her back, breathing hard and watching the stars sparkle in the night sky. Her hair fanned out around her head, brushing her cheeks. She heard Herman cough when he surfaced.

"Are you okay?" she asked, trying to look at him with as little movement as possible.

"Amazing," he said. His grin took up his entire face. "Just winded."

"Yeah," Mara agreed.

Herman pointed to their right. "The boat's there, about five hundred meters. What's the plan?"

"We climb on board, free Katherine, subdue the captors, and take the ship home."

"Oh, okay," he said. "If that's all."

"You can stay in the water," Mara said.

"No." Herman turned and swam human-style in the direction of the boat.

The call from her superior was still strong in her mind as Mara followed Herman. The people who had been assigned to Caleb understood the unspoken plea that accompanied their job. Please keep the elephant alive.

But it hadn't been enough. The love of other Weights, made desperate by what was at stake, could not lift the pain. Another elephant had agreed to spend the necessary time as a human to cross the ocean for him, but even that might not have been enough. In the end, it was Caleb's choice whether he wanted to live with the weight or not. Mara couldn't change that. There were only four elephants left now.

The only Blue Whale in existence.

Her hands touched the wood sides of the boat and she tried to keep her breathing quiet, to no avail. They circled it, and when they found no easy way up, Mara swam away and changed. She charged the boat and jumped, hoping she wouldn't hit the side, especially in front of Herman. She flew over the railing and changed, hitting the deck with a splat that dragged at her skin.

The ship was dark, the captors hopefully asleep. She anchored a rope as best she could with hands that shook, and tossed it to Herman. He pulled himself on board while she tried to calm her exhausted heart. If she couldn't stop shaking, she wouldn't be much use against an attack.

Herman leaned against the railing, his eyes roving over the deck. They passed Mara and returned, widening slightly. He met her eyes and winked. "Hey there."

Mara huffed and pointed toward the cabin. "They should be in there," she whispered. "Let's check below for Katherine."

Herman kept his gaze on the cabin while Mara lifted the creaky trapdoor. She slipped down the ladder and squinted through the dark. Boxes crowded the sides of the ship, leaving little room to move. She risked saying, "Katherine?"

Something shifted to her left. "Who's there?"

Mara crouched before a tiny cage, just big enough to squeeze the girl into. "Hey sweetie," Mara said, smiling her relief. "I'm here with Herman. We're getting you out of here."

The men had secured the cage by placing a heavy box on top of it. Mara lifted it off and while she focused on not falling over, Katherine pushed the lid up.

"You're naked," she whispered.

"I'm like you," Mara said.

"Mara!" Herman hissed down. "They're waking up."

"Don't move," Mara ordered him. She crouched in front of Katherine. "You need to change. Now. Can you do that?"

Katherine nodded and her small human form sucked in on itself, until a seagull stood among a pile of clothing.

"Good girl," Mara said. "When we get to the deck, fly. We'll be right behind you." She picked up the bird and held her in one arm while she climbed the ladder.

Herman was leaning against the cabin door, shoulders straining as the men inside gave muffled shouts. "I may have moved," he said. He lifted a hand in a wave. "Hey, Katherine."

Mara growled under her breath and released the seagull. Katherine gave a hop and took off.

"Don't move!" A man stepped out from the other side of the cabin. Mara felt the pressure of the gun over her heart, far away as it was. To Herman, he said, "Step away from the door."

"Do you want me to not move or move? Because it's a bit—"

"Move! Or I shoot the woman."

Herman stepped away from the door, his gaze on Mara. He smiled, a question in his eyes. Mara tilted her chin up.

"Politicals?" Mara asked the gunman, as his friend stumbled out of the cabin.

The man snorted. "Something this amazing? I'm not wasting my intel on those zealots. Two of you will fetch a better price than one."

"I think," Herman said, "you'll find us a bit more troublesome than one small bird."

The gun shifted to Herman. "And what are you?"

The last eyes the man ever saw were the Whale's. "I'm the leper of the sea."

He changed, a sudden disappearance of a man and the overwhelming presence of a Blue Whale. His side smacked Mara and she flew off the ship and into the water. She changed with the crash of the ship breaking, amplifying the tearing sensation she always experienced.

Herman seemed to enjoy the destruction part a bit too much, and as he thrashed on top of what remained of the boat, Mara made a note to ask him exactly how much he loved *Moby Dick*.

When she tasted blood in the water, they started their return. A seagull followed them, gliding on the air to keep with their slow pace. The sun was breaking over the horizon by the time they dragged themselves onto the beach, far from the cameras at the docks.

Mara carried the seagull up the beach with Herman trailing her. She stopped at a tent near the tree-line.

"Police," she croaked. "Get out."

The tent jerked and a man unzipped the opening enough to stick his head out. "Oh, hi, Herman," he said. His eyes went over Herman, then Mara. They jerked away at her expression and he gave Herman a wink. "Nice."

"Give me your fucking phone," Mara said.

He handed it to her and she walked away, ignoring what Herman might be saying. She called her captain.

"I have Katherine. You'd better come up with a story fast."

* * *

Mara sat on what remained of Herman's porch, sipping lemonade and watching the considerably closer ocean. The sun warmed her puffy hair all the way to the roots and made her sigh with contentment. "So what's it like being the town hero?" Mara asked.

"Bit traumatizing, to be honest. It's not every day a guy goes swimming with his new cop friend and discovers a missing child and a much abused boat. Hit a rock, so I hear."

"The FBI bought it. The debris had moved inland enough for it to be believable. At least, more so than the truth. I feel bad for Shelly though."

"Don't. She met a nice FBI chick yesterday. She doesn't know that the lawyer was interested in me, and how I might benefit her bank account."

"We obviously need to vet our human lawyers better. Try some questions like, 'How do you feel about kidnapping?'" Mara laughed at her own joke and found she was in no hurry to stop. Katherine's kidnappers were presumed lost at sea, and Mara found she couldn't feel bad about that. The lawyer had given up the names of the men she hired to capture Herman, and they had been taken into Weight custody. He was safe. Herman's house could even pass for the unfortunate victim of a cliff collapse, if no one looked too closely. Katherine was unharmed, and it looked like Mara would get to visit her new lightweight friend soon. All was well.

"Will you be going back soon?" His voice was too casual.

She looked at Herman but he kept watching the water. His shakes weren't so bad now. "I thought I might take some vacation time, actually," she said. His eyes flashed to her. She took another sip of lemonade. "It's become apparent to me I'm one of the worst swimmers alive. Thought you might help me change that."

Herman grinned and failed to quiet it. He looked away and leaned back into his chair. "I'll check my calendar."

ANZU, DUBA, BEAST
FAITH HUNTER

"We will hunt. Ready yourself. We leave after dusk. Gee."

I hated orders. But I owed Girrard DiMercy—the vampires' Mercy Blade—a hunt, which he had won from me in return for information. Gee had a good memory, but his timing sucked.

I flicked the note against the fingers of my other hand, thinking. With vamps and their playthings, you have to be one step ahead, and thinking things through had proved better than attacking first and asking questions later.

Gee expected me to shift into something like a hawk or an owl and hunt at his side, while he shifted into the thing he really was under layers of glamour. If that happened, he'd set all the parameters and I'd be little dog to his big dog—earth bird to his Anzu. So far as I knew, the feathered Anzu were not native to earth, and had once been worshipped as storm gods. Big honking storm gods with claws, wings, a raptor's beak, and attitude.

"Does Leo know about this invitation?" I asked, crumpling the note. Leo was the fanghead-vampire Master of the City of New Orleans and my boss. Gee's boss too, in a way.

The blood-servant-messenger's face broke into a smile that said I had asked a question he could answer. "Yes, ma'am. He knows. My master said, 'May your hunt be bloody. May you rend and eat the flesh of your prey.'"

"Well crap." I had *plans*. I was spending a four-day weekend with my sorta-boyfriend, eating and sleeping and everything my heart and body desired, in bed. *Plans*. And the following Tuesday, I was flying to Asheville, North Carolina, to spend a few days with my BFF Molly, to see the ultrasound of her baby, the one where the doc tells if it's a boy or a girl. And then I was gonna pick up my Harley, Bitsa, from the repair shop in

Charlotte. Finally. *Big plans.* Leo liked jerking my chain, and he would feel just peachy messing with my life.

But...it was only Wednesday. The hunt we bargained for was for twenty-four hours. I should be back by Thursday night. Friday morning at the latest. I'd still have a few days to myself and my honeybunch. Plus, Gee didn't know that I had aces up my sleeve. Well, not exactly aces. More like Jokers, both of them wild, cards that didn't belong in the deck of cards the Mercy Blade expected to deal. "Hmmm," I said.

The helpful human said, "Mr. DiMercy and the Master of the City have requested the courtesy of a reply."

"Did they, now. Well, tell them I said this." I shut the door in the servant's face. Turned the lock. Pulled my official cell phone, the Kevlar-cased one that allowed the Master of the City to track me, listen in on me, and read all my texts. It was daytime and he was probably in bed, but no way could I just take this. Vamps had a thing for pecking order. I couldn't refuse the invitation, but I was neither blood in Leo's fangs nor at the bottom of the suckhead hierarchy. I was the Enforcer to the MOC. This required more finesse than my usual hammer-and-machete-style of retort.

I scrolled for Leo's number. It was listed under Chief Fanghead.

As a skinwalker—a supernatural being who can shape-shift into animals, provided I have enough genetic material to work with—I've actually flown, and not just in planes. But Gee might not know that. A familiarity with flight was my first wild Joker.

Deep in the darks of my mind, my Beast huffed. *Eat order from Gee,* she thought at me. Beast didn't like it when I took the form of an animal other than hers—the puma concolor—the mountain lion. She especially didn't like flying.

We made a promise, I thought back at her. I wandered to my room as I punched Leo's number.

Promises are stupid human things. We are Beast. Eat note.

Beast is opinionated, with a mind and feelings of her own. I had pulled her soul into my body in an act of accidental black magic when I was five years old, while fighting for my life. That was back in the eighteen hundreds. Skinwalkers, even the two-souled, can live a long time.

The cell trilled the first ring. Thinking that I would balk at the order, Leo would keep me waiting.

My second wild Joker was a blue feather. Not so long ago, I came upon the glamoured body of a slain Anzu. She had looked perfectly human, albeit dead, except for the bright blue feathers on the floor around her body, downy and fluffy, catching the air currents and waving at me as if alive.

I hadn't intended to take a feather. I had forgotten I had stolen one. I'm guessing that Beast did it while I wasn't looking, a theft she had accomplished using my hands while my mind was occupied with more important things, which is scary in all sorts of ways. I hadn't discovered the feather until much later, in my collection of magical trinkets, but had never used it because taking the form of a sentient being was one of the darkest kinds of evil. Black magic. Unless I had permission. "Jane," Leo answered my call. "You have refused Girrard's invitation."

"Nope. But I need to talk to Sabina." Sabina was the woo-woo priestess of the Mithran-Vamps and she lived in the vampire cemetery. I'd need permission to enter.

There was a long pause, and I was sure Leo's brain was clicking through all the possibilities of why I'd need to talk to the eldest of the local Mithrans. "One moment."

A much longer pause later, I heard the sounds of movement and the shush of fabrics and soft-voiced instructions. The ambient noise changed and I knew I was being put on speakerphone, which made no sense. Until a voice spoke. "I am here," Sabina said.

I blinked and opened my mouth. Closed it. This saved me hours of afternoon traveling across the Mississippi and back. But I had to do this right. I drew on the scraps of vamp etiquette I had learned in my time as Leo's Enforcer and said, "Sabina Delgado y Aguilera, outclan priestess of the Mithrans, keeper of the sacred grounds, keeper of the Blood Cross, arbiter of disputes, I have a question and...uh...and I wish you to determine if the path I wish to take is one of sin."

"If I say it is sin, will you take another path, my child?"

"Yes."

"Speak."

I took a deep breath. "I want to know if it's black magic for a skinwalker to shift into the same kind of creature as Gee."

The silence on the other end of the connection was total. And then, in the background, Leo laughed. It was one of those vampire laughs, the kind that writers and producers and other creators of fiction got right. Seductive, warm, enticing, like heated silk sliding across my skin. A laugh that reminds you vamps are predators, built to seduce and charm before they kill. The liquid notes cut off in mid-peal, interrupted by a gasp of surprise or pain.

"You wish to know if this will turn you to the path of *u'tlun'ta,*" Sabina said, "the demon your kind becomes when they eat of sentient flesh."

Chills raced over me. *U'tlun'ta* was what my kind became when we got old and went insane and started eating people. "Pretty much, yes."

"Is the Anzu alive, and will you eat her flesh?"

"No!" I looked at the blank screen in revulsion, put the cell back to my ear, and said, "No. She's dead and I didn't kill her."

"What do you use for the snake that resides in the heart of all beasts?"

The words Sabina used froze me for several heartbeats. They were skinwalker words, for a skinwalker concept. "A feather," I whispered.

"With this action, you walk the sharp edge of a blade between light and dark. You do not cross that edge into darkness, but if you slip, you may bleed."

"I'll try not to slip."

The call went dead. I dropped to my bed. I had no idea if I'd be able to shift into an Anzu. No idea if there was enough genetic material in the core of the feather to allow me to shift. No idea if Gee would kill me at first sight. Or, for that matter, how much an Anzu weighed. Even though I'm a magical creature, I am still bound by the Law of Conservation of Mass/Energy. Taking on extra mass or leaving part of myself behind is dangerous. Flying by the seat of my pants never got any easier. No winged pun intended.

Stepping around piles of clothes and boots, junk mail, and a small stack of the *Times Picayune*, I picked up my gobag and shook the grindylow out of the folds. The neon-green, kitten-sized thing spit at me and showed me her steel claws. "Stop that," I scolded. She wrinkled her nose at me and leaped to my shoulder. Grindys kill were-creatures. It's their mission. This one liked nesting in my clothes. Absently, I patted her, and she cooed at me, nuzzling under my ear.

I packed a special gobag with a change of clothes, lightweight shoes, and my cell phone. I laid out the weapons candidates and then weeded them down, ending with a nine millimeter, extra mags, six stakes: three ash-wood, three sterling. And one vamp-killer—a steel-edged, long-bladed, silver-plated knife created especially for beheading vampires.

It's what I did, or had done, prior to taking the gig as Leo's Enforcer. I was a rogue-vamp hunter. And no way was I leaving home without the tools of my trade.

Packed, I left my room and skidded to a stop. My business partners were standing in the foyer just in front of my bedroom door. Alex Younger had a mulish set to his jaw, though at nineteen, he pretty much wore that expression all the time. Eli Younger, the elder Younger, stood with arms crossed, a speculative gleam in his eyes. I handed him the note.

He un-clumped it, read the three sentences, and some infinitesimal hint of tension in his face relaxed. "Payback's a bitch," he said, giving the note back. And I wasn't sure who was getting paid back, me for making a bargain, or Gee for enforcing it. "I guess you won't be needing us?"

I shouldered my gobag. "I have no idea where we'll fly for this hunt, but Gee said something about elk or moose when this first came up, so I'm guessing somewhere far north."

Elk? Moose? Beast perked up. *Moooses and elks are bigger than cows?*

Pretty much, I thought back at her.

Do not eat note.

I chuckled and passed the grindy to Alex. "Start your vacation early. Go play. Take in a movie, go visit Sylvia, start a new video game. Whatever. I'm sure I'll be somewhere way off, where there aren't many people. And then I have plans."

"*Fly for this hunt?*" Eli quoted me.

"Yeah," I said, going for casual. "Thought I'd try to shift into an Anzu."

Things took place behind Eli's eyes, things too fast to catch, but the tension was back, hiding beneath the skin of his face. "Watch yourself," he said, heading up the stairs to pack a bag. "It's hunting season in some northern states and it would ruin my weekend if you got shot out of the sky. I'd have to go find your body. Track down and kill whoever shot you. Spend the rest of my life in jail. Totally not in my long-term plans."

"What my bro said." Alex tossed me a box wrapped in brown paper and tied with twine. I caught it as he continued, "But I'll be here, so keep your official cell on, and wear that." He pointed at the box. "I can track you anytime you're within range of a tower or within range of a satellite, which should be nearly universal coverage these days. If you stay too long in one place, I'll assume you're in trouble and send Captain America." He thumbed at his brother.

* * *

Sunset had freshly bruised the skies. I was in the backyard, holding the Anzu feather, sitting on chilled boulders, naked except for my gobag (full of clothes, weapons, and equipment) and the necklaces around my neck. My gold nugget necklace and the new tracking necklace—looking like gold, but much more useful—and gobag were extra loose. I took several slow breaths. Concentrated on my heartbeat. Let my shoulders droop. The first stars came out as the sky darkened. I dropped into a meditative state, reached down into the tip of the blue feather, into the snake that lives at the center of all creatures: the double helix of DNA, as understood by the Cherokee of my own time. My skinwalker magics rose, vibrant, luminous, the silver and gray of the Gray Between. I dropped deeper, into the dried flesh at the base of the feather.

Anzu genetic structure unfolded before me.

The DNA wasn't a double helix, common to Earth creatures. It was a tangled mass of strands, spun in circles, glowing like glass, pale blue and green light. One ovoid spot in the slowly spinning circle was denser and darker. It opened its eyes and looked at me. Unfolded slowly. The genetic structure was a snake, holding its own tail in its mouth. *Ouroboros*, the name came to me. The ouroboros focused on me, in the Gray Between, a place where energy and mass are one.

The snake opened its mouth. Let go of its tail. And struck. Before I could jerk away, snake fangs pierced me. Pain shot through me as if I had been hit with a Taser. I screamed. Bones bent. Darkness took me, blazing and icy.

* * *

I woke. The night was cool, humid, strangely scented. Chemical stinks of exhaust, gasoline, diesel fuel, coffee, food, and hot grease were familiar, but sights and sounds were different. The world was orange and silver, my vision so intense it was like looking through a scope, each line of light and shadow vibrant and intense. Something moved. My eyes found it instantly. Even in the dark, I could see individual hairs on a small mouse, hunting along the brick wall, hear its nails click on the concrete.

The music from a club several streets over was a booming din that hurt my ears. The house band's off-key rendition of One Way Out would have made the Allman Brothers cringe. A motorcycle engine in the distance was cutting out. Cars motored through the French Quarter. A jet overhead slowed, descending for landing.

I lifted my arms and my right fingers brushed the wall nearest, ten feet away. I jerked back, rolled to my feet, and looked around, my head swiveling and turning; I had shifted shape. A warbling sigh sounded in my throat as I took myself in.

I was blue and scarlet and some sort of glowing color that might only be seen in ultraviolet. The glowing feathers were up under my wings and on my belly. A darker version overlay the tips of flight fathers and tail feathers, glowing with black-light intensity to my bird eyes. My feet were long, with clawed toes, ten inches from back claw to longest toe claw, with glowing orange skin over knobby joints. My beak was pointed and curved, a vicious hook on the end. It matched my orange legs. I spread my wings again, carefully, inspecting sapphire flight feathers, with a band of scarlet near my shoulder and another on the back of my neck—which I could see with the head-swiveling thing I could do. I had a twenty-foot wingspan. I shivered, settling my feathers, and I could feel each one as it found its place. I was freaking gorgeous. I also wasn't hungry, which was a change from all my other shape-shifts. Usually I had to fuel my shifts with prodigious amounts of food, but something about the soft-lit magic trembling along my wings suggested that I had pulled the energy from elsewhere.

Beast can kill many mooses with claws and strong beak, she thought.

My hearing grew clearer, sharper. People were talking *everywhere*. A whiteout of noise.

In the house, I heard Eli speak, his voice soft and dangerous. "Bro." My head tilted that way. "You go out there and I'll deck you."

"But it's been an hour. Aren't you *worried* about her?"

"No." But there was the sound of a lie in the single word. *Aw*. Eli was concerned about me. I should razz him for it.

But...I was shaped wrong to go inside. I was shaped wrong to open a door. I imagined raising my huge foot and trying to grip the doorknob. I laughed at the vision, the sound warbling, unexpectedly loud. The back door opened on the last note. "Jane?"

I froze. But...parrots could talk. I warbled again, trying to say hello. It came out a rippling trill. As Eli and the Kid raced out, I tried again, and this time, there were words mixed into the warble. "Thish ish *warble warble* intersh-ting."

"Janie?" Alex asked.

"Babe?" Eli asked. And he started laughing.

I lifted a clawed foot and said, very distinctly, if slowly, "Crack your skull like walnut."

Eli shut up, but there was still laughter on his face. The Kid went back inside where I could hear him laughing his head off saying, "Big Bird. Big blue bird. Holy shit." Laughing so hard he couldn't breathe.

I narrowed my eyes at Eli.

"Babe. I know you could crack my skull like a nut. But you're also funny looking."

I swiped at him with my wing, which banged into the porch support with a thump that freaking hurt. I warbled a word that I never would have spoken in English. Which made Eli laugh harder. Mid-laugh he drew a weapon and injected a round into the chamber. Aimed at me. I ducked. But he didn't fire.

Air whooshed down. Nearly knocked me off my perch on the cracked boulders. A foreign warble, an interrogative, carried on the air as I regained my balance. I turned to see an Anzu, smaller than my hundred forty-five pounds but a far brighter blue, alight on the brick wall surrounding the backyard.

He gleamed in my bird vision, ultraviolet blues and purples and a shocking ruby at shoulders and throat. He smelled like feathers, heat, and the down we line our nests with. He settled his feathers and cooed.

"Gee?" I managed.

"Jane? How have you...?" his words wisped, warbling but crisp and clear.

"Ummm. I had a feather." The consonants sounded like sharp *tocks*, but it was understandable. Sorta.

"You took a feather from Urggggllllaaammmaaah's body." He tilted his head. "Did you ask her consent?"

"She was kinda dead. So I asked Sabina. She said it was okay."

"Did she?" Gee considered that. "This is acceptable to me. Come. We must hurry or our prey will escape us."

I cocked my head at my partner. "I'll call when I'm back." He nodded. I hunched down and leaped, hopping to the top of the brick fence surrounding the backyard. It was easier than I had expected.

"Tis only the launch that is difficult." Gee said, trilling what might have been laughter, expecting me to face-plant. He threw himself into the air.

I know the glory of soaring, wingtips splayed, tail feathers twisting in subtle harmony with updrafts. And how to land, wings tilting just so, feathering down into a controlled fall with flight-feather positional changes and wing angle alterations, the variation slowing the descent, carrying me to a perch.

I gathered myself and dropped down until my knobby toes touched my breastbone, a position I might achieve in human form—if I broke my legs first. I leaped and threw out my arms. *Wings*. Air caught beneath me and I beat down. The long wingtips hit the earth and brushed brick before I managed a second stroke. And then I was lifting, wind in my face, air heavy, full of moisture. I tucked my feet, caught a rising thermal over the street, hot asphalt stink in my lungs. Beat downward again and again.

Below me, New Orleans glittered like diamonds, the Mississippi a black snake slithering through. I caught a second thermal and soared upward, Gee just ahead. I adjusted my flight position to his left, which decreased my wind resistance, things I knew by instinct and genetics. We rose higher, leaving the earth behind. Intermixed below us I could see circles and triangles in all the colors of the rainbow and long lines of something blue below the surface.

In this form, I could see magic far better than I could in human or Beast-form. The magic of full circles and smaller workings. And the long blue lines beneath the surface were...ley lines. I had never seen them like this before. And they were so beautiful they made my soul ache.

Anzu is good, Beast thought at me, sniffing the air. *Like Anzu.*

I cooed back at her.

I had no idea where we were going and I didn't care as my wings carried me, untiring, across the darkness of the world. Hours passed.

* * *

After midnight, Gee descended toward the faint lights of a small township. In the distance, ley lines glowed bright. They seemed like a nexus of some sort, a snarled clump of earth magics. I knew next to nothing about ley lines but they looked dangerous. Overloaded. As we spiraled down, they fell from view and I smelled freshwater lakes and streams, the richness of untouched earth and uncut forests, stone, crude oil, and much more faintly, the stink of old blood.

The scent grew stronger. A lot of old blood. And the stink of were, species unknown. It was a type I had never scented before. Not wolf, not big-cat, something more musky, though the scent was overpowered, fading even as we flew by.

Gee circled and dove, alighting on the edge of a house roof. I landed atop an abandoned car. The huge ranch house was in a clearing, at the end of a long empty road, the sharp piney scent of trees all around, trying to overcome the stink of vampire and human blood. The battle was at least a month old, the season having frozen, melted, and washed most of it away. What was left was the stench of fury, desperation, fear, and death.

I remembered Leo's words, quoted by the blood-servant who had delivered my invitation. "May your hunt be bloody. May you rend and eat the flesh of your prey."

Leo had known what Gee was taking me to hunt. "Well, crap," I said.

Gee trilled with mocking laughter.

Beast, who had been remarkably silent, growled to me, *Jane should have eaten note.*

I squatted down on the hood, chest to toes, and fluffed my feathers against the cold, trying to piece together the battle. My Anzu night vision picked out the entire house as if it was day, not darkest night, body fluids glowing as if they were under a black light.

The attackers came in through the front door, through the front windows, through the garage doors at the back, like a home invasion on steroids. The damage looked as if battering-rams had been used, huge holes punched right through the thin wood of the garage door, the front door knocked off its hinges, the frame shattered. I leaped to the front door and leaned inside.

The fight had been bloody, but the invaders hadn't used guns. All the gunfire destruction was from the back wall and hallway, toward the entrances and windows. At least five vamps and ten humans had died in the parts of the house I could see. And so far as my senses could tell me, not one of the attackers had been injured. I still couldn't identify the species of were, their scent hidden beneath the grizzly stinks of death.

There were no bodies. They had been carried off and buried or burned. But the crime scene hadn't been worked up. There was no crime scene tape, no sharp smell of fingerprint powder, no carpet taken up for analysis. The house hadn't been cleaned. Something was really wrong here.

* * *

"You coulda warned me to bring a coat," I grumbled as we trudged down an unpaved road, pea-gravel crunching beneath my thin-soled shoes. Suddenly, just bam, the road became paved, for no reason, but it was easier to walk, so I wasn't griping. I crossed my arms over my chest and hugged myself for warmth. Gee seemed unaffected by the cold, but glamour and shape-shifting were very different things. I was cold and starving. He wasn't. "Where are we? It's still fall and there's freaking snow on the ground."

Gee drawled, "We have alighted in Foleyet, little goddess, a tiny hamlet in Ontario, Canada."

"I'm not a goddess," I said by rote. I checked my cell. Nothing. Nada. No bars. *Ducky. Just freaking ducky.*

Gee turned off the road and around an abandoned building, the windows boarded over. The back door opened before us, light pouring into the night. The herbal stink of vamp and the rancid smell of old blood boiled out. I dropped my arms, leaped back a dozen feet. When I landed, I was holding a silver stake and a vamp-killer. Gee laughed, sly, mocking.

Holding the door was a vamp, a tribal woman, black-haired, black-eyed, tall and lean, similar to my own six feet of height and build, but she was utterly gorgeous. "It's our honor to receive the Enforcer of the Master of the City of New Orleans," the vamp said. "Why do you draw weapons?"

I slammed my weapons back into the sheaths. "Because I wasn't informed I would be meeting with Mithrans," I said, catching up with Gee. "Your species likes to play games." And I stuck out my foot, neatly tripping Gee over his own feet and mine, feeling better when Gee landed face first in the hard dirt and dusting of snow. "His does too. My apologies," I said to her. I drew on my training and said, "Additional apologies for my scent. It's considered a provocation by many Mithrans and that's unintentional." I took the two stairs and stopped in the doorway.

The woman leaned out and sniffed delicately before backing inside, her hands indicating welcome. "Namida Blackburn, of Clan Blackburn. We'd been told you smelled of predator, but all I detect is wind and storm clouds."

Interesting. "No insult was intended with the weapons," I said. I turned around and shut the door in Gee's face. My big-cat liked to play games too. Grinning, I faced Namida. "How may the Enforcer of the MOC of New Orleans assist you?"

* * *

The problem was simple, and not. Something were-tainted had attacked the local vamps, every full moon night for the last three months. In multiple attacks, three blood-families, vamps and their humans, had been decimated in remote areas, killed, eaten. The MOC of New York had declined to assist. The MOC of Toronto had declined to assist. The MsOCs of Chicago, Montreal, and Minneapolis had declined. In desperation, the local vamps had contracted (for an outrageous sum) the werewolf clan of Wisconsin. The wolves had flown in, taken one sniff, returned the down payment, and flown out. The Montana wolf clan hadn't returned calls. The local law and the Canadian Mounted Police had declined to assist, calling it a suckhead problem.

I could see why. The photos of what, in my part of the world, would have been crime scenes were horrible, and I had seen some pretty horrible stuff in my time. "I'm not familiar with many were-creatures. What do you speculate?"

"If it was a natural creature then I'd say a small, deformed brown bear." She shuffled the photos and showed me a clear print, one in a pool of dried blood. "Eh. The claws are too long and wide but the paw shape is bear. They grow to a thousand pounds. This one's four hundred?" she guessed.

I frowned and pulled the borrowed flannel shirt and down vest tighter across me, swirling the caramel-apple-flavored moonshine she had poured for me. Moonshine was the drink of choice here, not the New Orleans' tea or coffee. "It smelled like were," I murmured, "but even at four hundred pounds, the Mass to Energy Ratio is off for the average human-to-were conversion." And then things came together: the magical fuel for the shift to Anzu, the timing of this hunt. The sight of the twisted ley lines we had seen in the air. Magic here was messed up. So were physics. So were the weres. "Well dang," I muttered.

"What?" she asked.

I waved it away. "Nothing. Leo wanted it taken care of, so I'll take care of it," I said, sipping the moonshine and finishing off the pile of smoked elk meat and fresh bread. It had assuaged the hunger from my shift. Anzu magic only worked to fuel the shift one way, and I had eaten enough for four humans, but Namida didn't begrudge my caloric needs. "I'm on salary. What does Leo get out of this deal?"

"We align with him." The words were spare, without emotion.

"Uh huh." Namida and Leo had negotiated under the vamp system of parley, kinda like a peace treaty with the white man, with just about that much fairness. I'm Cherokee, so I know how "fair" works. "Fine. I'll need stuff, to include clothes, weapons, food, maps, and something that carries the weres' scent. Leo will reimburse you for my supplies."

Namida's eyebrows went up in amused surprise.

I canted my head, wearing a half-smile. "He sent me in return for your loyalty. I say he pays for expenses. In the long-run, you might have gotten the worst part of the bargain. Of course if I get killed on this gig, then I got the worst part." I checked my cell phone which displayed local time, so I'd acquired a signal at some point. I still had hours before dawn. If I was lucky, I'd find the weres' hidey hole before morning, shift, and come back in my human-form and shut them down. Nights were long this time of year.

"Thanks for the meal." I handed her my partial list of weapons, and her eyebrows went up again. Yeah. It was a lot. But if I could hit the were-creatures with fragmentation grenades, or their hidey-hole with the C4, I'd injure them enough to take them down, no matter how big they were. And I wasn't too particular about bringing in magical killers of humans alive and uninjured.

"Gee, you can come in," I said, without raising my voice.

The back door opened and Gee DiMercy minced in. He looked like a twenty-one year old Mediterranean man, delicate and pretty in the shadows, until he got a good look at our hostess and he suddenly morphed into something older and harder. The shift looked like a trick of the light, but I knew better. Light didn't make you suddenly six inches taller and give you a three-day beard. Gee was now a black-haired, blue-eyed warrior, tough and elegant all at once, the kind of man who can track, shoot, and dress an elk without breaking a sweat, and dance a gavotte at a black-tie soiree in the evening.

"Madam," he said, taking her hand and bending over it in European old-world charm. "I am Girrard DiMercy. You are Namida? You are as beautiful as your name. Star Dancer, yes?"

The vampire tilted her head, amusement sparkling in her black eyes, with a hint of interest. "You speak Ojibwe?"

"Sadly, no. But I knew a Chippewa woman by that name, many seasons past. She was lovely, but never so lovely as you."

Namida laughed and looked at me. "I see why you tripped him." She slid her hand from Gee's. "Kill the things that are killing my people and you have my permission to court me, little *misericord*. Until then, you two need to get cracking, eh?" Namida went to the far corner of the abandoned room and brought back a plastic baggie. The closer she got to us the worse the stink. She held it out. "One of my people managed to hurt the attackers. These are three samples of blood that isn't human or Mithran. Good luck." With that, she walked past us and out the back. She paused there, one hand on the door, and said to us, "I'll have all this stuff," she waved my list in the air, "by dawn." She closed the door behind her.

Gee stared after her, a hand on his chest and murmured, "I am in love."

"Uh huh." I pushed him to the door. Outside, Namida was gone, the night even colder. I opened the baggie and stuck it beneath his nose. Gee nearly threw up, but now we both had the scent. I placed the baggie beneath a rock on the top step. Between retches, he managed to say, "Duba. Kerit."

Using a cell phone provided by Namida, I wiki'd it and discovered that the Duba kerit was a cryptid, a creature never proved to be alive, also called Ngoloko, Nandi, Chimosit, and other less pronounceable names. It was a half-bear, half-hyena, and it was carnivorous, vicious, and nearly impossible to kill, except with silver. It also ate the brains of its victims—so, zombie were-bear-hyenas. Bears were solitary except for mothers and cubs, and hyenas lived in groups, making our prey an improbable were-hybrid. One that stank and scared the crap out of Gee. *Just ducky*. But we had its scent. Anzu had a great sense of smell and were able to follow a scent over very, very, *very* long distances. We walked out of town and I made Gee turn his back so I could strip, repack my gobag, and shift again. Back on the wing, we soared over Foleyet in widening circles. A snow storm blew in, ice stinging my eyes. I discovered that I had nictitating membranes and the discomfort eased.

Within an hour, a hundred miles from Foyelet, we caught the scent of the were-Duba. Heard screaming. Gunshots—two shotgun blasts.

I tilted my head down and folded my wings.

"Jane! No!" Gee shrilled.

I dove at the surface. The piercing wind whistled sharp. Lights below were blurred by snow and driving wind. A dozen rounds sounded from semi-automatic handguns. I smelled the stench of blood, human and Duba. The smell of wood-smoke.

The screams cut off.

A large log-cabin came into view, metal roof, smoking fireplaces, backyard fenced with tall planks. Cars inside the yard. Children's toys. A green and blue swing set.

I landed hard. The gobag slammed forward. My body rocked with momentum, wings slashing out to catch my fall. My wing hit some*thing*. *Duba*. It was holding a human head in its claws. It dropped the head and charged.

In the moment of attack, everything slowed, a thick, gluey bending of time. The falling snowflakes sluggish. The spin of the head the Duba had been chewing, its long, blond, bloody hair in a whirl, bearded face with two inch fangs. True-dead. My own body still tilting. My chest hitting the ground. The thing in mid-leap, hyena jaw and ears, bear nose and shoulders, hyena forelegs and bear back, paws a mix of the two. Bloody snout. Black-spotted tongue. Huge.

Scent and sight of a child in the broken window, her face filled with fear and fury. Smoking gun her hands. The stink of silvershot in the were-blood.

The Duba's mouth opened, roaring. It leaped toward me.

I'd have died. But Gee hit the earth running, in human form, swords drawn. He attacked. Time crashed back over me. A tsunami of sound. The swords of the Mercy Blade whirled into the arcane forms of the Spanish Circle—*La Destreza*. The attacking Duba flipped to the side in mid-leap and landed near the Anzu. Already bleeding. The swords were a cage of death that cut and cut and cut. The Duba bled, the silvered blades like acid in the wounds. The stink of silver and Duba blood filled the small area. The Duba screamed in fury.

Other Duba raced from the house into the black night, carrying various body parts. *Dinner*. One turned and looked back at us, roared. The reverberation beat on my ears like a bass drum.

I caught my balance and screamed an Anzu challenge.

Stupid. Stupid, stupid, stupid. Like I could fight in this form.

The Duba who had screamed raced toward me. I folded my wings and slid between two of the parked cars. And thought about my human form. So very different from the form of the Anzu, so banal and ordinary and...*Prey,* Beast thought at me. She took over the shift and forced me away, a clawed paw on my mind.

Bones shifted and broke and slid and cracked into place. Muscle reformed. Feathers became pelt. Beast screamed our challenge.

Leaped to the top of nearest car, long tail spinning for balance. Saw Duba attack Gee from behind. His head in her claws. She was mammal, and carried milk for young in long teats. The male Gee had fought was dead at her feet. *Mate. Duba female killing Gee.*

Leaped again, rotating body and tail. Stretching out front claws. Landed on top of female Duba. Bit her head. Blood was hot and stinky. Like meat of old possum on hot road, long dead. Killing teeth scraped skull, holding. Reached around and sank claws into Duba throat. Ripped with claws, tearing and shredding flesh of throat. Blood flew. Duba let go of Gee. Mercy Blade fell. Bloody heap of flesh.

You can kill the Duba or help Gee, Jane thought at me. *Not both.*

Female Duba shook self like dog in water and raced for broken wood of hole in fence, black night beyond. Beast sank claws in. Duba leaped. Jagged spines of bloody wood bit into Beast flesh at shoulders and back. *Should let go.* But twisted forelegs in moves had seen Gee's sword make, claws biting deep.

Duba fell. Beast tore into throat, savaging flesh. Tore off Duba head. Spine cracking. Carried it to lighted side of fence. Raced to Gee. Dropped head. Gee blood everywhere. Gee could not heal self of injury. Needed Jane. Needed hands and—

"I got this."

Whirled. Paws and claws out, head down. Snarled. Saw little girl who stood at window. Little girl holding gun and rags and...with fangs. *Is not child.* Was small vampire female.

"Don't make me shoot you, eh?" She held up gun. Pointed at Beast. Beast snarled. Looked to Gee. Growled. "Go change shape," she ordered. "I talked to Namida Blackburn, so I'm unimpressed with the display of teeth. Go." She shooed with hands as if to a send a kit out to play in grass. Beast snarled again and walked back to cars. *Changed.*

* * *

I was shaking badly, hunger pulling up through my body. It felt as if someone had reached through me, grabbed the soles of my feet, and pulled me inside out. But eating would have to wait. There were injured here, piled among the dead. And not enough saving hands. Using supplies given to me by the small vamp, working with those less injured, I bandaged and applied pressure, squeezed bags of fluid, forcing saline into the living, trying to stabilize blood pressure. It had been a long time since my emergency medicine class and my skills were rusty. But the humans here were skilled, and together we kept the less horribly wounded alive until a vampire could feed them, or heal the wounded with their blood or saliva. It was messy.

Dawn came before we could finish and I helped the vamps, their humans, and a badly wounded Gee into the narrow stair leading to the lair beneath the cabin. They would spend the day drinking from one another to heal. Seeing a vamp's lair was a rarity, usually a sign of great trust, but this time it fell under the category of emergency. I was alone when I closed the hatch beneath the kitchen table and heard the bolts ram home.

"Just me and the bodies," I said. Which was bad. Vampires who couldn't be saved had to be killed true-dead or risk rising as revenants—mindless eating machines akin to Hollywood's worst Zombies. That meant they had to be beheaded, thankfully not a job I had signed up for. I called Namida. She was old and powerful enough to be able to answer the phone after dawn, tell me where I was (at the Johnson Clan, which gave me nothing but a name, though every little bit helped.) She promised human assistance and cleanup via helicopter, which was pretty cool.

There were four tiny silver linings to the night: no one had died in the kitchen, the kitchen was fully stocked with meats of all kinds, the stove was hot, and so was the shower water.

* * *

I was gone by the time the helo showed up. I saw it through the low-lying clouds as I circled the Johnson Clan holdings and found the scent I was chasing. The Duba. I beat my wings and followed the stink. I found their den a hundred miles or so from Foleyet. It wasn't far as the Anzu flew, but the den was underground. According to the Internet there were no mines in the area, but the opening into the low hillside looked like an old mine, ancient timbers shoring up the entrance, iron rails leading in, the area denuded of trees, spotted with rusted vehicles, buildings in disrepair. The site, whatever it was, had been empty for a long time. I circled, looking for two things—a back entrance and signs of magic. I spotted them both instantly. There were three back entrances, all stinking of Duba and death and broken magic. The mine centered on the crisscrossed ley lines, the jumbled, twisted energies I had seen earlier. It was a place of intense earth magics, where normal—assuming there was a normal—were-creatures had been altered, possibly on the cellular level, by the concentrated, warped energies. *Bad place,* Beast thought at me. *Do not go in.*

Good advice, I thought back. The last time I went into a mine I nearly died. That wasn't happening again, especially into a mine flooded with sick magic.

Nothing about this hunt was proving easy. I flew back to the Johnson Clan cabin, shifted, dressed, and checked my cell. I had a signal and placed a call to Alex Younger back home, set the GPS system in the new necklace to broadcast my position, and ate again. Around me, humans carried out the last rites offered to the vamps they served. It was bloody. Messy. Their grief awful.

I was tired. Too tired. Shifting so many times was using up reserves I didn't have and eating up more calories than I could take in, even with Anzu magic fueling half the changes. In human form, I ate. And ate. When I could talk, I questioned the visiting humans and found that Namida had sent what I needed. She had also sent a special human, Masie, who had mad skills with explosive weapons. Handy, that.

Leaving the others burying the dead and cleaning up, we two flew to the mine again, this time on the helo they had come in, the craft loaded with explosives. At each of the three back entrances, Masie set explosives, enough C4 to bring down the tunnels and maybe half the mapped cave. The rumble and slam of explosive might was satisfying and properly climactic, dirt, smoke, and debris flying, the ground vibrating like a drum. There was no way to know if Masie had saved us the trouble of killing the weres. Not yet. We'd have to wait until dark. So we set up cameras at the remaining front entrance to track activity and took the helo back again.

* * *

At sunset, Gee and I landed at the mine and shifted shape. This time I had sufficient clothes, borrowed from the Johnson Clan and smelling of vampire and unfamiliar humans, but better than the cold I'd have been otherwise.

"You found the den," Gee said, when I came out from behind a dilapidated building. He sounded surprised, which was mildly insulting. Deep inside, Beast hissed at him.

I said, "Yeah. Their den is a mine that angles into those ley lines we saw, which are twisted and knotted like a snarl of yarn. The energies coiled there are where I figure the Duba came from in the first place. Some were-creature holed up inside and was changed by the magics down to the genetic level. That change was passed along to the bitten progeny."

"Ah," he said, excitement lacing his words. "We will hunt them in the mine?" I could smell anticipation on him.

"Not exactly," I hedged. I would fulfill my deal with the Anzu to the letter and not one iota more. My plan was down and dirty but effective, and did not include exposing him or me to the gene-altering energies. Or an underground hunt.

"What do you mean, 'not exactly,' little goddess?" he asked, suspicion in his tone and body posture.

"Ummm...that?"

His scent underwent a distinct change at the sound of a helo, the blades cutting the air with a deep thrum. "What have you done?" he asked.

I didn't answer, but I didn't let him from my sight either.

"You steal the hunt from our bargain?"

The helo dropped through the cloud cover and hovered twenty feet overhead, the downdraft beating the ground, the thunder of the engine like a thousand drums. This was a big-mother-of-a-bird. From the fuselage, something dropped, stretched out in the air, and landed, softly as a hunting big-cat. And then raced inside the mine. Gee hissed. I laughed.

"This was to be *our* hunt," he said.

"We hunted." When he started to object I said, "We flew. We tracked. You killed one. I killed one. I have officially completed my part of our agreement. We. Are. Done."

From the mine entrance I heard screams and yowls and sounds that might emerge from a hellpit.

His voice toneless, knowing I wasn't to be moved on this, Gee said, "There is no honor in this battle."

"No," I acknowledged, my voice as dry as his. "No honor at all."

"Why, then?"

"They bit humans. Those humans will likely become were-Duba. Were-Duba are worse than werewolves. Insane. Violent. Once they shift, they'll be killed." I frowned at the mine pit. "By their loved ones. Besides, hunting were-creatures has never been the job of a Mercy Blade or an Enforcer. It's the job of a grindylow and by the sounds, she's doing just fine."

Gee said, "When first we met, I thought you foolish, inept, and too gullible to work for the Master of the City. But you have grown shrewd, crafty as a cat in your dealings with the Mithrans." It didn't sound like a compliment but I didn't react. He looked up at the sky. "There are still moose and elk to be hunted and eaten, and a night of flying before us. Shall we?"

I looked at the mine and back to him. "Let me slip into something more appropriate." As the sounds of death echoed up from the mine and the last rays of sunset streaked the sky purple, I slid in to the shadows, stripped, stuffed my clothes into the gobag, and found the shape of the blue-feathered Anzu. With the Mercy Blade on my tail feathers, I streaked for the sky.

SHIFTR
PATRICIA BRAY

New luxury apartments in Manhattan's trendiest neighborhood. Open concept floor plan, cathedral ceilings, hardwood floors, and granite throughout. Residents of The Heights enjoy the best of city living with 24x7 concierge service, private gym, lunar activity rooms and direct access to High Line Park. Two bedroom, two bath units start at $1.5M. Call now to reserve!

I shut down the condofinder app just as my tablet chimed, reminding me that the development meeting was in ten minutes.

Apartments started at $1.5M, but if you wanted something in the upper floors, with a private balcony, you needed at least $3M. And I know it's a stereotype, but we caprids like to be up high. There's something viscerally satisfying about being up looking down, even when we're in our human form. If I was going to buy a place, it was going to be as close to the penthouse as I could afford. I'd spent too long sharing a cramped basement apartment in Brooklyn while we got the company off the ground. With less than two months to go before the company went public, I was looking forward to the day when I could cash in and reap my well-earned rewards.

As I went by Bob Sinclair's office, I poked my head in. The rest of us had cubicles, but he had actual walls, the one concession to a tech startup's supposed egality was the lack of a door.

"Bob, we need a decision on the security verification interface. Do we keep using Formbook's external authentication? Or do we bring it in-house and do our own?"

Bob looked up from his smartphone. Odds were good he'd either been sexting or doing his own bit of online window shopping. As CEO, he was my boss, but until recently we'd rarely seen him in the office and had no idea what he did day to day. Bob liked to call himself "the idea man" and it's true that Shiftr was originally his idea. Smart enough to recognize that he didn't have a clue how to write an app, he'd brought me on board to develop it, then begged and borrowed enough money to get us started. While I coded, he'd been making the rounds of the party scene, convincing people to give the app a try. These days he was consumed with the lawyers and money guys, which meant the rest of us could focus on keeping the internet's hottest app up and running.

"I've told you before, Tess, it's Robert," he said. Roe-bear, as if he'd ever been any closer to France than the bar at La Maison.

I resisted the urge to roll my eyes. Both the company and Bob had been going through a PR makeover as we got ready to launch ourselves on Wall Street. Bob now wore tailored suits and his office featured faked vacation pics from Alaska and the Pacific Northwest. While he never outright claimed to be an ursid, he didn't deny it either.

As a woman working in tech, I got it. Speciesism and sexism were both illegal, but also pervasive. CEOs were overwhelmingly from one of the privileged classes—canids, felids, ursids, or raptors. If the investors felt more comfortable dealing with Robert the purported ursid, then that was their problem.

"Security?" I prompted him. "I know it's going to push back some of our other projects, but it's the right thing to do. Using Formbook puts us at risk if their developers screw up. I'd rather invest the money to get this done right than have to do an emergency fix down the road."

Bob shook his head. "You're overstating the risk. I had Jamal take a look and he agrees with me. What we've got now works, and it's more important to get Humr up and running so we can prove to the investors we're not a one-app company."

Bob was a marketing guy, not a coder. In the beginning he'd trusted my decisions, but as Shiftr grew from a niche app to a media darling, his self-confidence had risen and he'd insisted on signing off on all major development decisions. And Jamal, his eyes firmly set on my job as chief technology officer, was quick to pander to Bob's every whim.

The job had stopped being fun a long time ago. These days it was less and less about the coding and more about office politics. I was counting the days until the stock launch, when my stake in the company would translate into a huge cash pile. If I walked away before then, I'd get only a pittance.

At this point I barely tolerated Bob, and the feeling was mutual. But until the launch, we needed each other.

From the corner of my eye I saw Alyssa Wang approaching. The Asian lioness had been assigned by Meyers, Sanchez & Ingraham to guide us through our initial stock offering, and while she had privileged access to the inner workings of the company, that didn't mean I wanted her to see the founders fighting with one another. Not to mention that every time she and Bob got together, they generated stacks of paperwork for me to sign off on. Best to make a retreat before she got any ideas about inviting me to join them in their strategy session.

"Okay, I'll tell the team that Humr is a go," I said, giving in to the inevitable.

I grabbed a fresh cup of coffee before heading to the glass-walled conference room affectionately called the goldfish bowl.

"I'm telling you, he's a Benjamite," Paul was insisting as I walked in.

"No, he's a monoform," Sheila retorted and a shiver of revulsion ran around the room.

There was no question in my mind who "he" was.

Officially I had no knowledge of the betting pool development was running, trying to guess Bob's wereform. Unofficially the guesses were a source of amusement on slow days. Jamal was the only one who had loyally plunked his money down on Alaskan grizzly bear, while most of the rest were split between various canid and felid forms. Sheila had picked rat, and doubled her bet last week.

"Paul, I hope your code is better than your logic. Benjamites believe technology is even more sinful than their wereforms. You won't find one living in a city, let alone working here," I pointed out.

And as for monoforms, the last supposed monoform had died in the London Zoo during Queen Victoria's reign. Today it was commonly accepted that the poor individual had been suffering from an extreme case of Emergence Dysfunction. These days ED was easily treatable, the recognizable blue pills available at any pharmacy, but in the past it had been a virtual death sentence.

"I'm sure I've seen his profile in the database—BobBearXXX, looking for cross-species hookups," Elena said.

I could see Jamal getting ready to object on Bob's behalf, so I cut the discussion short. "Any one of us dumb enough to have a profile on Shiftr deserves what they get. That said, let's refrain from speculation on wereforms unless you're all looking forward to another HR seminar on workplace sensitivity."

I took a sip of my coffee, then swiped my tablet, activating the link with the livescreen at the front of the room. "Okay folks, in the interests of not spending all day here, let's go through the list." A few taps brought up the open work queue. "Jamal, Humr is a go for phase two."

"Robert told me last night, so I've already got my team working on the next phase," Jamal said without looking up. "Ken's team will be running field tests with us this weekend."

Jamal kept typing away at his laptop, apparently too busy to pay attention to a mere staff meeting. It was such an obvious power play that it should have been laughable, but I couldn't afford to take him lightly, not while he had Bob's backing.

"Glad that you're on top of this, I know Bob has high hopes for Humr." From the look of the faces in the room, Bob and Jamal were among the few who did. The success of Shiftr was rooted in its uniqueness. People arranged hookups based on their wereforms, knowing nothing about the other than a photo and their list of kinks. You could browse profiles online and set up a meet, or run the app in cruising mode on your phone and it would beep when you were in range of a likeminded Were. What had once been confined to underground clubs and seedy backalleys—and was still illegal in several Southern states—was now just a few screentaps away.

By contrast there were already dozens of apps out there for conventional dating. Even with the best interface and matching algorithms Humr was unlikely to make much of a splash.

"And you can have Ken's test group after the fifteenth, not before. Next time check with me first before you poach resources."

Jamal raised his head and glared. "But Bob said—"

"The full moon is this weekend, and we all know what that does to the app usage. Ken's team will be backing up user support. I'm sure Bob will be happy to explain why we can't afford the bad publicity associated with any outages in our premiere app."

I turned my attention to the opposite side of the room, making it clear he was dismissed. "Sheila, how close are we on the Kanji 2.0 launch?"

As each team member went through their status, I paid attention to not only what they said, but how they said it. A few of the long term employees, Sheila among them, were still firmly on my side. But the majority of the room spent as much time looking at Jamal and checking his reactions as they did mine. It wasn't open revolt...yet. But it was clear the power was shifting. I couldn't wait until Jamal screwed up, as he inevitably would. It was time to take a more active approach.

* * *

My opportunity came on Thursday, as I overheard Bob and Jamal making plans to meet up after work. Our high tech office layout offered zero privacy, so if they were plotting something, they'd need to meet somewhere else. And with the full moon occurring in the early hours of Saturday morning, this would be the last night off any us got in the next few days.

I'd heard of the place they were going to, a cigar bar down in the financial district. Yelp described it as cozy, which meant that they'd spot me long before I got close enough to eavesdrop. But where Tess wasn't welcome, Kevin would fit right in.

Bob left the office at five, as was his habit. Soon after, Jamal began packing his things, proclaiming his intent to finish his work at home. I grabbed my bag and headed to the gym.

The ultramodern building where we had our offices included its own private gym and multiform locker rooms. While city living was designed for humans—what I liked to call the default setting—workplace rules required reasonable accommodations for wereforms. In some places that meant a single unisex stall for shifting, but our gym had two dozen private shiftrooms able to accommodate a wide variety of forms.

At five-thirty, Theresa Garan walked into a shiftroom. Fifteen minutes later, Kevin Chase walked out.

The biggest secret at Shiftr wasn't Bob's wereform. It was that his co-founder was a chimera.

Chimeras had been the stuff of legends, worshipped in some cultures, condemned in others. It had only been within the last decades, with the advent of DNA analysis, that scientists recognized chimerism as a legitimate biologic phenomenon. Kevin was the remnants of my unborn fraternal twin. I'd had no reason to suspect his existence until the day in my teens when I shifted to my weregoat form, then shifted back as Kevin not Tess.

Kevin was a fragment, not a whole person. He had my brain, my memories, and my skills. In either form I could type dozens of words per minute, but couldn't carry a tune. Those similarities aside, Kevin was unmistakably male, in appearance and scent. He even had his own driver's license, thanks to a judicious bit of hacking. Only a handful of people knew of his existence, and Bob was not among their number.

Leaving Tess's distinctive messenger bag behind, I headed out to meet my liftshare driver. A crisp hundred dollar bill ensured that I reached The Smoker's Den before Jamal. From there it was a simple matter of using Kevin's height and broad shoulders to push my way into a spot at a high top table, next to where Bob was waiting.

I wrinkled my nose against the smell and vowed to shower as soon as I could.

Jamal arrived when I was still on my first scotch. As he and Bob went through the ritual of selecting their cigars, then trimming and lighting them, I edged closer.

"I don't know why you put up with her. She never listens to what I say and belittles me in front of the others," Jamal whined.

"She's afraid of you," Bob said. "She knows you're better than she is."

I snorted, pretending to be amused by something on my smartphone. If Jamal had been Bob's first hire, Shiftr would never have gotten off the ground.

"I still think you should get rid of her."

"Tess is too big a part of Shiftr—having her leave before the IPO would be a red flag for the investors. We wait until after the stock launch—"

"You mean after she realizes she's screwed," Jamal broke in, with an ugly laugh.

"Exactly." Bob said. "Smart enough to code but dumb enough to sign anything put in front of her."

I took a sudden gulp of my drink to cover my unease. I'd expected to find Bob and Jamal plotting, looking for ways to consolidate their hold over the development team. I hadn't expected to find them declaring my downfall a fait accompli.

I thought about the stacks of documents that I'd been presented with over the past months. I'd read them all before signing—well mostly, anyway. At least skimmed them, even on the busiest days. I couldn't have missed anything vital, right?

The sinking feeling in my stomach said otherwise.

* * *

Bob and Jamal didn't have anything else of interest to say, so I'd gone back to the office, made copies of all the confidential-not-to-be-copied docs I'd signed and then dropped them off with a friend of a friend who specialized in business law. Something I probably should have done before signing them. By then it was Friday, and Shiftr usage started rising as the full moon approached.

It was possible to shift on any day of the month, but most of us felt that extra urge when the moon was full. Like an itch that needed to be scratched. Even at work it wasn't uncommon for folks to shift for at least part of their day. Bob had never done so, of course. But others had. I'd done it just last month, using the opportunity to test the new voice interaction upgrade.

In the old days people had lived together in clans made up of the same wereforms. Shifting was a social bonding activity, renewing ties of family/pack/flock/herd. Even in the city, like tended to gravitate to like, and those who shifted usually did so with others of their kind. When I'd first moved to Brooklyn I'd spent full moons with my second cousin and her family.

Shiftr users weren't interested in sharing kinship or finding potential mates. They were looking for one night hookups—sometimes multiple hookups a night. Wereforms-only, the app deliberately blocked sharing of details of their human lives. If you wanted anonymous no-string-attached sex, intra- or interspecies, then Shiftr would find you a match. Usage peaked at the full-moon, when inhibitions were lower, and moon-madness made a convenient excuse for infidelity.

We got some unexpected publicity when a conservative French politician called out Shiftr as a prime example of the immorality infesting modern society. New user signups in Europe spiked, then just when we had those handled, the load sharing complex in Atlanta crashed after a lightning strike fried their main transformer. We'd managed to switch to the backup site before most users noticed the problem, but it was one thing after another all weekend.

By the time Monday came the tech team was ready to crash. Hard. We staggered in to the office like extras from a zombie film. It wasn't till that afternoon that I had time to open my mail and look at the reply I'd received from the attorney. I read his message three times. Then, without a word to anyone, I packed my things and left.

I was three beers in by the time Sam Tate joined me at the bar at Altered States. A neighborhood bar in Brooklyn, it catered to wereforms looking to inflict serious damage on their livers. No dating, no hookups, just hardcore drinkers sharing their misery.

"Tailsmacked," Sam told the bartender, as he took the stool next to me. He looked me over. "Is that your first?"

"Third," I said. I had a rule when I counted beers. It was one, two, three, three, three...

Sam shook his head, knowing better than to challenge the count. We'd met through a mutual acquaintance when we were searching for cheap apartment sublets. Before meeting Sam I couldn't have imagined living with a rodent—let alone that I'd one day call him my best friend. But the wereguineapig was a genuinely good guy, and even after he'd left to move in with his partner we still stayed friends. He was the only one outside of my family who knew about Kevin.

Sam was two drinks in, and I was still calling this number three, even as my elbow kept slipping off the bar. Ordinarily I wouldn't let myself get this drunk in a public place, but with Sam in his biker's leathers, I knew no one would bother us.

"You know what the worst part is? I let them do this to me. I trusted them. Him. Bob, err, fucking Roe-bearrrrrrr, the wannabe salmon muncher."

"And you're cut off." Sam signaled to the bartender who swapped my pint glass for a mug of coffee before I knew what was happening.

"No—" I protested.

"I'll listen to you whine, but I'm not dealing with you puking."

The few brain cells that were still sober agreed that Sam had a point. Not to mention that if I puked in here I'd never be let back through the doors again.

"You still own forty percent of the company, right?" Sam asked.

"Yup," I said. The "p" sound amused me, so I repeated it again. "Yup. But because I'm a moron, I signed papers agreeing to transfer the bulk of the assets to a shell company in Delaware. Where I own less than two percent. When the stock goes public, Bob and his friends will be worth tens of millions each, while I'll be lucky to get a million for what they've left me."

Not much to show for four years of my life spent living and breathing Shiftr, 24x7.

"You were stupid and you got screwed. Happens. You can't kill Bob..."

There was a brief pause as we contemplated whether or not killing Bob was truly off limits. Though upon reflection Bob's heirs would get his shares, so while it might be satisfying, it wouldn't undo what had been done.

I shrugged, and Sam took that as a signal to continue. "There's no point in sticking around. Go on to the next thing, and find a place that will treat you right. You know Wei's been trying to poach you for HeritageNet for months now."

"Still sucks."

"Agreed," Sam said. Then, because he was a true friend, he let me order another beer.

* * *

The next day I mainlined coffee and ibuprofen, then put in a call to Wei Chen. By noon I had a signed offer letter, blessed by my newly retained attorney.

I told the development heads first. Jamal did a poor job concealing his glee. The rest expressed various degrees of regret. Most seemed to accept my explanation that I was leaving for a smaller company where I'd get the opportunity to play with new technologies rather than being in a project management role. Sheila and a handful of other long time employees probably realized that I had decided to jump before being pushed out, though none of them pressed me on why I was leaving before the presumed stock windfall. Ironically they were in better shape than I was—their bonuses were specific dollar amounts written into their employment contracts, rather than shares of stock in a company that could be stripped of its most valuable assets.

I left the daily development meeting and went straight to Bob's office, where he and Alyssa were reviewing the investors' package. I leaned in and said, "Bob, Alyssa, sorry to interrupt. Just wanted to let you know that I've told the development team, and made sure Sheila and Jamal are up to speed on all the open projects. I'll drop my badge and tech off with HR on the way out, okay?"

Bob's jaw dropped, while Alyssa merely blinked slowly. "You're leaving?" she asked.

"Yes, I thought Bob would have told you," I said, with the determined cheerfulness of a woman with nothing to hide. "Shiftr is great, and I know it will go on to even better things. But I miss the startup days, and the chance to be a part of a small team. I promised Bob I would stay to lead the security upgrade, but since he decided to stick with Formbook, it was a good time for me to move on."

"Dozens of apps use Formbook for verification, there's no need for us to invest personnel and time in developing a replacement for something that already works," Bob said, quick to leap upon any hint of criticism.

"And dozens of other app owners agree with you," I said. Left unsaid was the part where the other applications were much lower risk. If someone linked your Formbook id to your MyTunes account, the worst you could expect was some ribbing over a fondness for 90s grunge. But if they found your Shiftr account, the results could be devastating.

Bob opened and closed his mouth, for once at a loss for words. It was a good look on him. I had counted on Bob's pathological need to appear in control. He didn't want to appear blindsided, not in front of an outsider. He had no way to keep me here—I wasn't even required to give two weeks' notice.

"I'm surprised that you are leaving before the stock launch," Alyssa said.

"There's no reason for me not to, is there?" I wanted to make it clear that I knew what the score was, even as I refused to give Bob the satisfaction of watching me beg for what I was owed. Instead I turned to Alyssa, as if hers had been an honest question rather than an attempt to find out just how much I knew. "Bob has full confidence in Jamal to run the tech side. When HeritageNet asked me to help them enter the mobile space, I couldn't pass it up."

At the mention of HeritageNet, Bob relaxed. The genealogy website was lightyears from Shiftr's target population. While the investors might ask questions about my decision to leave, this wasn't the PR disaster it would have been if I'd left to join a competitor or start my own company.

I let Bob say the expected things about how much he was going to miss working with me. He wished me well at my new job and equally insincerely I wished him and Shiftr a bright future. It helped that I didn't have to fake my excitement, though that had as much to do with the backdoors I'd left in Shiftr as it did with my new job at HeritageNet.

* * *

As expected my departure from Shiftr made a brief ripple in the tech news, but as launch day approached and Bob and Jamal dominated the news coverage, most reporters seemed to forget that Jamal was a recent hire and not the original developer. The careful reshaping of history left no room for anyone not in Bob's inner circle. Even Sheila—who'd pioneered Shiftr's multi-language support, transforming it from a US-centered app into a global powerhouse—was rarely mentioned.

I did a few interviews, being careful not to criticize the Shiftr team, while at the same time mentioning that different development priorities were part of the reason why I'd left. Most interviewers didn't even bother to print that part. But they'd remember it, when the time came.

I'd forgotten how much fun it was to be immersed in developing a new app, writing, testing, and patching modules as fast as I could type. HeritageNet had started as a place to share genealogical information and piece together family trees. The single most comprehensive repository of birth and death records available, they'd only just begun to mine the data that they'd collected over the years.

The new app would turn genealogy on its head. Enter the information for yourself and your intended partner, and it would not only trace your family trees back for generations, it would also predict your children's wereforms. No guessing whether or not your partner was the true bred were-they claimed to be. No accusations over a child whose wereform harkened back to a long-forgotten ancestor. Simple, easy to use, it would function as both a standalone app and a plug-in for MateFinder. Better yet, I'd get a cut of the revenue. Not Shiftr level money, but enough for a down payment on that high rise apartment.

As for Shiftr, using the backdoor I'd left in the system, I created a profile for Maskboy91, a Scottish polecat, whose id indicated he'd signed up in our first year of service. Logging in from a burner phone, from time to time I updated the profile with both positive and negative feedback from various other Shiftr users. Maskboy91 had a favorability score of sixty percent, on the low side, but enough that he was still getting meetup requests.

On the day Shiftr went public I met Sam at Altered States. I ordered a scotch, then pulled up the live coverage on my tablet. As the barman grunted, I turned off sound and turned on the closed captioning.

By the time I'd switched from scotch to counting beers, it was all over. Shiftr had gone public at just over ninety dollars a share. Not quite the hundred dollar target Bob had originally been hoping for, but still an overwhelming success story by anyone's standards.

I raised my half-empty pint glass. "To Bob, may he get what he deserves."

"Hear, hear!" Sam clinked his glass against mine.

That afternoon, an anonymous message highlighting one of the security vulnerabilities of Formbook appeared buried in a hackers hangout on the darknet. Twelve minutes later, a comment seemingly from a different part of the globe speculated on what that vulnerability might mean for other apps that used Formbook logins.

And then I waited. And waited. After a month I was debating whether to drop more clues or hack Formbook myself.

Nearly two months after the company went public, I woke to news alerts with such lovely titles as "What stinks at Shiftr?" and the entirely delightful "SKUNK BOY!" overlaying Bob's DMV photo adorning the front page of the Daily News.

Shiftr's stock lost half its value on that first day. Bob the presumed ursid had been a Wall Street darling, but investors felt betrayed when confronted with evidence that he was actually a polecat. Not only a polecat but one with a history of unsavory hookups on Shiftr.

Those who could have forgiven his form were less quick to forgive the poor judgment shown by his choice in partners.

It did no good for Bob to deny that the profile was his, not when it was demonstrably linked with his authorized Formbook account.

Attention quickly turned to Jamal, and the numerous missteps made in response to the security breach. Users signed in to Shiftr using their Formbook ids, which included true form verification using their driver's license. While the user's personal information and Formbook login were never publicly displayed, the linkage ensured users couldn't run multiple profiles or falsify their wereforms.

When notified of the breach, Jamal had kept the site up and running while his team frantically tried to come up with a patch. This meant that Bob was merely the first of those exposed to the public eye. By the time he finally shut the site down, the damage was done, and a steady stream of the rich and famous found themselves issuing press releases.

As the stock continued to fall, investors clamored for action. Suddenly my name as trending in the news, along with that interview I'd done for Tech Hour, where much was made of my comment about Shiftr's security protocols. After being ignored for months, I was now hailed as a visionary who'd been pushed out by an incompetent and greedy CEO.

Days later we launched HeritageNet's FamilyMaker app to favorable reviews and steady downloads that outstripped marketing's most optimistic projections. Headlines lauding me as a technical genius ran side by side with stories of Shiftr's continuing mishaps. I had "Tess Garan, the Woman Who Gets Things Done in Tech" printed out and framed.

I moved into a high rise condo in the trendiest part of Hell's Kitchen, and bought Sam all the top shelf vodka he could drink.

It had taken four years for Bob to climb from unemployed marketing guy to Wall Street fame and fortune. It took less than four months for it all to come crashing down around him.

The end, when it came, was swift. As I was leaving work for the day, my personal cell rang.

"Theresa Garan?"

"Speaking." I recognized the voice, but decided to make her work for it.

"This is Alyssa Wang, I'm sure you remember me. Let me cut to the chase—I represent the investors who have taken control of Shiftr. Bob Sinclair has resigned as CEO, and we're looking for someone to take charge. Someone with the tech savvy to restore user confidence and rebuild shareholder value."

"Let me tell you what it will cost you," I said. And then I smiled.

SNIFF FOR YOUR LIFE
PHYLLIS AMES

Daniel Rathbone stepped briskly through the scattered leaves that threatened to obscure the sidewalk on the two block walk from the bus stop to his downtown Portland office. There was an undertone in the misty, autumnal air today. Something more than the reek of car and bus that, no matter how much he was exposed to it, his WerRat senses could not filter out. Other scents, each with their own story, tantalized his analytical abilities: the burnt coffee smell that emanated from the chain shop on the corner, the faint reek in the empty alleys where he caught the acrid odor of his lesser brethren. He absorbed the aromas and promised himself he'd explore them later.

He wriggled his nose, trying to identify the new scent. It eluded him.

He let the awareness slip away as he plodded up the granite steps to his office building. It was old and beautiful—marble, glass, and brass. Well actually it wasn't his, but like all of his kind, he made wherever he was his own.

A skateboarder with ubiquitous earbuds brushed his shoulder as he cleared the first step. The grungy kid (male body type—female scent) mumbled something that might have been an apology, or just as easily might have been a sneer at the squat bulk that was the hallmark of a WerRat. The bulk was deceptive. His kind were built short, barely five feet-four, and wide. Visually appearing about two hundred pounds, he was actually only one-forty, spread evenly over a broad base, with low density bones that distributed his weight.

Daniel's ears didn't work nearly as well as his nose, so he dismissed the skateboarder as just another inconvenience of modern "civilized" life.

Not his concern.

His nose twitched again. He stroked his cheek where his sensitive whiskers should be. The odd chemical smell had grown briefly stronger, then faded—as if someone had carried it closer to him, then took it inside the building.

Someone? Maybe the skateboarder?

Not his concern.

He longed for his ancestral home in Central Africa where life moved at a slower and more natural pace. No skateboarders in a hurry to nowhere, brushing by an invisible old man. No rancid chemicals. Only the clean scents of decay, the sweet scents of a termite mound, the cool but, even in human form, terrifying scent of the predator snake. The bad parts of his home were all better than a city. But so far as cities went, he liked Portland.

He stepped lightly up the remaining eight broad steps to the front door of the twelve story Art Deco building with a stained glass dome. As he pulled the heavy glass door open, he truly became Daniel Rathbone, CPA. Here, life had meaning for him. He had accounts to balance and expenditures to curb. Lawyers! They thought they were made of money. This was his concern.

At least the lawyers in charge of the office understood his sensitive nose and banned perfume and other artificial scents. In this modern human world, a mere WerRat had to choose his employers carefully. He'd looked a long time before he met the chief WerCougar in the Pacific Northwest, who was also a high-powered lawyer who knew the difference between a WerRat and a packrat, even though, to his embarrassing regret, they exhibited similar hoarding tendencies. But those tendencies had business worth, and even a WerCougar knew the value of a good comptroller.

Daniel stepped to the right upon entry, behind the dark mahogany counter that marked the forbidding barrier of a reception desk, and commandeered the old iron cage elevator original to the building. No one willingly shared the cramped space with him. Being fat, or at least appearing so, did have its advantages. Clients, of course, made use of the central, more spacious elevator paneled in mahogany and maroon-flossed gold wallpaper.

The elevator ground to a jarring halt and voices from the hallway became audible. "This guy really as good as his reputation?" The voice came with a new scent: a lighter, sweeter oil than the heavy grease that dominated the elevator. Gun oil—he knew it well. He backed out of the elevator, pulling the folding metal door closed. This allowed him to announce his presence. It didn't seem to matter. A second voice, one he knew well, responded with the low catlike tone only a Wer would recognize.

"Trust me, he has the best nose on the west coast. Besides, he's the only WerRat within fifty miles. His office may look like a packrat lives there, but he knows where every sheet of paper is at any given moment. *And* he will know if anything is missing and who took it." The hand that clamped firmly on his back told him that Stefan Treganis, the previously mentioned WerCougar and his boss, had added the last for his benefit.

Daniel preened a bit at the praise, and turned to acknowledge whoever this gun-wielding man would turn out to be. He smelled suspicion and disbelief on the stranger—acidic, similar to the strange smell outside. He also carried the actinic odor of the Wer. Odd he hadn't noticed it before.

Wolf probably. They carried the remnants of their last meal a lot longer than normals or other Wer. *Steak, barely cooked, topped with garlic and butter*. Too much garlic. Must be of Italian descent from the Midwest. Either that or FBI—they loved their garlic. And the FBI had only one known WerWolf working for them: Joe Bradbury the originator of the covenant of protection/cooperation between the Bureau and the Wer communities.

Something was up.

None of his concern. Except he was a WerRat and they apparently needed his nose.

Daniel nodded and grunted a greeting to Stefan. They silently stepped aside and he proceeded them into his space with a barely audible sigh of contentment. He didn't turn aside until he had crossed the room to where his custom-made chair awaited him behind the broad, cluttered desk.

From his post he could see his boss standing purposefully in the center of the room and the Wer with the gun leaning casually against his door.

Daniel stopped short before sitting. His nose quivered. He turned his head right and then left. He paused at every ten degrees of arc to sniff the air.

"What did you take?" he asked, then raised a malevolent glare to the man with the gun. "A folder of janitorial services requisition forms." He reached a finger to touch a spot in the disheveled mass of papers on the edge of his desk. An elegant brown paperweight, one of many similar creations scattered around the room, marked the appropriate pile. The glass had been burned brown in the catacombs beneath the Chernobyl reactor. There were heroes at Chernobyl who were never on film.

The man with the gun, and assumed federal agent of some ilk, retrieved the folder from under his suit jacket, revealing with a shocking lack of subtlety the pistol nestled firmly in a shoulder holster.

Daniel crossed the room in broad strides, for him at least, and snatched the precious papers out of the man's hands. He leafed through the folder to check; one never knew how sneaky the Feds could be under their rather blatant displays of authority. This Wer might be the alpha in his pack, but WerRats looked to no one but themselves for help or rules, or anything.

The assumed fed smiled sheepishly and, at Stefan's invite, entered Daniel's office.

He noted the magnificent pieces of glass that covered the surfaces of Daniel's office. Not all Wers had such symbols of rank within their own arcane hierarchy, but for the WerRat, glass was gold. He paused to admire the display of glass fountain pens standing neatly in their back-lit case of deep, dark mahogany. A collection such as this might have once represented the WerRat equivalent of a crown, but in truth, eBay was the source of more of the collection than royal birth. There were a few gifts from hero-worshipping underlings, but only a few.

The assumed Fed, having paid appropriate homage to the collection, abruptly turned to face the most powerful man in the law firm: Daniel, the man who controlled the check book. "I apologize, Mr. Rathbone," his eyes flickered to Stefan, "I meant no dishonor. But your kind are rare and I *have* to know the depth of your abilities."

The flickering glance told Daniel the true source of the apology. A warm flush of annoyance rose.

"Dishonor?" he said, and locked his glare on the man. "How can you dishonor something you do not know well enough to honor?"

The probable Fed seemed taken aback. Daniel gave him no quarter. "Do you know that in Africa, my kind are heroes for our work sniffing out landmines? We have saved thousands of children, farmers, and others who would otherwise have been killed or maimed. We do this as part of the covenant made with the gods thousands of years ago, to contribute to the survival of humans. Something other Wer forget."

"Your work in the minefields of the world is indeed heroic. You among all the Wer have honored our purpose and our past well." The presumed Fed placed a clenched fist against his heart and nodded his head, a gesture of respect and conciliation. "Which is why I have come today." He held out a hand. "My name is Joe Bradbury, and the city needs your help."

He reached under his suit jacket and pulled out an oblong box. "A token of respect and an acknowledgement that we need your service." He lifted the top off of the box and held it toward Daniel.

Daniel didn't need to look at the empty spot in his prized collection of pens to identify the slim blue glass object in the box. It was the one pen he did not have. It had been one of the pens used to sign the ill-fated agreement that led to the League of Nations. He could smell the horrifying memories of war that had driven the world to see the need for peace.

"I do not need to be bribed to assist the FBI," he said as he reached out and took the pen.

He set the small box on the desk and held the pen up to the light, then lifted the glass cover on the case and slipped the pen into the vacant slot, relishing the moment of satisfaction that warmed his chest as he closed the case. The pen gleamed in the light.

"What exactly do you need? Does your errand have something to do with the odd smells in the street I sensed this morning?" He pushed down the sudden eagerness to serve, to please, that pushed at his gut. He wanted to be involved, to be on the inside of a true Wer job.

"Possibly," Joe said cautiously. "We know that an anti-Wer terrorist group has put together a powerful bomb. Evidence tells us that Portland is the target."

Daniel wrinkled his nose. The odd scent forced itself to the forefront of his mind. "Portland is big."

The confirmed Fed looked at Stefan and then to Daniel. "The WerCourt Headquarters is in Old Town."

Stefan blanched, turning his already pale skin to a bleached leather sheet. "The Shanghai tunnels converge under the WerCourt. The network is extensive, running from the harbor up into the West Hills. A bomb there would collapse the foundations of every building for blocks."

"And we have a time," the Fed said. "Whatever it is, it happens at noon today."

Daniel checked his calendar. Noon today, October 18. He couldn't think of any historical event to commemorate today. Except...

"Who would know that eighty-five thousand years ago today a super volcano in Indonesia blew enough particulate matter into the atmosphere to cause a *ten year* winter? Who would know, besides the Wer, that this event triggered the beginning of the Wer?"

Now it was his concern.

"Our history has been passed down among my people, word for word, since the beginning. In each village, the strongest and best hunter was given the ability to shift into the shape of the apex predator of the region, to hunt for his people so that humanity might survive the endless winter, but only on the three nights of the full moon can we shift so that the prey might recover from the chase and survive too," Stefan chanted.

"How do you know the exact day?" Joe asked. "It's not like documentation exists. It is our legend and our religion to be sure. But I've never heard a specific date mentioned."

"My people remember and commemorate the day each year with rituals and fasting," Daniel said solemnly. "The calendar changes, the ways of keeping time change, but we know the importance of remembering. Our terrorist also knows the significance of today. His...no, *her* target is important to the Wer."

"Her?" Joe asked. "You've already seen her?"

"I smelled her as I came into the building this morning."

"Not my building," Stefan gasped. "I have things to do, papers and computer records that must be secured." He fled the office. In seconds, Daniel heard the antique elevator engage.

"What do you need?" Joe asked, leaning forward with his hands flat on Daniel's desk.

"Someone to disable the bomb, once I find it. I know nothing of these things."

"Done."

Daniel heaved himself upward from his chair, discarded his jacket in an untidy heap, and placed three glass pebbles in his pants pocket. His left hand caressed them, sliding fingertips over their smooth surface, tumbling them together.

His mind began sliding sideways.

He dropped the pebbles and freed his hand. Outside. He must be less exposed before he dropped into a hunting trance.

"Will they attack the WerCourt?" Daniel asked.

"If I knew that, I wouldn't need you," Joe snarled. His wolf was very close to the surface and the full moon was still twelve days away.

Daniel tumbled the glass pebbles in his pocket again for reassurance. Three. Still three of them. None had gone missing.

Joe calmed himself. "The WerCourt Headquarters is the only thing that makes sense."

"Send your bomb squad to follow me."

"Rathbone," Joe said.

Daniel stopped at the exit from his office.

"I've lost two teams already on this. One came back dazed and disoriented. They breathed a hallucinogenic gas engineered specifically for Wer. The other team is missing entirely."

Daniel nodded. "I know how to do this." He slipped off his shoes, then, with a tug, his socks. His toes curled against the cool, hardwood flooring. He felt as if his whole body breathed for the first time in hours.

"Call me when you know something. Anything."

Daniel was already scuttling for the elevator. He wanted desperately to drop to all fours and *shift*. But the moon was wrong. The process would take too long—even though he was a born Wer, a true Wer, and could *shift* anytime. Unlike the bitten, dependent upon the moon for assistance, he had alternatives.

Instead of departing the elevator at the ground floor lobby, he punched the button for B2 and slid a key card into an innocuous slot. The doors closed. The car did not stop at B2, but continued downward.

When the doors opened, the immediate scent of damp, earthy air filled the elevator. He could hear pumps working in the background. Only ten feet of cement and rebar separated him from the water table. Blocks away, the river lapped at the sea wall.

His nose crinkled in distaste. A WerWolf had been here recently. He sniffed again. A female. The skateboarder.

Was she part of the ant-Wer clan?

No time to ponder the implications. For the first time in his life, he regretted the absence of a cell phone, not that it would be much use in the subterranean maze. The elevator emergency phone normally connected directly to building maintenance, but he tapped in the override code and dialed the Fed's number. He didn't need to look at the card. He remembered.

Daniel spat his terse warnings into the phone even as he shed his clothing. He cast a brief glance to where he knew the camera focused on him, wondering for a moment if there were any information to be gleaned from the potential records. Joe would know and deal with it.

He dropped to the ground, leaving the phone dangling and the line still open.

His bones ground into new conformations. Slowly; too slowly this far away from the full moon. His ears extended. His body hair became a smooth black pelt. Whiskers sprang free as if spring loaded beneath his skin and eager to twitch as they filled his brain with new sensations.

In one leap he cleared the safe confines of the elevator and landed in the crude tunnel that led north, toward Old Town. The bomb smell sharpened. And something else he didn't remember from his first encounter with it on the street: *glass*. The bomb contained glass. Lethal shrapnel. A weapon against any who tried to disarm it and failed.

He loped less than a block in the lightless tunnel. His nose twitched in offense with every step across broken ground. Something new tugged at his nose and whiskers. *Gas*. The Fed had said his people had been attacked by a hallucinogenic gas. A lesser nose would not detect this pocket of altered air. He took to the walls, clinging to tiny ledges and pipes that ran along the curve of the ceiling. The air was lighter and cleaner here.

But...

Wriggling his nose once more, he realized that the *something* under the chemical smells was natural gas. It had probably been leaking from the pipes under the street, or from one of the old buildings, for a long time.

A very long time.

Gas at these levels, plus even a tiny flame, meant a huge boom rushing through the tunnels, undermining many, many buildings. How many would collapse? He calculated the force of the blast. The bomb could be tiny and still deadly.

He hurried his pace.

A branch westward to his left he ignored. At the next juncture he knew the straightforward tunnel looped around and headed back south within a few meters. In the darkness, the unwary would not notice the curving path.

He veered sharply right. The smell of the river slammed into him, blinding his nose to all else.

He paused and took the time to sort through the myriad watery scents. Plain water, algae, fish, garbage, drugs. That was the river. Crumbling mortar, baked clay in the bricks, minerals from the earth, and...and that ever-present natural gas. He'd passed beyond the concentration of the hallucinogens.

His whiskers picked up the brick arches supporting the tunnel roof. His paws felt the smooth rectangles separated by crumbling mortar.

Dim, dangling lightbulbs showed him how the space opened into a "courtyard" with several choices of direction. This section was part of the public tour. He had to pause and remember the scent he followed. He sorted through a century and a half of the odors of fear and despair when these tunnels were used by sea captains and pimps to restrain the latest crop of desperate humanity they sought to enslave aboard ships bound for the Orient or brothels throughout the world. Many captives had died here. Their ghosts lingered, distorting everything.

And the pervasive scent of the river added chill to the awfulness.

He forgot to use his nose.

His instincts told him to turn around and run back to safety, but his folk had overcome their fears to sniff out landmines for humans to disable. He had to overcome his own sense of impending doom. If that bomb went off, nowhere in downtown Portland was safe. Thousands of innocents depended upon him to find that bomb so the Feds could disarm it. If they had time. His gut felt the tug of the sun's gravity. Noon approached.

Something unnatural with an underlying petroleum base crept through his fearful shivers. He forced his senses awake again and clamped down on his instinct to run.

He caught the after-scent of many humans and their liquor from the antique saloon with access to the tunnels. Not that way. The bitch would not want to take a chance on being seen.

Angle left, north by northwest, toward the west hills. But not that far. Just away from the river and the docks.

He crept along, hugging the left hand curve where wall met ceiling. His whiskers twitched and his nose cringed. Not far now.

If he'd still been in human form he'd have broken out in a sweat.

Two more steps. He'd passed the source.

He dropped to the floor and backed up. A slight angle to the right and one step forward. He lifted his snout and his whiskers bristled. It was here.

An inch forward, then another one. He let his snout circle. Tight at first, then wider. There!

The bitch had removed a brick and stuffed the explosive into its place. The brick was...was...*there* on the floor, three paces to the right.

Daniel allowed himself a hysterical chuckle. If he'd traveled the floor, he'd have stumbled over it and discounted it as insignificant, along with all the other debris.

Back to work. He lifted his snout and sniffed for a trace of the bomb squad. Nothing. He was the only creature down here. The Fed was late.

And Daniel was out of time.

He needed his hands to remove the bomb from its niche and to disable it.

He willed a surge of adrenaline to begin shifting.

Three long minutes later, chilled air brushed against naked skin. He lost the tactile sensors in his whiskers.

But his nose remained offended.

His eyesight, always weak, had trouble picking out details from the dusty low-watt bulbs yards behind him. Tentatively, he reached out and touched the plastic-wrapped brick of explosives. Four wires dangled from the end, tucked tight against the adjoining bricks.

Gently, he traced the wires down. One was a bit pale. Yellow he guessed. The others would be red, blue, and green, each with a different purpose. He didn't know which did what. The few crime dramas he'd watched indicated that if he pulled the wrong one, he'd get automatic detonation.

A red LED light flashed on from another brick-sized device on the floor. Sixty, fifty-nine...

"Oh crap!"

He didn't know if he had disturbed the mechanism by tracing the wires, or if the bitch had found a safe haven and triggered it.

Either way he was out of time.

Thirty-two, thirty-one...

What should he do?

Before panic set in, he scrabbled the brick from its resting place, yanking all four of the wires loose at the same time.

"I am a hero rat, worthy of my people," he proclaimed loudly.

As the echoes faded, he folded himself around the brick and dropped to the floor. Less than one heartbeat later a sharp burn pierced his chest and darkness folded around and through him.

Complete darkness. His awareness faded with the muffled sound of a small explosion.

* * *

"Daniel?"

A muffled whisper penetrated the blackness.

"Daniel?"

The voice sounded a little louder and more precise, but so distant. And there was something between him and the sound.

He wriggled his nose and caught a whiff of blessed oxygen. More than a whiff. Someone pressed a plastic mask over his nose and mouth.

"It's me. Joe."

That explained a lot.

Then memory and pain slammed into him, took over his mind and emotions. There was nothing but the pain, centered in his chest.

Pain and glass. The bomb had contained glass beads as a form of shrapnel and seven of them had lodged in his chest. How fitting that he'd absorbed some precious glass in his final act.

"You need to change, Daniel. I brought your epi-pen to help."

Daniel cracked open an eye; the other seemed swollen shut.

Change! That's what he needed. The discomfort of shifting, then shifting back was nothing compared to the overwhelming *pain*. And there was a numbness around his nose.

"I brought help," Joe said.

Three bulky shadows paced behind him, between them and the light at the "courtyard." They each carried a powerful flashlight. Since Joe was a Wolf, he'd bring WerWolves. Their constant pacing, bulky bodies, and slightly hunched posture told him what they were, even without smelling them. Their distressed jeans and plaid flannel shirts over dingy T shirts identified them even more. "No bomb squad?"

"They fell to the hallucinogen. It was dissipating, but not fast enough. I watched them either drop or wander off, so we held our breath as long as we could and made it past the pocket. Now, I've put all the scattered body parts I could find close by. As you change, they should reattach in their proper places." He shone his flashlight on a small pile of gory bits, including a severed arm. "Make sure you remember to hold your left arm in place for a couple minutes, even after you change."

Daniel forced himself to nod acceptance, rather than slink back into gibbering horror or blind oblivion.

"You did good, Daniel. Here's the epi-pen. The adrenaline rush will help you change. But you have to will it to happen."

Even through his damaged nose, Daniel smelled something. Something wrong.

"Gas," he croaked.

Joe looked away from him, working his own nose. "Crap. The perp didn't need much in the way of explosives. The gas would have ignited and burned the entire tunnel system. Good thing for you it was such a small bomb. A bigger one and we wouldn't be able to save you. But we'll have to hurry and get you out of here. Marcus, find a cell signal and get some help down here. And shut off the gas mains!" Then he removed the mask from Daniel's face.

Something stabbed into Daniel's thigh. Instinct took over. He closed his eyes, gritted his teeth, and willed his Rat to come forth.

Oh, Gods! It hurt. His joints twisted. His whiskers drooped as they slid outward. His feet and hands cramped as they curled. And his arm...he couldn't find his left arm!

Joe held it against his body. One of the other Wolves guided his right paw to hold it in place.

And then it was done. He lay on his back and panted. Even the ignominy of exposing his belly didn't give him the energy to move.

Joe looked at his watch, lips moving as he counted at the seconds.

"Can you walk?" he asked.

Daniel shook his head. Even with help, he didn't think he could roll over.

"We've got to go before the gas takes us out." He grabbed the oxygen away from Daniel, took a long inhale and passed the device to his companions.

"How much time does he need before he can change back?" asked one of the pacing Wolves as he handed the mask back to Joe. His flashlight bobbed and highlighted circles of space all around him.

"I'd like to give him another five minutes to make sure that arm stays in place. Help me turn him over."

With much grunting and growling from the Wolves, and whimpering from Daniel, they managed to rock his body until his own momentum carried him over. Brick, rocks, and other rubble pressed into his belly. If he could feel that more intensely than the itching ache in his shoulder as the bones knit—or the horrific open wound in his chest as it closed, leaving the glass beads inside him—then he must be healing.

Not fast enough. The gas was making him sleepy.

"Don't you dare pass out again!" Joe shouted, demanding Daniel's attention. Then Joe shoved the mask over as much of his snout as he could. The flow of untainted air filled him and gave him the courage to push downward with three limbs and get his belly off the ground. One more sniff and he found he could limp along.

It was a long walk. He had to concentrate hard on putting one paw forward at a time, followed by another. The weakness of the half-knitted left foreleg hampered his balance.

He hardly noticed the gas smell. He hoped it had faded some as they left the higher concentrations beneath Old Town and approached downtown.

Three quarters of the way back to the elevator, they ran out of oxygen.

Daniel nudged Joe with his tail. Then he tried to stand on his hind legs. The best form of communication he had.

"Okay. Here's my epi-pen. You've got to change quickly so we can get back to safety."

"Gas company's on its way," the rearmost Wolf said, pocketing his cell phone. "We've got seven minutes max to clear out, leaving no traces."

Joe stabbed Daniel with yet another dose of the blessed epinephrine. The rush of blood through his body and the hyper-alert spinning of his mind followed.

He willed the change, letting it flow over him, not fighting the discomfort, just letting it happen.

It was over in only a little more than the thirty seconds it took with the aid of the full moon's gravity.

Light spilled out from the elevator, the door propped open by yet another Wolf. They'd come further than he thought. It was going to get very crowded in that elevator with five Wolves and an oversized Rat.

At least someone had respected him enough to fold his clothing neatly. He donned his pants one handed, even managed the zipper by himself. But the shirt...He paused, panting with weakness, sweat slicking his body, one arm in a shirt sleeve and the other still dangling uselessly. Joe took over, rearranging him as he pulled the left sleeve over the damaged arm first, then helped him twist to clothe the more mobile right arm.

At last they were ready to present themselves to the regular world, disheveled and beaten down, but not defeated.

"The bitch?" Daniel asked when they'd cleared the basement level.

"I have deployed the troops to hunt her down. Thanks to you, they have her scent. We have a picture from the elevator camera. She won't get far."

"Damage?"

"Weakened foundations of the WerCourt Headquarters. Minor, thanks to you. But they'll have to vacate until it's all shored up and retrofitted."

"Explanations?"

"Gas leak caused a minor explosion. The gas company has everything under control, including finding the leak and patching it."

"Needs an upgrade of those ancient pipes."

"The story of our lives. Almost all of the infrastructure needs upgrades."

Daniel wheezed acceptance. He really needed to get back to his numbers. Numbers were enough excitement for him.

"You really are a hero, Daniel. Worthy of your kind. Thank you."

Daniel nodded and began totting up the accounts payable in his head.

Author's Note: Want to know more about the real hero rats?
http://www.greatbigstory.com/stories/the-bomb-sniffing-rats-saving-limbs-in for how man's best friends save lives in Mozambique.

ABOUT THE AUTHORS

Award-winning author **DANIELLE ACKLEY-MCPHAIL** has worked both sides of the publishing industry for longer than she cares to admit. In 2014 she joined forces with Mike McPhail and Greg Schauer to form eSpec Books (www.especbooks.com). Her published works include six novels, *Yesterday's Dreams, Tomorrow's Memories, Today's Promise, The Halfling's Court, The Redcaps' Queen*, and *Baba Ali and the Clockwork Djinn*, written with Day Al-Mohamed. She is also the senior editor of the *Bad-Ass Faeries* anthology series. She can be found on Facebook (Danielle Ackley-McPhail) and Twitter (DMcPhail, eSpecBooks). To learn more about her work, visit www.sidhenadaire.com, www.especbooks.com or www.badassfaeries.com.

PHYLLIS AMES loves tramping through the forests of the Pacific Northwest with camera and binoculars. Her most treasured moments are catching sight, and photos of elusive black-tailed deer, bear cubs, coyotes, and yes, a blurry image of a cougar leaping from the roof of an abandoned cabin into a tall Douglas fir (much too blurry and indistinct to post). She is more afraid of things that go bump in the night than the shadowy depths of forest trails.

MIKE BARRETTA is a retired U.S. Naval Aviator who currently works for a defense contractor as a pilot. He holds a Master's degree in Strategic Planning and International Negotiation from the Naval Post-Graduate School and a Master's in English from the University of West Florida. His wife, Mary, to whom he has been married to for 26 years, is living proof that he is not such a bad guy once you get to know him. His stories have appeared in *Baen's Universe, Redstone, New Scientist, Orson Scott Card's Intergalactic Medicine Show* and various anthologies.

ANNELIESE BELMOND writes Sci-Fi and Fantasy novellas and short stories while she avoids polishing her novels. She is the author of the Star Mage Novella Series. When she's not writing, she's binge-watching TV and thinking about plot. She is a graduate of the Alpha SF/F/H Workshop for Young Writers. You can say hi to her through her website: http://www.anneliesebelmond.com/
Facebook: https://www.facebook.com/writeranneliesebelmond/

SARAH BRAND is a graduate student at the London School of Economics and an alumna of the Alpha Workshop for Young Writers. Her fiction has also appeared in the anthology *Athena's Daughters vol. 2*. She can be found at sarahbrand.com or on Twitter as @sarahbbrand.

PATRICIA BRAY is the author of a dozen novels, including *Devlin's Luck*, which won the Compton Crook Award for the best first novel in the field of science fiction or fantasy. A multi-genre author whose career spans both epic fantasy and Regency romance, her books have been translated into Russian, German, Portuguese and Hebrew. She's also crossed over to the dark side as the co-editor of *After Hours: Tales from the Ur-Bar* (DAW, March 2011) and *The Modern Fae's Guide to Surviving Humanity* (DAW, March 2012), *Clockwork Universe: Steampunk vs. Aliens* (ZNB, June 2014) and *Temporally Out of Order* (ZNB, August 2015). Patricia lives in a New England college town, where she combines her writing with a full-time career in I/T. To offset the hours spent at a keyboard, she bikes, hikes, cross-country skis, snowshoes and has recently taken up the noble sport of curling. To find out more, visit her website at www.patriciabray.com.

DAVID B. COE is the award-winning author of nineteen fantasy novels. His newest series, "The Case Files of Justis Fearsson" (*Spell Blind, His Father's Eyes*, and *Shadow's Blade*) is a contemporary urban fantasy with a "Were" twist. As D.B. Jackson, he writes the "Thieftaker Chronicles," a historical urban fantasy that includes *Thieftaker, Thieves' Quarry, A Plunder of Souls*, and *Dead Man's Reach*. He lives on the Cumberland Plateau with his wife and daughters. When he's not writing he likes to hike, play guitar, and stalk the perfect image with his camera.
http://www.DavidBCoe.com
http://www.davidbcoe.com/blog/
http://www.dbjackson-author.com
http://www.facebook.com/david.b.coe
http://twitter.com/DavidBCoe

FAITH HUNTER, fantasy writer, was born in Louisiana and raised all over the south. She writes two contemporary Urban Fantasy series: the "Skinwalker" series, featuring Jane Yellowrock, a Cherokee skinwalker who hunts rogue vampires, and the "Soulwood" series, featuring earth magic user Nell Ingram. Her "Rogue Mage" novels are a dark, urban, post-apocalyptic, fantasy series featuring Thorn St. Croix, a stone mage. The role playing game based on the series, is ROGUE MAGE, RPG.

www.faithhunter.net
https://www.facebook.com/official.faith.hunter
https://www.facebook.com/faith.hunter?fref=ts
@hunterfaith
http://www.yellowrocksecurities.com
www.gwenhunter.net

SUSAN JETT used to work for Sea Shepherd, but has always found the idea of swimming in anything deeper than a lap pool utterly terrifying. Now she lives about 20 miles from the ocean in an old farmhouse where she and her husband both write stories and try to civilize a small human. Find her online: Twitter @JettSusan and www.susanjett.com

KATHARINE KERR lives in the San Francisco Bay Area with her husband, two cats, and a vagrant skunk. Although she spent her childhood in a Great Lakes industrial city, she became a confirmed Californian at age nine, when her family relocated here. She's the author of the "Deverry" series of epic fantasies, the "Nola O'Grady" series of light-hearted urban fantasy, the "Runemaster" duo, and a few science fiction works, mostly notably *Snare*.

ELIZABETH KITE lives on a mountain located between Las Vegas and the desert. When she's not tanning by moonlight, you can find her next to a good cup of tea. Twice a year, she puts on a corset and pretends to be an escaped French nun while her husband plays a dashing bard. Her bookshelves are running out of space. Visit her on twitter at @Kitewrites.

GINI KOCH writes the fast, fresh and funny "Alien/Katherine 'Kitty' Katt" series for DAW Books, the "Necropolis Enforcement Files," and the "Martian Alliance Chronicles" series, as well as many other novels, novellas, and short stories. As G.J. Koch she writes the "Alexander Outland" series and she's made the most of multiple personality disorder by writing under a variety of other pen names as well, including Anita Ensal, Jemma Chase, A.E. Stanton, and J.C. Koch. She has stories featured in a variety of excellent anthologies, available now and upcoming, writing as Gini Koch, Anita Ensal, and J.C. Koch. www.ginikoch.com

ASHLEY MCCONNELL's first novel was a finalist for the Bram Stoker Award. Since 1990, she has sold horror, fantasy, and numerous media tie-in novels, as well as a handful of short stories and assorted articles. ("A"

and "the" featured prominently among them.) She is responsible for the erratic publication of the Bloodstained Bookshelf, a list of forthcoming traditionally-published mysteries at http://mirlacca.com/Bookshelf.html, and has a column in the Novelists, Inc. newsletter on Links You May Have Missed. She is currently owned by two horses and far too many cats.

SEANAN MCGUIRE lives and works in the Pacific Northwest, where she attempts to keep her massive blue cats from eating people. She writes a lot of things, because otherwise she stops sleeping. Sleep is good. She is the author of quite a lot of books, and takes quite a lot of naps. Keep up with her on Twitter at @seananmcguire or at www.seananmcguire.com.

ELIORA SMITH lives in Central New York with two cats and an ever-growing collection of dragons. In addition to writing fiction and poetry, Eliora makes jewelry. "Among the Grapevines, Growing" is their first published story, however some of their writing can be found at their sporadically updated WordPress blogs, Words of Realms and Scribbling on Seashells. They can be found on Twitter @Disabled_Dragon.

APRIL STEENBURGH is an author and freelance eBook formatter living in the Finger Lakes Region of New York. She shares her home with a lively band of animals and a very understanding partner. When not writing, she can be found working as a librarian at a local community college and as president of the Southern Tier Animal Rescue Network. Online, you can find April at https://aprilsteenburgh.com/
or https://www.facebook.com/fireun.

JEAN MARIE WARD writes fiction, nonfiction and everything in between, including novels (2008 Indie Book double-finalist *With Nine You Get Vanyr*) and art books. Her stories appear in numerous anthologies, such as *The Modern Fae's Guide to Surviving Humanity*, *The Clockwork Universe: Steampunk vs. Aliens*, and *Tales from the Vatican Vaults*. The former editor of *Crescent Blues*, she co-edited the six-volume, 40th anniversary World Fantasy Con anthology *Unconventional Fantasy* and is a frequent contributor to BuzzyMag.com. Her website is JeanMarieWard.com.

ABOUT THE EDITORS

PATRICIA BRAY is the author of a dozen novels, including *Devlin's Luck*, which won the Compton Crook Award for the best first novel in the field of science fiction or fantasy. A multi-genre author whose career spans both epic fantasy and Regency romance, her books have been translated into Russian, German, Portuguese and Hebrew. She's also crossed over to the dark side as the co-editor of *After Hours: Tales from the Ur-Bar* (DAW, March 2011) and *The Modern Fae's Guide to Surviving Humanity* (DAW, March 2012), *Clockwork Universe: Steampunk vs. Aliens* (ZNB, June 2014) and *Temporally Out of Order* (ZNB, August 2015). Patricia lives in a New England college town, where she combines her writing with a full-time career in I/T. To offset the hours spent at a keyboard, she bikes, hikes, cross-country skis, snowshoes and has recently taken up the noble sport of curling. To find out more, visit her website at www.patriciabray.com.

* * *

JOSHUA PALMATIER is a fantasy author with a PhD in mathematics. He currently teaches at SUNY Oneonta in upstate New York, while writing in his "spare" time, editing anthologies with fellow zombie and co-editor Patricia Bray, and founding the anthology-producing small press Zombies Need Brains LLC. His most recent fantasy novel *Threading the Needle* (July 2016) continues a new fantasy series begun in *Shattering the Ley*, although you can also find his "Throne of Amenkor" series and the "Well of Sorrows" series on the shelves. He is currently hard at work writing *Reaping the Aurora*, the third novel in the "Ley" series, and designing the kickstarter for the next Zombies Need Brains anthology project. You can find out more at www.joshuapalmatier.com or at the small press' site www.zombiesneedbrains.com. Or follow him on Twitter as @bentateauthor or @ZNBLLC.

ACKNOWLEDGMENTS

This anthology would not have been possible without the tremendous support of those who pledged during the Kickstarter. Everyone who contributed not only helped create this anthology, they also helped solidify the foundation of the small press Zombies Need Brains LLC, which I hope will be bringing SF&F themed anthologies to the reading public for years to come...as well as perhaps some select novels by leading authors, eventually. I want to thank each and every one of them for helping to bring this small dream into reality. Thank you, my zombie horde.

The Zombie Horde: Danielle Ackley-McPhail, Carol J. Guess, J.R. Murdock, Brian Quirt, Greg Resnik, Emy Peters, Julia Haynie, Heather Fagan, Kristy K, Evenstar Deane, Andrija Popovic, Cheryl Preyer, Susan B, Evaristo Ramos, Jr., JP Frantz, Michael Skolnik, Joelle M Reizes, Lorena Dinger, Kathleen T Hanrahan, Derick Sweat, Sandra Ulbrich Almazan, Tony Finan, John P. Murphy, Sheryl R. Hayes, John McNabb, Fen Eatough, Megan Beauchemin, Karl Maurer, Al Batson, Lim Ivan, Teresa Carrigan, Sheryl Ehrlich, "Gorgeous" Gary Ehrlich, Diana Castillo, Keith E. Hartman, Duncan & Andrea Rittschof, Leah Webber, Claire Sims, Ruth Stuart, Sofie Bird, Halcyoncin, Jean Marie Ward, Jeff Gulosh, Henry Lopez, Kristine Smith, Sharon Stogner, John Sturkie, Tommy Lewis, Max Kaehn, Elaine Tindill-Rohr, Chris Loeffler, Kerry aka Trouble, John Sapienza, Kathleen Ferrando, Gary Phillips, Kathy Martin, Sally Novak Janin, Matt Keck, Lea Zane, Amanda Johnson, Holland Dougherty, Russell Ventimeglia, Roy Romasanta, Ed Ellis, Steve Lord, Terry Hazen, Nathan Hillstrom, David Hill, Fred Herman, Elizabeth McKinstry, Joanne B Burrows, Lisa Padol, Mia Kleve, Angie Hogencamp, Hisham El-Far, Eleanor Russell, Anthony R. Cardno, Sabrina Poulsen, Jenn & Drew Bernat, Patti Short, Christopher Mangum, Larisa LaBrant, Jenn Whitworth, Debbie Matsuura, Elizabeth Kite, Morgan S. Brilliant, Tina Noe-Good, Rosanne Girton, Juli, Wolf SilverOak, Marty Tool, Carey Williams, Jaime C., Chris Barili, Denise Murray, Matt B, Scott Raun, Dino Hicks, Darryl M. Wood, Douglas Mosman, Peter Donald, R. Hunter, Steve Weiner, Krystina Harrington, Chris Brant, Andrew Neil Gray, Stephen Ballentine, Nancy Pimentel, Corey Terhune, Josie, Peter Thew, Ian Harvey, James Conason, Linda Pierce, Jeremy M. Gottwig, Ben Stanley, JE Chase, Jay Zastrow, Galena Ostipow, Sue C., Barbara Silcox, Michael J. D'Auben, Stephanie Lucas, Brad Roberts, David K. Mason, Dina S. Willner, Dustin Bell, Marsha Baker,

Alice Bentley, Lisa Kruse, Jessica Reid, Helen Cameron, Pam Blome, Brenda Moon, Kate Nelson, Lex, Jo Carol Jones, Beth aka Scifibookcat, Janito Vaqueiro Ferreira Filho, Cyn Armistead, Lorri-Lynne Brown, Jason Palmatier, Dustin Bridges, Katherine S, Pat Knuth, Derek Hudgins, Cullen Gilchrist, Jonathan Collins, Ian Chung, David Perlmutter, Camron S, Keith West, Future Potentate of the Solar System, Amy E Goldman, Pat Hayes, Maggie Allen, Cathy Brown, Evan Ladouceur, Sue & Rich Hanson, Cheryl Losinger, Ragnarok Publications, Katherine Malloy, Kristie Strum, Elizabeth Inglee_Richards, Leann Rettell, The Hoose Family, Holly, H. Rasmussen, Anne Rindfliesch, Deborah Fishburn, M. Calistri-Yeh, Patrick Dugan, Steven Mentzel, April Steenburgh, Deanna Harrison, Shauna Roberts, Sara R Marschand, Katherine & Elizabeth Rowe, Bill Simoni, Elizabeth Vrabel, Wendy K Cornwall, Bonnie Warford, Robert Gilson, Chan Ka Chun Patrick, David Zurek, Sean Collins, Laurie Treacy, Jake, Chrissie, Grace & Savannah Palmatier, Steph am I, Chrysta Stuckless, David Decker, Rachel Sasseen, Sarah Liberman, Shannon Everyday, Robert Elrod, Crazy Lady Used Books, Will Carlson, Joey Shoji, Colleen R., Gayle, Liz Harkness, Svend Andersen, Vicki Colbert, Mandy Stein, Erik T Johnson, Patricia Bray, Eddy Black, Shawn Fennessey, Robby Thrasher, Chad Bowden, J.V. Ackermann, Brook West, James H. Murphy Jr., Sharon Wood, Ann Leveille, Jerrie the filkferengi, Stephanie Wood Franklin, Jo Dawn Good, Aurora N., Jef Ball, Sarah E, Keith Hall, Melanie McCoy, Malevolent Media, sam murphy, Rissa Lyn, Lark Cunningham, Clarissa Floyd, Barbara White, Crystal Sarakas, Danielle Shaw, Jonathan S. Chance, Craig "Stevo" Stephenson, Cynthia Porter, David Medinnus, Daniel S, Mark Hirschman, Simon Dick, Diane Bekel, Galit A., Sarah Cornell, Yankton Robins, Alexander "Guddha" Gudenau, M. Menzies, Michael Bernardi, Janet L. Oblinger, RKBookman, Fin & Fisher, Morva Bowman and Alan Pollard, Vamsi, SwordFire, Ash Marten, Annika Samuelsson, Michele Fry, Michael Kahan, Jerel Heritage, David Eggerschwiler, Alexander Smith, Jennifer McGaffey, Shirley, Mark Phillips, Gavran, Priscilla, Janet Yuen, Colette Reap, ARFunk, D-Rock, John Dallman, Megan Hungerford, Dina B., Lesley Smith, William Hughes, Justin, Karl Jahn, Alexandra Garcia, Ilona Fenton, Andrew Taylor, Thomas Zilling, Lesley Mitchell, Mark Newman, James Spinks, Gabe, Alysia Murphy, Lirion, Robert Maughan, Beth LaClair, John Green, Adrian Cross, Chris Matosky, Lawrence M. Schoen, Jean-Pierre Ardoguein, Cate H, Nathan Turner, Eagle Archambeault, Sarah M Stewart, Leila Gaskin, Gilvoro, Todd V. Ehrenfels, Brendan Lonehawk, Kevin Winter, Elyse Grasso, Sarah Brand, Stephanie Cheshire, RiTides, Mandy Wultsch, Jen Woods, Mark

Kiraly, Misty Massey, Hamish Laws, Jenny Barber, S Whitaker, Chris Gerrib, Lisa "Flaptain" Stuckey, Margaret St. John, John W. Otte, K. Hodghead, Kathryn Whitlock, Vicki Greer, Gail Z. Martin, Shawn Marier, Alon Ziv, Morten Poulsen, Epiphyllum, H Lynnea Johnson, Janet Armentani, AM Scott, Mike Hampton, Elizabeth A. Janes, Jen Edwards, Stephanie Louie, Kitty Likes, S K Suchak, Christian Lindke, Andy Clayman, Mollie Bowers, Leanne Wu, Aaron Canton, Michael Roger Nichols, J.L. Gerrard, Starr Iraklianos, Keith Jones, Sidra Roman, Kaitlin Thorsen, Karen Haugland, Evergreen Lee, Dave Entermille, Margaret C. Thomson, Adriane Hughes Ruzak, Mervi Mustonen, Laura F., Jeanne Hartley, Jody Lynn Nye, Melinda Hunter, William Pearson, Chris Huning, Damia Torhagen, Marti Panikkar, Tal S, T. England, Niall Gordon, Jörg Tremmel, David Drew, Kevin Niemczyk, Tiago Thedim Dias, Lee Dalzell, Lisa Mitchell, The Mad Canner, Wayne L McCalla, Jr, Paul Bulmer, Jill B, Tony Fiorentino, Elaine Walker, Iain Riley, Judith Mortimore, Jeffry Rinkel, Tanya Koenig, Sam Karpierz, Ty Wilda, Robert Farley, Axisor and Mike, Orla, Heather Parra, Donna Gaudet, Missy Gunnels Katano, Kathy Robinson, Silence in the Library Publishing, Peter Young, Katrina Knight, Harvey Brinda, Marc D. Long, Hugh Agnew, Leah Smith, Catherine Gross-Colten, Deirdre M. Murphy, Michelle L, Laura Sheana Taylor, Sarena Ulibarri, Patrick Thomas, Kelly Melnyk, P. Chin, Tory Shade, GriffinFire, Elektra, Jennifer Scott, Brian, Sarah, and Joshua Williams, Jeffery Lawler, Cliff Winnig, Ludovic Mercier, Rebecca M, Damon Eric English, Jules Jones, Felicia Fredlund, jasperoo, Mariann Asanuma, CE Murphy, Pete Hollmer, Michael Hanscom, Peggy Martinez, Deirdre Furtado, Zen Dog, Andrew and Kate Barton, David Rippere, Gina Freed, Amanda Power, Diego Comics Publishing, Dani Bednar, Stephen Leigh, Sandra Komoroff, Noah Nichols, Samuel Lubell, Fred and Mimi Bailey, Lennhoff Family, Thomas Santilli, Delanda Scotti, S Ruskin, Amanda Weinstein, Waylon Adams, Camden C, A fan of words, Leshia-Aimée Doucet, Yair Goldberg, Barbara Hasebe, Jennifer Berk, Marc Tassin, Phyllis Dennis, Heather & Zachary Jones, Kerri Regan, Lori Joyce Parker, Timothy Nakayama, Jamie FitzGerald, Nirven, Darrell Grizzle, Robert Parks, Limugurl, Shannon Kauderer, Bobbie Heft-Eggert, WOL, Rhel ná DecVandé, Laura Wenham, Angela Butler, Belkis Marcillo, Erin Penn, Stephen Kissinger, TOM HAINES, Jenifer Purcell Rosenberg, Victoria, James Nettles, Liz H, Jenny Schwartzberg, Alien Zookeeper, C. R. Washington, Steven Halter, Chaddaï